REVEALING THE REAL DR ROBINSON

BY
DIANNE DRAKE

THE REBEL
AND MISS JONES

BY
ANNIE CLAYDON

MILLS &
BOON

Now that her children have left home, **Dianne Drake** is finally finding the time to do some of the things she adores—gardening, cooking, reading, shopping for antiques. Her absolute passion in life, however, is adopting abandoned and abused animals. Right now Dianne and her husband Joel have a little menagerie of three dogs and two cats, but that's always subject to change. A former symphony orchestra member, Dianne now attends the symphony as a spectator several times a month and, when time permits, takes in an occasional football, basketball or hockey game.

Cursed from an early age with a poor sense of direction and a propensity to read, **Annie Claydon** spent much of her childhood lost in books. After completing her degree in English Literature, she indulged her love of romantic fiction and spent a long, hot summer writing a book of her own. It was duly rejected and life took over. A series of U-turns led in the unlikely direction of a career in computing and information technology, but the lure of the printed page proved too much to bear. Now she has the perfect outlet for the stories which have always run through her head, writing Medical Romance™ for Mills and Boon®. Living in London, a city where getting lost can be a joy, she has no regrets for having taken her time in working her way back to the place that she started from.

REVEALING THE
REAL DR ROBINSON

BY
DIANNE DRAKE

MILLS
BOON

To Swede. You were my first true inspiration.

First published in Great Britain 2013
by Mills & Boon, an imprint of Harlequin (UK) Limited.
Harlequin (UK) Limited, Eton House, 18-24 Paradise Road,
Richmond, Surrey TW9 1SR

© Dianne Despain 2013

ISBN: 978 0 263 89877 4

Harlequin (UK) policy is to use papers that are natural, renewable and recyclable products and made from wood grown in sustainable forests. The logging and manufacturing process conform to the legal environmental regulations of the country of origin.

Printed and bound in Spain
by Blackprint CPI, Barcelona

Dear Reader

Welcome back to Argentina! I love jungle settings, don't you? In this series, which started in Texas with THE NO.1 DAD IN TEXAS, then travelled to Argentina in THE DOCTOR'S LOST-AND-FOUND HEART, I've decided to let Dr Ben Robinson stay in the country that captured his heart and fall in love. And fall in love is exactly what he does, in spite of fighting it every step of the way. But the heart always triumphs over the obstacles, and in Ben's case there are devastating obstacles.

Back in the day, when I was a young nurse and not yet the critical care nurse I turned out to be, I was assigned the one duty I always knew I didn't want: the burns unit. I'd been warned about the kind of suffering I would see there, and it was a given that the work would be difficult. I didn't fear hard work, but I didn't know if I'd have the heart to take care of the suffering I would encounter. But I was new, barely out of school, and couldn't refuse the assignment.

Yes, I did see suffering such as no one could anticipate. What I also saw, though, was the courage and spirit in my patients. In fact for my first few days on duty there my patients were the ones who helped me through, and I truly believe that was the first real lesson I ever had in the nature of human resilience.

My character Ben Robinson has suffered devastating burns in the past, and in REVEALING THE REAL DR ROBINSON you'll see some of the same resilience I saw in my patients. This story is about the true triumph of heart and soul in spite of overwhelming odds.

I'm on Facebook now, so please come visit me there at: http://www.facebook.com/DianneDrakeAuthor. Or check out my website at: www.DianneDrake.com. E-mails are appreciated, too: Dianne@DianneDrake.com

As always, wishing you health and happiness!

Dianne

CHAPTER ONE

BEN ROBINSON threw back the peeling wooden shutters, inviting in the crisp morning air. There'd been a dusting of snow in the valley overnight, for which he was glad. New powder on the ski slope, and one more day of skiing left before he returned home—it was perfect. Absolutely perfect.

In fact, everything about this holiday had been perfect. First time off in half a decade, first time in that half decade he'd almost relaxed. Tuscany in winter had been his dream, the one he hadn't expected to achieve given the way he lived his life. This was the best, though. He'd slept late every morning, then every night dined on his favorite indulgences—pastas and sauces and desserts—all of them sure to add an inch to his waistline. In between his indulgences, he'd explored the fairy-tale villages unchanged over the past two centuries, with all their little shelters for shepherds on the high pastures and the breathtaking succession of age-old churches, hermitages, castles and fortresses.

And he'd met Shanna. She'd shared some of that with him—the late-night dinners, the explorations. All very free and easy, but all very nice.

Ben's thoughts immediately turned to...well, whatever it was that had developed between them. Friendship? Brief acquaintance? Ships that passed in the night? Whatever it was, it was done. She'd had her plans for the day, he'd had his, and tomorrow he'd be gone. So there it was, come, gone, pleasant memories in its wake.

No, he hadn't had a holiday fling in the traditional sense. No kisses—not even a farewell kiss other than a peck on the cheek. No sleeping in late with her in bed next to him. Certainly no intimacies shared across the table during a late-night dinner. Then last night it had turned into a simple parting of the ways after a pleasant evening without any promises for his last day. Not even a mention of him leaving. But that was the way he'd framed it, wasn't it? Keep his distance. Enjoy the companionship, but not too much.

Play it safe.

Admittedly, for a moment or two, he'd wondered what might have happened between them if he'd let it. But he didn't even let that get past the wondering stage. No reason to because he would go home to Argentina *alone*. Continue his medical practice *alone*. Live his life *alone*.

And Shanna... A wistful sigh escaped him. He hoped she would come to the café this morning, the way she had every morning for the past two weeks. One last look would make his day seem a little better. But he wasn't counting on anything. He never did.

"Is that seat taken?" a familiar voice asked, twenty minutes later.

"Could be," he said, without looking up at her, for fear she'd read eagerness in his eyes. "If the right person asks politely."

"Who would she be?"

"Someone who would change her plans for the day. Ski with me now, shop tomorrow when I'm gone." Said in a matter-of-fact manner, taking great care not to sound hopeful or anxious.

Shanna Brooks. She was bundled up to the eyes with scarves, hat pulled down that almost covered her eyes and wisps of copper hair escaping their confinement, the way he'd come to count on. Breathtaking however she appeared. As she slid into the chair across from Ben, he couldn't help himself. He had to look across at her beautiful green eyes so full of life.

"That could be me," she said as the wraps came off her, layer by layer.

Had he really gotten up and walked to the table at the back of the café that first day she'd approached him? Pure insanity. But in his defense he'd stayed the next day and every day after that, feasting his eyes at the ritual of her revealing, the slow peeling away of scarves and hats and mittens. After all, he wasn't dead, just alone by choice, or design, or whatever the hell it was that had constructed his life to turn out the way it had. "But the question is, is it you?"

Frowning as she tossed her knit cap on the ledge of the picture window next to their table, she appeared to be thinking about her answer. "Did you ever consider that you could go shopping with me?" she finally asked. "Instead of me skiing with you?"

"No," he said, sounding too abrupt even to his ears. So he pulled back a little. "I'm on a mission. Twelve straight days of skiing without breaking a leg."

"What if your luck runs out and this is the day you come off the slopes with a tibia fracture?"

"Open?" Meaning bone protruding.

"Too much risk of infection," she said, tossing her mittens aside then starting to unzip her ski jacket. "I like to keep my fractures a little more straightforward. But I am thinking a tibial shaft fracture of some sort might be good." Something breaking between the knee and ankle.

"Maybe a tibial plateau fracture?" Just below the knee. "Could be you accidentally hit one of those little mogul hills, popped up, crashed back down."

"No, I don't think so. Too much risk of late-onset arthritis with a plateau fracture. How about a tibial plafond fracture?" Closer to the ankle. "It has the same degree of seriousness, same lengthy recovery, but less of a risk for long-term disability."

She smiled brightly, then nodded. "Good idea. And I'll make sure I'm there after the surgery with all my bundles and packages, because I'm going shopping this morning."

"More scarves, hats and mittens?"

"A girl can't have too many."

"But knowing how I'm going to injure myself on the slopes this morning, would you actually choose mittens over my wounds?" This was dangerous territory. Too close to being flirty. He knew that. But after nearly two weeks he was still no closer to learning why she'd quit her medical practice than he'd been that first day when he'd shunned her at breakfast, only to find her seated next to him on the lift up the mountain.

"Mittens over wounds because I'm still on leave."

He faked an exasperated expression. "You created my injury, the least you could do is patch me up."

"Wrong specialty," she said.

"What was your specialty?" he asked. "Before you quit?" She hadn't told him. In fact, they'd been five or six days into their relationship before she'd let it slip she was a doctor. Odd thing was, she'd known he was. That had probably been the most he'd revealed about himself, yet she'd kept their similar backgrounds to herself.

"It wasn't bones," she said.

Her eyes turned distant. He could see it, see her shutting out whatever it was that seemed to be skimming the surface of her unhappiness. Or aversion. "Never cared much for bones, either. Not after I broke my big toe once."

"Skiing?" she asked, turning to face him but obviously not focused on the conversation.

"Ever heard of turf toe?" Where a person propelled themselves forward by pushing off on the big toe, resulting in their weight shifting to their other foot. If the toe stayed flat on the ground and didn't lift to push off, the joint injury, associated with athletes who played on artificial turf, resulted.

That caught her interest for real. "You played soccer? Or football?"

"No. I was chasing an angora goat."

Her eyes widened. "Not sure I want to ask why."

He chuckled. "Nothing…untoward. My parents raised goats and sheep for the wool. The one I was shearing got away."

"Hence turf toe. But that's a ligament strain, not a break."

"Or in my case both."

Laughing, Shanna said, "Poor Ben. He doesn't even get the glory of claiming some great athletic accident. You don't really tell many people you had a goat injury, do you? Very embarrassing, Ben. *Very*."

"So would someone pointing out how embarrassing my embarrassment was." He flagged over the server, who immediately brought cups of coffee to the table.

"I don't suppose I could coax you into a send-off mimosa this morning, could I?" she asked. "Since this is our last morning together."

"Coffee's good," he said. Revealing a goat injury was enough for one day. No need to reveal any more than that.

"Champagne and orange juice is better." She paused, thought for a moment. A knowing expression tracked across her face in delayed measures as the full awareness of what she'd just realized finally struck her. "But you don't drink at all, do you? Not a drop."

"How do you figure?"

"When we've had dinner I've had wine a few times, yet you've always ordered..." She shrugged. "You're right. Coffee's good. And you should have told me, Ben. I wouldn't have..." Shaking her head, she picked up her coffee mug and held on to it for dear life. "I know we're not involved, but you should have told me."

"There's nothing to tell." Such a huge lie. But why say anything and ruin a little light flirting, a few pleasant meals, a couple runs down the slope? There was nothing sloppy, nothing sentimental about the two of them and he'd appreciated that because it had been a step totally outside his normal self. Now, though, it was time to step back in, and inside Ben Robinson there was no need to tell anybody anything about himself. Those who knew knew. Those who didn't never would.

"Nothing except a drinking problem? In the past, I'm assuming. It would have been nice to know, because I wouldn't have had wine—"

"Wouldn't have had wine?" he interrupted. "What people do or don't do around me doesn't bother me. I'm not influenced."

"Maybe you're not influenced, but I don't like being insensitive. If you'd told me..."

"It would have changed things between us. You would have been a little more on guard. Or wondered what caused me to turn into an alcoholic, which I am, by the way. That wasn't the kind of relationship we were having." And now started the awkwardness between them, when all they should have been doing was having a carefree last day. It was another perfect example of why he didn't get involved.

She'd peeled back one of his layers and discovered the first well-guarded aspect of a man called Ben Robinson. Yeah, he was an alcoholic. Yeah, he did still struggle with the temptation occasionally, even though he hadn't taken a drink in a decade. Yeah, it was a social barrier.

"Or it would have been a reference in passing. Not everybody is harsh in their judgments, Ben. Trust me, I understand how moments of weakness can escalate. But you're right. We didn't establish the kind of relationship where confessions were required. Anyway, I've enjoyed our connection for what it was—a few hours of fun with a man who speaks my language. It made my sabbatical easier." She reached across and squeezed his hand. "Although I *am* sorry you struggled with alcohol, Ben. Glad you made it through, but sorry for whatever took you on that journey." She fixed her gaze on the view of the mountain as she let go of his hand.

Then breakfast came, they ate, made light conversation about insignificant things, endured more silence between them than they had before. And it was over. Done. They descended into that so-called mutual parting of the ways of infamous fame and he went to ski while she went to shop. Afterward Ben Robinson, forever alone as he'd pledged himself to be, spent the thirty-six hours that came in a plane or between flights wondering why the hell he hadn't just lived in the moment for once. Or lived *for* the moment.

"Because reality returns after the moment," he muttered to himself, fastening his seat belt as he prepared for the last stretch of his journey home. Fourteen hours in the air left him with a lot of time to think, a lot of time to regret.

"Coffee, tea, soft drink? Glass of wine?" the flight attendant asked him as he tried stretching out his lanky legs in too tight a space. "Or a cocktail, sir? We have all the standards—gin, vodka, Scotch…"

Glancing at the beverage cart, he saw the array of small booze bottles, all ready for pouring. Except he didn't drink anymore. That was what he'd told Shanna, and that was the way he'd lived his life for a long, long time now.

Even so, nights like this weakened his resolve. Made it tougher on him to fight when he wasn't sure what he was fighting more—the booze, or himself.

Then he thought about Shanna's green eyes, and the way she'd looked at him that first morning when all she'd really wanted was the view of the mountain he had. He'd seen vitality, a spark that had made him change his ways for the duration of his holiday. He'd opened the door just a crack to let somebody in. Only now the holiday was over and Shanna was but a memory. And like every other time he'd been tempted to break his resolve, he'd take a deep breath and remind himself about his responsibilities. Then stay on track. "Water, please," he told the attendant. "Water will be fine."

"Okay, Ben Robinson, just who are you?" Two days ago he'd left her sitting in the café, wondering what it was about her that clearly hadn't inspired his trust. And it wasn't just about his drinking. It was about everything. They'd spent some nice time together, but every minute of it had shown her how obviously distant he was. More than that, how distant he wanted to stay. Being alone together—that was how she'd felt when she'd been with him. Alone. They'd shared a ski lift, shared meals, shared a few walks, shared time. What he hadn't shared had been himself.

"So who are you, really?" she asked her computer screen as she typed his name into a search engine. "And why are you in Argentina?" The even bigger question was, *Where in Argentina?* Because it was only after he'd gone that she'd realized she didn't know. Realized she didn't even have his phone number. Realized he had merely been a stranger passing through, stopping for a few moments without making a connection.

Except he had. She wasn't sure what kind it was, but here she was, looking for information about him, wondering what it was about Ben Robinson that pulled her in.

Maybe it was a simple thing, really. He was so found, and she was so lost. *Found* had a certain sense of stability to it. A security she'd thought she had but had then discovered it had all been an illusion. Ben didn't give in to illusions. Didn't even let them come near. Sure, it was a harsh way to live your life, but there was safety in that harshness, and that was what she needed—that safety. Because the rug had been pulled out from under her. All those things she'd defined her life by—gone now. One tug and she was flailing.

But Ben had flailed, hadn't he? The scars on his neck accounted for some kind of flailing. So did the alcohol. He'd recovered, though, and that was what eluded her. How to recover. How to even start. Or where to start. Which was why she was keying in his name and connecting it to Argentina medical facilities.

Her life was open now. She had no place to be and nothing to do until she figured out how to be someone else. A journey to start over—that was essentially what she was about. And Ben knew that journey. It was, in a word, *dispassion.* It's where he lived, where he succeeded. It's where she needed to live and succeed if she were to continue in medicine. Because if she couldn't find that place in her own soul, what she loved would destroy her. So her choices were two: learn how to separate herself completely from her passion; or walk away from it altogether.

That was why Ben fascinated her. He'd separated himself. She'd seen that the first morning he'd refused to sit across the table from her, then later sitting shoulder to shoulder on a ski lift with her in near silence. Yet he was a doctor. Owned a little hospital. It didn't seem to jibe. Or maybe it did. Maybe Ben was the master of that separation she needed to find, and embrace.

"I'm probably crazy, Ben," she said to the screen as a series of links popped up, none of them leading her to her object of fascination. "But I don't think we're through. If I can find you…" she said to the next futile attempt. The one after that she cursed, and the one after that she merely grunted at. But the next attempt…maybe not so futile. "Are you my Ben Robinson?" she asked the figure who finally popped up on her screen. Handsome, not a particularly friendly smile on his face. Same eyes, only hidden behind glasses. Shorter hair, no three-day growth of beard covering his face.

"Dr. Benjamin Robinson, owner and director of…" Shanna breathed a sigh of relief. No, she wasn't crazy. She was simply looking for a way home and Ben was the map. So, with that in mind, Dr. Shanna Brooks booked a plane ticket, packed her bags and headed to Argentina.

"Are you finally back in the swing of things?" Dr. Amanda Kenner asked her brother. "Or do you need some holiday recovery time?"

"Another week or two in Tuscany would work. But if I can't have that then, yes, I'm back in the swing of things." He gestured for her to follow him through the central ward in the forty-patient-capacity hospital called Caridad. There were no epidemics now, thanks to Amanda's husband, who'd solved a recent crisis with giardiasis. But there were still patients to be seen, and he was glad to be back on steady ground. This was where he belonged, and as much as he'd loved Tuscany, waiting another half decade for his next holiday would suit him fine. Getting away was good, but this is where he belonged.

Although…his thoughts drifted back to Shanna. Thoughts filled with regrets and missed opportunities. He was a normal man in those things, had desires, hopes and dreams. But he also had his reality, the one that told him who he was every time he looked into a mirror. And that was the fact of his life that never changed.

"You couldn't stand being away any longer," Amanda teased. "In fact, I'm surprised you stayed as long as you did."

"It was a nice place. Good food, the best skiing I've ever done. And Signora Palmadessa ran an outstanding little inn. But it was a holiday, and we can't spend our lives on holiday, can we?"

"Am I hearing some sadness in your voice?" Amanda asked.

He shook his head. "Exhaustion. It was a long trip home." Emotionally and physically.

Before they walked through the doors of the ward, Amanda stopped in front of her brother and studied his face for a moment. "You met someone there, didn't you?"

He nodded. "Not like you think, though."

"But you fell in love with her. You had a holiday fling and fell in love."

"No fling, no falling in love. She was just a nice way to pass some pleasant hours. Someone to take the stigma off eating alone. No big deal, really."

"Then why the wistful sigh?"

"Not wistful. Agitated. I have patients to see and you're standing in my way."

"I'm sorry it didn't work out, Ben. Whatever it was between you, whoever she was, I'm sorry it didn't work out, because I was truly hoping you'd meet a beautiful Tuscan woman who'd steal your heart at first sight, then you'd have some kind of wild adventure with her. Maybe even get married and send me an email telling me you were staying there to have a full life and lots of babies."

She backed away from Ben and brushed tears from her eyes. "Anything that makes you happy...that's all I want. All I've ever wanted for you."

"I know and I appreciate it. But I'm reconciled to what I have, what I am, Amanda," he said gently. "It's taken me a lot of years to come to terms with it, but it's a decent choice, all things considered. So now it's your turn to comes to terms with it. Okay?" Being alone *had* been his choice since he'd been fifteen. More strongly confirmed at age twenty-two with a fiancée, Nancy Collier, who'd gasped, but not in ecstasy, the first time they'd made love. Or attempted to.

The look on her face then the apologies and the discomfort...no man wanted to face that. But what he'd faced that day, even more than Nancy's repulsion over his physical scars, had been the fact that this was the way it was always going to be. One look at the monster, and people turned away. And that was what unleashed the real monster.

Now it was easier to not let them look.

"No, it's not okay. Your choice is too hard, Ben. You're too hard on yourself, and it worries me, because if someone wonderful did come along..."

Someone wonderful, like Shanna... "It is what it is. My life is good, I'm not alone." Subconsciously, he brushed his fingers across the scars on his neck. "And you're too sentimental right now. Pregnancy hormones running amuck with your emotions, or something like that. How's my nephew, by the way?" he asked, fervently hoping to get off the circumstances of his life, for which there was no solution. "I've missed him. Wondered how he was settling into family life." He was referring to Ezequiel, the twelve-year-old Amanda and Jack had recently adopted. Also the sure proof there were happy endings out there. Just not for him.

"He and Jack are out on a medical run, but they should be back in a couple of days. Jack decided it's good to take Ezequiel with him whenever he can when he goes out on short trips. It gives them some quality father-son time, and also gives Ezequiel a sense of purpose, pretending to be a doctor's assistant." She smiled with pride. "My new son is like a sponge. He absorbs everything, and he's so anxious to learn and experience new things. I think he might be a doctor someday."

"Children have so many expectations at that age," Ben commented as he stepped around Amanda and pulled open the door to the women's ward. He'd had those same expectations once. Not about being a doctor so much as the other things life might hold in store for him. In his youthful naivety he had just been waiting for the world to open up for him so he could take whatever he wanted.

Then one day it had ended. *Everything.* No more expectations, no more youthful hopes and dreams because those didn't happen where he'd spent the next year of his life—in a burns ward, fighting for his life, going through skin graft after skin graft, battling any number of opportunistic infections trying to kill him by various degrees.

Those had been the days when his expectations had turned away from the world and centered only on surviving through the next few minutes, the next hour, the next day.

"I'm sorry it didn't work out," she said as they walked shoulder to shoulder to their first patient. "Your affair in Tuscany. I'm sorry it didn't work out."

"There was nothing to work out," he said, stopping short of the bed where his first patient was dozing, then turned to face his sister. "See, that's the thing. She wasn't into me. If she had been, I wouldn't have spent those few days with her. That's the way it is, Amanda, and it's not going to change." He gave her a squeeze on the arm. "I love you for trying, but you've more important things to worry about now. And in the meantime I've got a middle-aged woman, bad diet, uncontrolled diabetes to look after."

"Do you remember that treehouse Dad built us?" Amanda asked.

"The one where I wouldn't let girls inside?" he replied, wondering where this was going.

"But I always managed to get in, Ben."

"And left dolls there."

"I knew you didn't want a sister, knew you felt threatened when Mom and Dad adopted me. I was only five, but I could see it in you. See the resentment and the fear that maybe they were replacing you with me. It shows, Ben. It always shows on you."

"But we eventually had fun there when I finally managed to get rid of the dolls."

"And the pink curtains Mother made for the treehouse."

Good memories, those days when his family had been happy. They were good to hold on to, especially when the darker days had prevailed. "So, are you thinking we should build a treehouse for Ezequiel? Is that where this conversation is leading?"

"You know it's not," she whispered, fighting back tears. "In the days before you accepted me as your sister, you hid in that treehouse. Refused to come out. I watched from my bedroom window. Could see you in there angry, hurt... crying. Ben, you have to come out of the treehouse. You can't spend your whole life hiding."

"I run a hospital. I work twenty hours a day, seven days a week. That's not hiding."

"There are different ways to hide, Ben." She swiped at her tears. "Anyway, you've got patients to see, I've got patients to see…"

"I'm fine, Amanda," he said as she walked away. She didn't answer, though. Just kept on walking. And he…well, he just tried to blot it out of his mind. What else was there?

"So, I didn't expect to see you back here so soon," he said, turning his attention to his patient as he pulled up a chair next to the bed, and sat down. "It's only been three weeks, Maria, which means we need to talk again about the things that can happen to you if you don't take better care of yourself." Said to a lady who was eyeing a plate of pastries next to her bed, left there by a too-sympathetic husband.

Sighing, Ben began the spiel he'd used on her ten times before. Apparently to no avail again. But he understood. It was never easy giving up what you loved, or what you wanted, no matter what the reason. Sometimes, though, life was just plain cruel and forced it on you. "First, you could have heart complications…" Something he assiduously avoided in his personal life.

CHAPTER TWO

"THAT way," the disagreeable driver grunted. The filter of his cigarette was stuck between his lips, just hanging there, no more cigarette left to smoke. "I don't go there."

"I'm not surprised," she quipped, tossing her oversized duffel on the ground outside the taxi, not expecting the driver to help her. Which he didn't. But he was quick to extend his meaty hand out the window for a tip. The only tip she wanted to give him was to quit smoking and adopt a better disposition, but handing him a few pesos was easier. So she handed him a fist full of notes, then watched as he counted his money, grunted, then drove off without a care or concern over how she was going to accomplish the next leg of her journey.

For all she knew, she was nowhere near the village, called *Aldea de Cascada*—village by the waterfall—which she'd been told was also called *Aldea de Hospital,* thanks to Ben's hospital.

Major disillusion certainly caused major life changes. And the gnats swarming her, either to glom onto the carbon dioxide was she exhaling or the sweat she was sweating like she'd never sweated before, were sure testament to that.

"Okay," she said, picking up the duffel and slinging it over her shoulder, which threw her off balance and sent her tumbling backward a couple of steps. "Just do it. You want your life back, this is how you'll get it."

Shanna gained her balance at the same time she gained her bearings, and headed off down the narrow grassy path she hoped would lead either to her destination or to some-place where someone else could point her in the right direction. At this juncture, there weren't many options. The sun was already getting groggy in the sky, so if she didn't land somewhere soon, the chances looked good for her spending the night out here. Not an appealing thought, sleeping alone in the jungle where who knew what kinds of predators were lurking.

Thing was, the darned bag weighed her down, which slowed her down. But leaving it, maybe coming back to-morrow to get it, wasn't an option. If something happened to it, if it disappeared overnight… She hadn't brought much on this journey, but she wasn't about to do without the few creature comforts she'd included. So she redoubled her efforts, focused only on the trail ahead of her, and bore down for the march. Thinking on every step of it how she was going to explain herself to Ben without looking like an idiot, a total lunatic or both.

A few casual days in a tiny Italian village weren't enough to compel anyone to do what she was doing. Es-pecially given the way those days had gone. He'd been there but, in so many ways, he hadn't been. And that was what she needed to learn from him. How to switch off her feelings and simply get on with it. That's the way he lived his life, being an outstanding doctor, no emotional involvement attached to it. Precisely what she needed to learn. And now she'd traveled halfway around the world to get it, or come to terms with what she would do with the rest of her life if she couldn't. Because heart-on-the-sleeve medicine didn't work in the Brooks medical world.

"Ayúdeme por favor. Mi madre fue mordida por una serpiente. Está muy enferma. No puede mover. Pienso que se morirá. Ayúdeme por favor!"

A young girl, probably no more than ten, appeared on the road and grabbed hold of Shanna's duffel. Not to steal it. Shanna understood that. The child was terrified because, from what Shanna could gather, her mother had been bitten by a snake. *Una serpiente.* Wasn't moving. Possibly dying, or already dead.

"Is she breathing?" Shanna asked instinctively, before she'd had a chance to think that the girl probably spoke no English. *"Respirar. ¿Respira su madre?"* she repeated, grateful for some family urging in the direction of languages.

"Yo no sé. Está en el suelo, como duerme. Pero yo no sé si puede respirar."

Unconscious, on the ground. Status of her breathing unknown. *"¿Sabe donde el hospital es?"* She was asking the girl if she knew where the hospital was.

The girl nodded then pointed straight ahead on the trail.

"¿Es muy distante?" Very far?

The girl shook her head. *"No."*

"Bueno. Por favor, corre al hospital, los dice lo que usted me dijo, y los dice que hay ya un médico con su madre, pero necesitan alguien que puede ayudar a conseguirla al hospital." She was telling the girl to run ahead to the hospital for help, but the look on the girl's face indicated she either didn't understand or might be afraid to do so. *"¿Lo que es su nombre?"* she asked the girl as they made their way through the grasses.

"Valeria," she said.

"Eso es un hermoso nombre." Beautiful name.

"Agradecimiento."

Valeria smiled politely with her thank-you, even though

she was so scared. Shanna was impressed by the girl's manners, especially given the circumstances. Grace under pressure. Something she needed to master. *"¿Y qué es el nombre de su madre?"*

"Su nombre está Ines."

The mother's name was Ines. Just as that little bit of knowledge sank in, they rounded a clump of tall pampas grass, where Ines was sprawled on the ground. Breathing, thank God! But barely.

Shanna dropped her bag to the ground, knelt to open it, then had second thoughts about snakes. Pit vipers were prevalent here. At least, that was what she'd read on the plane. That, and so many other disjointed facts about Argentina. So she stayed half upright, half bending, and grabbed the few medical supplies she'd been allowed to carry in. No medicines, just equipment. Which wouldn't save the woman's life. *"Soy médico, Valeria. Pero debo ayudar. Por eso yo deseo que vaya al hospital."* I'm a doctor, but I need help.

Back home, help had been at hand with just the push of a button. Out here, she didn't know. And as she wrapped her stethoscope around her neck and clicked on her penlight, she wasn't even sure the kind of help she might have had back home would do much good, given what she was already seeing in Ines.

Truth was, if the bite had come from a pit viper, the only possible treatment was antivenin. *"Debo ayudar."* Yes, she needed help, especially when her first take of the woman's pulse revealed tachycardia. Pulse much too fast and starting to skip some beats. In addition, there was swelling on her left ankle where the bite area was, not only very puffy but red and hot to the touch.

Shanna imagined other symptoms had occurred while the child had waited there with her mother, probably hoping someone would come along to help them—difficulty with speaking, muscle weakness, dizziness before passing out, excessive sweating, blurred vision, maybe even some paralysis.

While she'd never had to treat a venomous snake bite as a family practitioner, she'd certainly studied them in medical school. Which was nothing like encountering one in front of her. Because what she remembered from her studies was that without fast treatment death followed coma. And the blue tinge developing around Ines's lips was a precursor to death.

"¿Puede correr al hospital, Valeria?" Even though she asked Valeria again to run to the hospital, Shanna wasn't sure it would make much difference. Time was elapsing and she had no idea how long ago Ines had been bitten. But the woman was still breathing, which meant there was still hope. Only at Ben Robinson's hospital, though, and only if Ben stocked the right kinds of antivenin.

The child tugged on Shanna's shirt. *"Sí, puedo. Pero tengo a amigos cerca que puede ayudar a llevar a mi madre allí. Creo que sería más rápido."*

She had friends who could carry Ines there faster. Shanna kept her fingers crossed as she shooed Valeria off to fetch these friends. *"Tan rápidamente como usted puede,"* she urged the child, even though she didn't know if Valeria's fast would be fast enough.

In the meantime, Shanna kept vigil over Ines, washing the snake wound the best she could with bottled water. There'd been a time when making a tourniquet had been the field standard in care, but studies had proved that when a tourniquet was applied, the poison was likely to concentrate where the tourniquet was cutting off circulation, increasing the chances of amputation or even a faster death. Then there was the idea that cutting the wound and sucking out the poison could improve things. Unfortunately, too many people had died from sucking the poison into their own lip or mouth cut.

So now she had to sit and wait, feeling as medically ineffective as she had that day when she'd promised her patient, Elsa Willoughby, a kidney transplant. Not a simple thing to promise, granted. But Elsa had been in a bad condition, which should have put her at the top of the list for an available kidney. What she hadn't expected, though, had been the hospital's refusal to allow the procedure once a kidney became available. A refusal that had come from her grandfather, and been upheld by her father and several other doctors bearing the Brooks name. It was like they'd turned into a wall of opposition because she'd had a patient who needed an operation they didn't want to grant.

Your patient is too old, her grandfather had stated. That, and another dozen reasons that had got Elsa rejected from Brooks Medical Center, a conglomerate of three hospitals, nine clinics and fourteen other miscellaneous medical services.

Eventually, the county hospital had taken Elsa, but too late. Her condition had deteriorated to the point that she had no longer been a good enough candidate for a transplant anywhere. She'd gone back on dialysis to await her fate, which had come just four months later.

Shanna still had nightmares about the day she'd had to tell her patient she could do nothing for her, that the medical system she'd loved and trusted had failed her. She'd had a small *breakdown, meltdown,* whatever the term du jour turned out to be. Had spent the night alone, crying, angry, doubting everything about what she was doing.

Next morning she'd gone to her grandfather one more time, trying to persuade him to change his mind. But his was a mind that wouldn't be changed. *"Given your emo-*

tional involvement, you may be better suited in an admin-istrative role than the actual practice of medicine," her grandfather had said. An administrative role because she cared? It's why she'd left medicine and had gone looking for a better way. Or a different way. Or any way at all that would define her place in medicine. And if it wasn't out there, then what?

Ben Robinson. He proved it was out there. Everything she'd seen of him proved it. And to gain some of what he had, she'd do whatever she had to.

Except here she was again. Not being able to treat a patient. So she spent the next several minutes doing what she'd done with Elsa after she'd broken the news. She sat and held her patient's hand, felt her own pulse jump every time Ines twitched, felt her own breath catch each time Ines's breath went raspy. Heart-on-her-sleeve medicine. Even deep in the jungle she could feel the disapproval of the entire Brooks family.

Luckily for Ines, that wait wasn't long for only min-utes after Shanna had settled in she heard quite a clamor coming from the trail. Not just one or two people. Prob-ably not even three or four of them. In fact, by the time she was on her feet, twenty or so people were standing in front of her, hefting a bed. Not a stretcher or some make-shift rig to transport Ines but a single-size bed, mattress, blankets, pillows and all. She'd never seen anything like it. So much response, so much concern... "Put her..." she started to instruct, but the will of the people took over, and before Shanna could blink, Ines was lifted into the bed, and the bed was being whisked down the trail. All she could do was follow.

Which she did, for about half a mile. Then, at the entry to a small wooden building, everybody stepped back for her to go first, after which several of the men followed her in, leaving the bedframe outside and carrying Ines gently on the mattress.

Shanna spotted Ben immediately, and even in the urgency of the moment her heart clutched. Was it excitement to see him, to start her medical makeover? Or was it merely excitement for medical help for her patient? She didn't know which, didn't care. Ben was bent over an empty exam table in what she presumed to be the emergency area. He was adjusting a light, not even aware yet that she was in the room. "Is that table taken?" she asked, smiling when he looked up at her.

"I'm supposing this is not a coincidence, you being here?" Ben asked. He gestured for Shanna to sit down across the table from him. They were in the doctors' lounge, a tiny place with a table, two chairs, an old sofa, a refrigerator and barely enough room to turn around. Sparse of comfort and cramped, but well used by Ben's largely volunteer staff. "Which means you're stalking me, correct?"

She grasped the cup of yerba maté he'd made, a tealike drink popular in Argentina, like it was her lifeline. Ben had mentioned it was his favorite, but she hadn't quite acquired the taste for it yet, like she hadn't yet acquired the taste for the changes she needed to make in herself.

"Believe me, I had thirty hours to think about it on the flight. You know, questions you'd ask. Answers I'd give. What would sound plausible, what wouldn't."

"Plausible would be good," he conceded, still absolutely bewildered by her being there. Wondering, also, if he was hallucinating or under some kind of other spell that plucked his thoughts from his mind and turned them into reality. Because he'd thought about her in every unoccupied moment since he'd left Tuscany. She'd even managed to creep into a few of his occupied moments. And now here she was, like he'd ordered her up and, *poof,* she appeared. "But under the circumstances, difficult. You followed me halfway around the world, and I'm trying to imagine how plausible any explanation for that could be."

"Other than stalking you," she said quite brightly. Taking a sip of the maté, she let the bitter taste mellow out on her tongue for a moment, then nodded as she swallowed. "Which I'm not. At least, not in the traditional sense."

"Okay, then tell me what's the *untraditional* sense." It was flattering that she'd followed him here. At least, he thought it was. Or hoped it was. Because there was the distinct possibility that Shanna Brooks was some kind of lunatic, and he'd completely missed that in her back in Tuscany. Blinded by the aura, oblivious to the reality? No, that didn't make any sense because he'd looked into her eyes more than once, and there was nothing to suggest anything wrong with her. In fact, one of the things he'd been drawn to had been her spark, her vitality, which shone in her eyes.

"It's hard to explain. I…I need something different."

"You needed something different so you stalked me and ended up in my jungle hospital. Which, by the way, isn't on the map, or any global tracking system I know about. So you had to put some effort into finding me." These kinds of things never happened to him, and he wondered if he should pinch himself to make sure he was awake.

Shanna shrugged. "You're right. You're way off the map. But you'd mentioned you were in Argentina, and I'm resourceful. So, here you are." She took another sip of maté, watched him carefully over the top of her mug.

"Yes, here I am." So was she being deliberately vague, or was she as unsure of herself as he was sensing, putting forward the brave front with nothing behind it to back it up? Because Shanna Brooks seemed almost as surprised to be here as he was to see her here. "Several years, now, which gets me back to my original question…"

"Why am I stalking you?" She drew in a deep breath. "The answer is…I want to be like you. So who better to show me how to do that than you?"

Now he was back to the theory that she might be a lunatic. "What you're telling me is that you want to be like a recluse doctor who's running an isolated, struggling volunteer hospital in the middle of a jungle?"

She smiled. "Not sure it does. So you're thinking I'm crazy, aren't you?"

"Probably not crazy enough to medicate you. But odd enough that I might have to keep an eye on you, take away sharp objects, limit your prescribing to sugar pills."

Shanna laughed. "Don't blame you. In the same position, I might also be calling for a security guard."

"If we had one," he said. "Which we don't. So what didn't you tell me back in Tuscany that I obviously should know since you've set your sights on…me?"

"That's a fair question, I suppose."

"Which you're going to answer, I suppose?"

She sat her mug down on the table and simply studied him for a moment. Looked deep into his eyes, never breaking contact for what seemed like an eternity. Then she drew in a deep breath, let it out slowly and smiled. "You deserve an answer, but it's not necessarily the real answer because…"

"Because it's hard to explain," he filled in.

"Harder than you can know."

"Then, start at the beginning."

"The thing is, every story has so many beginnings. With this one, let's begin where medicine and I came to a parting of the ways. For the sake of keeping this brief, let's just call it a discrepancy of idealisms, and move on from there. After I hung up my medical diploma, I went on a road trip. You know, in search of myself, in search of truth, maybe in the higher sense in search of the meaning of life.

"Who knows what I was in search of but, whatever it was, I met you and I liked the way you talked about your medical world. Thought maybe I might like the way you actually deal with it, as well. And I'll admit I probably got caught up pretty easily as I didn't have my own medical world any longer."

"Cutting to the chase," he interrupted. "You followed me here to study me."

"Like I said, it sounds crazy. The only thing I know for sure is that I don't know anything. I loved being a doctor, think I want to keep doing that. But…" She shrugged. "You need volunteers, and I'm here to volunteer."

They hadn't talked about this in Tuscany, and it was something that should have come up when they'd discovered they were both physicians. Of course, how much had he told her about himself? Not much. Shanna had done the same, so he couldn't fault her for that. "Well, you're off to a good start, showing up at my door with your own patient."

"Then you'll let me stay?"

He'd seen good medical skill and that was almost enough to hire her on the spot. But he was cautious about the people he brought in, even if he had spent time with them on holiday. So while his impulses were telling him one thing, his head was still ruling him. It had to because his only priority was Hospital de Caridad. "You show up on my doorstep and declare yourself ready to work, and think I'll just let you start working?"

"I was hoping. And you can do an internet search on me."

"Oh, I intend to." Although what he'd seen of her already told him everything he needed to know. That, and there was no reason to doubt she was who she said she was. Still, those were personal feelings getting in the way, and whatever was going to happen with Shanna had to be kept professional. From here on out she wasn't a wishful memory left over from holiday but one of his volunteers. One of the many who got treated no differently than anyone else. In a way, that was too bad, because he'd like those wishful memories.

"You're a cautious man, Ben Robinson."

"Have to be." He smiled. "You never know who's going to pop out of the jungle and ask for a job."

"Look, I appreciate the opportunity. Just tell me what you want me to do, then point me in the right direction."

He pointed at the door. "Evening house calls. You can come along…observation only for now, just to see how we operate. Then after you're rested…" A sly smile crossed his lips. "And fully checked out, we'll get you on the full schedule." He wasn't sure why he was asking her to tag along, especially as he intended to treat her the way he did all his volunteers—none of whom ever accompanied him on his house calls. Normally, he enjoyed these evening rounds alone, because they got him away from the routine grind and gave him time to walk and think. It was a pleasant way to spend his evenings, yet here he was disrupting himself, and not sure why.

Shanna laughed. "You really don't trust me, do you?"

"You know how that old saying goes, something about keeping your friends close and your stalker closer…."

"Enemies," she corrected. "Keep your enemies closer."

Except he didn't see anything in Shanna that would make her his enemy. If anything, what he saw was…gentle. Compassionate. "For now, let's just keep it at stalker."

"So, do you have a bed for a stalker someplace?" she

asked, taking her last sip of mate then pushing back from the table.

Since Amanda and Jack were still occupying the guest cottage until their own cottage was built, and all the volunteer rooms were full, there weren't many options left open. His cottage was built like all the others, two small residences per cottage, divided by a central corridor. As hospital owner, he claimed privilege and took up both residences in his cottage, using one for living and one for storage, because he valued his privacy. Looked like he was going to have to share, though. An idea with a certain jumbled appeal. "I occupy half the cottage around to the side...you walked right past it when you came in."

"Half a cottage?"

"Don't require much."

"So what you're telling me is we're sharing quarters? I'll take the part you don't require?"

"Something like that. You'll get your own room, as well as your own bathroom and a very small living area. So I'll have someone move my things aside and make room for you." Everything in that cottage was the sum total of his life, all of it packed into three or four boxes. Bottom line, there wasn't going to be much of his life to move aside.

"Very practical," she said. "Me being your stalker, and all."

He cleared his throat. "Well, then..." What else was there to say after the most beautiful woman he'd ever set eyes on called him practical? The answer was...nothing. There was nothing to say. Not a word. When a woman saw a man as practical, that was as far as they would go. But that was what he wanted, wasn't it? The two of them going nowhere except on some house calls. Yes, practical was right where he needed to be with her. Right now, though, getting what he wanted didn't feel so good.

CHAPTER THREE

"Who is she?" Amanda asked, waylaying her brother in the hospital hall and practically shoving him into a supply closet. "And why is she staying in *your* cottage?"

"Technically, the cottages are meant to be shared by two. So she's not really staying in my cottage so much as she's occupying the other half of a cottage that was designed to be used by two people."

"Quit being evasive," Amanda scolded. "I want to know who she is and if she's the one you met in Tuscany. Oh, and why she's here."

"It's not what you think," he told his sister.

"You don't know what I think."

"Yes, I do. It's the same thing you think every time you come up with the crazy idea that I might be getting involved with someone."

"So, are you getting involved with...?"

"Shanna. Shanna Brooks. And, *no*...notice the emphasis I place on the word *no? No,* I'm not getting involved with her. But, yes, she's the person I met in Tuscany."

"And *didn't* have an affair with."

"And didn't have an affair with," he repeated.

"Yet she followed you here?"

"Yes, but I'm still trying to process the reason." Saying she wanted to be like him could be open to so many interpretations. "I think maybe she's just looking for some variety in her medical life."

"Medical life. So she's what? Doctor, nurse, technician?"

"Family-practice doctor. Burned out, I'm pretty sure."

"And she's looking for a nice jungle hospital to rejuvenate her?" Amanda shook her head, smiled. "Don't be naive, Ben. She's looking for *you* to rejuvenate her. Notice the emphasis I place on the word *you?* And I couldn't be happier for you. It's about time you crawled out of your deep, dank hole and did some real living."

"It's a normal hole, and I live just fine in it."

Amanda's curiosity relaxed a bit, and she arched playful eyebrows at him. "Well, whatever it's about, you have very good taste in roommates. In fact, that's a Robinson trait. Just look what happened to me and my roommate." She patted her rounding belly. "It worked out pretty well."

"Because there was something there between the two of you to work out." He held out his hand to stop her from saying the words he knew she'd say. "I'm fine. Just leave it at that, okay?"

"Yeah, well, a beautiful woman just followed you halfway around the world. I'd say that's better than fine, and as for leaving it alone…" Amanda gave her brother an affectionate squeeze on the arm then spun away. "Think I'll go help our new volunteer get settled in."

"She's going on evening house calls with me."

"Like I said, I think I'll help our new volunteer get settled in…later."

"Leave it alone, Amanda," he warned. His sister was a free spirit, which was both endearing and, right this very moment, aggravating.

"According to you, there's nothing to leave alone."

"So let's keep it that way." There were times, though, when he wished he didn't have to.

"You chose a beautiful area," Shanna said, trailing along behind Ben. His long legs kept a brisk pace and while she was tall, just a few inches shy of his six-foot-two frame, with long legs herself, she was struggling to keep up with him.

"It chose me," he said brusquely. "There was a need here, and I had the means to do something about it."

"So you set up a hospital, just like that?" He seemed the type who could. Efficient, not a speck of nonsense in him. She wondered, for a moment, if Ben ever had fun in life, then dismissed the thought when she remembered that her life didn't afford much fun, either. Not even after she'd walked away from medicine and, effectively, everything else in her life. Her goal then had been to see the world, have a good time, forget what frustrated her, what made her angry or sad. Concentrate only on what was good in the moment. Then get back to her life and see how it worked out. This was now the working-out part and fun didn't matter. It was time to be a doctor again but without the emotional involvement that always got in her way.

"Easier said than done. But from a simplistic viewpoint, yes. I set up a hospital just like that. With my sister. She's only just started working here full time, but she's been my partner from the beginning."

"Why Argentina?" Was it easier to fight his demons in such an isolated place? Maybe working so hard with so few resources helped him cope.

"Before you ask, no, it's not about isolating myself from the world because I'm an alcoholic and the temptations here might be fewer. They're not. And I don't consider this isolating myself from the world. My parents were humanitarian workers here for a while. And my sister's native Argentinian, from a region south of here."

"I'd wondered if it might have something to do with your…shall we call it *demon*. But it's not, and—"

"Not, it's not," he interrupted.

"Then I'm glad Argentina comes naturally to you. Choosing where you want to be because it's the right fit or because of the emotional involvement makes your existence there easier. Oh, and just for the record, you overcame a problem, and I admire that. I hope it's not an issue for you, because it's not for me."

"You're the only one I've ever told, Shanna."

"And that's as far as it goes. I hope you'll trust that, because we all have our past mistakes. Believe me, I have my share." Rebelliousness, a husband she never should have married. Definitely a few mistakes there. "But live and learn, or live and wallow. What you're doing here in Argentina isn't wallowing, and that's what matters."

He nodded, seemed to accept that explanation from her, then smiled. "No, being in Argentina isn't about wallowing because I've always loved it here. The people are great, and they're also very appreciative of our efforts—even the little things that don't matter so much in most medical facilities. You know, give them an aspirin for a headache and they're thankful. Back home, you give a patient an aspirin and, well, let's just say it's not likely to be received in the best spirit."

Something she understood completely. Her family employed a cadre of lawyers to keep all things worked out, including the irate patient who might refuse an aspirin for a headache then turn around and sue because she'd wanted a narcotic. As part owner of Brooks Medical Center, Shanna understood that all too well. Which made Ben's set up here seem all the more appealing. "Well, I may need an aspirin for some legs aches if you don't slow down. You're tall, long legs, I'm having a hard time keeping up."

He stopped, measured her up, nodded. "Somehow, I don't think you've ever had a hard time keeping up. In fact, I'm betting that in one way or another you're always out in the lead."

"Not all the time," she said, hearing the sadness starting to slip into her voice. "Sometimes I'm so far behind I'm not sure I'll ever catch up."

Ben stopped. Turned to face her. "Which has nothing to do with our walking pace."

"Nothing." She was surprised by his responsiveness. Had she made a cryptic remark like that to her ex-husband, he wouldn't have caught on. But Ben did. He absolutely did, which tweaked a change in her opinion of him. Made it a little softer in her estimation. And a little less dispassionate.

"If I slow down, are you going to tell me why you want to be like me? I'm not sure I like the idea of being watched that closely."

"Some people might be flattered."

"Or suspicious," he countered.

"Or hanging on by a thread."

"Let me guess. You've come to a crossroad, don't know which way to go, so your choice is to copycat me?" He resumed walking, but much slower this time. "Let me tell you, Shanna. That sounds crazy."

"I know. But all my options at that crossroad are leading me to another career path."

"Then flip a coin."

"Would, if I could. But it's not that easy."

"Sure it is. You're a family practitioner. That seems like a pretty good path to me. So stay on the path you're already on and figure out how to make it work. If you still enjoy practicing medicine."

That was exactly what she was doing, trying to figure out how to make it work. But Ben didn't need to be privy to these things about her, especially the part where she wanted to figure out how to separate herself from the emotion the way he did. Telling him everything would only make him wary and watchful of her weaknesses, the way her grandfather had been.

Here, at Caridad, she had the perfect opportunity to work one on one with the exact kind of doctor she had to become in order to survive—the doctor who didn't flinch or cry when her patient died, or didn't get so emotionally invested she lost sleep, couldn't eat. Her grandfather had called her a sissified practitioner. Her father had backed that up and no one else in her family had come to her defense, which meant they all agreed to some extent, if not totally.

But, then, look at them, the stalwart Brooks family doctors—her parents, grandparents, brothers. Why would they back her up when they were so entrenched in the Brooks family ways? She was the ousted, the one who didn't fit. If she wanted back in, she was the one who had to do the changing. Thing was, she wasn't sure anymore if she really wanted in, and maybe that was what bothered her. However it went, for now, she was exploring options, and Ben was the best option she'd come across. "I love practicing medicine. But for the moment I'm openly observing all paths and leaving it at that." Such a confusing place to be.

"Well, in that case, this path leads to Vera Santos, who had a stroke about a year ago. She gets along fairly well, takes care of her grandchildren during the day when their parents are working, and she has a passion for eating anything and everything that will elevate her blood pressure."

That caught her interest, shook her right out of her confusion. "What medication is she on? Chlorothiazide or furosemide?"

"No medicine. But she's eating more fish and grain. Garlic, too. And she's currently concentrating on eating more vegetables and fewer sweets."

"Is it working?"

"Marginally. Her blood pressure is still high, but not as high as it was when she had her stroke last year. Which I'd consider progress."

"Progress would be convincing her to take a pill."

"Which she won't do because she doesn't trust our kind of medicine."

"So she doesn't get treated? Her medical condition is like a ticking time bomb, Ben. You know the statistics, she's ten times as likely to have a second stroke because she's already had one and her hypertension isn't controlled. I mean, how can we let that happen?" It didn't seem acceptable, especially with a condition that could kill her. And there she went again, heart on her sleeve and emotional involvement she shouldn't be having.

"She does get treated, Shanna. She's on a better diet, she's losing weight—doing nicely at it, her blood pressure is lowering, and I check her once a week. More, if she's not feeling well. And the big thing is, if she refuses my treatment, and I have offered a variety of options, including pills, I can't force it down her throat."

Ben held the gate open for Shanna, then followed her up the path to the front door. "We deal in realities here. It would be nice to give her a pill, but the reality is, she's allowing me to do only what she wants me to do. It's all I have to work with. I don't like it, because my preference

would be something more aggressive. But it's not my preference, so I have to make do and be glad she allows me to
do what I'm doing. The alternative could be doing nothing at all."

And there was his practical side, the one that didn't
jump in with both feet and get emotionally tangled up at
the start. "But she knows the consequences. I tell her every
time I see her. Don't like the result, but it's her decision to
make, her consequence to deal with."

Shanna knew about choices and consequences. She
was living the consequence of her choice now. Somehow,
though, losing a family, which she feared was part of what
was at stake for her, didn't equate to losing a life, which
was exactly what Vera Santos had at risk here—her life.
So who really cared that she was already over the emotional edge for this patient? It wasn't like her grandfather was standing there, calling her a sissy for caring. He
wasn't. Quite simply, Shanna wanted to help Vera Santos
and that didn't make her a sissified practitioner, no matter what anybody said.

"What if I can persuade her?" she asked. "What if I can
get her to agree to take the pills?"

"That sure of yourself?" he asked.

"That sure of human nature." She knocked on the front
door, then smiled at him. "And of myself."

"Well, if you're that sure, here's the deal." A mischievous glint popped into his eyes. "You get her to agree to
the pills and after house calls I'll show you around the village, take you to dinner at the cantina."

She liked the glint, liked this unexpected side of him
because previously, when they had been in Tuscany, he'd
never initiated the plans. Whatever they'd done with one
another had been more as a result of them mutually stum-

bling into something together. So Ben asking…that was a nice touch.

"Then get yourself ready for the pay-off, Dr. Robinson," she warned, "because I'm ready for that night on the town."

"But here's the flipside. What do I get in return if she doesn't agree?"

"She'll agree," Shanna said quite confidently.

"But if she doesn't, what's in it for me?"

She thought hard for a moment. "A humble apology for being wrong?"

"Not enough."

His face was totally expressionless and someone who didn't know him might have thought he was being unfriendly. But he wasn't. Ben was reserved but never unfriendly. And that elfish little glint was still in his eyes. "I know you love yerba maté tea, that you drink it every day. What I'll do is brew it and bring it to you whenever you want it, for one entire day. Medical rounds and patient emergencies excluded, of course."

"Tea, but for an entire week, *and* a humble apology. Then the bet's on."

She liked this side of him more and more. Not playful but light in a cautious, grounded sort of way. Like taking the step, but conservatively. Something she needed to learn, actually. "You're a hard man, Ben. But I'm not worried, because I'm going to win," she said as she stepped up to the door to address the woman who had opened it and was now standing there watching the two of them banter.

"Buenas noches, Sra. Santos," Shanna began. *"Me llamo Dr. Brooks. Trabajo en el hospital con Dr. Robinson. La razón que estoy aquí esta noche es que quiero hablar con usted acerca de cómo puede quedarse sano y continuar cuidar de sus nietos."*

"Really?" Ben said. "You're going to use her grand-

children as the reason for her to take her medicine? Isn't
that being a little manipulative, telling her you want to
talk to her about how to stay healthy so she can take care
of them?"

"Not manipulative. Smart." Shanna looked up at him,
smiling. "And you're just annoyed you didn't think of it
first."

"How do you know I didn't think of it first? Or already
tried it?"

"Because, like I said, you're annoyed. If you'd already
tried it and it didn't work, you'd be laughing at me. And
if you'd tried it and it had worked we wouldn't be making
a house call." She stepped through the door Mrs. Santos
held open for her, then turned back to Ben. "Is dancing
included in that night on the town, by the way?"

His response was to roll his eyes, exaggerate a sigh and
follow her inside. No answer, no smile. Faked annoyance,
she realized. Which meant his exterior wasn't as hard as
she'd thought it was. That came as a surprise. Actually, a
huge surprise. But, sometimes she liked surprises.

"Okay, so you win," Ben said, stepping around Shanna on
the path back to the village and doubling his pace. Five
house calls, and they were finished for the evening.

"Spoken like a man who's going to grudgingly pay off
his wager." She was barely keeping up with him again and,
truth be told, she was almost too exhausted to care if he
left her behind. Everything about the past few days had finally caught up with her, and the adrenalin edge had worn
off. There were no big plans left in her for the rest of the
night, except to get back to her room. Forget the tour, forget everything else. All she wanted to do was concentrate
on putting one foot in front of the other enough times to
get her where she wanted to be—in bed, asleep.

"Spoken like a man who actually wishes he'd thought of your idea first. What you said to convince Vera Santos to take her medicine was nothing short of brilliant. And, yes, I wish I'd thought of it."

"What?" Shanna sputtered, pausing a moment to catch her breath.

Ben stopped and turned around. "You heard what I said. No need to repeat myself just so you can gloat."

"Only gloat…a little." Suddenly so exhausted she felt paralyzed, her words barely managed to escape her lips.

"Shanna…" He took two steps back toward her but she held up her hand to stop him. "Are you okay?"

"I'm fine. Just a little more tired than I'd expected. Wasn't easy getting here."

"Jet lag, humidity…"

Nodding, Shanna drew in a deep breath. "Is it a rough life out here, Ben?"

"Not particularly. There are differences, but you get used to them."

"I hope so…" Straightening, she started down the path again and had almost caught up with Ben when he turned and continued his own trek, but even at his much slower pace she couldn't keep up. So she didn't even try. Instead, she lagged back and watched him walk. *Man with a purpose,* she thought, noting his long, deliberate strides. *He calculates everything about his life.* Evidenced by his squared shoulders. Not a movement in him without a specific intent. Maybe that was good, all things considered. But she couldn't help wondering if it was also lonely.

Another couple of dozen steps forward, and Ben was totally out of sight, which was just as well because a little cleared patch beside the road called her name. She wanted to sit down. In fact, she dropped her backpack to the ground with that intent, but thought about Ines and the snake then wondered about what other animals might be lurking in the dark, ready to get her.

"Jaguars," Ben said, stepping up behind her. "Cougars, and the occasional boar. Plus the snakes, which you already know about."

Gasping, Shanna spun to face him. "Where did you come from?"

"You weren't keeping up so I rounded back. Saw you contemplating a little rest by the side of the road and figured that if you were as smart as you seem, you were probably wondering what kinds of animals out here might get you if you sat down. Oh, and I originally came from California, if that's what you're asking."

"It's not funny," she snapped. Her heart was pounding so hard it hurt, and she was barely able to breathe, he'd scared her so bad.

"No, being out here alone at night is never funny. It's one of those differences you have to adjust to."

"Do you routinely take all your volunteers to the jungle at night and scare them to death?"

He chuckled. "Hadn't ever considered it, but it does sound like a good indoctrination idea, doesn't it? Especially since you'll never come this way at night again without being cautious."

He'd actually laughed. Attempted a little humor then laughed. She'd heard it in his voice, wished she could have seen it on his face. "I know I told you you're a hard man, Ben. But I'd like to add cruel to that, as well. You're a hard *and* cruel man. Has anybody ever told you that?"

"Once or twice. But I like to think of myself as a man who doesn't want to see his volunteers get eaten. Which probably wouldn't have happened to you as there hasn't been a sighting of a jaguar near here in years. Still, better to be safe than sorry. Right?"

Not only was he laughing, he was sounding quite chipper. Was this Ben in his element? she wondered. Ben synonymous with the night? Happy in his separation? That analysis didn't seem right. He might put on that dark front—a psychologist would probably say it was meant to keep people away. Yet she saw something else, something behind it, and it wasn't dark at all. In fact, it was quite the opposite. "Did you ever consider that it might be better to warn me rather than scare me?"

"And you're the type who'll listen to a warning? Because you seem just the opposite. You know, the one who has to find out on her own. Learn her lessons the hard way. Confront the jaguar head on to prove there's really a jaguar there."

He was right about that, but she didn't have to admit it to him. "In other words, learn my lesson by getting myself eaten?"

"Why are you really here, Shanna? And don't tell me it's because you want to be like me, because nobody who knows me wants to be like me."

"But I don't know you. All that time we spent together in Tuscany and I really don't know any more than what I see when I look at you."

"That's not why you came to Argentina, to get to know me. And maybe you're here because of that crossroad you've come to. But this is a drastic change from your life, as well as a drastic change from the way you practice medicine. There's nothing here that's easy. Not even the village path."

"Maybe I'm looking for drastic and difficult."

"I'm not buying it. What you're telling me may be partial reasons, but in total I'm not buying it."

"You don't have to. As long as you let me work here,

we'll both get what we need. Why complicate it with anything else?"

He shrugged. "Guess we don't have to, do we?" Taking a few steps closer, he bent and picked up her backpack. "Look, it's getting late. I have a couple of patients I want to check on before I grab a of couple hours' sleep, so we need to hurry this along." Then he slid his arm around her waist, clearly for support rather than anything else. "Lean on me and we'll be back at the hospital in a few minutes."

"I'm sorry, Ben. Normally, I have more stamina than this. I really didn't expect to get this tired as I haven't done much of anything for a while now."

"Nothing to be sorry about."

That was all he said. For the rest of the way back they walked in silence. She was glad for the assistance. Snuggling into his side maybe a bit more than she needed to as they walked, she was glad the assistance was coming from Ben.

CHAPTER FOUR

"MY BROTHER thought I should look in on you, and I wanted to meet you…considering what I've heard." Amanda sat a tray of coffee and pastries on the nightstand next to Shanna's bed. "I'm Amanda Kenner, by the way. Part-owner of the hospital and resident pediatrician. And impressed as all get-out that you followed Ben from Italy to Argentina."

"What time is it?" Shanna responded groggily, pushing herself part way to a sitting position. Last night was a blur. Ben had helped her back to the hospital, then she'd practically fallen through the door to her room, and right this moment she didn't have any recollection of tumbling into bed or anything else past the door. Yet here she was, dressed in yesterday's clothes, stretched out in bed and feeling rested. And her only concession to undressing was that her boots and socks were off. Had Ben done that? Had he actually removed them for her?

"It's a little after noon. I'd thought about waking you for breakfast earlier because you missed supper last night, but Ben said you needed sleep more than you needed food, so I waited as long as I could. The thing is, if you're going to volunteer here, I really need you on the work schedule for this afternoon. Normally, we like to give our volunteers a couple of days to acclimatize, but we're in a pinch."

"Sure, I can work." Shanna struggled to a fully upright

sitting position, brushed back her hair with her fingers and tried to stifle a yawn. "And about me following Ben here, yes, I did. But it's not what it looks like. I'm not really stalking him."

Grinning, Amanda said, "Well, whatever your reason, we're glad to have you. Caridad is always in need of good volunteers and from what Ben described about your *grand* entrance, you're good. So, about going on duty later..."

She liked Ben's sister. She was as outgoing as Ben was closed in. And Amanda clearly loved her brother. Had some hopeful expectations for him in the relationship department, too, Shanna guessed. "Not a problem. But would you mind if I took half an hour to eat, then grab a shower before I start work? I'm used to putting in the hard hours, but what I've done here so far has been a different kind of hard and I'm a little slow readjusting."

"I'll bet working at your family's medical center was very hard. From my own limited experience of owning Caridad, I know I work longer and harder than I ever did when I was on staff in a hospital back in Texas. Something about the responsibility of ownership that drives us to do more, I think."

"Does Ben know who I am?" she asked, quite alarmed. Leading off with her family and their medical empire wasn't something she was comfortable with, so she didn't. In fact, it never came up in conversation unless the other person asked, because she'd learned, early on, that being the youngest child of a medical dynasty carried a stigma of sorts. Or unrealistic expectations. Sometimes it simply put a target with a bull's eye on her forehead. *Look at me.* She hated that notoriety. Hated the attention because for her, her motivations weren't about being part of the illustrious Brooks family. They were about being a doctor. And while the two should have been one and the same, so often, it seemed, they weren't. Not to her, anyway. Although the rest of the family would dispute that.

"Yep, he knows who you are. Told me where to look you up, actually. But as you didn't know he knows, I'd better warn you, in case it comes up, that my brother applied for a residency at your hospital."

That surprised her. "He was a resident there?" She didn't recall him, didn't recall seeing anything in his brief online bio about him working there, didn't even recall his name from back in the day, and she and Ben should have, at the very least, crossed paths for a year or two in one hospital hall or another as she was thirty-four and he was only a couple of years older.

"No, he wasn't. He just applied for the position. And was rejected."

Shanna opened her mouth to speak but didn't know what to say. "How?" she finally managed.

A passing sadness crossed Amanda's face, followed by a smile. But not the cheery smile that had been there. "Bad attitude. Impeccable academic credits, medical aptitude that couldn't be touched by anyone else. But a pretty big chip on his shoulder. Don't worry about it, though. He eventually landed at a hospital in New York City that was a much better fit for him."

Odd revelation. She didn't know what to make of it. "So, how do I react to that?"

"You don't. Ben doesn't carry grudges."

"Then I guess I should say that's a relief because I want to stay here for a while."

"It's a relief only if you want long, hard hours, no pay and lots of bugs," said Amanda as she swatted a mosquito on her arm. "Which is probably what you'd get at Brooks Medical Center, minus the no pay and bugs. *Especially the bugs.*"

"Money's not a problem, and bugs I can deal with. I liked entomology when I was in college. Used to torment my brothers with bugs instead of the other way around. Always found it was a good way to get even with them... drop some kind of bug in one of their shoes, put something crawly in a school backpack." Smiling at the memory, she scooted to the edge of the bed, picked up the cup of coffee and took a sip.

"Now I feel human again," she said on a sigh.

"Ben and I didn't torment each other so much as conspire together. We were always out to conquer something... mostly the kids who lived down the street. They were bullies. Maybe not in the literal definition of how we see bullies today, but they called us names, threw things at us, ganged up to keep us from walking by their house. So Ben and I were allies early on."

"That's nice," Shanna said wistfully. "My family was never close. Everybody was...busy. Stodgy. They worked, didn't have much time to stay home. Consequently, John, Adam and I were raised by a very caring nanny who tried hard but who couldn't quite instill in us that sense of family. So we weren't close the way you and Ben were, and I think because I was the youngest I was the one who was always trying to get noticed the most. Hence the bugs."

"Family dynamics," Amanda said, patting her tummy. "I'm beginning to see them from the other point of view."

"And it's good?" Shanna already knew the answer. Amanda had the contented look of a woman who had it all. A look to envy.

"Like nothing I would have ever imagined. Anyway, take an hour. Get yourself up and ready for work, then have a look around the hospital. I've got you scheduled for our Emergency, which isn't really much of an Emergency. But it gets busy, and we're down one doctor until my husband gets back…"

"Jack Kenner, right?"

At the mention of his name Amanda smiled from ear to ear. "You know who he is?"

Shanna nodded as she took her next sip of coffee. "He's a big deal in epidemics. We had a situation once at Brooks Medical Center, tried to get him to come and figure it out. He was tied up in Africa somewhere, dealing with malaria. My grandfather offered him an insane amount of money to drop what he was doing and come and help us. Wanted to send the family jet to get him. But your husband had integrity. Stayed where he was." One more sip. "Can't wait to meet him, and it'll be an honor to step in for him."

"I expect Ben will step into Emergency to check on you. But if he doesn't, I'll have one of the nurses help get you situated."

As it turned out, getting situated was an understatement. An hour later, when Shanna entered the room designated as Emergency, she was besieged by patients, dozens of them surrounding her immediately, wanting to see her, trying to tell her what was wrong, trying to grab her attention first. The doctor on duty, a small, thin, older man by the name of Vance Hastings, looked like he was about to become one of the patients himself.

"Getting too old for this," he wheezed as he dabbed his forehead with a handkerchief. "Ten-hour shifts at this pace are for the young." He finally managed a smile at Shanna. "But if you need help, I might have another hour or two left in me."

Shanna chuckled. "How about I prescribe bed rest for now, and if I need you later on, I'll come and get you?"

"Bless you, my child. You've just saved an old man's life."

His friendly smile was nice, very soothing. Yet she wondered why he pushed himself so hard when it was so clearly difficult on him. How difficult, she couldn't have even begun to guess until the end of her first hour on shift, when she'd already seen ten patients and was beginning to question if she'd be able to hold out for another nine hours.

"It's overwhelming, isn't it?" Ben said, stepping into the cubicle where she'd just dressed and bandaged a little girl's foot and sent her back to her mother's arms.

"Is it like this every day?" she asked, leaning against the wall, trying to take a two-minute break.

"Some days it's worse."

"So, conversely, some days it's better?" she asked.

"No, not usually. At least, not during summer. People are active, they get hurt more, other weather-related things pop up. It'll slow down when the weather cools, though. Not that you'll be around long enough to see that."

"Big assumption to make, isn't it? Especially when I stalked you halfway around the world just so I could do what I'm doing."

To help her, he pulled the paper cover off the exam table and replaced it with a fresh one, then set about the task of restocking the table-side tools. "It's also a big assumption to make, thinking you'll want to stay that long. I'm a boring man, Shanna. I work and that's it. So once you've started to observe what you think you want to observe in me, what you're going to find is…nothing. And if this fascination with me is the only reason you're here, you'll be long gone before the cool weather hits."

"But what if I'm not, Ben?"

"Are you challenging me to another wager? Because this is the one you'll lose."

"If I lose, I'm your yerba maté tea slave for the duration of my stay, whatever that turns out to be—I'll give you adequate notice if I leave, by the way. And if I win, the first thing I want is a humble apology. Next thing is my morning coffee served to me in bed. Amanda did that for me this morning and it was nice, so I want a morning coffee slave for the duration of my stay."

"Which is going to be over long before cold weather strikes." He smiled. "No matter how adequate your notice is."

"Do you want me to leave?" It seemed like he might, but she wasn't sure. Then she saw it, the distance in his eyes replaced by that glint. It was his giveaway, she realized. A little tease, an invitation to advance, but only a little.

"I never like to lose a good doctor. But I have an idea Brooks Medical Center never likes to lose a good doctor, either. Especially one who comes with the Brooks name."

"How long have you known?"

"I did an internet search before I took you out on house calls. Back in Italy, unraveling your curious background didn't seem necessary because it had nothing to do with my hospital. And going for six days without telling me you're a doctor is curious, Shanna. But the moment you invaded my Emergency it not only became necessary to find out about you, but urgent, given your intention to volunteer.

"Yet you didn't say anything to me?"

"And yet I didn't say anything. People are entitled to their privacy, Shanna. Everybody, including Shanna Brooks, who was made assistant head of family practice only days before she left. Or, as the hospital's public statement put it, went on an extended personal leave for rest and relaxation before assuming her next level of duties. The thing is, I figured if you wanted me to know who you were, you'd tell me. You didn't, so I didn't see any point in worrying about it."

"We had a difference of opinion—my grandfather and

I. Over a patient's treatment. As a result, I realized I had some thinking to do, and I couldn't do it and still continue to work."

"Did you go against the status quo?"

"Tried to. At the time I didn't even realize that's what I was doing. My patient was in end-stage renal disease, I put her on the transplant list. My grandfather took her off because she was older than the hospital protocol called for. I argued, he won, she died."

Ben whistled softly. "I'm sorry. It's always tough when you can't do anything."

"It's even tougher, Ben, when you're part-owner of a family business and the family turns against you."

"You took it personally?"

"Yes, I did. Very personally. I should have been able to save my patient. Her family expected that of me, I expected that of me." She shut her eyes, trying to blot that day from her memory—the day she'd told Elsa the bad news. Heart on her sleeve all the way, and she didn't care. Alone in her office afterward, she'd cried, kicked the trash can. Been called weak by her grandfather. *Do you think you're going to survive in this profession, Shanna, if you're weak?*

Weak. That one, single word had forced her decision. "It's like there's always been this undertow, something churning underneath the surface waiting to pull me under. I always fight hard against it. I was fighting hard against it for my patient, but…" She shrugged.

"I wasn't strong enough when I should have been. So it took me a few weeks to tie up all my medical loose ends, then I went to Tuscany for a holiday, to think… My family has a home there and it seemed like a safe place to be. And the rest, as they say, is history. Here I am." Yes, here she was, wondering if she ever could be strong enough to survive as a doctor or if her emotions would always get in the way.

"Here you are, and Caridad is glad to have you. But I'm wondering if you should have stayed at Brooks Medical and worked it out, rather than coming here."

"The problem is me, Ben. Not Brooks Medical Center. And, no, I couldn't have worked it out there, couldn't have worked *me* out there. But don't worry. I'm not going to jeopardize anything at Caridad. Not going to let my problems overshadow my work. Not going to suddenly figure out which path to take and leave you in a lurch. If that's what you're thinking." If he wasn't, he should be. But she hoped he wasn't, because what Ben thought about her mattered. She wasn't sure why, exactly. She only knew that it did.

"I didn't think you would."

"What makes you so…trusting? If a doctor came to me the way I came to you, I wouldn't do what you've done."

"It's not that I'm trusting. I just don't expect anything from anybody. That way, whatever happens happens. And I don't get disappointed. That's as far as I let anything go. The way I want to live my life, and I'm happy with it."

That might be the way he lived his life, and maybe he was happy with it, but why did she see a distant sadness in his eyes so much of the time? Could it be this wasn't the way he wanted to live his life but the way he thought he had to?

"Anyway…" She pointed to the adjacent room, one half the size of the closet-size room in which she was working "I noticed it's set up for patient care. If you're not busy right now, would you care to see a few patients in there rather than letting that space go to waste?"

"Spoken like a doctor who's used to being in charge," he said, smiling.

"Not as in charge as I used to think I was." She turned then headed to the door, on her way to the hall to call her next patient. "Tomorrow night good for you?" she tossed over her shoulder on her way out.

"For what?"

"Dinner. You still owe me that night on the town, and I'm ready to collect. I'm scheduled for a back-to-back today and tomorrow, which means by tomorrow evening I'll be free." She spun to face him, not expecting him to be so close on her heels—so close they could have kissed. "So, dinner?" It was the first time she'd really noticed the extent and severity of the scars on his neck. Oh, she'd seen them, hadn't paid too much attention. But this close she knew that what was visible on Ben was only a small part of it. She also knew the suffering that had come with them.

"Barring medical emergencies, mud slides and pestilence, I think I might be able to manage dinner," he replied, stepping back from her.

She laughed. "I've never had pestilence used as an excuse to stand me up."

"Not stand you up per se. Just warning you that if pestilence happens…" Rather than finishing his sentence, he brushed by her and went to the waiting area and called the next patient, while Shanna stood back and watched. Beautiful man, amazing physique, accentuated by the fact that this was the hospital where they didn't have to wear scrubs and white jackets if they didn't want to. Ben was dressed in a casual pair of tan cargo pants, along with a baggy camp shirt, long sleeves rolled up to just below the elbows. He exercised, kept himself in superb shape, which was evidenced in the muscles that rippled underneath all that fabric. Brown eyes, casually shaggy brown hair…the substance of dreamy sighs, she thought.

Yes, he was definitely a guy who could make a girl go

giddy with his good looks. But he was locked up so tight. Maybe because of his scars, maybe because of something else. Which really didn't make a difference, or shouldn't make a difference. She was only here to learn from him, and not get goose bumps from just looking at him.

Shanna followed Ben to the waiting area to call her next patient, brushing her arm, trying to rid herself of her goose bumps.

Time passed so quickly she felt like her head was swimming. One minute she was in the middle of yesterday's shift, now it was the end of the next day, she'd worked twenty hours out of the last thirty, and every single one of them had gone by in a blur.

Even more amazing was the fact that she'd never worked as hard in her whole life, or felt so good about her accomplishments. Little things. Sore throat. Bug bites. Cuts. Sprains. Pregnancy checks. All of that, and her body wasn't protesting…yet. Of course, she could be on an adrenalin kick, or maybe it was the evening ahead with Ben that was giving her this late burst of energy.

Either way, she was charged, raring to go.

The funny thing was, she hadn't been out on a date of any sort in, what? Definitely not since the divorce five years ago. Add two years of marriage to that, most of which she hadn't even lived with her husband…now that she'd done the math, she was suddenly nervous. Which showed itself when Ben knocked on her door and her reaction was a little clutch in her heart and a little catch in her lungs. Then that last quick look in the mirror to make sure she was presentable, even though Ben had already seen her covered in the best the jungle had to offer.

"It's not a date," she said aloud as she dabbed on a bit of lip gloss, ran her fingers through her hair to give it just a little more wild edge and headed to the door. "He's paying off a bet." Doing the honorable thing.

"I have to be back on duty in an hour," he said, right off.

Her formerly clutching heart sank a little, but she smiled through it. "And I have a date with a riveting medical journal, so that works out, doesn't it?" A reactionary riposte, she knew, but it was the best she could come up with.

"Then I guess we'd better hurry." Ben didn't come in. Instead he stepped back from the door and actually started to walk down the corridor. Not as an escort, but as someone to follow.

"I guess we had. You go on ahead, and I'll catch up." With that, Shanna dashed back into her room, grabbed a tissue and wiped the gloss off her lips, then found a rubber band. When she caught up to Ben, who was halfway off the hospital compound, her hair was pulled back into her workaday ponytail.

And he didn't say a word about it. Not one darned word. In fact, he barely spoke as they walked down to the village, not hand in hand. Not even together, as his pace was always about two steps in front of her. The place where he seemed to want to be.

Then, apart from the expected conversation—*it's a nice night, we're having nice weather*—the other little bits of conversation focused on patients and hospital supplies, and by the time they reached the edge of the village proper, Shanna was so annoyed by his rude behavior she blurted out, "How about we just skip this whole thing, since it's obvious you don't want to do this?"

Ben stopped a good five feet ahead of her but didn't turn to face her right away. In fact, it took him several seconds before he spun around. "It's not that I don't want to do this. It's that I *don't* do this."

"What? Take a night off?"

"No. I don't take women to dinner. Or anywhere else, for that matter. Remember how I told you I was boring? Remember how we simply met up in Tuscany but never really went together? Well, this is part of it. I *do not* date. Not ever."

This was something she hadn't seen coming. Not at all. "Because you don't like women? You're gay?"

He actually laughed. "I love women. The only gender for me, actually. But I don't get involved with them."

"How would you define involved? Because in my world a one-hour night out on the village doesn't constitute an involvement."

"Especially in a ponytail?" he asked.

Now she was perplexed. Noticing her quick hair change would indicate a signal of some sort. She just didn't know what kind of signal. More than that, she didn't know what kind of signal she wanted. Because, like Ben, she didn't get involved, and she had a divorce certificate to remind her just how messy an involvement of a personal nature could be. "You noticed?"

"I'm not oblivious, Shanna. Maybe a little obtuse in some matters, but I do notice the things around me."

"Obtuse by design," she commented, even though she was still keeping her distance.

"Not denying it."

Well, at least he was honest. No way she could fault that. "As long as we know where we stand," she said.

"See, that's the thing. You may know where you stand, but I don't. I don't even know why you're here. The real reason. Not the one you're giving me."

"And that bothers you?"

"What bothers me is that I planned an hour for this dinner, and we're standing in the middle of the road, wasting it."

See, there it was again, the nagging reminder that Ben didn't want this. And it wasn't only about dinner. Which made her wonder how she was going to stay close enough to watch him when all he wanted was to keep her at a distance. She'd hoped something would come of this evening, even if he'd reduced it to mere minutes.

Now, though, it felt like he was even shutting that down to her, so what was the point of continuing when it was obvious his conversation would not go much beyond the weather or the patient with severe eczema? "You know what, Ben? You're off the hook. I relieve you of your obligation to take me to the village. You can have your hour back, okay? Have fun with it."

With that, she spun around and marched as hard and fast as she could back to her room, where she slammed the door, kicked a wooden footstool across the small confines, then threw herself down on the bed and simply stared up at the ceiling.

Okay, so maybe she did let her emotions get in the way. And maybe he wasn't the one, and this wasn't the place. But she wasn't ready to concede that her grandfather was right about her, because that doomed her to a career she simply didn't want. Even thinking about spending every day pushing papers and fiddling with mundane business things made her queasy. That wasn't her idea of being a doctor, but it was all her family was offering unless...

"Unless I learn to be more like Ben and less like me." That reality caused a hard lump to form in her throat. Being like Ben wasn't a victory. It was a concession. "Just do it, Shanna," she said, staring so intently at the lovely little *mariposas*—butterflies—taking up residence on her ceiling light that a bang on her door startled her.

"Go away," she shouted, knowing instinctively it was Ben coming to make amends.

"By my watch, I still have a little over half an hour coming to me," he shouted back.

"Consider it my gift to you. And don't you dare tell me you've marked it down in your calendar and you can't change it."

"I did. It's in ink, so it's impossible to change," he countered.

In spite of herself, she laughed. Ben Robinson might have the social skills of a pink fairy armadillo, an Argentine animal that possessed the ability to bury itself completely in a matter of seconds if frightened, but Ben's armadillo ways were engaging in some respects. "If you promise not to bury yourself in the dirt the instant you step inside, the door's unlocked. Come in, if you want to."

"I'm not sure…was that an invitation?" he asked, pushing the door open.

"If you want it to be." Surprisingly, she wanted him to open that door.

"Look," he said, stepping over the threshold yet not entering the room, "I live a very secluded life out here, forget how things are supposed to work sometimes."

"Like common civilities?"

He nodded. "I, um… No excuses. I was rude and I'm sorry. I so totally avoid all the social trappings that I forget how people might have certain expectations of me in those areas, since I don't have expectations of myself. I didn't mean to offend you, Shanna. In fact, I was looking forward to—"

"An hour," she interrupted.

"Okay, you're going to get another apology because I realize that timeline was uncalled for. That was me, trying to play it safe."

"Safe from what?" she asked, sitting up and scooting to the edge of the bed. "From me? Do you think I have *those* kinds of intentions? You know, follow you all the way from Tuscany to wherever in the world this is just to seduce you? Because if it was seduction I wanted from you, I'd have gotten it over with in Tuscany, and right now I'd be sipping wine in a Paris bistro instead of lying in my bed watching bugs in Argentina."

"What else am I supposed to believe? You tell me you're here so you can be like me, and if that's the case then you're certifiably insane. And I don't think you're insane."

"I need a new dedication in my life, Ben, and I wasn't finding it where I was. You intrigued me in Tuscany and that's why I came here. The kind of dedication you have is what I want to develop in myself." Dedication, meaning *dispassion* or *distance*. Which she would never, ever say to him in those terms because that would be hurtful. Ben didn't deserve that.

He shook his head. "All I see when I'm watching you work is dedication. You're involved, Shanna. And passionate. How can that *not* be dedication?" He stepped into the room, took a few more steps forward, then extended his hand to her. "Anyway, let's not ruin the rest of the evening with philosophical conundrums. Come on, get up. I owe you a dinner."

She looked at his hand for a moment. Soft, gentle. The kind of hand that could stroke a woman into easy submission. "I'll go, but only because it's in ink on your calendar and, God only knows, you can't change it once it's in ink."

"I wrote it in ink because I didn't want to find an excuse to get out of it."

"But an hour?" she asked, taking hold of his hand and tingling to everything she'd expected his touch to be. Tingling *and* goose bumps.

"That gave *you* your out, Shanna. I'm not the most engaging person to be around so I figured an hour was time enough to eat and for you to make a polite exit once you realized that anything more than an hour with me would turn into misery. So, yes, an hour. But let's add an option to that."

"An option for what?"

"More. There's nothing written in ink underneath that hour."

"So I get to negotiate for another hour if the first one goes well?" Normally, this was where she'd have simply shoved him out the door, by brute force if necessary, then locked it after him. But she did have those tingles and goose bumps to contend with, whatever they meant. Besides that, Ben fascinated her. His odd outlook on life could be her starting point.

"If you want to negotiate. Not sure that's going to happen, though."

"Pretty sure you're that boring, are you, Doctor?" she asked, standing. "Do I feel another wager coming on? Because I like to dance, so it might involve a tango. Just thought I should warn you."

What was it about her that intrigued him? She was pretty. Downright beautiful, actually. Red hair like he'd never known red could be. Sensual, soft. And green eyes the color of emeralds. So, in spite of his empty heart, there were so many reasons to look. He was human after all. But what else? Her infectious personality? Because Shanna had the ability to draw people in, and he wasn't denying that he'd been drawn in, starting with that first morning in Tuscany when she'd approached him and he'd walked away.

And too many stray thoughts long after that. Now, thinking about the two of them in a tango, specifically a sultry Argentine tango...he could almost feel her leg snaking up his, feel her thigh pressed to his.

When he realized where his thoughts were taking him, Ben expelled a sharp breath. No way in hell that was going to happen. He wouldn't allow it. And that was where his mind stayed for a good part of their walk to the village— on the things he wouldn't allow.

Except the list was provocative, because everything he forbade himself was everything he wanted, and the more he tried to force it away, the more it pummeled him. It was only when they were seated across from each other at the *restaurante aéreo fresco* and Shanna was studying the menu scribbled on a chalkboard hanging on the outside brick wall that he was able to force himself to relax a little. Otherwise he was well into his second chance at an evening he didn't want to ruin, on the verge of ruining that, too.

"If I could make a recommendation, *bife a caballo* is excellent. Beef is the traditional evening meal here, and *a caballo* means—"

"On a horse?" she asked.

"I forgot you speak the language."

"Some. It was the second language in my home when I was growing up."

"I'm guessing a Spanish-speaking nanny?" He smiled as he flagged down the server, a young girl who didn't look to be more than fifteen or sixteen. Glancing back to acknowledge him, she was moving slowly, holding her back. Looked exhausted, so he gave her the okay sign and a smile, indicating he wasn't in a hurry.

"Best nanny in the world—one of the Brooks family perks."

"Spoken with a hint of disdain."

"Not disdain so much as disappointment. I love Asuncion. Would trust her with my own child, if I had children. The thing is, I would raise my own children and not leave that to the nanny. Her job would be as caregiver when I wasn't there, not stand-in parent. But when I was growing up, she was my stand-in parent because my parents were so involved in the hospital. I'd go days without even seeing them. Wouldn't even see them when they were home."

"I met your father the day your grandfather rejected me for a residency position. He was…formidable. Not much separation between your father and your grandfather, actually."

Shanna tensed. "I'm sorry you were rejected, Ben. My grandfather is a very hard man. He has his ideas and he doesn't budge."

He reached across the table, squeezed her hand. "But I benefited from his rejection because I found a hospital that taught me what I needed to know about surviving in the kind of practice I've set up here. It was rough, but it was also good, so I should probably thank your family for turning me down because your grandfather was correct when he told me my personality was abrasive and I was too argumentative to succeed in their residency program."

"Were you really abrasive and argumentative?" she asked. "Because I can't see that. Socially distant bordering on cold or aloof maybe. But abrasive and argumentative?"

He chuckled. "Talk about abrasive."

She smiled. "Sometimes the truth is harsh. But that's how I see you…most of the time. It's not a criticism, though."

"It's not harsh. The truth is the truth, but it's not always so nice to hear. Anyway, back then I was abrasive and especially argumentative. Lots of axes to grind, I suppose. And it's still in me, if I want it to be."

"Do you want it to be?"

"Not for a long time. Behaving that way doesn't prove

anything and, in the end, the only one truly hurt is yourself. So why bother when it doesn't get you what you need?"

"What do you need?"

"A tiny hospital in an isolated area of Argentina."

Shanna sighed, slipped her hand out of his and relaxed back into her chair. "I'm still sorry my grandfather rejected you, but I'm glad you got everything you wanted in spite of him."

"One of life's little ironies is that I didn't get what I wanted at the time, but what I needed found me when I was ready for it. It worked out the way it was meant to." But it wasn't all good with her. He could see it in her eyes, in the way her shoulders went so rigid. Her new *dedication* had something to do with her family, and it was about a lot more than an argument over the treatment of an end-stage renal patient. Asking her about it would signal involvement, however, so he opted for the safe route.

He deferred back to the menu. "Anyway, *bife a caballo* is a steak topped with a couple of fried eggs, with fried potatoes and salad on the side. It was a traditional meal before the gauchos set out on their horses to tend to their ranch—hence the equine reference in the name. Not what I'd care to eat before I go horseback riding, but to each his own, I suppose."

"Sounds…huge. But I like food, so it'll work."

"Bife a caballo. Make that two," he said, holding up two fingers to the young server, who'd finally made her way to the table, seeming awfully glad to stand there and rest while he and Shanna talked. "With lemonade?" he asked Shanna. Then confirmed it to the server when Shanna said yes. *"Dos vasos de limonada también, por favor."*

"So now that the dinner necessities are taken care of, and I've apologized on behalf of my family, although I doubt they'd actually ever apologize to anyone about anything, is this where we discover we have nothing to talk about, or so many things in common we won't be able to stop talking?"

"The former for me," Ben said. "Keeps it simple."

"What's wrong with making it complicated?"

"Complicated takes too much effort. There's too much responsibility involved, and I have enough of that with the hospital. Don't care to go looking for more."

"Makes sense to me," she said, knowing it did but simply not feeling the substance of it. "So, in the spirit of simplicity, how about we come up with a list of complicated topics we're not going to talk about? You know, set our boundaries?"

"Sounds like something I'd say."

"I know," she said. "Isn't that great? Since you recognized it, that means I passed my first test at being like you!"

"Are you always this direct?" he asked.

"No, but that's one of my off-limits subjects."

"Like why you're here is?"

She stared at him point-blank. "I already told you why I'm here."

"And I told you I don't believe you."

"So, let's add that to the list. Also my family, and my family's hospital."

"Which would all be interrelated with your reason for setting limits on what we can talk about, I'm guessing. And that's probably off limits, too." She was different. Fresh. He liked the honesty, even if it was a bit quirky and definitely brutal.

"You're right. Off limits."

"Which pretty well limits us to medicine."

"And the weather," she added, smiling. "I'm always up for a good, rousing discussion on heat and humidity."

"Unless it's one of my off-limits subjects." Said with a deadpan face.

"In which case, I'll talk about this really advanced case of lupus I treated in one of my patients a while back, and what happened when we—"

He thrust out his hand to stop her. "*We* would imply your medical colleagues or your hospital, and I don't want you breaking any of your conversational boundaries. Just trying to stick to our rules of engagement."

"So, in these rules of engagement, medicine's basically out?"

He faked a frown. It was silly chatter, he knew that, but it was the first time he'd just let himself go in a conversation other than with Amanda and Jack in so long he couldn't remember. With Shanna, it was fun. Nonsense, but fun. "Not out, totally. But I think we'll have to be very careful how we proceed." Very careful, indeed.

CHAPTER FIVE

"You barely touched it," Ben said as the server was clearing the table of dishes. "If you didn't like it, I'm sure there's something else on the menu…"

Laughing, she held out her hand to stop him. "That's not it. Everything was delicious. But they served me enough to feed a family of four for a week. How's anybody supposed to eat that much?" Shanna glanced over at his plate, saw it was empty. Practically licked clean. She shrugged a fake wince.

"Except you, apparently. And, might I add, I'm impressed, unless you have the metabolism of a bird. In which case, I'm still impressed, but not as much."

"I think I skipped a couple meals today, maybe one or two yesterday, probably all of them the day before."

"Sounds like you need a keeper." Which sounded way more involved than she'd intended it to. Of course she was safe on the domestic count, being a woman who'd never cooked a complete meal in her entire life, to the annoyance of her ex-husband, who'd wanted both professional status as well as a domestic diva in his little woman.

"Or maybe I could simply use four more hours in the day, with an extra day tagged on at the end of the week."

"Four more hours and one more day in which you'd forget to eat. So, I have a question."

"Off limits?"

"Shouldn't be, but I don't really know since we never got around to discussing what's off limits for you. Anyway, it's about Tuscany. You don't seem like the type of person who'd ever want to take a holiday, yet there you were, all relaxed..."

"Until you sat down at my table."

"That *did* disrupt you, didn't it?" she said with a smile.

"Not as much as looking up and seeing you standing there in my emergency room a few weeks later."

"Unavoidable. Both times, actually. You were sitting at the table I'd sat at every morning for a month, and I didn't want to miss my view. It's spectacular. Something I looked forward to. And there was nothing I could do about barging into your Emergency because I had a dying patient and yours was the only Emergency in a hundred miles. Anyway, back to Tuscany. What was that about? Because men like you who won't take time off to eat also won't take time off to go skiing."

"It was about a Christmas gift from my sister and her husband. We'd had a stressful few months, learning things about our parents we didn't want to know. Amanda and her husband had their time away when they married and they thought I needed some downtime, as well. I'm not so much of a recluse that I could turn it down. Besides, I'd always wanted to go to Tuscany."

"I wouldn't have guessed you for the Tuscany type."

"Me neither, actually. But even now and then even someone like me has a need for something nice."

"Ben, I didn't mean..." Too late. The moment her words were out, that little bit of abandon she'd caught a glimpse of in him retreated to distant icebergs. Now there he was, all rigid and brooding, just like the way he'd been that morning in Tuscany. In other words, her evening with Dr. Ben

Robinson had ended the way it had started. Badly. "I'm sorry. I didn't mean to imply you wouldn't want something nice, like a holiday in Tuscany."

"You're right, though. It wasn't me. It was the person who stepped outside me for a few days."

"We create who we want to be, Ben. That's the easy part. The hard part is figuring out who that is. And I liked the man I met in Tuscany, otherwise I wouldn't have spent time with him. But I like the man in Argentina, as well. He's different. Not as relaxed. Underestimates himself in huge ways, but every bit as likeable as the man I met in Tuscany when he wants to be…which isn't enough."

"When he wants to be. See, that's the crux of the matter, isn't it? I don't really care if I'm liked as a person. Being respected as a doctor is more important, and as often as not it's easier not being liked."

"Really? You're serious?"

He shrugged. "I'm not a disagreeable person, Shanna. At least, I try not to be. But as far as extending myself so someone can like me, or be my friend…it doesn't matter. Being alone is fine. I'm used to my own company, and I can accept that."

"Because of your scars?" she asked, and instantly regretted it, because he tensed up. The strain was obvious at once in his face, in the way he squared his shoulders and sat up straighter in his chair. "Or is that an off-limits topic?" she asked quickly,

"My scars have nothing to do with anything and, yes, I prefer not to talk about them."

His voice couldn't have been any stiffer. And just like that, their evening together was over. He distanced himself and she could see he wasn't coming back around anytime soon because he was exhibiting all the telltale signs—

looking around, glancing at his watch, huffing out impatient sighs.

She hadn't meant to turn a pleasant time into one where half the people involved didn't want to tolerate the other half, and it was painfully obvious Ben didn't want to tolerate her right now. Fighting himself not to show it, and losing the fight.

"Okay, I'll add it to the list. Anyway, I, um…I need to get back. Reading to do… And sleep. Lovely dinner, though. Very…" She stood, pushed the chair back so hard it toppled over, hitting the plank floor with a hollow thud. One of the servers pushed through the crowded tables to right the chair, and she was grateful for the distraction as Ben was simply sitting there, staring at her, so untouchable on any level that all she wanted to do was get away. "Thank you," she managed, after the server had scooted away.

"Wouldn't you care to stay and have dessert or coffee?" he asked, trying hard to force pleasantries into the clumsy moment.

"If I go now, I can read one journal article and still have ten hours of uninterrupted sleep before I'm back on duty. Win-win for me." She smiled, but the sentiment behind it was…well, she wasn't sure. Let down, maybe?

Finally, he stood. "Look, I'm sorry this is so awkward. Like I told you, I don't do this, Shanna. Don't go out, don't socialize. Don't have pleasant conversations with beautiful women. Now you see why."

"What I see, Ben, is a man who holds himself back. If that's your choice, then it's your choice. But if you're doing it because you think your scars really matter to me, or because you believe you can't socialize or you're not good at it, you're wrong. Because I did have a lovely evening *with* you, up until the moment you decided to check out of our date because I mentioned something that was, apparently, on your list. You underestimate who you are, Ben. And you underestimate how people view you."

"Or I know how people view me, and I've put myself in a place where it doesn't matter anymore."

"It matters, Ben. And I'm sorry for your isolation. So now I'm going back to my room. Please, stay here. Have your dessert and coffee. Don't worry about me. I'll be fine getting back on my own." It wasn't the worst date she'd ever had. That would have been the one where she'd met her ex-husband—a night of business transactions, pure and simple. Oh, he'd been charming enough. Hadn't checked out on her like Ben just had. But he hadn't really been there, either. Probably because he had been daydreaming his way to Chief of Surgery at Brooks, a sure promotion when you married the collective owners' daughter, granddaughter, sister, whatever you wanted to call her. The thing was, that bad date had ended in marriage two months later. This one…it wasn't going to end in anything. Ben wore his intentions looped around his neck the way he did his stethoscope.

On her way down the road Shanna glanced back at Ben, who was paying the server and probably thinking about the faster path back to the hospital. Admittedly, she was disappointed to see him concentrating on counting out change and not even watching to see if she'd taken the correct road back. Which she had, but it would have been nice to see him return a glance with a little bit of concern when she'd looked back at—

Shanna stopped in midthought, blinked. Automatically switched into doctor mode. Sucked in a deep breath and spun round, then covered the fifty or so yards back to the restaurant before the server had collapsed all the way into Ben's arms. "Symptoms?" she shouted at him over the gasps of the crowd.

He was holding her, half suspended in the air, lowering her gently to the plank floor by the time Shanna literally hurdled over the stone wall surrounding the restaurant's outdoor tables and was at his side. Ben went to his knees with the girl, starting his first assessment of her. "Fever," he said as several patrons came running over to watch, tightening into a narrow circle around Ben and Shanna. "Pale. Shallow respirations. Clammy. Shanna, could you get these people to move back?" he yelled to her over the din.

Without a moment's hesitation she stood and took command of the crowd. *"Por favor. Todos retroceden. Somos médicos. Debemos alojarnos para revisar a esta chica. Por favor, retroceda."* With her words she stepped into the crowd, literally spreading her arms and forcing them back, farther and farther, until the restaurant owner, Señor Raul Varga appeared, and asked everyone standing around outside to, please, go back into the restaurant and have a *yerba maté* or a *licuado* courtesy of the restaurant.

"Thank you," Shanna said, on her way back to help Ben.

"Will she be okay?" Varga asked. "She's my daughter. Graciela."

"You daughter…" Shanna mused. Then asked immediately, "Has she been sick lately? Doing anything different from what she normally does? *Anything* out of the ordinary?"

He shook his head. "Nothing that I can remember, except she's been complaining she's tired. My wife usually knows these things better than I do, but she's away, taking care of her mother. And I think my daughter is doing this for attention because she has to take over some of her mother's duties for a while and she doesn't like it."

Not likely, Shanna thought. Not with Ben down on the floor with the girl, doing a frantic check. "But other than tired, have you noticed anything else about Graciela?" Varga was not a wealth of information, and she understood he was frustrated with a situation he didn't know how to control—a teenage daughter—but she had to keep pressing him. "Think about it. Was there something you wouldn't normally pay any attention to?"

He frowned. Rubbed his forehead. "Maybe. It was a nosebleed. Is this bad? Is she really sick?"

"When was that?" Shanna asked anxiously. "The nosebleed. When was it?"

"A few days ago. Then she was sick to her stomach. Vomiting a little. But I think it was on purpose." The increasing worry on his face said just the opposite.

"Anything else?"

"Let me think, please." Varga shook his head, shut his eyes.

"Has she had a headache?"

He nodded. "Yes! A little, maybe. She's been working hard, complaining because she wants to do other things. But I thought she was playing sick so she could go to Buenos Aires with her friends. They had a trip planned to visit the *Museo de Arte Latinoamericano,* and I wouldn't let her go because I needed help here. So I thought she was being…how do you say, *petulante?*"

"Petulant," Shanna said, realizing this was far more than a case of a teenage girl trying to get her own way. "Look, I'm pretty sure Dr. Robinson's going to want Graciela in the hospital, so if you have a vehicle…"

"A truck," Varga said, full concern finally registering on his face.

"Good. Go bring it to the front of the restaurant. And let me tell Dr. Robinson we'll be ready to go in a few minutes." After she told him what she suspected.

"My Graciela is that sick?"

"I think she is." She gave him a reassuring squeeze on his arm. Poor man had thought he was dealing with a contentious teenager, not a very sick one. "But we'll know more once we get her up to Caridad."

"Slow pulse," Ben said, when Shanna returned to him and knelt down. "Respirations still labored but not getting worse. And without a thermometer I'm guessing three or four degrees of fever."

"Specifically, *yellow* fever," Shanna said.

Rather than questioning her, Ben looked over at her, frowning. "How so?"

"History of bloody nose the past few days, nausea, headache...with a slow pulse and a fever... Am I wrong?" she asked, wondering what his intent stare was about. "Is that why you're frowning at me?"

"That's a frown of admiration," he said, "because I think you're spot on."

"But you already knew, didn't you?"

"Saw her having some back spasms earlier, so I was guessing. Nothing confirmed, though."

"Well, I may be late with the diagnosis, but I've got a truck ready to take her to the hospital. Unless you beat me to that, too."

He smiled. "It was a brilliant catch, Shanna, for someone who's never practiced in the jungle before. You, um... you haven't practiced in the jungle before, have you?"

A brilliant catch? That pleased her, actually. She'd had compliments before. Lots of them, some because she'd done something good and more than a fair share of kiss-up compliments because she was a Brooks and someone wanted something from her, or her family. But Ben's praise was genuine, and it felt good. "No, I haven't. Just imagine what I could do if had," she said just as Varga rolled up outside in his truck.

Forty minutes later, Graciela Varga, who was floating in and out of consciousness, was isolated in a small hospital room as far away from the rest of the patient rooms as possible, one of three Ben used as his intensive care. He was overseeing the administration of IV fluids when Shanna entered the room. "What's next?" she asked him. Except for the last few minutes, trying to explain to Graciela's mother, by phone, what was going on with her daughter, and at the same time trying to console an unconsolable Raul Varga, she hadn't been more than a few feet away from Ben since they'd admitted the girl.

"Wait and see. Since there's no treatment, we treat her symptoms, keep her fever down, keep her hydrated and make sure she doesn't get a urinary infection or pneumonia."

"What about the village? If we've got one case, aren't we at risk here for more?"

"In the two years I've been here, I've made sure as many people as were willing were vaccinated. So I'm not expecting an outbreak. Maybe some isolated cases, but nothing we can't deal with." He looked point blank at her. "Have you been vaccinated?" he asked.

Her reply, "It left a tiny pinprick scar. Want to see where?"

He didn't answer, of course. Instead, he handed her the chart. "She's yours. If you have any questions about what to do, ask."

"And I'll bet you're off to do a midnight run of yellow fever vaccinations. Right?"

"Am I that transparent?"

"Of course you are," she quipped, then headed off to the medicine room to see what kinds of antibiotics they had in large supply, just in case. The thing was, Ben wasn't really transparent in any sense of the word. In fact, if ever she'd known anyone who'd be difficult to see through, it would be him. He held tight to every little nuance of himself, didn't let anything go without a fight.

The reason she'd known he'd go back to the village to administer vaccinations was because that was the little piece of him he'd let her see. He was a humanitarian, so human-centered that the needs of the village came first. "And tomorrow you'll sleep," she murmured.

Ben was someone to admire in a world where people like him usually went unnoticed. In Ben's case, unnoticed by choice. Another of his off-limits subjects, she guessed as she started counting the various vials and pill bottles of penicillin.

"So, why am I here?" she mused as she shifted her count to the doxycycline. "To be like Ben." The thing was, she wasn't seeing Ben in the same light she had when she'd come here. And that was where it got complicated, because what Ben displayed on the outside and who he was on the inside weren't anywhere close to being the same.

And the more she watched him the more she wondered if she might not be patterning herself after the wrong perception of Ben Robinson. Because the man coming into view wasn't the person she wanted to be but one she might want to…have. Yes, that was definitely complicated.

"Which is why you need to go south and stay there with Jack for a little while," Ben argued with Amanda.

"I've been vaccinated, and I'm not going to catch anything."

"And I found three more mild cases of yellow fever last night." He pointed to her rounded belly. "Do I have to remind you…?"

"That I'm pregnant? No, Ben. You don't. And I'm being cautious."

"Not cautious enough. And Jack agrees with me on this. You shouldn't be here until we know if these are just isolated cases or a full-blown outbreak. And he does miss you. So does your son."

"If I leave, you'll be short-handed," she argued

He glanced at Shanna, hoping for some support. In these arguments with his sister he never won. Never had. Probably never would. And she was correct in that she wasn't at risk of catching yellow fever. Still, there were always the oddball cases. "Just go. Make me feel better. For once, let me win an argument."

"And I can cover for you," Shanna volunteered. They were sitting in the cramped lounge. Ben was all rigid on the wooden chair in the corner, Amanda was sitting on the two-seat sofa, with her feet up, and Shanna was sitting cross-legged on top of the table, a pseudo-meditative position, not that she was meditating there, more that it was the only place to sit comfortably with the other spots occupied. And she was tired to the bone. Run ragged these past twenty-four hours. Hoping for an adrenalin push to get her through the next several.

"Starting now. Which means…" She swept her hands in a shooing motion. "Go. Get out of here. We're fine."

"That's not the point," Amanda said, looking first at Shanna then at Ben. "My brother overreacts."

"And my brothers overachieve," Shanna countered. "They're not going to change. Doubt Ben will, either."

"So you're taking his side?"

"No sides to take. You've got a lovely husband and son out there who'd probably be overjoyed to have you spring an unexpected trip on them. Take it from someone whose ex-husband wasn't so lovely—join them. Enjoy what you've got. Let Ben quit worrying about you."

"You have an ex-husband?" Ben asked, totally flummoxed by her casual announcement. Somehow he'd never pictured her married. Or involved. Or anything. Stupid of him, really. Why wouldn't she have an ex-husband/or a current one, for that matter? Even an involvement. Shanna was sensational. Could have her pick of men. "Would he be off limits?"

Shanna shook her head. "Not off limits. Just not worthy of wasting good breath on. He happened at a time when I wanted a pat on the head from my family. As it turned out, he wanted my family's name. Daddy shoved him in my direction, not sure what came after that, but two months later we were married. I like to think of it as a marriage of inconvenience, because nothing worked out with it, except he got himself into my family, even took the family name. The only good thing that came of it was the divorce."

"He actually took your name?" Ben asked.

"In a hyphenated version. Dr. William Henry Morrison *hyphen* Brooks. I wanted to add the initials BD after that, for Big Deal, because that's what he thought he was. But he didn't think that was funny."

It was, though. And Ben laughed out loud at the mental image he was forming of Dr. William Henry Morrison *hyphen* Brooks, Big Deal. "So *you* divorced him, not the other way around?"

"I divorced him, and I would have done it twice if I could have. Although, as a parting gift, I let him keep my name, and my family let him keep his position at Brooks. In deference to my ex, he's a good doctor, brilliant neurosurgeon, and he's turned himself into the third son my father never had. No bitter feelings, though. William got what he wanted and I got my freedom back before we did anything like that." She pointed to Amanda's belly. "Speaking of which, do you need helping packing your bag, Amanda?"

"You're not the most subtle person I've ever met," Amanda replied, pushing herself up off the two-seat couch. "And while I appreciate the offer, I'm not going to take much with me. Just enough clothes for a few days. Oh, and, Ben…" she turned a pointed stare on her brother "…since you're forcing this on me, I'm going to raid supplies so I can take some things down to the orphanage. If there's anything you don't want me taking, let me know."

"I already have a couple of boxes packed for Richard out on the porch, ready to go." He glanced at Shanna to explain. "An orphanage we help support. Richard Hathaway operates on meager supplies—more meager than we do—and we try to help him out where we can."

"When you don't have enough yourself?" Shanna asked.

"That's why I named the hospital Caridad—charity. We do what we can when we're able. Not everybody's fortunate but everybody's deserving."

"What you're deserving of, Ben," she said, uncrossing her legs and scooting herself to the edge of the table, "is some sleep. We've got two other doctors up and working right now and we can handle anything that comes in. So don't argue with me, okay? You look tired. Go take a nap, and I'll come and get you if we need you. Maybe fix you some of that yerba maté tea after you get up, even though I didn't lose the bet."

"You know me. Yerba maté is hard to resist." So was Shanna. And as much as he hated admitting it, he *was* feeling tired, more so than usual. Maybe a nice, cool shower then a couple hours' sleep would do him some good. "Okay, I'm going. No argument," he said, also standing. On his way out the door he gave his sister a squeeze on the arm. "Tell Jack to tie you up, if that's what it takes."

"I love you, too," Amanda replied, laughing. She turned

to Shanna. "And you get to tie him up, if that's what you have to do."

"I heard that," Ben shouted from down the hall.

"I meant you to," Amanda shouted back.

"My brothers and I were never like that," Shanna said.

"You mean close?"

"Close, friendly. My whole family's demeanor is...I guess the best way to describe it is that we keep ourselves emotionally separated. I mean, there's love, don't get me wrong, but we don't show it. Don't acknowledge it. Most of the time we just have our own agendas."

"Even when you were children?"

"Especially when we were children. Because we were in training then."

"Training for what?"

"To be who we were supposed to be—a Brooks," Shanna said with a wistful smile. "You're lucky to have a brother like Ben. Lucky to be so close."

"I know," Amanda said as she exited the room.

A cool shower and a nap—not quite as good as Tuscany, but he'd take it. At thirty-six, he wasn't exactly old but the muscles were tightening up on him a little more often these days. The body wearing down a little faster. Oh, he could still keep up the pace. Keeping it with a nap thrown in made it easier, though. Especially on days like today where he just felt beat.

With a weary sigh Ben stripped himself bare in his room then trudged to the bath, taking care not to look in the floor-length mirror as he passed it by. Why torture himself? Truth was, he'd thought about having it removed and keeping only the shaving mirror in the bathroom. That would have been another cop-out, though, and in a life filled with too many cop-outs with bad results already, this one just didn't measure up.

So he simply plodded on by, headed straight to the shower and stepped in, hoping the cold spray would chill some sense into him. Because, damn, he had Shanna on his mind. Couldn't get her out of it. Couldn't quit thinking about her married, or not married, or sitting across the table from him all bundled up until only her eyes were showing.

She'd hit him hard, which was why he turned on the water full spray and let its moderately cool pelting sting his skin. He didn't need to be thinking about her, not in the way he was trying to avoid. Even now, in not thinking about her, he was thinking about her so intently he felt the ache start in his groin. Then the throb. Before it went further, he punched the water faucets off, grabbed a towel and slammed the shower door back so hard it broke off its hinges. Not that it mattered, because they were his hinges, weren't they? So he could break them any damn way he wanted.

Although to break them because he was thinking of Shanna—that wasn't acceptable. Nothing about the crazy way he felt when he was near her was acceptable. So, after a hasty hit with the razor to his stubble, and a comb through his hair, he threw on a pair of cotton boxers and a T-shirt and tumbled into bed, face first, already worrying that he wouldn't be able to take advantage of the next couple of hours.

Too often he didn't sleep even when he had the time off, like he did right now, because his head was filled with so many things—the hospital, his mother, who was fading away to old-age illnesses, his sister, a long life of emptiness ahead of him. Mind-sucks was what he called them. A litany of stresses meant to keep him awake.

Right now, though, it wasn't a mind-suck that wouldn't let him close his eyes. It was Shanna. And the instant she popped into his mind, that ache in his groin wasn't far behind. "Damn," he muttered, turning over and staring up at the ceiling, starting to count the revolutions of the overhead fan.

He was somewhere near a thousand revolutions when the ache subsided.

He was closer to two thousand when he finally dozed off.

Yerba maté tea. Herbal, grassy taste. Chock full of caffeine. And to her tongue peculiarly bitter. But Ben liked it. Lived on it, as she hardly ever saw him without a mug of it in his hand. It did smell lovely steeping, but sometimes the senses were deceptive. Her senses about Ben? Not deceptive as much as confused.

What she wanted to see in him was definitely there, but the whole picture was different. What she'd thought was a healthy wall of dispassion wasn't dispassion at all. He drove himself harder to take care of his patients than anyone she'd ever known. Like spending an entire night knocking on doors to look for people who needed vaccinations. Or pacing the hospital's halls hour upon hour, simply looking in on patients, attending to the little things like drinks of water and cool compresses.

Last night, or more precisely the small hours of the morning, she'd peeked into the children's ward only to find him sitting in a rocking chair, rocking a toddler to sleep, needing sleep himself as much as the restless toddler did. There was no dispassion in that. Yet the message he flashed clearly when anybody looked was, *Keep away.*

"So, who are you, Ben?" she asked as she placed the teapot on a tray and headed out the kitchen door with it.

A minute later, standing outside Ben's door, she was trying to figure out the answer to her question and waiting for him to respond to her first knock. Neither thing happened, so she shoved the question aside and knocked again, only to be met with no response. "Ben," she finally called through the door. "Your yerba maté tea awaits. Open up."

Again, nothing. Her third attempt came with a twist of the knob, and she found the door unlocked. Shoving it open a crack, she didn't enter, but called, "Ben, it's time to wake up and smell the tea. You in there?"

Only silence greeted her. A good hip shove to the door opened it, and she stepped inside. Saw him stretched out in bed. Long, muscular. The sight of him nearly took her breath away, he was so gorgeous, just lying there in sleeping innocence. She couldn't help staring for a moment. Admiring the physical aspect of him. Definitely a man who brought some kind of response to the surface, and it was a whole lot more than tingles and goose bumps. Clearing her throat, trying to avert her thoughts as well as her eyes, she began, "I brought you some—"

But Ben finished her sentence and ended her mood when he lurched up in the bed, and bellowed, "What the hell are you doing in here? Get out, Shanna!"

His voice and demeanor startled her so badly she stepped backward, tripped and dropped her tea on the floor, breaking the teapot and cup and splashing the yerba maté all over the wall and floor in the entryway. In her scurry to sidestep the mess, she didn't see Ben jump from the bed and practically sprint across the room. But she heard the bathroom door slam, and the only thing she could think was that he must have been sleeping so soundly she'd startled him out of a dream.

"I'm sorry," she called to him. A frantic look for rags

or a towel to clean up the mess netted nothing. "I thought you'd like some tea before you went back on duty…"

"I'll clean it up," he shouted, his voice flat, inhospitable. "Just leave me alone and shut the door on your way out. And in the future, when I want tea, I'll take care of that on my own."

She'd made an effort, and even though it had turned out badly, that was all she got from him? *Shut the door on your way out?* She wasn't angry. More like hurt. Okay, so maybe she'd overstepped the mark, and maybe she shouldn't have barged into his room because he was, after all, a very private person. But, darn, she hadn't expected this reaction. Hadn't deserved it either, in her opinion. Well, so much for trying to be nice. "Fine," she snapped. "I'll shut your door."

She really wanted to slam it, but she didn't. Instead, she shut it quietly, listened to the hollow click, then went across the hall to her own room and listened to her own hollow click. It really wasn't right, feeling so dejected about what had just happened, but she did. And for the next ten minutes she sat on the edge of her bed, wondering why she'd bothered in the first place.

Was she simply trying to get Ben to like or notice her, the way she'd spent a lifetime trying for those very same things with her family? Or were her feelings for Ben turning into something she'd never counted on?

Neither would come with a happy ending because they were hinged on something in Ben that wouldn't be budged. Yet here she was, trying to budge him anyway, when she was the one who needed budging.

For the first time it occurred to her that Ben wasn't going to be able to teach her what she wanted to be taught. Which meant there was no reason to stay.

Except she wanted to. And that was the thought that sent her running for the shower, to wash off the tea and, hopefully, wash away some of the confusion. Because she really, truly didn't want to leave here, and the only reason that could be happening was that she was falling for someone who would never return her feelings. And that was what had got her here in the first place—her feelings.

CHAPTER SIX

HE REALLY wanted to lob the damned medical reference book at the wall. In fact, it was in his grip, ready to go, and the only thing stopping him was that someone out in the hall would hear it and come running. Then there would be questions, and he'd have to make up answers because he wasn't about to tell anybody that he'd spent the last two hours fretting over things he couldn't control. So what if she'd seen him…all of him? Did it make any difference? They weren't involved, weren't going to get involved. And she was a doctor after all. She'd seen scars. Even ones as bad as his.

But the look on her face…had he imagined it there? Or really seen it? Because it was no different than the look on Nancy's face that day he'd trusted her enough to let his guard down. Nancy had gasped. So had Shanna. And Nancy had turned away. Shanna? He didn't know what she'd done because she had been so involved in reacting to her spilled tea that he'd seized that opportunity to run for his clothes.

He shouldn't have yelled at her, though. After all, he was the one who'd invited her to stay in his cottage. Sooner or later she'd have noticed more than the few scars that showed on his neck. She would have seen those on his arm, shoulder, chest, down his belly to his hip, and halfway down his leg. It's who he was. *What* he was. And Shanna was perceptive. She'd already asked. Already started connecting the proverbial dots. Alcohol in his past, scars… And a lot more hideous dots to connect.

Tension running the length of his arm, Ben gripped the medical reference book so tight his knuckles turned white, then he stared at the book, willing it back to its spot on the shelf lest his frustration got the better of him. Normally, these things didn't matter. He resigned himself to what he could and couldn't have, and got on with life. But Shanna…why the hell was she stirring up these longings after he'd put them to rest? After he'd convinced himself it didn't matter anymore? And there were so many regrets attached to those longings. Damn, he had a list of them.

Ben looked at the book in his hand again, started to relax his grip then without thought or further provocation hurled it at the wall, knocking his medical diploma to the floor, along with the photos of his parents. It hit so hard it actually dented the wall. Didn't break through so much as dimple it. But it was a dimple heard up and down the hall outside because immediately someone knocked on the door. Then there were shouts. And more knocking.

"I'm fine," he shouted out to them, trying to maintain more control in his voice than he felt. "Just dropped something." More like his self-confidence dropping to the floor, shattering.

"Don't suppose a pot of yerba maté would fix something for you, would it?" one familiar voice rang out.

Naturally, she would be there to hear. Humiliation heaped on his earlier humiliation. Still, just hearing her voice, even though it was locked away on the other side of the door, made him unbend just a little. "But didn't you break my teapot?" he yelled back when he was convinced he could control the sharp cut that wanted to overtake his voice. Normally he wasn't this edgy. Normally he let these things go without acting out. Normally… What the hell was normal, anyway?

"I bought you another one in the village. Actually, I bought two, just in case."

Just go away, he thought. *Please, just go away, Shanna.* Even as he was thinking the words he was on his way to open the door to her. No barriers in place to stop him. "Before you come in, not a word. Okay? I'm just like everybody else. Get angry. That's all it was. Me getting angry." He pointed to the book. "I'm sorry about earlier, too, when you came to my room, and now I'm just…"

"Letting off a little steam."

"A whole lot of steam. Sometimes it builds up."

"I know the feeling. I threw a chair through a plate-glass window once," she said, bending down to pick up his diploma and photos from the shards of broken picture glass. "Meant to do it, too."

In spite of himself, Ben laughed. "I can picture that."

"You can?" she said, looking up at him. "Nobody else in my world could. In fact, they were pretty indignant about the whole thing, about how I'd had the audacity to react."

"React how?"

"In opposition to my family. I was fourteen or fifteen. I had a boyfriend. You know, love of my life and all that. And I wanted to go somewhere with him…don't remember where." She laughed. "Don't even remember his name. But my father refused to let me go because the Brooks family was going to be hosting some kind of event…we always hosted events. So, true to my teenage nature, I threw a tantrum." She stood and handed the photos and diploma to Ben.

"My tantrums were pretty much overlooked, though, because they were…quiet. No throwing books at the wall and breaking glass. More like a very passive *please let me.* Except that never got heard. Or if they heard me, they ignored it. So this one time I decided to get their attention. Actually, it was the beginning of several times I tried to get their attention. Other stories for other days because this was the beginning of Shanna, the wayward teenager."

"Who threw a chair out the window as her prelude." An image he liked.

"Actually, it was an antique Windsor sidechair worth about fifteen thousand dollars. Broke it to pieces. Dozens of pieces. No way to have it restored."

The smile on his face widened. "But did you feel better afterward?"

"Did you feel better after you threw the book?" she countered.

"A little," he admitted.

"A lot," she admitted. "Probably because that one act got me the first honest reaction I'd ever seen from my father. He was really…mad. Yelled at me. Stood over me when I cleaned up the broken glass. Took away all the privileges a girl that age has. *For a month!*"

"You liked that?"

"What I liked was knowing that I had the ability to make my father respond."

"Which you used over and over?"

She shrugged. "Like I said. Stories for another day."

"So, overall, how did that turn out for you?"

"Don't know yet. Time will tell, I suppose, because I'm still wayward, or willful, or whatever you want to call it. Look, I'm going to run down the hall and grab a broom and dustpan to get the glass cleaned up. You get to clean it up, though."

"After which you're going to suspend my privileges for a month?"

"Only if you want them suspended, Ben."

She was like a magnet. He couldn't help himself. As much as he didn't want to be drawn, he was. "Guess that depends on what's being suspended, doesn't it? Like my common sense," he said. "I'm really sorry about earlier, Shanna. You caught me…off guard."

"We all have our moments. Don't worry about it."

"But you didn't deserve one of *my* moments. They're…"

"Intense?"

"That's putting it mildly." Only there was nothing mild about his reactions. Most of the time he held them back, but with Shanna…seeing him figuratively bare came close to seeing the worst of part him, the part that still festered. And he couldn't deal with her seeing that. Just couldn't deal with it.

"You've got a way to go to equal some of mine, Ben." She smiled. "Like I said, we all have our moments, and a couple of mine really stand out."

"That bad?" he asked.

She laughed. "Worse." Spinning, she headed off in the direction of the supply closet, and while he was tempted to step out the door and watch her when she turned and scurried down the hall, he didn't. An old-fashioned page over the loudspeaker called him to Pediatrics, where Nurse Teresa Vera stopped him just short of entering the ward. "We've just readmitted Maritza Costa. She was complaining of another cold, had a little congestion in both lungs. Dr. Francis saw her in Emergency a little while ago and decided to have her stay."

Maritza Costa, a beautiful little girl with a bad heart. He didn't have the facilities here yet to treat her the way she needed, and her parents didn't want to send her to another hospital. Truth was, the child needed surgery very badly. Attempts to seal the hole in her heart through a cardiac cath had failed, and now it was a waiting game. Waiting, and a lot of finger-crossing, because Maritza wasn't going to get better without the surgery, and their best hope at present was to pray she didn't get worse. With an extra prayer tossed in that her parents would have a change of heart. No such luck, though. "Any problems other than congestion? Did you run an EKG?"

"EKG showed no significant changes. And no other medical problems except…"

Vera paused, obviously not sure that she should proceed.

"Except what?"

"She hasn't smiled, Doctor. Not once."

In most patients that wouldn't be considered a symptom, but in Maritza it was a huge sign that something else was going on because, no matter what else was happening to the child, Maritza smiled her way through it. It was something everybody at Caridad counted on. "I'll go and take a look, see if I can figure it out."

"I promised her ice cream but she says she's not hungry."

"Well, bring some anyway, and let's see what we can do."

In Pediatrics, Maritza had her own private bed, the one on the end where she could look out the window and watch the main street of the village. "So you're back again?" Ben said, pulling up a chair and sitting down next to her. Right away he saw it—the listlessness in her eyes. All the brightness usually there had drained away.

Maritza nodded but said nothing.

"Maritza, sweetheart, where don't you feel good? Can you tell me if something hurts, or just doesn't feel right?"

She shrugged and looked away. But not out the window. More like, she was staring off into space.

"It's okay if you don't answer me, but I'm going to listen to your chest now. I need to figure out what's making you feel this way." He placed the stethoscope into his ears then leaned over to have a listen to her chest. Definitely congestion. Wheezing bilaterally. "Could you turn over on your left side just a little?" he asked, then listened again when she did. "That's good. So, do you have a sore throat?" he asked. "If you do, I understand why you're not talking. It hurts to talk, doesn't it?"

She nodded.

"Can I have a look at your throat?" he asked, fishing through his pocket for his penlight. "I'm going to put a tongue depressor in your mouth, Maritza, so you may gag a little bit. But it will only take me a few seconds to look." Which was what he did. Quick peek, pink throat. Not flaming red, thank heavens. No fever either, according to her chart. But he still had a nagging suspicion...

"Three ice creams," Shanna said, carrying three bowls to the bedside, one of them so heaped with ice cream it was dripping over the sides. She looked at Maritza and smiled. "He really likes ice cream," she said, perching herself on the edge of the bed, handing Ben's bowl to Ben, setting her bowl aside and scooping out a spoonful for Maritza. "All they had in the kitchen was vanilla, but if you have a favorite flavor, I can look for it next time I'm down in the village."

"Vanilla's good," Maritza whispered, then took the spoon from Shanna, looked at it for a moment and finally lifted it to her lips. Took a tiny bite, winced when she swallowed and tried again.

"Maritza's been with us before," Ben explained, picking up his bowl of ice cream then standing. He ducked out of the cubicle, gave his ice cream to the only other child in the room today, ten-year-old Nayla, admitted with appendicitis and now excited to be the lucky recipient of the largest bowl of ice cream she'd ever seen in her life. "Ventricular septal defect," he said, stepping back over to Maritza's bed.

"Repaired?" she asked.

Maritza shook her head as Ben answered, "No. Not yet."

She addressed the girl. "Have you been to see a dentist lately, Maritza? Someone who looked at your teeth?"

"Yes," she whispered.

"Your parents took you?" Ben questioned, picking up Shanna's bowl of ice cream and simply holding it. Better the ice cream than clenching his fists. But he was angry. Damned angry. He'd specifically told her parents… "Was that when the traveling dentist came through last week?"

Maritza nodded.

He gripped the bowl even tighter. So tight the chill of it, combined with cutting off the blood supply to his fingers, caused a dull ache to set in. "Well, I think maybe I should…" The things he wanted to say to them, and would force himself to hold back, were giving him a headache, especially after he'd specifically given them the list of things Maritza should and should not do. "Should go find some medicine for you. But it's going to be in an IV, Maritza. You remember what that is, don't you?" Poor child. She didn't deserve this.

"Yes," she whispered as she attempted one more bite of the ice cream, then set the bowl aside and slid down into the bed, ready for a nap.

"Good. You sleep for a while," Shanna said gently, pulling the sheet up over the child. "As soon as we get some of the medicine into you, you'll start feeling better."

Maritza nodded as her eyes fluttered shut, and Ben instinctively laid a hand to her forehead. Definitely a fever now. Too hot. Too sick. "Bacterial endocarditis," he said gravely. "And she belongs in a hospital that can treat her heart condition as well as… You know, I specifically told them not to take her to the dentist. He comes through every few months, and Maritza's parents asked me if it would be okay to set up an appointment for her."

"But they didn't listen," Shanna said, sliding off the bed. "Are you okay, Ben?" she asked. "You seem agitated."

"Try angry," he said, walking away from the bed. "Enough to throw more than a book, which I'm not going to do."

Shanna caught up to him and they didn't speak until they were outside the ward. "Why hasn't her ventricular septal defect been corrected?" she finally asked.

"Her parents won't let us send her to one of the hospitals that can perform the surgery. They won't go very far from the village, won't let their daughter go very far."

"But do they know it's a correctable condition? That the longer they postpone it, the more difficult it's going to be?"

"They know all that, but they believe that as long as they bring her here she'll be fine."

"And pretty sick now, with a heart infection." Because bacteria had entered her system through a dental procedure. Common and frustrating. "So, can we send her someplace else now? Because this is going to get tricky."

Ben stopped, leaned against the wall, shut his eyes, trying to mentally will away his headache. "I'll talk to them again, but I'm not holding out a lot of hope. Amanda and I have tried everything we can think of and so far it's falling on deaf ears."

"Or frightened ears," Shanna said sympathetically, immediately connecting to the pain and fear of Maritza's parents. "It's hard to move in a different direction when it scares you to death."

"But they know they can go to the hospital with her if we transfer her." He opened his eyes, straightened up.

"You're right, though. I'm sure they're scared to death. But so am I, because we could lose her."

"Look, how about you go and talk to her parents since you know them, and I'll get an IV started in Maritza. Then I'll get some blood cultures going so we'll know what we're dealing with. And, Ben, relax. You're looking as stressed as Maritza looks sick."

"Easier said than done," he said as she walked away. Especially when his stress was about Shanna.

"Another case of yellow fever admitted." Shanna caught up with Ben in the corridor between their rooms. "And Maritza's stable." It had been a long day and she was ready to be off her feet for a while. "Her fever was elevated this evening, but the antibiotics should kick that pretty quickly."

"And her parents are still refusing to let me send her somewhere else, so nothing's changed with that."

His emotional level over this was much the way hers usually was, and it was interesting to watch because in Ben it didn't look like a weakness, which was the way she characterized it in herself. "Did they ever tell you why they allowed the dental procedure?"

He leaned back against the wall, folded his arms over his chest. Sighed heavily. "It was a free exam. They were trying to be good parents, and they didn't think an exam qualified as a procedure."

Shanna winced. "Scraping one of those dental scalers over my teeth is more than a procedure. It's torture."

"Well, procedure or torture, either way that's what happened. Look, would you like to come in for a drink? Not yerba maté, as I know you don't like that. But I've got some killer fruit juice. Unless you've got something else to do."

"I'd love some killer fruit juice. Can you give me a minute to go…" She had been going to say "slip into something more comfortable," but that certainly had a sexual connotation, which had no application here whatsoever. "Go change my shoes."

"I'll leave my door open. And I promise not to over-react this time."

In the span of a minute Shanna slipped out of her long cargo pants and oversized camp shirt and into a clean pair of shorts, a fresh T-shirt and a pair of sandals. Now she wouldn't look so much like Ben, who also wore long cargo pants and a below-the-elbow camp shirt. Sexy look on him. Dreary on her. On her way across the hall she wondered if he might have slipped into something more comfortable, too, but as she pushed through his door she saw the same old Ben in the same old clothes. Oh, well. So much for wishful thinking. "I see you cleaned up my mess from this afternoon."

"Shall I grovel to you now, tell you how embarrassed I am?"

Laughing, Shanna waved him off as she crossed the room and sat down at his tiny kitchen table for two. "For what it's worth, I thought you looked…good. Every now and then I enjoy a good look at a guy in his boxers."

"I take it that's not on your off-limit topics."

She shook her head. "A girl appreciates what she appreciates. No reason denying it."

"And your ex?"

"Definitely didn't appreciate him in any capacity. On our wedding night I caught him doodling his new last name on a pad of paper. And that was the high point of our marriage."

"Ouch," Ben said. "All the hopes and dreams of a new bride dashed to pieces in a doodle."

"No hopes, no dreams and definitely no dashing. But that's when I started formulating my divorce plans. It had been a huge mistake, but I didn't realize it until I said 'I do,' and knew I should have said 'I don't.'"

"And you got out fast."

"No, he delayed it. Was afraid he'd have to let go of my family. So it took a while, but in my mind the marriage lasted three months, even though the paperwork said two years."

"Why did you do it in the first place? Were you really that desperate to get your family's attention?"

"We all have our flaws. Mine just happens to be trying to please a family who won't be pleased by me. They're... hard to deal with sometimes. They thought I should be married, so that's what I did."

"That's rough," he said. "My father was a very demanding man, kept lots of secrets, told lots of lies, but I don't think there was a day of my life that I ever had to fight for his attention. I'm sorry you've had to do that."

"You know what they say about how something that doesn't kill you only makes you stronger." She took a sip of the juice. It was pulpy, thick and cool, sliding down her throat. And it took long enough to slide that she hoped in the span of those few seconds their topic of conversation would switch. Talking about her failure to please her family made her seem weak, and she didn't want Ben to see her that way.

"So, do we talk about the elephant in the room? I know it's one of your off-limit topics but, Ben...I think we should just get it out of the way. You know, over and done with then move on to the next subject."

He looked across the table at her, didn't flinch, didn't blink. Didn't do anything until he picked up his glass of juice and took a sip. "I was burned," he said, setting the glass back down. "I was fifteen, got a little sloppy in some car repairs I was doing with my dad, and the result is what you see. Some scars."

Said much too casually. "How extensive?" she asked.

"Neck, shoulder..." He shrugged, shook his head. "Not worth talking about."

Because he'd never talked about it? She'd seen him run when caught exposed, she saw the kinds of clothes he wore to cover up. Something told Shanna the real scars weren't what you could see on the surface. "Maybe not, but I'm sticking to my guns."

"About what?" he asked, clearly relieved she wasn't pursuing the matter.

"Men in boxer shorts. I do enjoy a good look every now and then, and you were a good look, scars included. So, on that note..." she scooted the chair back and stood "...thank you for the juice and the company. But now I'm going to grab a couple of hours' sleep then go back over and sit with Maritza for a while." Handing the glass to Ben as she passed him, she swept by then paused halfway between him and the door and turned to face him.

"My family is all about exclusion, Ben. That's what I grew up with, what I got used to. It's not a good way to have your life develop around you and it's not a good way to choose your life. Whatever you've gone through, whatever else you've done, you don't have to be excluded, and you don't have to exclude yourself. You've proved your place in the world and that accounts for a lot more than... scars."

He didn't respond but, then, she hadn't expected him to. No good-night or parting words of support. He was Ben after all. And the more she knew him, the more she cared. Because with Ben there were no perceptions. He was who he was.

* * *

"How long?" Shanna yelled down the hall, already assessing her options.

"Less than five minutes," the nurse yelled back. "Her fever spiked, we tried to cool her down with a sponge bath, but when that didn't work, we called you, and in those few minutes she…"

She'd had a febrile seizure. Then her heart had stopped. "And what was her temperature last time you took it?" Resuscitation

"One hundred-five."

"I need epinephrine," she said, sprinting by the nurse who detoured to the medicine room while Shanna shoved though the pediatric ward doors just as Ben came charging in from the opposite direction. At Maritza's bedside one nurse and a volunteer from the village were already fully engaged in resuscitation efforts when Ben grabbed the laryngoscope and an endotracheal tube off the emergency cart and in two blinks had the breathing tube in place.

"I'll bag," the nurse volunteered as Shanna moved in to start chest compressions while Ben readied the defibrillator in the event Maritza's heart didn't resume its rhythm on its own. "I called for epi," she said as he stepped back to ready the defibrillator. "But I'd rather not interrupt the resuscitation to use it if we don't have to."

"Because?" Ben asked.

"Side-effects. At Brooks, we instituted what's being recommended internationally, which is high-quality, rapid CPR with minimal interruptions, including not interrupting to administer medication. I went to a conference in Oslo and researchers there…" She stopped. "Bottom line, keep the CPR going, do the drugs afterward. But you know that, Ben. Didn't you write a response to one of the journal articles on it?"

"You read my response?"

"I read several of your responses," she said, getting ready to step back so Ben could attempt a cardioversion— shock Maritza's heart back into a normal rhythm. Once she saw he was ready, she stopped chest compression for a split second, looked at the heart monitor, saw nothing but the tell-tale squiggly tracing of ventricular fibrillation, where the heart was jiggling but not beating, then moved into place with the paddles. "Back," she cautioned the nurse as she herself stepped away and allowed Ben to come forward and administer the first shock to Maritza's chest.

Everybody in the room held their collective breaths for a fraction of a second, watching the heart tracing on the portable EKG machine continue to waver across the screen. Then, just as Shanna positioned herself to start compressions again, the first blip appeared. Then the second, the third…

"Hold off bagging her," Shanna instructed the nurse as she put a stethoscope to the girl's chest to see what was going on in there. A breath sound, a heartbeat… It was amazing how, after a sputter, Maritza was breathing again, fighting against the breathing tube. Not awake yet but returning to life.

"Welcome back," Ben said to the child. Then he turned to Shanna. "Now we get her transferred. Her parents are going to listen to me or I'll be taking her to *El hospital para la Cirugía Cardiovascular* in Buenos Aires myself."

"We didn't call them," one of the nurses said. "Didn't have time."

Ben looked out the window at Maritza's view of the village, all of it lit up now, casting a yellow glow against the black of the night. "That's fine. I'd rather talk to them at home anyway. Care to take a walk with me?" he asked Shanna, then signaled for Dr. Francis to stay with the girl while they went to make the notification.

"It's easy for you, isn't it?" Shanna asked Ben a little while later as they approached the Costa home. "Taking charge the way you do."

"I've never thought of myself as a take-charge kind of person."

"But you step up when it's necessary and…lead. Make people want to follow. My father and my grandfather, too, actually, are great leaders, but they do it by force. They demand that people follow them, whereas you simply walk quietly and people want to follow."

She twined her arm through his, fully expecting him to shake her off, but he didn't. And for a few moments someone might have mistaken them for lovers out for an evening stroll, they looked so cozy and perfect together. Well suited, Shanna thought, even though she knew better. Her head was in a fantasy world. Ben was being polite, not shaking her off. That was all. For a little while, though, it was nice. And such a simple thing. She liked simple things. Too bad she hadn't known that years ago.

Of course, if she had, she wouldn't have met Ben. And the more she knew about him, and the closer they became, the more she was beginning to see how truly passionate he was. Of course, if she totally convinced herself she'd made a mistake then there was no reason to be here. She'd come to study the way he distanced himself from his patients when, in truth, he didn't. It was himself he distanced himself from. But she wasn't ready to make the full admission because she wasn't ready to leave. So for now she shoved it out of her head.

"Shanna," he said, before he knocked on the door, "it's been a crazy day from the beginning to the end and—"

"And we survived to face another crazy day tomorrow," she said, letting go of his arm. What was the point of holding on to someone who didn't want to be held?

"Yes, another day. Look, I'm glad you're here. Whatever brought you here, whatever's keeping you here, I'm glad you're here."

"I'm glad I'm here, too. None of this is what I'd expected but, it's good."

"What did you expect?"

She laughed. "In my isolated world I expected Brooks in a miniature version. Maybe with a few jungle creatures thrown in for good measure."

"Well, the jungle creatures I can do, but this isn't Brooks by any stretch of the imagination. In fact, Caridad is the anti-Brooks."

"You can say that again."

He landed his first knocks on the door. Then stepped back, shoulder to shoulder with Shanna. "Like I said, it's nice having you here, Shanna. You make Caridad better, and I hope that in spite of my ups and downs, you'll consider staying for a while because…" He turned to face Shanna, who was already facing him. "Because we're good together, as doctor and doctor."

"Doctor and doctor," she murmured, stepping up to him.

"Nice medical relationship," he murmured.

"Very nice," she practically purred as she looked into his eyes. "Very, very nice."

By the time Maritza's father opened the door to them, they were locked in an embrace, exploring the depths of their very first kiss. A nice kiss, Shanna thought as the yellow porch light flipped on. Nicer than any kiss she'd ever had. But from a man who would regret it the instant it was over.

CHAPTER SEVEN

THE kiss had been yesterday, today was life as normal. But nerve-racking, considering the dozen or so times she'd walked by Ben already, only to be greeted by the most clinical of nods, with nothing else. She had been right. He regretted the kiss. So now what? How did they get back to the place they needed to be in order to keep working together? Or was Ben actually able to turn it off that easily?

So much for a spontaneous moment gone bad. Although she'd enjoyed it. But that was as much time as she had to devote to thinking about it because her day was full. Her yellow-fever patients were all recovering nicely, Maritza was finally where she needed to be and her doctors there were cautiously optimistic about her recovery. Now Shanna had a dozen patients waiting for her in clinic and if she didn't grab a cup of tea for herself now—*not* yerba maté— it might be hours before she got the chance again. So, on her way to clinic, she ducked into the lounge, put a kettle of water on the free-standing electric burner and was starting to look through Caridad's stash of various teas when she heard familiar footsteps behind her. Immediately, she tensed up. But didn't turn around to face him.

"That kiss probably wasn't the most appropriate thing I've ever done, but I'm not going to apologize for it," Ben said, standing in the doorway, keeping his distance.

He was scowling, she imagined. "Do you want me to apologize? Because from the way you've been avoiding me…"

"Not avoiding you. Just trying to figure out how to handle it."

"It was just a kiss, Ben." Simple admission, complicated reaction. That kiss had shaken her to the soul. "People do it all the time."

"I don't."

Of course he didn't. Ben preferred sitting with his face to the wall. Except it hadn't been a wall he'd been facing when he'd initiated the kiss. And make no mistake, he'd been the one to pull her into him. And not so gently. Not roughly, either. More like possessively. Being possessed by Ben…she'd liked it.

She turned to face him. "It reminded me of the night Jimmy Barstow brought me home from a date. He escorted me to the front porch and we had that typically awkward moment most teenagers do, where you're not sure about the kiss. You know, will he, won't he? Should I, shouldn't I? Should I tilt my head? Open my mouth?"

"Did you?" he asked.

"Tilt, yes. Mouth, no. It was my first kiss, by the way." She wrinkled her nose at the memory. "Not good by any stretch of the imagination. But, still, my first. And in a fifteen-year-old's mind, so romantic."

"Let me guess. Until the front porch light came on."

"Not just a light, Ben. It was a floodlight. Lit up the whole front yard and halfway across the street, blinded me and my date. Then there was my father, who'd grown to about ten times his normal size, as I seem to recall. He was standing in the front door, arms folded across his chest, mean frown on his face.

"In one version of the story he's holding a shotgun and

in another he's got two growling Rottweilers on leashes, ready to rip through the screen door. Either way, my father posed this huge threat and that's the part of this story that's never changed."

"So, what did he do?" Finally, Ben's scowl melted down to pleasant interest. No smile there but nothing negative, either.

Shanna shook her head. "Nothing. I expected an earthquake, and got…nothing. He opened the door for me, thanked Jimmy for seeing me home safely, and that was that."

"Were you disappointed?"

"Maybe a little. Normally, the people in my life fight against me. I think just that once I wanted someone to fight for me. Anyway…" she turned back round to find her tea "…last night, it was nice. Don't know what it was about, but I hope it doesn't come between us because I enjoy being here, Ben. Like the work, like you…"

"You had your tongue down my throat," he said, in his typical businesslike voice.

Smiling, Shanna grabbed a bag of oolong then turned back to face Ben just as the tea kettle began its spindly prewhistle. "Consider yourself lucky. I never got that far with Jimmy. And Jimmy never got that far with me, the way *you* did." Just then the kettle erupted into a full whistle, and Shanna was grateful for the distraction because, yes, she'd had her tongue down his throat and, yes, she'd enjoyed it. And, yes, she'd do it again. That was the troubling part. Knowing what she knew about Ben, she'd do it again.

"I don't do this, Shanna."

He entered the room, stepped up behind her, so close behind her she could feel his breath tickle her neck. Then it happened again, tingles and goose bumps. Only this time she shivered. And she couldn't hide it. He was too close, and she could feel him staring hard at her. Turning around now would mean risking another kiss. But today she wasn't into risks because one more risk and things might change drastically. She didn't want them to so she kept her back to him. "But you did," she said, trying not to sound as unsteady as she felt.

"We let it get out of hand once, but it's not going to happen again because I don't get involved in relationships."

"Are you sure?" she asked. "Because yesterday you seemed like a man on the verge."

"I'm always a man on the verge, but I'm also a man who knows when he has to pull back."

"Then you're missing out, Ben." She sidestepped him to prepare her tea. "Because getting involved on some level is what life's supposed to be about. I'd be lost without my involvements. They've made me who I am. Even my bad marriage played a part in shaping me. Every person I've ever met, every patient I've ever known… It's not good, excluding everything you're afraid will get close enough to touch you."

She turned around. "And that's not just about relationships, Ben. It's everything. It's…life."

"Sounds good when you say it, and for you it probably works. Hell, it probably works like that for just about everybody. But I don't have enough in me to be *more* than what this hospital needs. It's my life, Shanna. Everything I am, and there's nothing left over."

"Then that's what you'll be contented with for the rest of your life?"

"That's what I've reconciled myself to for the rest of my life. My choice."

"Too bad, because everybody loses. The people who surround you. You…me. We all lose."

Ben didn't say a word when she picked up her mug of

tea and walked away from him. Even, steady footsteps on the corridor floor. Jerky, unsteady heartbeats inside her chest. Because he was watching her. She could feel it. One kiss. One impulsive little kiss with such an enormous ripple effect. Nobody, not even Jimmy Barstow, had ever evoked the uncertainty and excitement in her in a simple kiss the way Ben had. So now what was she going to do about it?

Nothing. He'd made himself perfectly clear. He was married to his work. And as for her, she hadn't thought straight about anything for months. So who was to say she was thinking straight about her feelings for Ben? She liked him. Liked him enough to kiss him, actually. Liked him enough that she hadn't stopped thinking about that kiss.

But was there really something more than that? Or had that kiss merely been a refuge on a very tumultuous journey? Take one step beyond that kiss and that was when the confusion took over.

So, she had to keep reminding herself that Ben was her refuge for a little while, and only a little while, and that was where she needed to keep him. Shove him back to the edges and she'd be fine. Of course, the way *he* wanted to be kept on the edges was going to make that pretty easy.

"No, I'm fine." Talking to her grandfather was like talking to a wall. Nothing got through to the man except what he wanted to hear, which, in this case, wasn't what she was saying. In his defense, he was a great healer, had the best medical instinct she'd ever seen. But the downside to that came with the little girl who had just wanted to crawl up on her grandfather's lap and have him tell her a story.

In her life there had been no laps, no stories. Only a grandfather who would spend an occasional evening explaining a coronary stent or an implantable cardiac defibrillator to a six-year-old little girl who was clutching a plastic model of a human heart rather than a cuddly teddy bear. "I'm in Argentina right now."

She waved to Ben, who was poking his head into his office to see who was tying up his landline. She grinned sheepishly as she held the phone receiver away from her ear, not really keen on listening to the same loud voice booming the same things he'd told her when she'd left home. "Just seeing the sights for now, Grandfather. It's a beautiful country. Great food. Nice people." Like he would be interested in anything outside his world. "Good health care, too."

Okay, maybe she shouldn't have tossed that last bit into the conversation, but giving good health care was what this sojourn was about. Why she'd left medicine, why she hoped to find her way back. Why she was so confused about how to do that.

"It's nonsense, Shanna." Miles Brooks spoke so loudly Ben grimaced from the doorway on the other side of the room. "A waste of time, and I'm not a patient man. We have a medical center to run here, and we can't keep your position open forever while you're off trying to discover yourself, or whatever it is you're off doing."

She regretted Ben had to hear this, but it was his office, and it had the only private landline in the hospital. Since her cell wasn't getting a signal, she didn't have a choice. Though she hadn't expected Ben to fold his arms across his chest, lean against the door frame and simply listen. Which was exactly what he was doing.

"I'm not trying to discover myself, Grandfather," she said, knowing that wasn't entirely true. There was some self-discovery mixed in there. For the most part, though, she knew who she was, so this journey of hers was more about reconciliation. That was the part that got confusing. She still didn't know what she was trying to reconcile herself to—who she was or to who she had to become. "I'm just taking time to see things I've never had time to see before."

"While we continue working to support your whim. It's irresponsible, Shanna. And it's not fair to your family. You have your obligations to this family and to the medical center, and you're beginning to run out of goodwill, as far as most of us are concerned. We gave you your time, didn't have a choice. But your time's running out."

She shut her eyes and tried blanking out the next two minutes because she knew her grandfather's lecture by heart, knew every word of it, knew every inflection in his voice as he reeled out each and every point in detail, all of them telling her why she was such a letdown to her family, why she was such a screw-up in her duties.

It was easy to shut out, though, and it wasn't like this was the first time she'd shut it out. But what wasn't easy to shut out was Ben hearing it. Two uninterrupted minutes of standing and listening to all the things that made her a colossal Brooks failure, and by the time she'd hung up the phone she felt like she'd been put through the wringer, not because of what her grandfather had said but because of what Ben had overheard. And might believe.

"So there you have it," she said, standing up. "My dirty laundry. Every last speck of it."

"He's not a friendly man," Ben commented, still not budging from the doorway. "The day I sat across the desk from him and he pummeled me with questions, I think I would have rather taken a physical beating. So, how are you doing?"

"Pretty much beat up. Used to it, though. My grandfather means well…"

"For the medical center? Or for you?"

"It's all interchangeable. In my family, by the time we're able to walk, we're already beginning to assimilate. And it's not necessarily a bad thing, Ben. I'm not complaining. Wasn't even unhappy. But…we're just not typical, and sometimes I think that typical might be nice."

"You're a good doctor, Shanna. He's anxious to get you back. I can understand that."

"See, that's the thing. He's anxious to get me back because he wants to win. Wants to get his way."

"Or get his granddaughter back."

She thought about that for a moment. It would have been nice to believe there was some sentiment attached to him wanting her to return, but there wasn't. She was, pure and simple, a practical matter. Her grandfather wanted her back on his terms and anything else disrupted his plans.

"What he doesn't like to lose is control. The thing is, Ben, I don't hate him. Don't even dislike him. My grandfather's a great man, he's been responsible for many advances in cardiac medicine. And look at the hospitals and clinics he's built. I'm in awe of him. And proud of him. But…" She shrugged.

"It's tough being the granddaughter of a medical legacy?"

"Something like that." Especially if you were in search of your own medical legacy and beginning to have grave doubts that it's out there. "My entire family is so driven by what they do there's no room for anything else. Fun for my father is lecturing at a medical conference. For my mother it's publishing another article on the latest discovery in cancer treatment…she's an oncologist.

"You know my grandfather, and my grandmother is dean of a nursing school. My great-grandparents are the same. Great-Grandfather founded the Brooks Medical Center, Great-Grandmother started one of the first schools of nursing in that part of the country. That's who the Brooks family is, and they've cloistered me, but not with bad intentions. They kept my brothers and me separated from all the things other kids our ages were doing because the world we live in is a perfect world...for the Brooks family purpose."

"But not for Shanna?"

She shrugged. "It's a safe world. A whole lot safer than anything outside it. And the people in it are happy, Ben. There's never been a time when I've believed anyone in my family isn't happy."

"Which means Shanna is..."

"Trying to find out if I'm really cut from the family cloth. I've got to know myself better before I go back." Not just know herself better but prove herself worthy. She had to change, or everything about her future with Brooks Medical Center would be changed for her. "And in the meantime I'm going to be checking Beatriz Rivas in a few minutes. Her baby's breech, and as she's getting closer to her due date, I want to see what I can do about turning it."

"An ECV?"

"I know there are a lot of various non-medical traditions on how to turn a baby—playing soft music at the pelvic bone so the baby will gravitate toward it, putting ice at the top of the abdomen so the baby will turn away from it. But an external cephalic version is relatively easy, and if it works it saves Beatriz from having a Caesarean section."

"You've done them before?"

Shanna nodded. "And had pretty good luck. It doesn't always work, but in my opinion it's always worth a try. And since you have that nice ultrasound machine..."

"Thanks to my brother-in-law. When he found out Amanda was pregnant, he ordered state-of-the-art everything for obstetrics. Otherwise I might have to sit near the end of the bed, strum my ukelele and hope the baby turns toward my music."

Shanna laughed. "I didn't take you for a ukelele man."

"I'm not. But my mother always thought I had the music in me, which I didn't, and when I was younger she bought me a mighty fine electric guitar and an amp that turns up so loud it would shake the currasows right out of the trees." He smiled. "Large birds. Size of a wild turkey."

"So you're a rock star."

"Hardly. Haven't touched a guitar since I was a kid. Wasn't very good at it when I did."

"Then the currasows are safe. Good for them, too bad for me. I'd have liked to hear you play."

"Trust me. When I was a kid, nobody liked hearing me play, but it didn't matter because I loved it. Loved the way I shattered windows, knocked things off walls...in the neighbor's house across the street."

It was a new way to picture Ben, talking about something he loved other than medicine. Something she hadn't anticipated but really, really liked. Naturally, her mind went wild with the thought—skin-tight jeans, ab-tight T-shirt, ripped, exposing flesh. That was an unexpected jolt of nice she hadn't seen coming, but one a girl could certainly enjoy lingering on for a while.

"What's the smile about?" he asked.

"Thinking about delivering Beatriz's baby," she lied. "She's thirty-seven weeks now, and I'm hoping I'll be here long enough to do the delivery. Want to help me with the ECV?"

Ben finally stepped into the office. "Give me five minutes, okay?"

"Five minutes. And, Ben, about that kiss..." She'd wanted it. No denying that. No telling him that, either. "I didn't come here to get personally involved, if that's worrying you. We made a mistake, it's over. Live and learn."

"Live and learn. And I'm sorry I put you through my usual reaction."

Shanna laughed. "One thing's for sure—you've got it down to a science."

"They say practice makes perfect."

But for Ben practice brought about heartache. She could see it in his eyes, and that sadness cut right through her. Which was precisely what her grandfather had lectured her about—she was too emotional to succeed at Brooks. So far, though, none of that was changing. And for the first time since she'd left she was beginning to wonder if she wanted to go back there. The question was always out there about her grandfather not taking her back, but she'd never thought she might be the one to sever the ties. It was on her mind now.

"And perfection takes practice," she said, still trying to come to terms with how she might be the one to cut herself off from her family, and not the other way around.

"Well, perfect or not, as a friend, do you want to go down to the village with me later on? Maybe have dinner, listen to some music? No off-limits lists involved."

It was really too bad she didn't want to get involved as much as he didn't want to get involved, because Ben would have been the one. Undeniably, unquestionably, the one. Really, too bad. "In what kind of time frame? I'm assuming you have a time limit on that."

He winced then smiled. "Okay, I deserved that."

Biting back her own smile, she arched playful eyebrows at him. "You're right, you did. So, how about we get through the ECV then see what happens afterward?"

"Fair enough."

She nodded then stepped out into the hall. "Five minutes, Ben." Five minutes to collect her wits, because Ben had just asked her out on a date, whether or not that was what he'd intended. And she'd put him off. Of course, if he'd been standing there in rock-star clothes rather than well-worn and faded scrubs... Thing was, in her mind right now he was in well-worn and faded scrubs, and looking as good as he would in rock-star clothes. Causing her breath to catch, her pulse to increase a beat or two.

Just a reaction to something that didn't exist. That was all it was. Nothing.

When he entered the obstetrics procedure room, the patient was on her hands and knees on the floor and Shanna was sitting on a stool, holding an electric toothbrush. This was where most doctors would have stopped whatever was going on, no questions asked, and quickly come up with another plan. But somehow the doctor with the toothbrush looked like she was totally in control of the situation, and if Ben hadn't already put his faith in her, it was clear from the expression on Beatriz Rivas's face that she had all the faith in the world. So he simply slipped in and took his place standing along the wall, watching and waiting for Shanna's next move.

"I had her start the rocking yesterday," she said to him. "I don't like to give anesthesia before the procedure. Don't even like using tocolytic drugs—" meant as a relaxer "—because they can increase the mother's pulse rate as well as the baby's heart rate, and lower the mother's blood pressure, which can put extra strain on her heart. And that's not to mention they can make her jittery, anxious and nauseated and also send her into labor. So I try the more natural approach, and pelvic rocking helps."

"Makes sense. But the toothbrush?"

"Actually, studies have shown that vibroacoustic stimulation can startle the baby into moving away from the woman's spine, which makes him or her more easy to turn. I just happen to like the buzzing sound an electric toothbrush makes. It's gentle, and I've had it work."

"But no ukelele?" he asked, smiling.

"Sorry. Your uke's untried, my toothbrush isn't." Grinning, she held it up, hit the switch, then let it buzz for a second.

"Somehow I don't see this approach being used at Brooks Medical Center. But I could be wrong."

She shook her head. "Not wrong. If any of my family members walked in on this…" Standing, she bent down to help Beatriz up from the floor. "Let's just say that any encounters you've had with my grandfather in the past would have been a walk in the park in comparison. So now…" She gestured for Ben to turn around as she helped Beatriz into an exam gown, but he chose to leave the room instead. Privacy was his own personal issue, which turned it into a priority for his patients. So often in medicine, when all the basic elements were broken down, and all the tests taken, the only thing some patients were left with was their self-respect. It was always his aim to leave that intact as well as add his share to it.

In this case, he was glad for a short reprieve, where he simply went to the desk across the hall and sat down. Too much work was finally beginning to catch up with him. He was a little achy today, with a bit of a headache. Nothing eight or ten uninterrupted hours of sleep wouldn't fix. Except he didn't have eight or ten hours anywhere in his schedule, and the foreseeable future wasn't going to be any different. Two of his doctors had left the day before and no one had come to replace them.

But in a week, he promised himself. When his new staff was on board and oriented to the hospital, when the final verdict that the yellow-fever cases were isolated and not an outbreak, when a couple of his more critical cases had turned the corner—that was when he'd take his eight or ten hours. Shut his eyes, hopefully dream of Tuscany...

"Ben," Shanna whispered, practically in his ear. "Wake up. Are you okay?" Asked to the accompaniment of gentle nudging.

A moment passed before he was aware of her standing over him, looking down. The back of her hand was laid across his forehead like she was a mother checking a child for fever.

"Don't know how it was where you went to med school, but where I went we had an actual class on catnapping. Taught us how, when, where to grab them, including standing up, leaning on a wall, napping with eyes open so no one will know you're napping..."

"Napping with a fever?" she asked.

He rolled back in his chair to get away from her. "There's a difference between warm and feverish. I'm warm. Need to take off a layer of clothing to get more comfortable."

"What are you denying, Ben?"

"Nothing."

"You're rundown."

"And I'm entitled to be rundown."

"But you got back off a holiday not so long ago."

"More rundown from that than from work."

"It's true what they say, isn't it?" she asked, spinning away from him. "That doctors make the worst patients."

"That would assume I'm a patient. I'm not." He stood, followed her to the exam-room door. "Look, I appreciate your concern, Shanna, but I'm not sick. I'll admit I'm tired, I'll admit I wouldn't mind getting a good night's sleep. That's as far as it goes."

"You're sure?" she asked, before she pushed open the door. "Because I can handle more if you need a day or two off to recover. Or even a night off to sleep. Like tonight. Skip the night on the town so you can sleep."

She spun to face him. Then simply stared. Looked deep into his eyes for so long he wasn't sure if she was assessing him for something or trying to discern a lie the way his mother used to do—that long, hard stare, followed by, "Benny, I know you're not telling me the truth." Only thing was, he wasn't lying about anything. He wasn't sick. Left to the scrutiny of an overly compassionate doctor, that might be the way it looked. But he knew his body…the good and the bad of it. Right now, he was tired. That was all.

Shanna cared. And she worried about him. Worried too much. It was a nice feeling, having someone worry about him outside his mandatory worriers—his mom, his sister and even to some extent his brother-in-law. Nothing he was going to get used to, though. Because Shanna was just passing through, like it or not.

Today, he didn't like it.

CHAPTER EIGHT

"So, WHERE do we begin?" he asked Shanna, deferring completely to her knowledge in carrying out the external cephalic version.

Shanna glanced at him, studied him only the way Shanna could—a hard, through-to-the-bone stare like she was seeing more than he wanted anyone to. Like she was trying to find the soul he fought to keep shrouded. Finally, she nodded.

"I'd like you to monitor the baby's heatbeat, Dr. Robinson, as well as Beatriz's vital signs. Her baseline is already charted, so I think we're good to go."

Smiling at her patient, she exuded confidence and caring. It was written all over her, everything she was, and everything that made her a good doctor. Ben liked the way she cared, the way she got involved. Doctors with that level of passion were hard to find, especially coming from the kind of institution Brooks Medical Center was, and he could understand why her family wanted her back. She was rare in the profession. Someone to admire for her compassion. "Good with that," he said.

"So, are you ready to get this baby turned over?"

"*Sí,* Doc Shanna," Beatriz responded.

First, she gave Ben a smile, then she turned her attention back to her patient. "Okay, first, relax. You may feel a little discomfort, but you've already had two other babies and this isn't anything compared to that." Handing Beatriz the toothbrush, she instructed her to simply hold it near the baby's head, then she examined the woman's belly until she found the baby's exact placement.

Glancing at Ben, she said, "Normally this is where I might do an ultrasound to determine the positioning, but baby Rivas has taken a mighty strong position against Beatriz's pelvis—his or her bottom is deeply seated there—so I'm going to tilt the head of the table down to help baby move away from there. Except..." she winked at him "...this table doesn't tilt, so guess what?"

He chuckled. "I'm going to make it tilt. Probably with a couple of nice big medical texts that work better to prop up a table than hit a wall."

Two minutes later, Ben was positioning them under the table legs, making a mental note to go looking for better exam tables whenever he had the chance. He was welcome to scrounge used equipment in any number of hospitals throughout Argentina. In fact, that was how he'd started Caridad—with scrounged equipment from other hospitals. For now the medical texts were much better suited under the table than against the wall, and Shanna was busy manipulating Beatriz's belly, turning the baby like it was something she did every day.

Watching her, feeling his admiration for her continue to spiral upward, he saw the good rapport she found with her patient. Saw the ease, the caring. Especially saw the way Shanna kept Beatriz smiling with her lighthearted chat about baby names, even though without painkillers the procedure could be excruciating, and probably was. All of it was amazing to watch, every facet of Shanna's bedside manner, every nuance of her skill.

"Okay, now. Just think of this as a tummy massage

with a little extra pressure," Shanna said while she oiled up Beatriz's belly then began in earnest the kneading that would turn the baby round, placing her left hand where the baby's head was positioned and the right at the baby's bottom. "You're definitely going to feel some pressure and discomfort, so let me know if the pain gets too bad because we can stop, and I'll give you something to ease it."

"Vital signs holding nicely," Ben said, feeling almost superfluous in the room now as Shanna had everything so much under control.

She smiled at him. "Well, up on this end I'm being kicked. Someone's really fighting me on this move. And from the force of the kick I'm betting we may have a future soccer star here." She leaned a bit more into Beatriz and alternately pushed then rolled the baby to a head-down position for a moment, pausing to slide the ultrasound probe over Beatriz in order to view the positioning. "Not bad," she murmured, twisting back so Ben could have a look.

"He's going to turn right back round, though, isn't he?" Ben asked. "Once you get him fully positioned."

"The stubborn ones usually do. Unless we hold them down for a while. You know, win the battle of endurance." She glanced up at him but didn't smile. Instead her expression was thoughtful, serious. "And that's a battle I always win, Ben. Against stubbornness, against anything else that gets in the way of what I need to do."

Was that a warning to him? "Your point being?"

"For future reference, that's all. You're pale, your eyes have dark circles under them and either you're going to take care of it or I will. Because you need to rest."

"Is it a boy?" Beatriz asked, totally oblivious to the subtext going on around her.

Returning her attention to her patient, softness came back to Shanna's expression. "Yes, I believe it is. And he's a big one. Looks ready for that soccer ball," she answered. "See, to the left? That's his head. And to the right, that's his..." Grinning, she moved back into position. "Definitely a boy, Beatriz. No doubt about it. Did you want a boy?"

Beatriz smiled contentedly. "We have two daughters. A son will be nice this time."

"So, boys' names..." Shanna said, pushing harder on Beatriz's upper abdomen as the baby finally started to co-operate and slide into place. "Esteban, Gerado, Miguel..." Sucking in a deep breath, she bit her bottom lip and pushed even harder. "Rafael, Raoul..." Another solid push, and this time when she sucked in her breath she held it and gave one last final prod to Beatriz's belly. Then let out her breath, smiled and nodded.

"And Nehuen, which means strong, because your baby is strong enough to give me quite a fight, Beatriz." She nodded Ben over to her side of the table then instructed him where to place his hands. "Dr. Stubborn, meet Baby Stubborn. You two should hit it off well. As for me, my back needs a break so, Ben, will you hold the baby in place for a few minutes so he doesn't reposition himself?"

He laid his hands on Beatriz's belly, let Shanna physically manipulate him to the exact spots she wanted braced, and the feel of her hands with oil on them, sliding over his hands, purposely splaying each of his fingers into po-sition...it was all he could do to focus on the fetal moni-tor. "Your technique was...I guess the only thing anyone could really say was flawless. When I've seen these done they were always more invasive, stressful. Is this some-thing you learned at Brooks?"

Twisting from side to side to relieve the tightness in her back, she shook her head. "No. We have an outstanding obstetrics department so once my patients are confirmed pregnant, I send them to the experts. Can't say that I've ever actually done the procedure at Brooks. But trying to make the ECV less stressful is something that made sense to me the first time I ever saw one done. I was still a resident, working through my obstetrics rotation. My advisor asked me to assist him in the procedure, which I was glad to do.

'But he was so…rough. Too rough, I thought. Didn't establish rapport with his patient, didn't use oil to make the rub more gentle. A lot of subtle deficiencies, I thought. Then when the baby didn't cooperate he resorted to using more drugs than I care to remember. Drugs were his first line of response and I don't necessarily believe in that if the ECV can be done without them. That's the way I am about everything—the fewer drugs used, the better.

"Anyway, that first time, all I saw was how scared the mother was and how oblivious to her needs the doctor seemed to be. At least, from my perspective, which could have been a little off since it was my first time. The next time he was called out to do an ECV, I asked him if I could try it and I pretty much did just the opposite of everything he'd done and it seemed to work. Could have been a different kind of response from the patient, could have been my ideas were actually good. Don't know. But I liked the result, and continued to use my way throughout the rest of my obstetrics rotation. Haven't done the procedure since then, though."

She twisted a little too hard to the right, winced, grabbed her lower back, then twisted back to the left to straighten out her kink. "Don't get me wrong. My advisor was an excellent doctor and an even better instructor, but somewhere in the mix I think he lost his bedside manner. Watching him, with all his excellent medical skills and his sub-par people skills was when I decided that a doctor's manner in healing is nearly as important as the actual healing."

"Well, however you accomplished it, this baby has surrendered peacefully. He's holding his place just fine." And so was Beatriz, who'd dozed off at the end of a procedure that was often traumatic. Shanna was right, though. The manner was important. And when that manner came from Shanna, it resulted in the smile like the one on Beatriz's face. Like the one he felt in his heart.

Now, even more than before, he wondered what had gone so wrong in her life, or her medical practice, that had caused Shanna to leave one of the most reputable medical institutions anywhere and come to the jungle. Especially one where she was part-owner. Before today, he'd thought it might have been impulse or wanderlust. Or that she was just someone traveling the world in search of herself. All those made sense to him and in so many ways he understood that. Of course, that was coming from the perspective of someone who'd searched for the same thing and walked away empty.

What didn't make sense about Shanna, though, was Shanna herself. Everything she did was well thought-out, nothing came without a precise motivation. And there was nothing about her that was lost. Or, at least, appeared lost on the surface. Which meant there was something much deeper going on with her. Something that made him wonder what would have caused her to pack it in and end up here.

He really wanted to think that the call of the humanitarian cause might have lured her, but he knew better. She had a reason for being *here*. And it was something she wouldn't, or couldn't, divulge to him. So, damn it, what was it? What wasn't she saying?

"Look, I think we're good here," he finally said. "Why

don't I go get one of the volunteers to sit with Beatriz for the next couple of hours, and if nothing changes, we can send her home?"

"I could use a break," she admitted. "Go somewhere and try to exercise out the knots."

"Your back aching that bad?"

She nodded. "It comes and goes. Usually just some kinks from an old injury."

"Another one of those Shanna stories? You know, the foibles of youth?"

Nodding, she said, "Big foible." She stepped aside as Consuela Alvarez made her way to the bed and turned to shoo Ben and Shanna on their way. "Big, *big* foible. My family had picked out some kind of surgery for me to pursue, but bad backs and operating tables don't mix."

"I don't see you as a surgeon. Not that you don't have the skill but you like the personal interactions."

"Precisely. But for the Brooks family, family practice is too mundane. Good for someone else but not us."

"Someone else, like me?"

"Obviously, I don't look down my nose at family practice, because it's what I chose. And I think you're a natural for family practice, but I could see you as a surgeon," she said.

He shook his head. "I thought about general surgery for a while. Couldn't see myself tied down to an operating room all day, so I looked for something with some variety. Which, for me, turned out to be what I'm doing. It's good, too, because I like being someplace where the expectations are different."

"You mean expectations of you?"

"No, not of me. But of medicine in general. The people here want to keep it simple. Pure. Maybe fundamental. They're happy to get penicillin, yet during my residency when I prescribed it for a patient I was told it was outdated, that there were better antibiotics, to at least prescribe one of the updated penicillins. Yet, plain, old-fashioned penicillin's a perfectly good drug that works, and it's a lot less costly than any other antibiotic on the market.

"Your ECV's another example. You tried the simple thing first, and it worked. So I guess what's maybe the most important thing to me is that I like the expectation that medicine can still be pure. Or fundamental. And that's not my patients' expectations. It's mine."

"Then you're a country GP at heart, aren't you?"

"And proud of it. The bigger medicine gets, the more impersonal it becomes. But when someone is sick and needs a doctor, they still want to feel like their doctor cares in something other than a corporate-detached kind of way. So long live the country GP, because that's where the true personal medicine is still being practiced."

"The country GP who has found himself happy in a jungle village. There's something quixotic in that, Ben Robinson. I envy you your choice. And your dream."

An expression crossed her face, one that was sad, full of melancholia, and that was when he knew, when he finally could see her conflict. Somehow Shanna was caught between two medical ideals, trying to figure out which one she wanted. That was probably a simplified version of it, but he'd bet his best stethoscope that was where it had all begun for her. "For me, it was a simple choice. I tried it on, it felt right. So I adapted it to fit me."

She smiled. "Well, I think the good thing is that your kind of medicine still exists to give medicine as a whole that more rounded, compassionate edge."

"Until it gets shoved so far back nobody can find it. It's already happening in a lot of places. The United States... Express the sentiment of being a country GP to your colleagues and they look at you like you're crazy. Make a house call? No one does it anymore. Go back to simpler prescriptions? Some pharmacies don't even stock them."

"But the country GP found his country, and his practice, didn't he? And he's practicing happily-ever-after. Isn't that the way it should be?"

"I don't know, Shanna. You tell me."

That sad, melancholic look passed over her face again. "When I was a girl, still in middle school, I accompanied my father on a lecture tour throughout Europe. He's the medical academic in the family. Anyway, most of the time he stuck to the large cities and universities, but in England he went to visit a former colleague who lived in some little village…I don't remember the name. It was old, coastal, very quaint. Buildings two hundred years old that would have been condemned for old age where I came from but still had a vital purpose in that village.

"And the people…they fished for a living. Worked so hard, and seemed happy doing it. There was actually still a millinery shop, Ben. Someone making hats, of all things. I mean, who makes hats?" Wonderment shone in her eyes. "It was the first time I'd ever seen anything outside my own life and I was in awe. I couldn't believe people lived like these people did.

"Anyway, my father's colleague turned out to be someone with whom he'd associated when he was guest lecturer at Oxford. Professor Augustus Aloysius Copp. He referred to himself as a licentiate in medicine and surgery, and I thought that sounded more important than just about anything I'd ever heard. Turns out he was a very important man in the medical field.

"But here he was in a fishing village, this man with the most impressive academic record, and he was working as a GP after such an illustrious career. Picking up his medical bag, walking out the door of his two-hundred-year-old cottage and making house calls on a regular basis to people who lived in other two-hundred-year-old cottages.

"My father and I tagged along with him one day and I kept wondering why Dr. Copp was doing it. It was hard work, all that walking, and he wasn't so young. All I knew was the medicine I saw in my own life every single day. It was very narrow, the way my life was. But, Ben, this was the first time I became aware that there *was* another way. Dr. Copp was happy, his patients respected him and he loved his patients. It was a simple system that worked and he said it was truly the way he'd always wanted to practice medicine."

"But that kind of a system's not for you."

She shrugged. "Not for me. At least, not in the life I have back at Brooks Medical Center."

"Yet here you are, picking up your medical bag and electric toothbrush and making house calls on a regular basis now. And you're enjoying it, Shanna. It shows all over you. How can you explain that?"

"I don't know. Maybe it's something about knowing how the world needs both Dr. Copp and Dr. Robinson."

"It also needs Dr. Brooks, wherever she decides she wants to be."

"*Whatever* she decides she wants to be," Shanna said, her voice bittersweet.

"You'll figure it out, Shanna. When you want to. But in the meantime..." He stopped at one of the exam rooms, opened the door and gestured Shanna in.

"What's this about?" she asked.

He held up his hands. "Good with aching back. Won't cure anything, but will sure make the aches of the moment feel better."

"Really? You'd do that for me?" Before he had a chance

to answer, she scooted into the room and was already half-way up on the exam table. "Never let it be said I don't take full advantage when something good is presented me. So, do you want my shirt off, Ben?"

He gulped. "Your shirt?"

"For the massage. Would it be easier without my shirt?"

Images of Shanna without her shirt flashed through his mind, exploded in his mind, sky-rocketed all around his mind, and it was all he could do to maintain his doctorly comportment. Bad idea, this massage. Especially when he didn't stand a chance of keeping it professional. At least, not in his mind—damned traitor to his resolves.

"No, leave it on," he said, wishing he didn't have to say that. But better safe than sorry. "I can get at the places I need without it coming off." *Unfortunately.*

"Lower back," she said, settling down. "Above the coc-cyx, just to the…" She sucked in her breath, held it for a moment as his fingers went, almost instinctively, right to the spot. "Yes," she murmured, hoping it didn't sound like a purr. "Right there."

"So, tell me the story of your back injury. Your big, *big* foible," he said as his fingers applied the first level of pres-sure. "And the tattoo. What's that about?"

"Tattoo's about my first real act of rebellion. Actually, the second part of my first real act."

"The foible?"

"Yes, the foible. After the whole window-chair incident, I decided I wanted horseback riding lessons. My parents refused. They didn't have enough time to take me, said it was too dangerous, kept telling me I had better things to do with my time. Take your pick. There was a counter-argument for every one of my arguments." She laughed.

"I will say, it was the first time they ever put up much of a united front against me. Most of the time they deferred me to the other parent, who deferred me back, turning most decisions concerning me into a volley between two parents who didn't know what to do with me and didn't want to take the time to find out. In the end, I usually got what I wanted because they got sick of the back and forth."

"Making you a very willful child."

He applied a little extra pressure just offside her tattoo, causing her to gasp, suck in a sharp breath, then let it out judiciously. "You really know where to hurt a girl, don't you?"

"On the back, or in the pride?"

"A little bit of both. But you're right. I was willful. Saw my advantages and took them where I could. Except about the horseback riding. I had no idea what to do against a united front. So I ignored their refusal to allow me to do it and did it anyway. One of my girlfriends had a beautiful chestnut mare boarded at a local stable so I'd go with her after school when she'd go to groom or ride her horse."

"And you rode her horse?"

"Not exactly. You know that part where you said I was willful..." She flinched again. "Are you doing that on purpose? Trying to hurt me?"

"You're tensing up."

Because his fingers on her felt so...good. Perfect. Like they were the fingers that should be massaging her back. "I'm tensing up because talking about my family makes me tense," she lied.

"Actually, you were talking about your friend's horse."

"*My* horse," she corrected. "There was a beautiful gray there for sale, so I bought her."

"You had that kind of money when you were a kid? Because when I was that age I was doing good to scrape together twenty dollars."

"No, I didn't have that kind of money, but I knew the

combination to my dad's safe so I took a little bit at a time, hoping he wouldn't notice it missing, or would think he'd miscounted last time he'd checked. Eventually, I had enough to buy a horse."

He chuckled. "Burglary. Good plan. Where I come from, that'll get you sent off to a juvenile correctional facility."

"Where I come from, too. But that's not what happened. I bought my horse, paid for riding lessons and to have her boarded with that money I was taking, and had a perfectly good secret going for over a year. Then I fell off. Got sloppy saddling my horse, didn't get everything cinched properly and took a mighty hard fall on one of the trails. Fractured my back, not seriously but serious enough that I had to be airlifted to a hospital by helicopter."

"Riding in a helicopter with a broken back usually isn't conducive to being kept secret."

"Especially when the helicopter sets down on my family's own helipad, even though I'd specifically told the pilot to take me to another hospital. Anyway, they'd radioed ahead, and when they pulled my stretcher out of the chopper, there to greet me were my parents, my grandparents and a few other family members. Imagine a whole platoon of Brooks medical workers standing there with scowls and folded arms... The scowls came only after they'd determined I was okay, by the way. But still..."

"Secret's out."

"In a big way. And I had to give my horse back. Then deal with the consequences of going into my dad's safe and taking the money, which turned into the kind of hospital duty no one ever aspires to."

"Did it involve bedpans?"

She nodded. "And that was one of the more pleasant aspects of my punishment."

He chuckled as he shifted the focus of his massage up a couple of inches. "Something tells me that didn't end the rebellion."

"Hardly. My physical therapist...beautiful man, my first adult crush, actually. Let me rephrase that—my first teenage crush on an adult. I fell in love with his tattoos probably more than I fell in love with him. They represented freedom and self-expression. Anyway, he had these big, muscly arms..."

"Unlike mine."

"You have nice arms, Ben. Small in proportion to Lance's arms, but you work out."

"How can you tell?"

"A girl notices these things, even under long sleeves." She noticed it was his muscles that tensed up this time. Could feel it in his touch, in the way he attacked her muscles, going from firm and gentle to nearly pinching.

"Had to start when I was a kid. Didn't see any reason to stop."

Something to do with his own physical rehab? She wondered about it, wanted to ask, but nothing in Ben made him seem inclined to want to tell her about his scars. So she didn't ask. Instead, she returned to her own conversation, trying to keep it light to make him feel at ease, because maybe if he stayed at ease, he'd talk about himself. She hoped he would, anyway.

"Like me. I didn't see any reason to stop rebelling so I got a tattoo. Thought about something dark and sinister like a skull or a snake. Decided I'd rather go artsy. Since I'd broken my back, I choose the Djed, had it put right over my own backbone. It's Egyptian, by the way. And it's believed that the Djed is a rendering of a human backbone. It represents stability and strength."

"Well, your Djed is artsy. Has a nice sarcasm to it,

doesn't it? A particularly explicit message, which I'm sure your parents didn't appreciate the first time they saw it."

"After I had it done I was actually going to keep it hidden, but something about a lower back tattoo and a low-cut swimsuit don't go together. We have a pool, and I was sitting out there one day, reading a book, and my grandmother saw it."

"Let me guess. She made a fuss?"

"That's not even the half of it. By the time the whole Brooks clan got through with me, you'd have thought I'd tattooed it in the middle of my forehead."

He moved his hands up another couple of inches, splayed out his fingers on either side of her spine, and applied a much deeper pressure than he'd been applying. "More bedpan duty?"

"Enough to make me the bedpan queen of the world."

"But you got what you wanted, didn't you?"

"My tattoo?"

"No. Attention. You're a smart woman now so I'm assuming you were a smart girl then. And smart girls know they will get caught stealing their father's money, and buying a horse, and getting a tattoo. Your crimes, Shanna, were all pretty obvious. Anyone looking would have noticed them, which is why I believe you did what you did. To see if your parents were watching."

She'd never analyzed her rebelliousness that way. To her, the things she'd done as a child had been pranks. Stupid, childhood whims. But cries for attention? "They were busy people," she said, not sure if she should defend them or defend herself.

"Busy people with a child who needed to be noticed."

Which had made her seem so willful. And she had been, but that was a long time ago. Still, what if that was what he thought of her now? What if he believed her turning up here was something done out of sheer, petulant willfulness? Everything she'd told Ben led her to that conclusion, so why wouldn't he be led, as well? "That's why you think I'm here, isn't it? You think I'm still the child who wants to be noticed? That coming to Argentina is just a step or two beyond my tattoo?"

Bolting up on the table, she twisted round to face him on her way off it. "Tell me, Ben. Is that the conclusion you've drawn? That I'm looking for attention so I came out here into the middle of nowhere hoping somebody notices me? That I'm being…manipulative?"

"You're not driven by selfish needs, Shanna. I know that. I don't think there's anything manipulative about you."

But there was, and that was when she realized it. She was here to use Ben as her means to being accepted back into the family, and into the medical center. Maybe she wasn't overtly using him, but using him as her role model to get something she wanted was its own brand of manipulation, and suddenly she felt ashamed. She should have been honest with him from the start, and take the consequences as they came. Now it was too late. Ben wasn't who she'd believed he was. Not at all. And to top that, she was falling in love with him.

"Look, I um…" Sliding to the floor, she paused for a moment, but couldn't find it in herself to look at him. "About tonight. I can't go to the village with you. And you do need your rest." She wanted to suggest another time, but she wasn't sure she should. Because to go much further with this, she'd have to tell him everything, and to do that would hurt a kind, decent man who didn't deserve to be hurt. *Hey, look, Ben. I came here to pattern myself after the coldhearted so-and-so I thought you were.* It made her sick to even think that had been her motivation.

"Anyway, I'm going to make sure Beatriz gets back home safely, then I've got some paperwork to catch up on. So..." There was nothing else to say, so she didn't. Sighing, she shook her head in despair, then walked out the door.

What was the point of any of it? It always turned out the same. He'd taken that step forward, and she'd stepped backward. He'd gone against his resolve, and it had turned out exactly the way he'd known it would. But there were times he just wanted to forget who he was, how he lived. Because, damn it, he was lonely. So lonely he had to force himself to face the next day. Every time he crawled out of his bed, it felt like something was ripping out his heart. And Shanna...he knew she wouldn't stay. But he'd wanted to forget that. Wanted to forget his past, forget everything.

But it didn't matter, did it? Or maybe it did. Because it hurt more than he'd expected as he hadn't been able to brace himself against her the way he did everything else. So, really, what *was* the point?

He was falling in love, which was tantamount to falling into a great abyss. That was the point.

CHAPTER NINE

"THEY'LL both be back next week," Ben explained to Shanna as the two of them shared a hasty breakfast at his tiny kitchen table, sipping coffee and eating *sandwiches di miga,* crustless sandwiches stuffed with red peppers, tomatoes, lettuce, ham and hard-boiled eggs. He was glad Amanda and Jack were returning to Caridad but concerned at the same time because, while his sister's pregnancy was textbook perfect, he knew she would throw herself into the work here the way she always did, and it worried him.

Of course, she was Jack's to worry about now. He was only the bystander, as it should be. In so many ways, though, he envied her the life she was building. Husband, son, baby on the way…he'd never dreamed of having those things. Why fool himself? Marriage, family, happily-ever-after bliss weren't in his future, and he'd known that for a very long time.

"So if I left, you wouldn't be in a bind?"

"You're thinking about leaving?" It didn't surprise him. Shanna needed more than this. She was too vital to contain here. He understood it, but he didn't like it.

"Maybe. Haven't really decided yet."

"Going back to Chicago? Back to your practice."

She shook her head. "I, um…I'm going back, but in a different direction. Going to step out of patient care, leave that for those more suited to it, and focus on hospital administration. Chief Operating Officer."

That surprised him. No, that shocked him. "Which means?"

"A lot of responsibility. I'll be accountable for the smooth and efficient operation of all our various facilities, including the management of the profit-and-loss statement for the hospital's business. I'll also oversee the integration of our strategic plan, and provide oversight for the development of high-quality, cost-effective and integrated clinical programs throughout Brooks Medical Center. Our management portfolio is diverse, Ben, and this position carries with it a substantial scope of obligation. It's a new position for Brooks Medical Center and my family feels it's best keeping it in the family."

"Then why are you here, working harder than you've probably ever worked in your life, telling me you want to be like me?"

"One last fling to see where I belong, I suppose."

"What you're telling me is that based on what you're doing here, you're going to return to Brooks and never see another patient again? How does that make sense, Shanna? Because that's not you. You love patient care. In fact, I don't think I've ever seen anyone love it the way you do. Anyone looking at you can see it. And anyone who knows you knows that not being in patient care will make you miserable. So why the change?"

"You adjusted to your life, Ben, based on your circumstances. That's all I'm doing—adjusting."

"But I didn't walk away from the one thing I truly love."

"I'm not walking away, either. Simply walking in another direction."

Something else was at the bottom of this because Shanna clearly did not want to make this move. Judging from the dismal look on her face, she knew it was a mistake. Yet for some reason he didn't know, she was about to go through with it. "Are you trying to get yourself even more lost?" he asked. "Because the minute you put on your administrator hat, that's what's going to happen to you, and I think you know that.

"Some people are born to be great administrators, Shanna. But some are born to be great healers, and that's what you are. Your heart, your soul…it's all about the care of others, and if you walk away from it, you're going to regret it every day of your life. And the down-to-the-soul kind of misery you're going to feel can cause you to do things to yourself you'd never believed you could." Alcoholism. Drug addiction. And worse.

"No, I'm not trying to get myself any more lost because I'm not sure it's possible to be any more lost than I already am," she said on a dispirited sigh.

"Then why leave here? We may not have all the whistles and bells you have at Brooks, but I believe you know who you are here."

"Why leave?" she asked, then immediately countered with, "Why stay?"

"Because you love the work, you can't deny that."

"Yeah, well, I love lazy days on a tropical beach, too. But not enough to spend the rest of my life there. Besides, you'll be back to full coverage, so you're not going to need an extra doctor hanging around."

"Don't make this about what I need or don't need for Caridad. We always need doctors. That's probably never going to change. So why are you really doing this?" Why the hell couldn't he just bring himself to tell her he wanted her here? That he liked having her around? That she made him feel…she simply made him *feel?*

Because that would call for a step further, a commitment he didn't have in him. Oh, she'd stay out of pity, or some selfless act that bound her here only as a doctor, because that was who Shanna was. In the end, though, she'd quit looking at him the way she had when she'd kissed him, the way a lover did. Seeing that look die was something he couldn't bear. That was why he couldn't ask her or tell her or beg her to stay. Because she would, but for reasons that would only hurt her.

"You've got more than enough volunteers to cover, Ben, so you really don't need me."

"But it's nice having someone here for…for continuity's sake."

She laughed bitterly. "That's me. Standing right in there for continuity's sake." She glanced down at the sandwich she'd been nibbling at for the past twenty minutes, then tossed it across the room, hitting the trash can with it dead center. "Look, I'm not going to leave you in a lurch, if that's what you're worried about. I may wear my heart on my sleeve when it comes to dealing with my patients, but I'm responsible."

Ben pushed back from the table so abruptly his chair toppled as he stood. "Whoever said you weren't?"

"Outright? Nobody. By implication? My father and my grandfather. My mother, my grandmother. My brothers. See, I'm the one who didn't fit into the mold, and maybe that's some of that willfulness from my youth hanging on. Maybe it's not. I don't know. But I do know this. There comes a time when you have to meet your life head on. This is my time. And my life…it is what it is." She spun, headed for the door, got to the doorway then stopped, and turned to face him.

"I love Caridad, Ben. Love what you're doing here. For me, that's always the problem. I love, and it gets in the way. You, of all people, should understand that, because you've managed to push all the love in your life so far to the sides I doubt you could even see it from wherever you choose to stand."

While she hadn't meant that to be cruel, what she'd just said slapped him so hard he could almost feel the literal sting. It was true, of course. Just not easy to hear. Even more difficult knowing Shanna could see that in him.

"I, um…I spare other people's feelings," he said with much more composure than he felt. "Because I know how it is to come face-to-face with a flaw. That's what I am, Shanna. A flaw. And I accept that because while people may take pity on me for a little while, it doesn't last. So why put anybody through that? Why put myself through it when I know how it turns out in the end? So if you see that as shoving love aside, then that's what it is. But that's me. It's not you. Love doesn't get in your way. It's what makes you who you are…a doctor who exudes passion and compassion. Losing that to paperwork is…it's unfortunate. And wrong."

"But what happens, Ben, when the passion and compassion get in the way of good doctoring?"

Now he had the perfect picture, the perfect understanding of what her family had done to her, and it made him sick to his stomach. "You said you wear your heart on your sleeve."

She nodded. Swallowed hard. "That's me. Heart on my sleeve. A real sissified practitioner because I get too emotionally involved."

"Who the hell ever said something like that to you?" Actually, he could guess. He'd met Miles Brooks once. Recognized his handiwork.

"It doesn't matter, because it's true. I get too involved. Lose objectivity."

"Your grandfather is wrong, Shanna. And it does matter. Your greatest ability is the way you empathize with your patients. You understand them in ways most doctors can't, and to berate that shows ignorance and intolerance. So why are you going back to a place where you can't be the kind of doctor you have a natural gift for being simply to try and fit yourself into a mold that will never fit you?"

"Because if I don't, it's not just my spot in the family medical practice I'll lose. It's my spot in the family. And in spite of who they are, or what they are, I don't want to walk away from them."

"Maybe you don't, but think about how they're willing to walk away from you. Look, Shanna, I know what it's like to have everything you've ever known taken away from you. After I was burned I spent a year, a complete year simply fighting to survive, and I gave up more times that I can probably remember. Not because of the pain, not because of the prospect of dozens of surgeries in my future, but because I knew that my old life was gone. I lost my youth, I lost my innocence and I lost everything I'd ever thought I would have in life because one simple thing I loved doing—working on cars with my dad—went bad in ways no one could have ever predicted.

"Trust me, it's not easy coming back from that loss. By the age of nineteen I was an alcoholic. Couldn't get through my day without bracing myself with a drink or two or ten. Then when that wasn't enough to get me through, I added drugs to that mix."

"Ben," she gasped, "I—I didn't know."

"Nobody does, outside my family. It was a bad time for all of us, but the point is I lost myself in profound ways I still don't understand. I couldn't figure out my day, let alone my life, because I was scared to death to face my loss. And that's what you're about to do. You're about to lose yourself in such a profound way because you're afraid to face the loss of your family. But the loss of Shanna Brooks is a far worse loss."

She swiped at the tears streaming down her cheeks as Ben crossed the room and pulled her into his arms. A place where she fit so naturally. It was a dangerous thing he was doing. But for the moment Shanna's need was greater than his, and nothing else mattered.

"You're a good man," Shanna finally said through her sniffles. She put her hand over his heart. "I don't know what you've suffered in the past, but you have too much goodness in your heart to shut out the people who see it, who want to be part of it." Her hand moved to the right, and came to rest on the buttons of his white camp shirt. "A few days ago, when I told you my goal was to lose myself…" She undid the top button of his shirt. "That's what you do, isn't it? Lose yourself, pray to God nobody finds you. It's no different than what I'm doing, is it? You isolate yourself in a jungle clinic for fear someone will get too close. I isolate myself in my family for fear they will turn their backs on me. Makes us quite a pair, doesn't it?"

There was nothing in him that was prepared to deal with this—with her brutal honesty. Because she was correct. It was easier being lost. "I tried the other way, and it didn't work."

She undid another button. "Because you didn't want it to work, Ben. You're a capable man. Maybe the most capable person I've ever met, so you're not going to be stopped at anything you truly want to do."

He raised his hand to cover hers, to stop her unbuttoning his shirt, because what she'd find underneath was so obscene, and Shanna was so pure. "What I want is my practice here."

"And to be left alone," she said. "You forgot to add that part, Ben. You truly, sincerely want to be left alone. Want to be a recluse, live your life out without anybody coming close. Then someday Amanda's children can talk about their odd uncle, the one who spent his life in this one-room apartment and only came out to work." She drew in a shuddering breath, then let it out and looked up at him. "I show it all too easily, and you hide it all too easily."

Without provocation, without warning, she pulled her hand away from his, then grabbed hold of his shirt and literally ripped it open, exposing every bare inch of his chest.

"Damn it to hell," he grunted, grabbing at the fabric, trying to cover himself.

"No," she said, her voice almost a whisper as she grabbed his hand. "Don't, Ben."

"You don't understand…" Shoving her hands off him, he spun around and literally broke into a run, to his bathroom, to his closet, anywhere to cover himself. Anywhere to get away.

But Shanna was too quick. She caught up, practically tackling him as she grabbed him from behind, and held on. Laid her head on his back, wrapped her arms around his waist and simply held on for dear life. For a minute, or an eternity…it all blended together. His needs, his desires, his reality… Then he snapped back to where he needed to be. "Don't do this, Shanna," he said. "Don't fool yourself into thinking that this could be something other than what it is. We're colleagues, that's all there is. That's all I do."

"But is it all you *want* to do?" she asked him. "Tell me the truth, Ben. Is that all you want of us?"

"All I want is…"

"To be left alone to practice your medicine. That's what you keep saying. And maybe you believe it. But I don't."

How could he do this? How could he walk away from her and not look back? He wanted her to stay. Wanted to live in the fantasy that everything would work out, that they could end up like Amanda and Jack, and work through the obstacles to find the love. But he knew better, because he knew himself. And Ben Robinson, as himself, was the one thing Shanna didn't know. She saw the doctor and the outward manifestations of the man, but the layers underneath were so grisly they would defy Shanna's usual sunshine optimism. To see that diminished or destroyed in her...he couldn't do it, because it was that optimism he'd first loved about her.

"We all make choices based on who we are, Shanna. It's one of those facts of life you can't escape."

Loosening her grip, she slid round to the front of him and gently pulled apart the ripped fabric of his shirt. "What if you make choices on the wrong perception of yourself?" Gently, so very gently, she traced her fingers over his chest, over his scars. "Could that be you, Ben? Could that be what you've done to yourself?"

Shutting his eyes, he was torn between the pure, physical want for her touch and the sure knowledge of what would come later. No one had ever come this close, no one had ever touched him this way. Not physically, not emotionally. From Shanna, he wanted it more than he'd ever wanted anything in his entire life. Being touched by her—that was all there was. Just this moment. Only her touch. It had to stop, though. He had to stop it. Yet the struggle was so fierce... "What I've done to myself is what I had to do. And I don't fool myself about anything." So true. But it was a truth not meant for her.

"But you're more than your scars, Ben."

Her fingers fluttered up and down his chest, her touch so light he could barely feel it. But the shivers he was holding back and the pure emotional arousal told him she was there. Dangerously there. "And you're more than your family," he managed to say, fighting not to let himself sound as ragged as he felt. "Shanna, don't. We can't…"

Swallowing hard, he tried to step back, wanted to step back, but as he looked down and saw her eyes looking directly into his, there was nothing in him that could make him move. She was so beautiful, and so innocent. The ugliness of the world had never touched her and, with all his heart, he hoped it never would. "You don't know what's involved here. Don't know me…"

"Touch me, Ben," she said, taking hold of his hand and guiding it to her chest, over her heart. "That's what I know. I want you to touch me." He was such a beautiful man, in every way she wanted. She could see that beauty, and feel it every time she looked at him, yet how would she show him what was so obvious to her? "And I want to touch you."

Reaching up to his face, she followed the line of his scars, starting behind his left ear and twining down, under his chin, across his shoulder, his chest, over part of his stomach. Then, stopped by his cargo pants, she let that impede her only a moment, before she unzipped him, lowered his cargos and his briefs, and continued tracing her fingers across his lower abdomen, over his hip and came to a stop where his scar did, halfway down his thigh.

She felt him shudder, felt his muscles tense, knew if she looked up she'd see how rigidly his face was set, see how tightly closed his eyes were. None of that mattered, though, as she touched her lips to the start of the scar on his thigh and followed the journey upward her fingers had just traveled downward. But when she got to midchest, that was where she ended, where she snaked both her hands around his neck. Where he surrendered and his muscles relaxed. Where she lost her soul and found her heart.

* * *

It was still dark outside, but she was awake. Had barely slept, thinking about how this had started with her exploring the idea of leaving, and how beautifully it had ended, lying here with Ben. No matter how beautiful, though, she was filled with trepidation, this queasiness in the pit of her stomach that wouldn't go away.

Too many of her thoughts were wrapped in so much confusion because, come first light, everything would be the same as it had been before they'd spent the night together. They'd escaped into each other for a while, which had only deepened her feelings for this man. Nothing had changed, though. Not in any real sense.

And she wasn't going to delude herself into thinking that one perfect night would transform anything. Her family didn't want her the way she was, and Ben didn't want her. Those were two hard facts she still had to face.

Ben...beautiful man. Everything she'd ever wanted. Kind, considerate and so compassionate. Yet he was still so guarded. Not able to let himself go. Or only going through the correct motions. She'd felt it in the way he'd held her, kissed her, made love to her. He'd allowed her only a small part of him, but she wasn't even sure which part that was. She wondered if it was simply the physical need he'd relinquished to her when all she'd wanted had been a piece of his heart. Consequently, in the afterglow, the emptiness had started to creep in.

So for now she'd accept it as it was and, come daylight, maybe she'd see it all differently. Or maybe she'd pretend a little while longer that when Ben opened his eyes he'd see the possibilities, not the impossibilities.

Falling in love shouldn't be this difficult, she thought as she turned on her side to snuggle into Ben, who was likewise on his side but with his back to her. Scooting over, she matched the lines of her body to his and placed her hand over his waist, just to feel connected. Maybe that was what she'd missed—the real connection between them. Or maybe she was simply reading her insecurities into a place they didn't need to be. Whatever it was, duty would be calling in another couple of hours, and she needed to be better rested. So she exhaled, relaxed, enjoyed the feel of him pressed to her, and...

She felt his muscles go tense. Then jerk convulsively. One hard, fast snap. Then his breathing turned shallow for a moment, almost like he was panting, and she was instantly alert. Did he feel warm? Too warm? Another hard jerk followed immediately by a third one...

"Ben," she whispered, giving him a gentle nudge on the shoulder.

His response was a groggy mumble. Understandable. He was sleeping, didn't want to be disturbed. But she propped herself up on her elbow and instinctively reached over him to feel his forehead. An old-fashioned diagnostic tool, but it worked. And he wasn't just warm, he was burning up. "Ben," she said, this time giving him a hard shake.

Again, he responded with a mumble, so Shanna rolled over, flipped on the light on the bedside stand, then rolled back to Ben and pulled him over onto his back. "Ben," she said, this time urgently. "Can you hear me?"

His eyes fluttered open. "I'm fine," he said, his voice unusually gravelly.

"Look at me," she said as his eyes sagged closed again. "Focus on me, Ben. Open your eyes and focus on me." Moving up to her knees so she could get a better angle to examine him, it occurred to her that he was completely naked and except for Ben's T-shirt, which she was wearing, she was nearly the same. "Come on, open your eyes," she said, patting both sides of his face to arouse him.

"I already focused on you," he said, opening his eyes and attempting a smile.

"You have a fever. You've been telling me you were tired, that you weren't sick. But now you have a fever, and it's high, Ben. I don't know how high, but it's high."

"You make me hot." He shook himself, shook his head, sucked in a deep breath. "But I'm not sick. All I need is some sleep."

While his words weren't nearly as garbled now, he was still too thick, too lethargic. "How long have you been feeling bad?" she asked. Taking his pulse—too fast. Feeling the glands in his neck—slightly swollen.

Instead of answering, he went back to sleep.

"Ben, please. Stay with me."

"I can't," he mumbled. "What I did... Horrible things. Let people down..."

She needed to examine him. *Really* examine him. But she was torn between dressing and running across the hall for her medical bag or simply calling Dr. Hueber, the on-call for emergencies tonight, and letting him make the assumptions he wanted.

Except assumptions might not be good for Ben's reputation, and she didn't want to jeopardize his hospital or his standing in the village, so she threw on her clothes faster than she knew she could dress, dashed to her room across the hall, then hurried back and practically tumbled back into the bed next to him to take his blood pressure. Low. Respirations normal, but on the shallow side. Pupils reactive, but a little sluggish. No huge concerns so far. Then his heart, and that was where the concern started. His pulse was thready, cutting in and out.

An infection? She'd seen him tired, seen him avoid meals, claiming he was too busy to eat. Those might simply be Ben, but they might also be symptoms of whatever this was. "Ben," she said, giving him a gentle nudge. "Wake up. Hear me? Wake up. I want to ask you some questions."

"Need a shower," he mumbled. "Make morning rounds..."

"No morning rounds," she said, scrambling from the bed and rummaging through his drawer for a pair of briefs. Once found, she put them on him, along with socks. She had no reason why those were important to her, but they were. She wanted him to look...professional when she admitted him to the hospital. So after the socks, on went a scrub shirt and pants, and that was where she stopped and called Hueber, and told him what was going on. His response was to send two volunteers and a stretcher and, within minutes, Ben was stretched out atop an exam table, where Dr. Hueber was hooking him up to a heart monitor while Shanna was busy starting an IV.

"When did this start?" Hueber asked.

"He was fine last night. We talked for a while after our shifts were over. Then this morning, when I went to make sure he was on morning rounds, he was like this."

"Noticed anything before this? I've only been here a few days, so I haven't really had the chance to talk to him yet. But if you've been around awhile, maybe you've noticed something."

"Maybe. He's been tired off and on, and doesn't have much of an appetite."

"Been fine," Ben interjected. "Working too many hours."

"Working too many hours doesn't get you in this shape," Shanna said, glancing nervously at the heart monitor. "So tell me when you started feeling bad."

"A few minutes ago."

She glanced across at Hueber, who was getting ready to

put an oxygen mask on Ben. "Now, be truthful with me, Ben. How long have you been feeling bad?"

This time he didn't answer. He simply sighed heavily and drifted off.

"I'm assuming he's current on all his vaccinations," Hueber said.

Shaking her head, Shanna shrugged. Honestly, she didn't know. Doctors were usually the worst patients so she wouldn't put it past Ben to let his vaccinations lapse. She hoped he hadn't, though, because that would be a starting point, where they could begin to rule out various conditions. She ran a hand over Ben's sweaty brow. "What have you done, Ben Robinson?" she asked, not concerned that Hueber was arching knowing eyebrows at her. "What did you go and contract?" And could they treat it here, or should they be looking for a lifeline out?

Hueber cleared his throat. "I don't suppose you've inspected him, have you?" he asked, then added, "In the professional sense."

"What do you mean?" she asked, the implication of Hueber's question not lost on her.

"For bites, cuts, rashes, those sorts of things. It's what we do here in the jungle because there are so many unknown variables we're not used to dealing with. You know, look between fingers and toes and all those other places you might not normally examine."

"No, I haven't inspected him. I only found him right before I called you." Technically, that was correct. Besides, it was none of Hueber's business that she'd spent the most amazing night of her life with Ben prior to that. At least, she hoped medical necessity wouldn't turn it into Hueber's business.

"Then while I go wake another doctor up to come work in Emergency, I'd suggest you inspect him. And keep your fingers crossed we find something easy to identify. Because Ben doesn't have the medical resources at Caridad yet to take care of him if we don't see something we can diagnose pretty damned fast, and have the means to treat." He sighed. "And don't fight me on this, but I'm going to line up medical transport for him in case we can't treat him here. Or he gets worse."

There wasn't an argument in her. What Ben was experiencing always came with the uncertainty of not knowing what came next. Truthfully, it excited her. Showed her a raw, new medical horizon she hadn't even known existed. In her heart of hearts she wanted to stay, wanted to be a part of everything Ben did here. Wanted to be a part of Ben. But staying came with the knowledge that she might never get from him what she needed, and how did someone who openly wore her heart on her sleeve survive that?

"What did this to you?" she asked as she examined his arms, first his left, then his right, noting the perfect flesh juxtaposed against the scars. "To have gone through what you did and get yourself to where you are…" Suddenly, the doctor in Shanna gave way to the woman, and she felt warm tears sliding down her cheeks. It didn't matter if Hueber saw, didn't matter what he knew. She was in love with this guy, didn't care if her heart *was* on her sleeve or if she was just plain sissified, like her grandfather had said.

Right now she needed to cry. For herself. For Ben. "When you're better, we've got some things to talk about, Ben Robinson," she managed through her sniffles.

He stirred. Opened his eyes and simply stared at her for a moment. Then he reached up and brushed a tear from her cheek. And went back to sleep before he could lower his hand to the bed.

She caught it as it dropped, and held on for a moment. "I'm going to get you through this," she promised, then kissed his hand and lowered it to his side. "Don't know what it is, but I'm a good doctor." Bending down to his ear, she whispered, "And you're a good lover. It's a combination we can work with, Ben. But you've got to get better first. Hear me? You've got to get better."

Rather than responding, Ben remained still, so for the next several minutes she searched him for anything that might indicate what was happening. But came up empty.

"His sister's here," Hueber said, poking his head through the curtain. "And her husband. They want to take over his case. Just thought you should know."

Shanna nodded, and as soon as Hueber was gone, she kissed Ben gently on the cheek. "I'll be back," she whispered. "I promise."

"What is it?" Amanda asked, the instant Shanna stepped into the hall.

"Don't know, so right now we're treating symptoms and watching him."

"That's not good enough!" Amanda snapped. Her husband, Jack, stepped up beside his wife and slipped a steadying arm around her waist.

"I'm Jack Kenner," he said, pulling his wife tight to his side.

"Nice to meet you. I'm Shanna Brooks."

"So, do you suspect anything?" Jack asked. "How was he acting before he got sick? Was he displaying any symptoms?"

"Tired, lack of appetite. Then this morning he spiked a fever, starting having a heart arrhythmia, compromised respiration. Became lethargic, not comatose but at times on the verge of going completely under. So far, though, he always rallies out of it. But each time it's dragging him deeper down."

"And you're sure these symptoms manifested themselves this morning?"

Shanna nodded, didn't say a word. But the implication wasn't lost on Amanda or Jack, both of whom had
the good grace to not ask. "I've asked him a couple times
lately if he's feeling okay, and he always said he's fine."
She shrugged. "But that's Ben, isn't it?"

"I want Jack to treat him," Amanda said. "There's no
time to soft-pedal this or spare feelings. Jack's the best,
and I want Ben to have the best."

Shanna knew Amanda was upset, and didn't want to add
to that, especially as she was pregnant. But she'd made a
promise to Ben she intended to see through. Ben trusted
that. Deep in her heart she knew he truly trusted that.
"With all due respect, Amanda, I need Jack in the lab. He
is the best, and he's the one who needs to do the tests. But
I need to do the treatment because I promised Ben I would.
So, if you'll excuse me, I'm going to draw the first round
of blood work, so Jack can have a look."

"Can I see him?" Amanda asked.

"In a few minutes. I'm in the middle of an exam, and
once I'm through with that, I'll let you know."

"He isn't going to…?"

Amanda didn't finish the question, but she didn't have
to because the unspoken word congealed inside Shanna,
clawed at her breath, clutched at her heart. "No. He isn't."
Words that shouldn't have been said as last time she'd
made that promise, she'd failed her patient. And if ever
there was a time she'd worn her heart on her sleeve, this
was it. It was time to face who she was, and accept it, for
Ben. That was the thought weighing on her as she went
back into the exam, followed by Jack, who insisted on
drawing his own samples.

"In my work, it's best to control all the variables." He

glanced briefly at Ben, then turned to the storage cabinet to pull out the various sample tubes he'd need and turned back. "Damned shame, what he's gone through," he said as he applied the tourniquet and started his search for a good vein. "He'd hate it, being exposed the way he is right now. Ben does everything he can to cover himself up."

"She's already seen me," Ben muttered.

Chuckling as he poked for a vein, Jack said, "So you're eavesdropping on us?"

"Some. Too much effort to open my eyes, but I can hear."

"Off and on," Shanna said, stepping up to the head of the bed with a damp cloth to wipe Ben's face.

"But everything was fine last night?" Jack asked. "And I'm not asking to pry. I need to establish a timeline."

"He was fine until a little before midnight, then..." Shanna shrugged, looked over at Jack, who was extracting his third tube of blood from Ben's arm, and smiled apologetically. "Then when I woke up just after five he was like this. First thing I noticed was how hot he was, then after I checked him I discovered the rest." Dipping the rag into a basin of cool water, she wrung it out and began to wipe his face again, but stopped. Held her breath, bent down, took a close look... "Hello, kissing bug."

Also called a triatomine bug, they hid in crevices in the walls and roofs during the day, emerging at night when people slept. "See, Jack, right there, next to Ben's left eye, that little bit of swelling." The triatomine's choice of human contact—the face. Hence the common swelling near the eye.

"She knows bugs," Ben mumbled.

"I may know my bugs, but this little beauty isn't one of my favorites," she said. It caused too much damage. Often killed its victims or rendered them significantly damaged

and disabled. Heart transplants were a frequent outcome
for the lucky ones able to survive to that point.

The outlook for Ben? She hoped good. She hoped this
was in an early enough phase that a sufficient course
of benznidazole, an antiparasitic drug, would be all he
needed. It was a long shot. She understood that. But she
also knew Ben. He was strong. A fighter. If will could win
this battle, he'd be good as new in due course. "Really,
Ben. A bee sting would have been easier."

"Never claimed to be easy," he said as his eyes shut.

"No, you didn't," she whispered, then looked across at
Jack, who was well into drawing the fourth and final tube
of blood. "Jack, besides the blood work you're going to do,
I'd like to get an abdominal X-ray, as well as do an endoscopy. Do you think Amanda will object?"

"You're Ben's physician," he said, "so do what you think
is necessary. And, by the way, good catch, Dr. Brooks. I
knew who you were before, but that officially turned you
into a jungle doctor." After he'd drawn the blood, Jack
pulled off the tourniquet then moved up to look at what
Shanna had spotted. To the naked eye the swelling was
nearly invisible. But it was there. He whistled as he pal-
pated it with his index finger to make sure. "Yep. Hell of
a good catch!"

"Well, it's barely there, but it's definitely a chagoma."

"And as it hasn't developed fully yet, I'm definitely
impressed."

Maybe he was, but he needed to reserve judgment of
her until later, after Ben had run his course with Chagas
disease, so named for the Brazilian doctor who had first
diagnosed it. Time, as well as treatment, would be the deciding factor, but time scared her to death as the course
of this disease was to start mild in the early stages, sometimes go away altogether, sometimes go dormant, only to

return with a vengeance after a while. Ben was definitely seeing the vengeance side, but she was praying it was the early stage of vengeance rather than the late.

"You stay with me, Ben," she told him three hours later, as she settled down into a chair next to his bed. "I don't want you going anywhere." They'd put him in one of the very few private rooms at Caridad after Jack had confirmed the diagnosis by identifying the parasites in Ben's blood, and after an abdominal X-ray and endoscopy had shown no intestinal, stomach or esophagus damage—the usual areas of damage in Chagas. And while Chagas wasn't contagious, and any other patient infected with it might have gone to the ward, Ben deserved his privacy. So much so, she believed, that she'd removed all the nurses from his care. He was hers to take care of, and hers alone.

So maybe it was the protective thing going on in her because Ben fought hard to protect himself. Or maybe it was just that she didn't want to leave him, didn't want to take her eyes off him. Didn't want to shut her eyes and not hear his breathing. Whatever the case, as she settled down she knew she'd be there for the duration, however long that was. After that…no clue. But for now her life was solved, even if that solution was only a temporary one. She loved this man and she was hoping the rest of it would fall into place.

"Damn it, Ben! I've spent a lifetime having difficult stuff, and for a change I needed something easy. But you're not easy. Not even close to it. So why did you happen to me?"

Naturally, he didn't answer. But that was okay, because she didn't have an answer, either. For now, maybe being clueless was enough.

CHAPTER TEN

"Not as good as Italy," Ben said, struggling to his feet. Eleven days flat on his back, except for trips to the bathroom over the past couple of days, and he was ready to get up and move around. But slowly, because the repercussions from being bedbound were screaming from every fiber and synapse in his body.

"What?" Shanna asked, holding on to him as she steadied him.

"Italy. The mountains, and the ski slopes. Nice way to spend my time off work. This wasn't. I hate being…"

She laughed. "Grounded."

"Grounded. Inactive. Treated like an invalid."

"But you are an invalid." They were heading outside, to a chair on the wooden porch.

"Because you've been waiting on me hand and foot. Being my *slave,* even though you didn't lose the bet." After he'd rejoined the so-called living, he hadn't really minded her taking care of him. In fact, the better he felt, the more he'd enjoyed it. Shanna had such a feminine touch, and that was something he wasn't used to, especially when it touched him.

"Haven't heard you objecting."

"I've been sick, not crazy."

"Anything you want before I go on duty?"

Glancing over at the clinic, the line of people waiting to be seen was winding its way around the corner of the building. Ever since word had got out that he'd nearly succumbed to the dreaded kissing bug, people were lining up to have every bug bite and nibble checked. He couldn't blame them. It was a frightening thing to be attacked in the night and never even realize it until you were sick. Or, in his case, almost dead. "I want you to take some time off. You're looking worn out."

"Wish I could, but I can't. Your doctor is absolutely adamant about you not coming back to work for at least three more weeks, which means somebody's got to see your patients while you're sitting here lounging around and drinking tropical fruit drinks."

"My doctor is overreacting. I'll be good to go in a few days."

"Your doctor scheduled you for some tests in Buenos Aires in a few days, and she's not taking no for an answer."

"I don't have any heart damage, Shanna," he said. Except for some residual weakness, he felt fine. Mentally, he was ready to get back to work, if not to active duty then consulting in some capacity. But she was being a real stickler, which he would appreciate for some other patient but not for himself. "All my vital organs are fine. Everything's fine."

"How do you know that, Ben? You were sick for weeks before you collapsed, and you didn't even know it."

"Because Chagas is asymptomatic in the beginning."

"Doesn't matter. I'm not clearing you for work, and that's hospital policy. Your policy. You have to secure your doctor's clearance to return to work after an extended illness."

He appreciated her diligence, but more than that he appreciated the feistiness in her. He'd been a grump these past several days and had caught himself arguing when there wasn't anything to argue about. Shanna had stood up to him every time, and he liked watching that in her. Part feistiness, part pure moral purpose. She was a fierce doctor. More than that, a true friend. Maybe the first one he'd had outside his sister since his childhood.

Loving her was complicating the situation, though, because things hadn't changed with him. At the end of all of Shanna's tender, loving care he'd still be who he'd been for the last dozen years, and she deserved more than that... better than that. "I can change the rules."

A sly smile slid to her lips. "Not without Amanda's consent. And she won't consent, Ben. We're on the same page when it comes to what to do about you."

"I feel..." Happy, actually. *Happy* wasn't a word that invaded his vocabulary too often, neither did it ever have a place in his life. But he felt happy and in odd, refracted moments, even though he didn't want his convalescence to end. It had to, of course, but he liked the attention. Especially Shanna's attention.

"Smothered?" she asked.

"Picked on." In a good way.

"Poor Ben. Terrible patient. Even worse in his recovery." She laughed as she spun away. "If I have time, I'll join you for lunch. And if you need anything..."

"I need to get back to work."

"Not happening yet, so deal with it." She waved goodbye, then hurried over to the clinic where the waiting crowd almost mobbed her as she tried to get through.

Shanna had brought new life to Caridad. And new inspiration. The place needed her more than it needed most of the equipment on his want list because she embodied what he wanted this place to be—the hope, the passion, the caring demeanor. But she was fully in doctor mode right now, and when that wore down a little, when she actually had time to figure out that they weren't a couple, or involved, or could never have a relationship, she'd leave, because Shanna was such a bright star in the universe and Caridad couldn't contain her.

So for the next hour, trying to keep his mind off what he couldn't have, he sat in the sun and endured an article with the dry title "Internal Jugular Vein Cannulation: to Turn or Not to Turn the Head." Dry reading to go along with the title, and in spite of the early hour he caught himself nodding off halfway through, where he was just beginning to read the section where cannulation times, success rates and correlation to neutral head position and forty-five-degree head rotation were being introduced.

That was when his eyes finally gave up the battle and sent Ben off to catch forty winks, or in his case an hour's worth.

He only woke up when an unfamiliar voice invaded the pleasant dream where he and Shanna were stretched out on a blanket, having a picnic down at *laguna ocultada*. They'd just decided there were things better to do than eat when—

"Dr. Robinson?" It was an older voice, a vaguely familiar one. "You *are* Dr. Robinson, aren't you?"

He opened his eyes, disappointed that his dream had been interrupted. "I am," he said, looking up at the man. Good-looking guy, vaguely familiar face, lots of white hair, age indeterminable as he didn't have a wrinkle. But he had...Shanna's green eyes. He'd recognize them anywhere.

"And you're Dr. Brooks?" Extending his hand to the man, he didn't even attempt to stand. Wasn't sure if his legs were quite steady enough, and pitching forward into Shanna's grandfather's arms wasn't an impression he cared to make. "Please, forgive my appearance."

He had on his usual cargo pants and white, long-sleeved

shirt, but his hair was unkempt, and he sported several days' worth of stubble. And he was barefooted. During his illness he'd discovered he liked going without shoes. A small step away from his cautious ways, but a nice one. "But I'm recovering from Chagas. Not up to speed yet."

"I trust it was caught early enough that you'll have full recovery," he said, taking Ben's hand. "Mind if I sit down?"

"By all means..." So, what was he doing here? Shanna hadn't mentioned anything about a visit. Or if she had, it had been days ago, when he'd still been too sick to hang on to much around him. Did she even know he was here? "Would you care for some fruit juice?" He pointed to the pitcher Shanna had left for him. "Or I can have some tea made. Yerba maté's quite tasty."

Miles Brooks rejected both offers and never fully settled into the chair. Instead, he sat on the edge, kept himself erect and, from outward appearances, aloof. His attire was something more suited to the golf course than the jungle. "My goal, young man, is to collect my granddaughter and leave here as quickly as possible."

"Shanna knows your plan?"

"What Shanna knows is that she doesn't belong here. She may have some wild, romantic notion that she's queen of the jungle, but her place is at her hospital, taking up her new duties, and once she's out of this environment, she'll remember that."

"You're really going to let her walk away from patient care to spend her days behind a desk?"

"Not let, young man. Insist. She has a good head for business matters, and a frail heart for patient care. What I've done is put her where she belongs."

"You put her where she belongs." No wonder Shanna was on a sabbatical. That was probably what he'd be doing too if Miles Brooks was what he had to face every day. "Shouldn't where she belongs be Shanna's choice?"

"When she works for me, no, it is not."

"Then that's too bad. Because I'd be willing to bet there's no one on your staff as suited for patient care as your granddaughter."

"I gave her the chance to be suited the way Brooks Medical Center needs her to be suited. But she failed, Dr. Robinson. Failed miserably."

"Failed what?" he asked.

"My ultimatum. After her sabbatical, she was to return to us as a doctor who didn't get emotionally involved with her patients, or as an administrator who would have no contact whatsoever with patients. Her emotions make her weak. She gets too involved, too caught up in aspects of a patient's life where she has no business. So I gave her a chance to correct that, to remove the emotion from her patient care and deal solely with the treatment. In other words, eliminate the involvement she seems to develop for the people she treats and simply do a straightforward job. It's what we expect from all our physicians, and Shanna is no exception.

"Oh, and she agreed to the arrangement, by the way. We didn't just shove her out the door. She walked away willingly, knowing what she had to do."

He didn't know how to process this yet. Didn't even know how to begin, he was so…numb. Shanna had agreed to her grandfather's ultimatum? How? Why? "And she's agreed to return to Brooks on your terms?" he asked, trying to blot out what was becoming glaringly obvious.

"If she doesn't return, the board has the right to sever her completely from Brooks, which would mean her part-ownership would dissolve."

"And she wouldn't be welcome in her family?"

"Really, that's none of your business, Doctor."

True, it wasn't. But now he had his answer and he couldn't simply blot it out. Because now he understood why Shanna had come here to be like him. In her eyes, he was like her grandfather. Cold, dispassionate. She'd come here to learn detachment from the master of detachment. He couldn't say it was a good feeling, being copied for the things he himself knew weren't good.

In fact, it felt downright awful, because he'd hoped she was here to observe and learn something else from him. Jungle medicine would have been okay. Running a small hospital would have been fine. Or maybe, in the wildest of all fantasies, she'd followed him here because she'd wanted to have some kind of a relationship, in spite of his platonic ways in Tuscany.

Well, it didn't matter what he thought, did it? Because what Shanna had come to learn from him was how to be a cold, impersonal bastard like her grandfather was. That was all she'd wanted—to figure out how to switch off her real self, the way he was so good at doing, and turn on the heart of stone. And she'd seen him as her perfect teacher. "You don't care what people want, do you, Dr. Brooks? Or what they're best suited for?"

"In my world, what I have to care about is that everything is run as efficiently as possible. We're a large institution, and silly sentimentality gets in the way. Shanna suffers from silly sentimentality, and the only way to reduce that is to remove its cause from her path. I know you run a hospital here, but I doubt you can even begin to comprehend to enormity of the task of running Brooks."

No, he couldn't imagine. Neither did he want to. "How did you find Caridad?" he asked, fighting back the thought of what Shanna really thought about him.

"You're easy to track. And I do remember you, by the

way. Young man with an axe to grind. My decision to refuse you for a residency was a good one and judging from the way you ended up, even better than I realized. You may think you're some kind of a Svengali, son, who's going to manipulate his way into the Brooks family and medical resources through my granddaughter, but it's not going to happen.

"It's a simple equation, really. Shanna back at Brooks Medical Center equals everything for her. Shanna staying at this little place you call Caridad equals nothing for her—no more partnering in our medical enterprises, no more position at the hospital, no more family, for the most part. If she turns her back on us, we turn ours on her. And somehow I have an idea you enter into the equation, don't you? I'm sure she's gotten herself all emotional over you. Young man with a tragic past. Now with a serious illness. That's her element, Doctor. It's where she deludes herself into believing she's delivering good patient care."

"You're a divisive son of a bitch, Dr. Brooks."

Miles Brooks laughed aloud over that. "Been called worse, young man."

"But have you been called shortsighted? Because believing that good medicine is practiced without emotional involvement is about as shortsighted as it comes."

"Fine. Run your hospital on any kind of emotion you want. But don't disrespect me because I don't choose to be the same kind of administrator you are. What I do works."

"And hurts your granddaughter. Can't you see that? She's as gifted a doctor as I've ever seen, and what you expect from her either diminishes or disallows that. And if you force her back to Brooks in an administrative-only capacity, it's your loss."

"Or, depending on the perspective, my gain."

"Add manipulative to my description of you, Dr.

Brooks. Because it's not Shanna you want. It's your victory over her."

"It's never occurred to you that her family loves her and that's why we want her back."

"No, because it's never occurred to Shanna that her family loves her." He watched the old man's face for some sort of shock, or anger, because that was an outrageous statement to make, as true as it was. Sadly, nothing registered on Miles Brooks. And that was when it hit him again. Shanna had believed she could learn from him how to be like this cruel excuse of a man.

"What her family loves, Dr. Robinson, is any equation that betters the hospital. Shanna is part of that equation. But do you fall into that somewhere? To get her, do I have to offer you something?"

"Shanna's too smart to get involved with me because she sees me as being just like you. She deserves better than me, and better than you."

"See, that's where you're wrong. You're nothing like me, because men like me don't have women like my granddaughter falling in love with them."

She was in love with him? It was everything he wanted to know, and nothing he wanted to know.

Miles Brooks arched bushy eyebrows. "You didn't know that? Because you conceal your feelings as poorly as my granddaughter does, which caused me to think you might pick up on the feelings of others as easily as she does. Doesn't matter, though. You'll stay here, she won't. She's a Brooks after all. We know where we belong. But I'm willing to make you part of this if that's how it turns out."

How it would turn out was that there was nothing for Shanna here, especially if what her grandfather said was true, that she loved him. And, damn, did that jar him. More than he expected. "Look, Shanna's in clinic right now, so please don't interrupt her while she's seeing patients. We're going to have lunch together in a while, and you're welcome to join us then. In the meantime, the brown building just to the front of the hospital has an empty room, and you're welcome to make yourself at home there, for as long as you stay at Caridad."

"Just for the night, son. That will give Shanna sufficient time to get her things packed, and for you to make your decision." With that, Miles Brooks stood, bowed slightly at the waist, and headed for the steps. "I understand that you're concerned for my granddaughter, and if you care for her the way I believe you do, you'll do what's best for her. So, please, have someone come and get me when Shanna is available."

Or never, Ben thought. *I'll never have someone come and get you, you manipulative old...*

"You're not supposed to be up and wandering around yet," Shanna said once she noticed Ben standing by the wall in her exam room, simply watching her bandage the lengthy cut to which she'd just applied twenty-two stitches on a little boy's left leg.

"I could have done those stitches. Simple thing, no physical effort."

"Or stayed put, like the doctor told you to do."

"I did, for a while. Read some. Had a visitor."

"Maybe you should have kept your visitor there longer so you'd have stayed down longer." She turned to face him. "Look, I know you're bored out of your head. I would be, too. But until we have some tests done that we can't do here, I want you resting. And we're not going to get them done until we can arrange a plane to get us there, which isn't until next week at the earliest. So, please, be a better patient."

He chuckled. "Deaf ears, Doctor. Your advice is falling on deaf ears."

"Don't I know that!" she said, then escorted the child out to the waiting room back to his mother. When she returned, Ben was seated on the exam table, legs dangling, the look on his face…well, she hadn't seen it before, couldn't determine what it was. But it was so serious it caused her to shiver. "You're not feeling well, are you?" she asked, stepping back into the room and shutting the door.

"I'm feeling fine," he said, patting the table next to him. "But we need to talk. I've already asked Dr. Hueber to cover the clinic for you for a little while so you don't have to worry about that."

"Maybe I should stand…" She didn't like bad news, and everything inside her screamed that this was bad. So bad, in fact, that last time she'd felt this way had been the day her grandfather had told her Elsa Willoughby had been turned down for a kidney transplant. That day had changed her life and, somehow, she knew this was going to be another life-changer. "Just tell me, Ben. Whatever it is, *please,* just tell me."

He patted the table again, and she climbed up next to him. Two people, sitting side by side, touching at the shoulders and hips, in an empty little room. Could have been intimate, but it wasn't. Ben knew that as he reached for Shanna's hand. Shanna knew that as she slipped her hand into his.

"Your grandfather is here," he finally said.

"What?" she sputtered.

"He was my visitor. He's come to take you home."

Of all the things Ben might have told her, this was the one thing she couldn't have anticipated. Her grandfather had come to get her. "Did he say why?"

"He said it's time."

"It's time because my family doesn't like to lose, and the longer I'm away from them the more they risk losing."

"Lose what? This isn't a game."

"Isn't it?" she snapped. Her body tensed. She could feel her muscles tighten, starting in her neck then working down to her shoulders, her back... "It's all about control, Ben. That's all it's ever about in my family, and I'm willing to bet my grandfather never once told you he'd missed me. And why my grandfather, Ben? I have parents—a mother and a father who could have asked me. Picked up a phone and asked. But they didn't because that's not the way my family is run. And we *are* run, Ben. Make no mistake about that. We're run like a business."

"Which is why you left them?"

She shook her head. "When that's all you know, you accept it. It is what it is. And it really didn't bother me all that much, to be honest." When she'd been allowed to practice as a doctor and not as an administrator.

"Something bothered you enough to get you here, Shanna. And I know what it is now."

"To learn from you, Ben. That's what I've always said." Her heart started to pound because Ben had figured it out, and it hurt him the way she'd feared it would.

"And what I've never believed. But your grandfather told me about his ultimatum."

In spite of the Argentine heat in the room, she shivered. "I'm not sure..."

"Yes, you are. After your sabbatical you were to go back to Brooks either as a doctor who didn't get emotionally involved with her patients or as an administrator. One or the other. In fact, it was an agreement you made with your grandfather, wasn't it? Learn to be more like him or, as it turned out, like me? Me and your grandfather, one and the same."

"No, Ben. That's not what I was doing."

"Really, Shanna? Can you really sit here and tell me that you don't see me as a replica of your grandfather? That you didn't come here to copy me just so you could get back into his good graces?" He pulled his hand away from hers and stood. Went to the window and stared outside. "Because that's what it was. The one thing I couldn't figure out about why you wanted to learn from me. I flattered myself in a lot of ways, trying to figure it out. Or should I say, deluded myself?"

"You're not wrong," she conceded. "But you're also not right."

"Which makes about as much sense as everything else." He turned to face her. "Couldn't you have been honest and up front? Told me you'd come to learn from my cold, detached, harsh, heartless, indifferent, insensitive, uncaring, unemotional, unloving, unsympathetic ways—take your pick, use one description or use them all because they all work. They're all what you think of me."

"What I thought of you, Ben."

"Like I said."

This couldn't be happening. She'd almost convinced herself she could stay here, do the work she loved, coexist with the man she loved even though he'd never return those same feelings. Because having even a small piece of Ben was better than not having him at all. Which was, ironically, where she was now.

She couldn't blame him for being hurt, though, because yes, those were the things she'd thought he was, the reason she'd come here. But the reason she'd fallen in love with him had been because he was none of those things.

"What else was I supposed to think of you?" she asked, fighting not to cry, not to drag the emotions into this that had gotten her into trouble in the first place. "In Italy, we shared time together yet you kept your distance. You did the polite, expected things, like opened doors for me, and deferred to my lunch choices. But you kept this icy distance. And, yes, I thought you would be the perfect role model for what I needed to accomplish if I wanted to go back to my hospital...*my* hospital, Ben. It's all I know. All I ever wanted to do was grow up and be like the rest of my family. And you seemed...like the rest of my family.

"So I thought maybe observing someone like them outside the whole Brooks atmosphere might be what I needed. You know, keep it objective. Do it someplace where there weren't so many expectations of me. So I chose you. After I met you, I thought you'd be the perfect person to observe. Someone exceptional in his skills yet separated by an emotional mile from everything but the pure aspects of doctoring."

"See, that's what I don't understand. Why do you want to separate yourself that way?"

She smiled sadly. "It gets in the way."

"How, Shanna? Tell me how?"

"I've always loved the connections we have as doctors, Ben. You know that about me. It's why I'm happy in family practice because I can have those connections. In medicine, we're fortunate because we can touch so many lives, connect to so many people. I truly believe, in ways I don't understand, that everybody is connected. Maybe it's as vague as we're simply connected by the universe, or maybe there's this personal connection we have to find for ourselves. Whatever it is, I like that connection, and tried really hard to find it with everyone I took care of.

"But then there was this patient...Elsa Willoughby. End-stage renal. I told you about her. Anyway, I was furious my grandfather took her off the kidney transplant waiting list. *Furious*. Because she might have had a good outcome.

I wanted so badly for her to live that my objectivity was totally clouded by my emotional attachment."

"Age aside, was she a bad risk?"

Shanna nodded. "Medically, she had problems. But I cared for her, and because of that I made promises I couldn't keep. Then she died, and I..." Okay, so the emotional block didn't work. Now there were tears running down her cheeks, and she didn't give a damn. "See, this is who I am," she said, swatting at the tears. "I lead with my heart and I can't change it. Although for a minute I thought if I watched you, I might find out how you did it, but you don't, Ben."

She sniffled. Looked up at him through blurry eyes. "You don't turn it off. None of it. You channel it differently, but you're not like my grandfather or any of the other people I've tried to emulate. I saw that in you almost immediately, and should probably have walked away before it came to...to this. Because, yes, I always knew I was going back to Brooks. That was the agreement. Return one way or the other."

"So you're going to return to something that will make you miserable?"

"We all learn to adapt, don't we? Just look at you."

"Did it ever occur to you, Shanna, that your emotional attachment to your patients is what makes you the extraordinary doctor you are? I've watched you, envied your confidence to become involved on the level you do."

"You don't have to be kind to me, Ben. I'll be fine."

"But will you be happy?"

Truly happy? No. Not without Ben. But Ben wasn't available, and the part of him she might have had earlier had vanished. "*Happy* is such a relative term."

"Okay, then skip happy. Will you be fulfilled?"

"Why do you care?"

"Because I care about you, Shanna. I'll admit I'm not sure how to get past all those things you thought I was, but that doesn't change the fact that I care about you, and I see you diving headfirst into the worst mistake you're ever going to make."

"So, what's my alternative? Stay here and work with the man I've fallen in love with, always knowing he doesn't want me? How does that make me happy or fulfill me?"

"You what?"

"Love you, Ben. And don't pretend you didn't know it. You did. But because you're not open to it, you've ignored it. But I don't hide things well, and you're not oblivious."

He sighed deeply. "Whatever you think you feel…"

"*Think* I feel? Whatever I *think* I feel? How can you say that to me?"

He sighed deeply again, and this time outwardly braced himself. "I've told you ever since you got here…"

She thrust out her hand to stop him. "It doesn't matter what you told me. Okay? Once again, I led with my emotions, and look where it got me. So why not go back to Brooks and be what I'm supposed to be?"

"Because it's not what you want to be."

"But I don't get to choose what I want to be, Ben. Wearing my heart on my sleeve the way I've been accused of doing so often hurts. And I can't be good at anything if that always gets in my way."

"Don't let it get in your way, Shanna. Embrace it."

"To what end? Because all I want is to embrace you, and a life here at Caridad with you. But you won't let me have that."

"Which is what I've been saying all along. I can't get involved with you the way you want to get involved with me."

"Because of your scars? Or the fact that you had a problem with alcohol in the past? Do you think so little of me, Ben, that I can't get past those things?"

"No, I think so much of you, because I know you can. I'm the one who can't. Every time I look in the mirror… it's there, staring back at me. And if you thought all those horrible things of me before… Shanna, there are parts of me that are dead. Nobody wants that around them. I don't want it around me, but that's how it is. How I am."

"Not dead, Ben. Maybe held back, but you have such a pure passion for medicine on a level I didn't even know was out there. I mean, here you are, this doctor who built a hospital out of a board and a couple of nails. There's nothing dead in that. And nothing dead in the man who made it happen, and succeed."

Good argument on deaf ears. She could see that in him, see him pull back emotionally. In his mind he was distancing himself even more, and that was what she couldn't endure. He wouldn't let her in. More than that, he fought to keep her out.

"You know, I was willing to take anything just to stay with you. I love the medicine here, and I love you, and I would have taken whatever you allowed me. But you're not allowing me anything, Ben. Nothing." So maybe it was time to go, to end it. To do some of that distancing herself, so she could figure out what came next. Because it wasn't Brooks.

Ben had shown her who she was, as surely as he'd shown her he didn't want her. Loving Ben had made her realize who she wanted to be, though. But it had also shown her what she'd never have, and she couldn't stay here, facing that pain every day. "Anyway, unless you need me, I'll be packed and out of here by tomorrow."

"You're welcome to stay and work. Caridad needs you, Shanna."

"But you don't. I'm sorry if I hurt you, Ben. All those things I thought about you as a doctor were wrong. You're amazing, and I hope you have a happy life. Oh, and just so you'll know, I'm not going back to Brooks, because you're right. The kind of doctor I am is fine. That's what you've taught me, and for that I thank you."

She loved Tuscany in the winter, and she was glad it was still winter here. Loved the amazing slopes of Garfagnana, even though she hadn't done any skiing since she'd arrived two weeks ago. Loved the Tuscan wines, even though she hadn't drunk any on this stay. Loved the fairy-tale villages, age-old churches, hermitages, castles and fortresses, although she didn't feel up to exploring them just now. But she loved Tuscany, just not as much as Argentina. Argentina was her past, however. Its memories her heartbreak.

This morning she simply didn't have the will to move away from this table. *Their table by the window.* Some might call her crazy, sitting there, thinking of it as their table, but it was. She could still feel Ben here, and that was where she needed to be for a while—in a place where she could still feel him. Love lingering, love dying, neither was easy.

But she didn't know how to move on yet. Maybe because she didn't want to, or because the anchor of losing the life she loved wouldn't allow it. Either way, she'd come here every morning the way she used to, and stare at the mountain. Sometimes she stared for minutes, sometimes hours. Then the rest of her day was lost in aimless strolling, uneaten meals and forced smiles for those who greeted her.

She wanted her purpose back, and Ben and Caridad were her purpose. Except she was unwanted there, even though there had been a time she'd believed that Ben loved her and, in the end, that love would break away everything that held him back. But that had been an illusion the way everything else had been. Two weeks ago, when she'd walked away, part of her had clung to the hope he'd run after her. He hadn't. Hadn't reached out to her in any way. And that wasn't an illusion. It was a reality, the one he'd tried to convey to her, and she wouldn't see. Yep, heart on her sleeve all the way. Too bad she couldn't have traded it in for blinkers, but what was done was done.

So now this emotional aftermath was hers to deal with, and the most she wanted to deal with was this table, this window, and the mountain she could see from it. Sighing, Shanna shut her eyes, trying to block out all the images that didn't want to be blocked.

"Is this seat taken?"

His voice came to her so clearly she could feel the tears welling behind her closed eyes. "No," she whispered, wishing the memory wasn't so vivid. By now it should have faded. She wanted it to fade.

"It's the only table with a view of the mountain, and I love to sit and watch it. It makes me feel like a part of something important."

It was so real, the memory of that day, the words she'd said to him, his voice... She opened her eyes, hoped he was there. But he wasn't. So she closed her eyes again, this time not even trying to hold back the tears that were starting to fall. *Please, go away,* she thought. *How can I get over you if I can't get away from you?*

"I'd never really looked at those mountains from this window, though. Not before you pointed them out to me."

"Ben," she choked, spinning around to find him standing behind her. "You... What...? Why are you here?"

"It seems I have a doctor who wants me to rest. So I came here to rest."

"Your doctor wouldn't have approved your trip halfway around the world. Not yet."

"He's a competent doctor. Great cardiologist. Pronounced me in good shape, no permanent damage. But in bad need of some serious relaxation. Thought Tuscany was a great idea."

"You went for your tests?" she asked.

"Actually, I caught a ride with your grandfather. You left before he did, and he had room to take me. Having a jet at your disposal comes with some advantages. He dropped me off in Buenos Aires on his way back to Chicago." Smiling, he said, "May I join you, Shanna?"

Oh, how she wanted him to. But he scared her, and she already hurt so badly. "I was just getting ready to leave, so you can have the table to yourself. It's better than sitting in the back, staring at the wall."

"What if I want to sit here at this table and stare at you?"

"But you don't, Ben." She swiped away the tears on her cheeks. Drew in a bracing breath. Squared her shoulders to face the hardest thing she'd ever had to do—reject Ben. Not for herself, though. For Ben. "Maybe you think you're doing the right thing, or trying to end something that never got started, but you don't have to do that. I lost my way for a little while, but I'm fine now."

"Which is why you're sitting here, crying?" He stepped around her, and took that seat. Then reached across the table and wiped away a stray tear with his thumb. "I'm sorry, Shanna. I knew you were falling in love with me, and I supposed there was a huge part of me that wanted you to."

Finally, she looked into his eyes. "But the warning was out there, Ben. It was always out there. Even that night when we made love, you didn't let me have all of you. I knew it. Didn't want to see it. But I did know it."

"But you didn't know me, Shanna."

"And I've apologized for that. I was wrong for assuming…anything."

He shook his head. "You were right for assuming everything. It's what I put out there for people to see, and you saw it. But only part of it."

"The part you wouldn't let me see."

"The part I couldn't let you see."

"Why not?"

"Because to admit it to you is to admit it to myself. And after I admit it, then I have to come to terms with how it's a part of me that doesn't fit into anything good, or noble, or all the things you think I am. It's a hard thing to do, see a flaw that can never be fixed. It's easier to ignore it than admit to it, because…"

"Because admitting it shatters the barriers you've put up around yourself to protect yourself from it. Then all that's left is vulnerability, and vulnerability can turn into such a deep, abiding pain if it's not tended properly."

"You're always amazing, Dr. Brooks."

"Not amazing, Dr. Robinson. Connected. And there's nothing wrong with that, as someone once told me. The thing is, all I've ever wanted in my life is to fit somewhere… somewhere I love, somewhere I want to be. And that was with you, which made me so vulnerable, because you shut me out every time I got close.

"Sure, maybe I could have hung around Caridad longer, waged a harder battle to get what I wanted from you, but what I've figured out is that I shouldn't have to fight for it. I fell in love with you for more reasons than I can count, and I'm still in love with you. I think you're in love with me, or you wouldn't have followed me halfway around the world. The feelings I have for you scare me, though, because you're who makes me vulnerable. But loving you makes me happy and hopeful. It's the same with you, I think.

"Loving me makes you vulnerable. But for you the remedy for that is to shut people out when they get too close. You shut me out because you don't know what to do with that vulnerability, and I don't want any more of that."

"It's conditioned in me, Shanna. Not meant to hurt anybody, but..."

"But protect yourself. I understand. People can be cruel, and I'm sure you've experienced more than your share of cruelty. So you keep yourself separate, push people away—"

"To protect them," he interrupted. "Them. Not me."

"Because you have scars? I don't understand."

"Scars," he said. "Deep scars."

"But this isn't about your physical scars, is it? It can't be, because that would make you...shallow. And you're not. So, who do you think I fell in love with, Ben?"

"You fell in love with an image. Someone you think is me, or you want to be me. But someone who isn't me."

"Who isn't you? The man in the café that morning who was so befuddled when a stranger sat down with him that he didn't know what to do? Or the man who spent the night knocking on doors, giving yellow-fever vaccinations to people who'd already refused them? Or spent the night, sitting in the chair at Maritza's bedside, watching her breathe, checking her pulse, reading—in very bad Spanish—bedtime stories to her?

"Tell me, Ben, which one of those people isn't you? Because the man who did all that is the one I fell in love with, the one I watched, and admired and realized he was worth everything I might lose if I stayed with him. And I want to stay with him, Ben. Now, even when I know you don't want me, I still want to stay with you, be a part of everything you are. Yet you're still pushing me away. You came all the way to Italy after me, and you're still shutting me out."

"You don't want to be part of everything, Shanna, because you don't know everything. And that's what I had to settle with myself before I came after you. What I had to face down in the mirror. Because you deserve to know everything."

"You mean before you push me away again?" she asked, withdrawing her hand from his. Glancing out at the mountain, she saw such majesty there. Looming over the entire village, it looked after the people, protected them, sheltered them, the way Ben did the people who came to Caridad. Yet there was a deadliness to the mountain. The snow that could take an inexperienced skier. The avalanche that could swallow up an unsuspecting village. No blame went to the mountain for these things, as the mountain lived up to its legacy.

So did Ben, and because she trusted in him with all her heart, she truly believed that no blame could go to him for whatever he perceived as his own deadliness. "You're right. I deserve to know," she finally said, hoping he understood where this had to go. Because this was up to Ben now. The rest of it was his to deal with because she'd gone as far as she could go. Loving him the way she did meant she would support him in anything, but he had to step up to take that support. With everything in her, she hoped he would.

"You flew from Argentina to Italy, but there's still one more step to take." The step where he proved his trust. Because in that trust she would find where she truly wanted to be.

He smiled, but sadly. "You see through me, don't you?"

"Not through you. But what I see encompasses some

of you. It has to encompass all of you, though. And you have to be the one to allow it."

"Or it encompasses none of me, which you'll understand when you know *everything*."

"That sells me short, Ben. After I've told you my feelings for you, I don't deserve that." Rather than responding, he stared out the window for a few moments. Were his eyes focused on the mountain, or on something so distant she couldn't begin to fathom it? She didn't know, so she waited because, ultimately, this would have to be in Ben's good time, or not at all. So, two, three, four minutes ticked off the clock in utter silence as she watched him barely blink, barely breathe.

Then it happened. He drew in a deep breath, held it for a second, and let it out. "You're right. You don't deserve to be sold short, and I'm sorry you thought that's what I was doing." Finally he faced her again. "I wasn't. But you were right when you said you scare me, because you do. More than anything in my life ever has."

"Why, Ben?"

"Because you make me realize I have to face things in myself that I've never faced. Ugly things, things I've done, things I don't want to be part of me but are."

"You're not alone, you know."

He nodded. "I know. And maybe that's what scares me most. I know how to be alone. Do a pretty damn good job of it. Anything else…" He shrugged. Shook his head. Drew in another deep breath and let it out. "I was burned, as you already know. Had thirty-three surgeries, and survived in spite of some pretty overwhelming odds against me. That's really just the preface, because the real story starts later, after those surgeries.

"It was this never-ending grind, going from one surgery to another, never having a life in between. But I managed it. Managed to move on, go to college, get myself into medical school. Deluded myself into thinking that my life could be normal, in spite of the stares and the things people said behind my back. Or even to my face. But people will talk, won't they? Most of the time I just shut it out. It was hard to do at first, but after a while it became easy.

"Then I met Nancy. Nice girl. Not the love of my life by a long shot, but I honestly believed I could find something with her. Long story short, my shirt came off, she gasped, drew back in unadulterated repulsion, and that's when I knew that I couldn't shut it out, that people would always react the way Nancy did. Which was an excuse. It wasn't Nancy's reaction that mattered. It was mine. I just found it easier to blame the whole succession of events that followed on the easiest target."

"Events, like drinking?"

He nodded. "It's easy to shut out a lot of the world when you're drunk. But I never could get drunk enough, so I started taking pills. I'm a doctor, had doctor friends. Easy access to whatever I wanted to medicate myself with. End result, an alcoholic who was also addicted to drugs.

"Two years of it, Shanna. Two years of wallowing. I managed to live my life through the first year of it, but couldn't keep going during the second year of it and got myself kicked out of my residency. It wasn't that I didn't want to be a surgeon. I was in the program, and got kicked out of it because being a surgeon didn't really work well with who I was turning into."

"But you pulled yourself out of it."

"Not at first. I took a year, and simply wallowed. The more I wallowed, the more miserable I was. Vicious circle. I tried a couple of twelve-step programs and failed. Reapplied to a surgical residency, was turned down. Decided to skip surgery and try for family practice, and your grand-father turned me down."

"You went to another hospital, though. You said it was a better fit for you."

"I went there as an outpatient in their drug and alcohol rehab clinic, ended up doing some volunteer work, then accepted a residency because no one else wanted to work there. It was old and underfunded and difficult, and they took me because no one else wanted the position. I will say it was the best thing for me because I saw medicine from a perspective I'd never have found at Brooks, and that's what made me able to come here and do what I do. But the way I was accepted there wasn't as a bright and shining endorsement of anything."

"Except a commitment to move forward despite the circumstances."

"See, that's the thing. I didn't have that kind of com-mitment. Before I ended up there, I'd got to the end of my rope, didn't see a way out. I was drinking, I needed pills just to get me moving, and my medical career was washed up. Nothing in that mess was moving forward."

"But look where you are. How did that person turn into the one who got you to Caridad?"

"Suicide. Or, shall I say, suicide attempt."

She gasped.

"What your grandfather turned down that day, Shanna, was me, at the bitter end. I went back to my hotel room, blamed him, blamed Nancy, blamed the world for the way I felt. Drank some more, popped more pills. I was just so... tired. So defeated. The worse I felt, the more I needed the crutches that were destroying my life—booze and pills. I can't even begin to realize, after all this time, the lengths I went to when I needed to find that numbness. A stronger man might have faced his fate earlier on, but I wasn't a stronger man. I was the man who made excuses.

"That's all I did until the day I quit. And don't get your hopes up about me. It wasn't a moment of clarity, or some great manifestation of what my life could become if I let my tragedy work for me. You know, make me stronger. In fact, what happened was one of the least noble incidents of my life. I...I..."

Shanna swallowed hard, suddenly understanding where this was leading to. The inevitable ending to the kinds of suffering he'd gone through. "You tried to kill yourself."

"I thought about it. Spent days and nights planning it. Even went out to this hilly area where I used to play when I was a kid and climbed up to the top of one of the peaks, and thought about stepping off. Must have stood on the edge a good two hours, looking down at what could have easily been my destiny. One step, and everything would have been solved."

"What stopped you?"

He chuckled, but bitterly. "Ironically, after all my self-destructive behavior, it turned out I didn't want to die. I'd worked too hard for too long trying to live, and here I was, on the verge of taking one step farther because... You pick an excuse. I had a lot of them, and they all centered on somebody else doing something to me when I was the one doing it to myself.

"That's when it all became clear. No voices booming at me from the heavens, no lightning bolts. Just some pretty deep soul-searching and the discovery that the world was full of people suffering far worse than me, who didn't give up, and who succeeded in doing what they wanted in spite of their suffering Then there I was, always looking for the easiest way out. The epitome of weakness."

"Or maybe that was the time when your true character decided to develop. We all get there in different ways, Ben. For some people it's easy. Who they are just manifests itself. But for others the journey is so hard. Maybe because what you're supposed to do in life is so immense, or difficult, you need to learn to deal with the adversities before you can accomplish great things."

"Yeah, well, tell that to my mirror, because every time I look in it, the person looking back looks weak to me. That's the monster I see, Shanna. Not the scars. Me. I know who I was, who I could become again. For me, every single day of my life is spent close to the edge. I'm still looking down, wondering what it would take to make me take that one step farther. How can I ask someone to be part of that?"

"But I know who you are, Ben. And when you're looking in the mirror seeing weakness, I'm looking in that same mirror at you, and all I see is unbelievable strength. To go from where you were to where you are now… Going through rehab, fighting to get back into a residency program. Setting up a hospital in Argentina. That's what someone in your life would be part of. What I would be part of, if you let me."

"That's what I want, Shanna. But what if I backslide? That's always a possibility. The biggest fear in my life. They teach you in the twelve-step programs that you're really only a step away from it at any given day, any given time. And it was so ugly. I was so ugly."

"Do you want to be with me, Ben?"

"More than anything. I want a future with you."

"Do you see marriage in that future?"

"I think I wanted to marry you the first time we sat here at this table together and you scared me so badly I ran to the back of the room to stare at the wall. But it's not that simple."

"I walked away from my life. Gave up a lot, actually. Stepped outside a medical practice I knew into something I had no idea existed. Turned my back on my family, who will now probably turn their backs on me. Fell in love with the most impossibly stubborn man I could have found, who loves me back but won't do anything about it. And you think that's simple?"

She scooted herself back from the table, then stood. "You know what? I'm tired of looking up at that mountain, wondering what's up there. Life's short, and we're wasting time. It's time to find out." She held out her hand to him. "I'm with you, Ben. But are you with me?"

Ben stood, then took her hand. "I'm with you."

"For the whole journey? Because that's what it's about. The whole journey or nothing."

He nodded. "I *am* tired of looking up at the mountain. I'm ready for the whole journey."

They stepped outside the café, and simply stood on the curb, looking up at the mountain together, Ben's arms wrapped around Shanna and Shanna leaning back into his embrace. "It's a long way up there," he finally said. "It'll take an hour to get to the lift and, depending on the lines of people, it might take us another hour to get to the top."

"Maybe even two or three," she added.

"Four. I think it's at least four."

"Then what do you suggest, Ben Robinson?" she asked, spinning round to face him.

"We get an earlier start at it tomorrow. But for now I know this bed and breakfast just up the street. Happen to have a room there, which I could probably switch to the honeymoon suite."

"That's what you want?" she asked him. "Are you sure? Because I haven't even heard a marriage proposal yet. So don't you think a honeymoon suite is getting ahead of ourselves?" She looked at his face, and for the first time since she'd known him saw no hesitance there. No distance. Nothing there but the glow of love, and trust, and the sure knowledge that this was where he belonged, where she belonged, where they belonged. And where they finally started, together. "So, will you marry me, Ben?"

"I thought you'd never ask." He pulled two boxes from his pocket and opened them. Wedding rings. Plain gold bands. "The custom is to wear the wedding band on your right hand until the wedding, when the priest blesses them and we move them to the left hand. These belonged to my grandparents, so they may look a little worn..."

"They're beautiful," she gasped as he took his grandmother's ring from the velvet box and placed it on Shanna's right ring finger, then kissed it. She did the same for him, and there, standing on a public street outside a little café, they made vows to each other. No priest, no formality, no legality. "I promise to love you and stand by your side forever, Ben Robinson."

"And I promise to love you and never shut you out of my life, forever, Shanna Brooks."

The traditional wedding kiss was a little salty for a quiet Italian village, but when they realized that they really did need to head straight to the bed and breakfast, in a hurry, and stepped back from each other, the small crowd that had gathered applauded them. Ben took a bow, Shanna curtsied, then they turned and strolled hand in hand to Signora Palmadessa's, where she threw rose petals on them when they entered.

"Almost a honeymoon," Ben whispered, as they sailed past the woman.

Shanna shook her head. Held up her ring, and smiled. "Doesn't matter which hand it's on. This is a real honeymoon."

"It's been sitting out there since this morning," she said, her focus on the large, wooden packing crate that had miraculously made it to Caridad. "Addressed to me. So I want to open it."

Ben laughed. Married legitimately a month now, he was only just beginning to understand Shanna and all her habits and personality quirks. It was a lifetime journey, he supposed, and one he was happy to take because marriage to her was everything he'd expected it to be. And so much more. In moments like these it made him wonder why he hadn't just married her at first sight then figured out the rough patches along the way, because doing everything together was so much better than being alone. "So open it," he said, handing her a pry bar then stepping back to watch.

"You don't think I can do it, do you?"

"What I think is that you can do anything you want."

She'd defied her family yet they'd come to Argentina for the wedding. A simple affair, really, where they'd moved the rings to their left hands, where she'd worn the traditional Argentinian blue petticoat under her white dress, where they'd danced the tango half the night. Her family hadn't stayed for the festivities. They'd literally flown in for the ceremony then left immediately after, but it was a start for Shanna, and she was cautiously optimistic for the future. Her grandfather had mentioned wanting a first great-grandchild. And he'd paid to have Ben's cottage with two separate apartments renovated into a single cottage for the two of them.

So maybe there were new things to explore with her family now that she wasn't part of the family business. However it happened, there were possibilities she'd never expected, and she was excited to explore them.

"I can't even budge the crate, Ben. It must have cost a fortune to have it shipped."

"It did," he said, grinning.

After taking several good whacks at the crate's top and loosening some of its nails, Shanna finally managed to wrestle the top of the box off, only to find it packed with foam peanuts and packing bubbles. But she tore at those like a woman possessed, throwing them all over the porch in her attempt to discover what was under them. Eventually, she saw it. "Ben, I..."

"You're not speechless, are you?" he teased. "Because if you are, I think I'll run and get the camera, because I'm not likely to see it again."

"How did you do this?"

"Bought it when we were in Tuscany, paid a company to ship it home—snail's-pace mail because I couldn't afford to express ship it."

She swiped at a tear sliding down her cheek. "It's ours, isn't it? Where we..."

"Met. Our table. Where we met. Where I fell in love with you." He'd bought the café table and chairs. "I didn't like the idea of other people sitting there, maybe damaging it or destroying it. Then I wondered about what would happen to it if the café changed its decor. So I bought it."

"Our table," she said, then ran across the porch, straight into Ben's arms. "Thank you, Ben. You don't know what this means to me."

"Want to show me?"

"In the middle of the day? You've got patients to see."

"Covered."

"And I'm behind on my charting."

"Charting can wait." He lowered his lips to hers. "Forever, for all I care."

"Why, Ben Robinson, whatever has come over you?"

"You," he said as his lips found hers.

* * * * *

THE REBEL
AND MISS JONES

BY
ANNIE CLAYDON

To the unsung hero

First published in Great Britain 2013
by Mills & Boon, an imprint of Harlequin (UK) Limited.
Harlequin (UK) Limited, Eton House, 18-24 Paradise Road,
Richmond, Surrey TW9 1SR

© Annie Claydon 2013

ISBN: 978 0 263 89877 4

Printed and bound in Spain
by Blackprint CPI, Barcelona

Dear Reader

One of the best things about being a writer is that you have the opportunity to travel, even if it's only in your imagination. So this book has been a real indulgence, because I got to set it in two of my favourite places—which just happen to be on opposite sides of the world.

For me, one of the best parts of travelling is returning home. But for Sara and Reece 'home' isn't just a different place on the map, it's an entirely different concept. The challenge that they face is not merely a matter of physical distance, and it's one which is far more difficult to overcome. I loved writing their story, even if they did have me tearing my hair out at times, and I was with them every step of the way on their travels, as they explored each other's worlds and began to find that home truly is where the heart is.

Thank you for reading Reece and Sara's story. I hope you enjoy it. I'm always delighted to hear from readers, and you can e-mail me via my website at: www.annieclaydon.com

Annie

**These books are also available in eBook format
from www.millsandboon.co.uk**

CHAPTER ONE

'I've got to go. You know that, don't you?'

They'd been through this already. Sara grinned up at her brother. 'Of course I do. I know what it's like to be on call. You can't tell a bush fire that now's not convenient and you'll be there in a couple of days.'

Simon smiled for the first time since he'd answered the telephone that morning. 'You grew up some time when I wasn't looking. I keep forgetting that.' He pinched the bridge of his nose, as if he still couldn't believe the evidence of his own eyes. 'Ten years is a long time.'

And a lot had happened in the years since they'd last seen each other. But this wasn't the time to dwell on that. 'If the boot was on the other foot, and that phone call had been for a paramedic, you wouldn't have seen me for dust. You need to go.'

Simon shrugged. 'You'll be here when I get back?' It was almost as if he thought she wouldn't. As if the bonds that they'd been carefully rebuilding for the last two days would break at the slightest touch. Sara could understand that too. She shared his fears.

'Where else am I going to go? By the time you get back I'll have got over my jet-lag, rearranged your house for you and taught Trader how to bark with an English accent.'

'I've still got an English accent.' Simon frowned. 'Haven't I?'

'Now you mention it, no. Not any more.' Simon's accent was pure Aussie to her ears. He'd changed in other ways too. No longer the lanky older brother, fresh out of university, who had clashed so violently with their mother and walked out of their lives for ever. He was broader, more thoughtful and a great deal more measured. Much tidier too. 'Did I say that I'm proud of you?'

'No. But thanks.' The smile he gave her was full of the warmth they'd once had. Simon heaved his backpack onto his shoulder and turned to face her squarely. 'I'll let someone know you're here as soon as I get to the CFA centre. There's a list of numbers on the pad in the kitchen, so call if you need anything. Someone will come by tomorrow if I'm not back.'

'I'll be okay. I'm not sixteen any more.'

'Bear with me. The fire's well out of this region and heading westwards, away from us, but if there is any danger someone will contact you and drive up here to get you. If you can put your valuables into one bag, well and good, but don't waste any time…'

'I know, I know.' Sara held up her hands. 'We've been through all this.'

'Right.' Simon still hesitated. Finally he leant in, giving her an awkward kiss on the cheek.

'Stay safe. See you soon.' Sara gave him a bright smile, and propelled him out of the door.

She'd been restless all day, and had hovered fitfully between being half asleep and half awake all night, but now something shocked Sara into wakefulness. The silence perhaps. Or maybe it was the insidious, nagging worry that she had tried think through logically but still couldn't quite put a name to. Even the feeble light of early dawn some-how seemed slightly menacing.

Simon might have come back while she was sleeping. The thought propelled her out of bed, and took her all the way to the large windows at the front of the house. Nothing. His car wasn't parked in its usual place, and his jacket wasn't hanging in the hallway. Sara knew that she wouldn't find him sleeping in his bedroom either, but she looked anyway.

She wasn't used to this. She'd dealt with her fair share of emergencies but waiting it out while someone else handled the situation was way out of her experience. Taking Trader for a long, brisk walk yesterday afternoon, without see-ing another living soul, had spooked her even more. She'd returned to Simon's beautiful house, switched on the TV and played one DVD after another, just to hear the sound of human voices.

She padded to the kitchen, the sound of scratching at the back door coming almost as a relief. Pulling back the bolts, she opened the door, and fifty pounds of Australian cattle dog, the only one of his kind that Sara had ever seen before, herded her deftly out of the way to get past her and into the house.

'Whoa, Trader.' The dog had followed her footsteps, trotting hopefully to Simon's bedroom door, and finding the room empty, was now pacing the hallway fretfully. 'He's not here. I'm on breakfast duty today.'

Trader was unsettled about something. Perhaps food would appease him. Fetching the plastic container that held his food, Sara made for the doors that led out onto the ve-randa, unlocking them and sliding them back.

Maybe the wind changed. Maybe it was just that she was outside the house now. The smell hit her like a slap in the face. Blown in on the breeze, like bad news from across the hillside, came the acrid smell of smoke.

Trader was at her side, pressing himself against her legs, and she staggered back. He nipped at her heels, trying to shepherd her back into the house, and Sara grabbed his collar. 'Okay, okay, have it your way.' Maybe Trader knew best. She certainly didn't know what to do.

Gathering up his bowls, spilling what was left of the water in one down her nightdress, she pulled the dog inside the house and shut the patio doors, locking them tight as if somehow that might stop a fire from getting in. 'You can eat inside today.'

Quickly she put Trader's food down for him on the kitchen floor and made for the sink to fill his water bowl. When she twisted the tap, nothing happened. Sara whirled around and saw that the LED lights on the fridge and the cooker were out too.

'Dammit!' No electricity meant that the pump from the water tank wasn't working. Turning the tap off, she poured some spring water from the refrigerator into Trader's bowl, then took a swig from the bottle. Maybe the hydration would help her to think.

This must be another fire. Unless the wind had changed and the fire that Simon had gone to was coming this way. Sara had no idea, and it didn't really matter. It looked as if the situation had changed, and so Simon needed to keep his promise and either come and get her himself or send someone. Any time now would be good.

The phone was dead and even though she knew her mobile was out of range here, she tried it anyway. 'It's only a little smoke, Trader. Smoke travels for miles, the fire's probably nowhere near us.'

Her assertion was born of hope rather than knowledge, but at least Trader's gentle, intelligent eyes looked convinced. Perhaps that was a good sign. Sara left him to eat, and ran to fetch the binoculars that Simon kept in his home office. Slipping outside, she trained them on the horizon in the direction that the smoke seemed to be coming from.

She could see the source of the black smoke, which billowed out from behind a fold in the landscape. It was impossible to gauge how close the fire was or which way it was headed, but the breeze in her face gave Sara a sickening clue.

'Oh!' Her chest and stomach tightened painfully, and she doubled over, trying to breathe. She had to get out of here. Had to get home. She had responsibilities.

Suddenly this whole trip seemed impossibly reckless. Gran had urged her to come here, and had even booked herself into respite care for three weeks, but that was just temporary. She was ninety years old, and completely dependent on Sara. What would she do if she didn't come back?

Simon would send someone. He had to. Their mother might have labelled her elder brother feckless, irresponsible and not worthy of a moment in their thoughts, but Sara knew that wasn't true. This time he was going to come through for her.

Self-pity wasn't going to get her anywhere. Emptying the contents of the kitchen drawers at least secured a battery radio and Sara switched it on, scanning for a local station. Surely they'd be putting out information on some kind of regular basis.

Carrying the radio with her, she quickly filled a couple of bags with what she hoped were Simon's most valued possessions and put them in the hall. She pulled on a pair of jeans and made her way around the outside of the house, pulling the fire shutters down over the windows and back door as Trader ran back and forth, trying to urge her away from the ever more pungent smell of smoke, which was beginning to hang in the air like a dirty fog.

A tone sounded from the radio, and she held it to her ear, straining to catch every word. It didn't help much, mentioning places that she'd only half heard of and could be anywhere, and fire alert statuses that could mean anything. She understood the urgency, though. *Evacuate. Be safe. Nearest low-risk area.*

There was nowhere to go. She was without a car and even if she could remember the way to the nearest town, she knew that trying to walk the twenty or so miles there would be madness. Simon had designed this house himself, and put all his architectural expertise and experience of local building techniques and conditions into it. The shutters were designed to keep burning embers from getting into the house, and the mud-brick walls would afford some protection if the blaze was not too intense. If the worst came to the worst, she and Trader were just going to have to sit it out and hope for the best.

The thought made her feel sick. Gulping back tears, Sara turned to the only living creature that might give her any comfort. 'He won't forget us, Trader.' The animal seemed to sense her anxiety and nosed at her hand. 'It's probably not as bad as we think it is. Perhaps the wind will change...'

She stiffened, straining to see, as she caught a glimpse of something that looked like more smoke, this time on the dirt road leading to the front of the house. There was movement, and the flash of something bright in the sunlight. Just as dread began to grip her, squeezing all of the air from her lungs, she made out what it was. A vehicle, moving at speed and kicking up dust as it went. It could only be coming to one place. That track only led here.

Not wanting to leave anything to chance, Sara ran back into the house, pulling the red tablecloth from the table and sending the wooden bowls in the centre of it crashing to the floor behind her. Whoever it was wouldn't be able to hear her yet, but she shouted anyway, waving the table-cloth over her head.

'Sit, Trader.' Sara strained to see any sign that the driver of the SUV had seen her. Nothing. She waved the cloth again and this time, through her tears of frustration, she saw something. Headlights, three short flashes and then a pause, and another three flashes. Just to make sure, she waved again. Another three flashes.

'Thank you.' She whispered the words under her breath, to no one in particular, her chest heaving. 'It's all right, see, Trader. Someone's coming.'

By the time the SUV had skidded to a halt outside the house Trader was barking joyfully, pulling her towards the man who swung the door open and got out.

She could have hugged him. If he'd been middle-aged, with a paunch, she might have. But this was the kind of man you didn't just walk up to and hug without having to accuse yourself of an ulterior motive. Tall, broad and with blue eyes, bright against his tanned skin. Thick blond hair that looked as if it hadn't been combed in a while, which just added to the general look of a handsome adventurer.

'Sara? Sara Jones?' He was striding towards her and she nodded, lost for words. 'Simon sent me to fetch you.'

This wasn't the moment to ask why he hadn't come sooner. Neither was it the time for the normal reservations about getting into strangers' cars. Trader seemed to know him and at his command gave off trying to lick his hand and trotted to the SUV, jumping in and settling quietly on the back seat.

'We have to hurry.' The stranger didn't seem disposed to stop for questions anyway, and had already taken the steps up to the veranda two at a time, twisting the handle of the front door and turning to her in surprise when it didn't budge.

'I've got the key here.' Sara hurried after him, pulling the single key from her pocket. In her agitation it slipped through her fingers, bouncing next to her bare feet on the decking and sliding through a crack between the boards.

At least he didn't call her stupid, but that didn't stop Sara from muttering the word under her breath. He shrugged, starting for the back of the house, and Sara ran after him. 'I locked the doors at the back too. Maybe we could lever one of the boards up. I think I can get my arm through…'

He looked at her in frank disbelief. 'Yeah, maybe. Stand back.' Before she could stop him he had shouldered the door and it burst inwards, snapping back against the wall.

'Did you have to do that?' The door had smashed into the table in the hallway, sending a glass bowl crashing onto the floor, and broken shards were everywhere. Just because her habit of locking doors was a little over the top for this neck of the woods, it didn't mean he had to go caveman on her.

He turned, taking her by the shoulders. 'Sara, we don't have any time.' The look on his face was making her tremble.

'But you can't even see the fire yet…'

'If you can see a fire, it's too late to run. At the moment we have two options, staying here to fight it or getting out. We're not properly prepared for the first and the second isn't going to be available for much longer.' He was focussed, calm, and Sara began to divine that breaking the door down had not been an overreaction. 'It's going to be okay, Sara, but if we're leaving, we need to do it now.'

There was something in his eyes that made her trust him. Something about the brief smile he gave her. She'd made a few bad decisions in her life, but hopefully this wasn't going to be one of them. 'Yes…okay.'

'Good. Thank you.' Before she could ask him what would happen next, he had lifted her up in his arms, carrying her into the house, his boots scrunching on the broken glass. 'Have you got a pair of heavy boots and a thick cotton jacket?'

'Yes. But it's too hot…'

'Heavy clothes will protect you. Cotton is less flammable than man-made materials.' There was no arguing with him, and Sara didn't particularly want him to elaborate on a situation where she might need heavy cotton clothing to protect her. Hopefully he was just being over-cautious.

He let her down, and she bolted to her bedroom. Now wasn't the time to be thinking that despite the smoky smell of his clothes the scent of his skin was alluring, or that the sheer power in his arms and shoulders was somehow reassuring.

When she emerged from her room, the hallway was empty of the bundles that she'd left there and her new companion was rummaging in the refrigerator, two large bottles of water under his arm.

'Ready to go?'

'Yes.' She mustn't hesitate now. Mustn't go and check the house to make sure everything was secure. If Simon had trusted this stranger, then she had to do so.

'Good.' He turned to her, kicking the fridge door closed. His gaze flicked over her with an audacity that made her shiver, and Sara called a mental reality check. He was just making sure that she wasn't wearing anything that might catch light. 'Have you got everything?'

'Yes.' Her passport and valuables were in the large leather handbag she had slung across her body. That was all she needed.

'Let's go, then.'

He hurried her to the SUV and then went back to draw the shutter down over the shattered front door. Sara craned her neck to keep the house in view as the car described a wide arc and bumped back down the dirt track towards the road.

'Reece Fletcher. Nice to meet you, Sara.'

'What?' All her attention was on the house, trying to fix it into her memory as if that would somehow ensure that it would still be standing when she returned. It had been Simon's dream to build this house, and the thought of it being reduced to ashes was impossibly cruel.

'Will you keep your eye on the road ahead of us for me?'

'What for?' She swung round, scanning the empty road, before she realised that Reece was just giving her something to do so she wouldn't be staring out of the back window of the car for the next five miles, straining for a last glimpse of the house.

'Just look.' His voice was gentler now. 'And if you could open one of those bottles of water, that would be great. You'll find a couple of plastic beakers in the glove compartment.'

'Right.' Now that they were on the road, the lines of tension in Reece's face had relaxed and Sara drew her sunglasses out of her bag and put them on, only partly to shade her eyes from the glare. At least when he'd been ordering her around, she'd been able to respond without feeling the need to cry on his shoulder.

Time for another reality check. She'd just been rescued. Wanting to cling to Reece was a perfectly natural reaction. Deal with it.

'Nice to meet you too, Reece. Thanks for coming.' She handed him half a cup of water and he downed it in one go, passing the cup back to her for a refill.

'No worries. I'll phone Simon when we get into range of a signal, let him know that we're on our way.' Although the road was empty, he was still watchful, his gaze flipping constantly from the road to the rear-view mirrors.

'Thanks.' Sara supposed that she ought to ask, even if she didn't much want to know why it had taken so long for Reece to come for her. 'Where is he?'

'He's okay, but he's in the hospital. No burns, but he has a compound break to his leg. That means—'

'I know.' Sara struggled to control the panic which rose in her chest. 'I mean, I know what that means, I'm a paramedic.'

He nodded slowly, as if he'd just remembered. 'Then you'll know that he needed an operation to set the leg. That was done last night, and he's awake now and doing well. He has a crush fracture in his lower back, but that will mend with rest. Some smoke inhalation, but it wasn't too bad.'

'What happened to him?'

'I don't know the details. He was working on a firebreak when he was injured. They brought him out and airlifted him to hospital. I'm on his list of people to call in case of an accident.'

It was obvious that Simon should choose someone who lived more locally than she did for that, but it still hurt. 'And he didn't think to mention that I was out here with Trader?'

Reece shot her a questioning look, the edges of his mouth turned down. 'He was diverted on his way into the CFA centre, never got the opportunity to tell anyone. And after he was injured he was heavily sedated most of the time. I didn't know you were here and assumed that Trader was with a neighbour and that the house was empty. If it's anyone's fault, it's mine.'

The way he sprang to Simon's defence so readily warmed Sara. 'No one knew.' She puffed out a breath.

He turned in his seat slightly, shooting her a quizzical look. 'How long *have* you been here?'

'Three days. We wanted a week to ourselves so we could do some catching up. Next week was going to be for introductions to friends.'

Reece chuckled. 'If he'd mentioned that, I'd have known what I had to look forward to when I came up at the weekend.'

Light dawned. 'So you're the doctor he talks about? Fletch?'

He grinned at her and Sara's fingertips began to tingle. So he wasn't just a handsome face, he'd been a good friend to her brother. Simon hadn't mentioned that Fletch was gorgeous but, then, she supposed he wouldn't have noticed. She'd noticed, though.

'What's he been telling you?' The engine of the SUV raced up a gear. Simon hadn't said anything about that easy, intimate grin either.

'He says…that you're a doctor. And that you've worked in lots of different places, from city hospitals to the outback. It must be interesting.' That seemed safe enough. 'What does he say about me?'

'That you were just a kid when he left home.' There was a trace of seriousness in his voice. 'I've obviously got some catching up to do.'

He was deliberately not saying everything, but now wasn't the time to start wondering how much Reece knew about the dysfunctional branch of Simon's family. 'So how come you got to drive all the way out here? Surely this is a busy time for you, with the fires and everything.'

He laughed. 'I've been working for a week straight now. When the call came in about Simon, I was just about to go off duty and catch some shut-eye. By the time I got to the hospital, he'd just woken up and was shouting the place down and I came straight here.'

'So…' Her brain was working overtime, trying to process all of the new information that had been thrown at her this morning. She decided to concentrate on the most immediate concern. 'How long since you've slept?'

He laughed. 'Just keep talking.'

CHAPTER TWO

SIMON'S kid sister had taken it almost as a personal affront when he declined her offer to drive. Reece was tired but he wasn't that far gone. And ever since he'd seen Sara he'd been wide awake. Her dark hair, cut almost boyishly short, emphasised the soft curve at the nape of her neck. Those large, grey eyes managed to be both seductive and intelligent at the same time. She'd buckled down and done what had needed to be done in a crisis.

Clearly she was stubborn too. 'I'm perfectly capable of driving an automatic. I drive in London every day. Have you ever driven through a two-mile traffic jam to get to a pile-up?'

She had him there. 'Okay, but the conditions here are different.' He couldn't quite divine whether she had been aware of the seriousness of the situation. She was either handling it extremely well or she didn't realise how narrow their escape had been.

'All right, then. What do I need to watch out for?' She obviously wasn't about to give up, and exhilaration flared in the pit of Reece's stomach.

'Kangaroos on the road, for a start.' He reckoned she hadn't come across that one.

'Simon's told me about not trying to overtake them. I reckon I'm in much better shape than you are to keep an eye out for anything about to leap out in front of me, and I know where the brake is.' She wrinkled her nose at him, and Reece wondered how long he could hold out if she was going to use such unscrupulous methods of persuasion.

She had half turned towards him in her seat, and even though he couldn't see her eyes behind her sunglasses, he was pretty sure that she was sizing him up. 'So are you going to stop, or do we need to do that thing they do in the movies, where they keep driving while they swap places? I've not done that before, but I can give it a try.'

He found himself wondering whether she would actually do it, and a laugh began to rumble deep in his chest, leaving him almost breathless.

'What's that?' Her attention was diverted for a moment and the tone of her voice changed. Reece followed the line of her pointing finger and saw a ute stopped at the side of a track leading to the road.

Without a word, Reece swung the steering-wheel round, bumping onto the cracked, dry earth. She had the presence of mind to hang on, and they sped towards the vehicle. The hazards were on, blinking a warning, or in these circumstances more likely a cry for help.

'There's someone in there.' She was leaning forward, trying to see through the dust. Reece jammed on the brakes, and before he could tell her to stay in the car, she had released her seat belt and had jumped out, running towards the stranded truck.

He was right behind her. A quick look told him all he needed to know, and he opened the driver's door and spoke quietly to the middle-aged man behind the wheel.

'What's up, mate?' Blue lips. Perspiration. Gasping for breath. 'I'm a doctor.'

'Bloody angina. Always seems to come on just when

you don't want it, eh?' The man seemed more annoyed than relieved to see them.

Reece resisted the temptation to roll his eyes. Bravado was just one of the unhelpful reactions that someone might have to a situation like this. 'Have you got medication? Pills or a spray?'

'Yes.' The man tried to turn in his seat and winced, clutching his chest. 'There's a spray in the emergency bag behind my seat.'

'I'll get it.' Sara was grinning, only a slight shake of her head betraying that she was probably thinking exactly the same as Reece was. Opening the passenger door, she clambered inside, tugging at the red canvas bag that was wedged behind the driver's seat. She managed to pull it out, almost falling backwards out of the vehicle, and unzipped it. 'Gotcha.'

'That's the one.' Disarmed by her smile, the man began to relax in his seat.

She passed the canister of nitroglycerin spray over to Reece, and he checked the prescription details on the label. 'Here you go, mate.'

The spray began to work, and almost before his eyes the man began to recover, the blue tinge around his lips fading. Reece straightened and beckoned Sara to his side, out of earshot. 'I'll check that the truck's running all right and then I want you to take my car. Keep going on this road for another thirty kilometres and we'll meet you…'

'I'll stay with you.' She grabbed the car keys from him and pocketed them. 'How long do we have?' She scanned the horizon, suddenly tense.

Reece didn't know. The fire might be coming this way and it might not. But by the time he got on the road again she could put at least five kilometres between herself and here and that could only be good. 'Not enough time to argue about it.'

'Perfect.' She turned on her heel and almost flounced the two steps back to the truck, bending down by the driver's door to talk to the man.

Reece sighed. The look on her face when she'd looked back in the direction they'd just come from told him that she had understood the risks of staying any longer, and her body language now showed that there was no changing her mind. And since he would have made the same decision in her place, he couldn't think of a single argument to persuade her differently.

'Right, then, Frank, if you're up to standing, we'll just move you round to the passenger seat and we can get going.' She gave the man a bright smile and he grinned at her. She had a way with her. No-nonsense, but with a lightness of touch that made even Reece feel better about the situation.

'Sure.' The man took her arm, leaning heavily on it, and Reece supported him from the other side. They slowly walked him around to the passenger seat and she folded a rug to make a support for his back, and buckled the seat belt over him.

'Where are we going?' That hint of tension had returned, although she hid it from Frank.

'It's thirty kilometres to the next town. I'll call ahead, see if an ambulance can meet us there.'

'Okay. I'll follow you.'

'Think you can keep up?' Reece grinned at her, suddenly relishing the chance to goad her a little.

Her cheeks flushed prettily and suddenly the day seemed a whole lot easier. 'I'll do my best.'

They leaned against the SUV side by side, drinking the takeaway coffee that Sara had got from the store in the

main street while Reece had been busy seeing Frank into
the ambulance. Trader lapped greedily at the water that she
had poured into a camping dish she found in the boot of
the car. 'So what was he doing out there? The guy in the
café said that whole area is on high alert.'

'It is. He'd been staying with his daughter for a couple
of days and he reckoned he'd nip back and get some things
from home. He would have been fine if the angina hadn't
slowed him up.'

'Hmm. So you gave him the talk about not being inde-
structible, then?'

Reece chuckled. He liked the way that she anticipated
him. The way that they'd fallen into an almost seamless
synchronicity back there. Just training, he guessed, hers
and his. 'Yeah. I imagine he'll hear it again from a few different directions.'

She shrugged. 'Well, as long as he listens to one of them.
We must be in mobile range by now.'

'Yeah. I'll call the hospital and get them to tell Simon
that we're on our way. We can stop by at my house first
and you can have a shower and change your clothes.' Reece
drew his phone out of his pocket.

She twisted her mouth ruefully and Reece wondered
what her lips would taste like. Sweet, he reckoned. Like the
rest of her. 'I'll take the shower, but I don't have a change
of clothes with me.'

'Wasn't that your case I put in the back of the car?'
The large, lightweight case with a strip of gaudy material
tied around the handle so it could be picked out easily at
an airport.

'Yes, but my clothes are in the chest of drawers in
Simon's spare room. I filled my case with his things.' She
shrugged. 'It's his home. I wanted to bring as much of it
as I could.'

Most women would have brought at least a change of clothes, but it seemed that Sara wasn't most women. She'd left behind practically everything she possessed in this hemisphere, putting her brother first. That simple act of selflessness made Reece smile.

'I'll call my sister, then. She's about your size. I dare say she can fix you up with something.'

She blushed again. Reece could really get used to that. 'That's okay. I have plenty of spending money. I can pop to the shops somewhere. I don't need much.'

Maybe not. But Reece could provide her with whatever she did need. She was his friend's sister, and she had no one else, which made her his responsibility now. 'I won't ask Kath to bring much, then.'

She nodded, head down all of a sudden, staring at her coffee. 'Thanks. Just a clean T-shirt would be great.' She drained her coffee, crushing the cardboard cup in her hands. 'Thanks for coming to get me. I don't know where I'd be right now if you hadn't.'

Her hands were shaking. She was under no illusions about the danger of the situation she'd been in.

'No problem. Do you want to drive while I make my calls? I'll programme the sat nav for you.' It might take her mind off the worries of the moment.

She nodded. 'Yeah. Thanks.'

'On the right, remember.' Reece tried to make a joke of it, but he was too tired to even see whether she got it or not.

'I remember. Get in, before I decide to leave you behind.'

He'd dozed fitfully in the car. As soon as he'd made his calls and there was nothing left to do, his body seemed to shut down, taking what it needed. Sara knew all about that kind of exhaustion. After her mother had died last year, finally losing her battle with cancer, it had been weeks before she'd been able to sit down without going to sleep. Gran had said she had slept off all her tears, gently making it clear that she disapproved of such a strategy, and in hindsight she might have been right.

The sat nav beeped in an indication that she was exactly where she was supposed to be. Sara nudged Reece gently, and he woke with a start, suddenly alert. 'Is this your house?'

'Uh?' He relaxed back into his seat when he saw where they were. 'No. This is my sister's house. Back up a bit, will you?'

Sara manoeuvred the heavy vehicle into the mouth of the driveway, stopping when Reece shook his head. 'Her car's not there, she must be over at my place. I'm just down the road a little way.'

'Down the road a little way' turned out to be more than four kilometres. Reece indicated an opening in the tall bushes that flanked the road, and Sara steered into it, the SUV dwarfing the small shiny runaround already parked outside the house.

'Here we are.' He grinned, stretching the kinks out of his back and shoulders. 'Hopefully, Kath's got the kettle on.' He opened the passenger door and almost fell out of the car, regaining his footing quickly. At his command, Trader suddenly woke from his repose and scrambled past Sara to follow Reece.

The house seemed far too big for one but, then, there was more space out here. There were large windows, a covered porch, and trees and bushes that were unfamiliar to Sara. It wasn't like home. From what Simon had said, it wasn't really a home to Reece either. Just a place to camp out until Reece's permanently itchy feet became too much for him and he upped sticks and moved on.

It was nice, though. An oasis of shade and weather-worn colours, which made up in charm for what it lacked in grooming. Reece fitted in here perfectly.

'Ah!' He was standing in the open doorway. 'I can smell fresh coffee.'

'Only because I brought it with me.' A woman's voice sounded from the hall. 'When did you last go shopping for food, Reece?'

He rolled his eyes and winked at Sara. 'I've been working.'

'Yeah, and what's your excuse the rest of the time?' A blonde, pretty woman dressed in shorts and a T-shirt joined him in the doorway.

Reece shrugged. 'No clue. Playing?'

Kath jabbed one finger at his ribs and Reece caught her hand, chuckling. Trader sensed that it was time to let off a little steam and threw himself against Reece's legs, demanding attention.

'Come inside.' Kath had broken away from Reece and was advancing on Sara now. 'Don't mind my brother, he's got no manners.' She grabbed Sara's hand and led her past Reece into the house. 'No coffee either, but at least I can do something about that.'

Kath stayed long enough to pour the coffee and unload the contents of two large shopping bags into the refrigerator. Then she took a last swig from her mug, professed herself delighted at having met Sara and apologised for having to run.

'Later, sis. I'll come by and pick Trader up this evening if that's okay.' Reece rose from the sofa and gave his sister a brief hug. 'Thanks for everything.'

'I just wish we weren't going away tomorrow. Perhaps I can stay behind a few days, Joe and the kids can manage on their own for a while...' Kath fisted her hand against

Reece's chest. Sara could never have done that with her own brother, and suddenly she envied Kath the careless gesture.

'Don't start trying to tear yourself in two again.' Reece held up an admonishing finger and Kath shrugged and nodded. 'If you can run some of that excess energy out of Trader this afternoon while we get sorted, that'll be fine.'

'Right. Later, then.' Kath grinned cheerily at Sara, and Trader followed her to the door with an air of almost palpable joy.

'At least Trader's found someone who's got their priorities straight.' Sara smiled, nodding at Kath as she jogged to her car, Trader trotting obediently behind her.

'Yeah.' Reece grinned. 'Cattle dogs can be a bit of a handful if they're not trained and exercised properly. Trader's ancestry is part dingo.'

'Yes, Simon told me. He said you helped him to train Trader.'

'Yep. He didn't have a clue where to start.' Reece shot her a quizzical look.

'No, he wouldn't. We didn't have pets at home. Too much mess.'

'That's a shame.'

'Yeah.'

Reece seemed to be waiting for Sara to elaborate, and when she didn't, he collected the empty coffee cups and put them into the dishwasher, leaving her to stare aimlessly out of the window. This sitting in one place, waiting to find out what someone else was going to do next, was the downside of being rescued.

'Right, then.' Reece obviously had a plan, even if she didn't. 'I expect you'll want to wash off some of that dust.' He turned, without waiting for her assent, and disappeared into the hallway. The only option available was to follow him.

'This is your room.' He flung one of the doors open and walked inside. 'The shower's through there, and Kath's left some things for you, so I hope you'll have everything you need.'

The room was bright and welcoming. Clean, cool shades of cream and green that just demanded you stay a while and relax. On the wide bed was a small pile of clothes, neatly folded. Next to it were towels and a small wicker basket containing soap, shampoo, toothpaste and some packages wrapped in paper. A large bunch of flowers sat on the table next to the bed, strange, brightly coloured blooms mixed with others that were more familiar to Sara.

This was a safe place, an oasis, where she could wash off the dust and sweat of the road. She couldn't accept it. She needed to stand on her own two feet. Make her own decisions.

'This is my guest room. It's yours for as long as you want it. At least until Simon gets out of hospital.'

From what Reece had said, that was going to be more than a week. 'I really can't impose. I'm very grateful for everything you've done already...'

'And what? Do you know anyone else here?'

No one. Apart from Simon, Reece was the only person who even came close to being a friend. 'I can book into a hotel. Near the hospital.'

'What, with Trader? Even if you find somewhere that'll take him, he'll get bored and tear the place apart.'

He had a point. 'Perhaps you wouldn't mind taking him. Just for a while, until I get something sorted.'

Reece rolled his eyes. 'Right. So I get to do a full day at the surgery then come home and take him out for a couple of hours to work off his excess energy. Anyway, what kind of person takes a mate's dog in and sends his sister to a hotel?'

Sara's hand flew to her mouth. 'I'm sorry. I didn't mean to…'

'Impose? You already said that. And you're not. You'll have to fend for yourself while I'm at work, but treat this place as your own.' He looked at his watch. 'It's half past ten now…an hour's drive to the hospital… We can catch our breath, have something to eat and be with Simon by lunchtime. What do you say?'

'That sounds wonderful. Thank you.' If she was going to stay here, she may as well do it gracefully. Her mother had told her that. Whatever you do, do it gracefully. Sara had been berated too many times for almost never following that advice.

'Good. Shall I call Simon, let him know that we're here, or would you like to?' He nodded at the phone extension next to the bed.

'I'd like to if that's okay.'

'Of course.' In one fluid movement he caught her hand, and Sara felt her cheeks redden. He produced a pen, pulling the cap off with his teeth in a gesture that was oddly almost piratical, and wrote on her palm. 'Here's the number. It's the main switchboard, but if you ask for Simon, they'll put you through to his room. Tell him that you and Trader are staying here.'

'Yes. I will. Thank you, Reece.' There was something else that she needed. The thought that Gran might have somehow heard about the fires was thudding at the back of her skull, like a headache about to happen. 'Would it be okay if I used your phone to call England?'

'Of course. Call whoever you want, you don't need to ask.'

'Thanks. I'll just be quick…'

He dismissed the notion with a weary gesture. 'Take as long as you like.' Turning swiftly, he strode out of the room and closed the door behind him. Sara heard the sounds of his footsteps along the hallway and another door opened. A thud as his heavy boots were dragged off and hit the floor. Then silence.

CHAPTER THREE

SARA had made her calls and taken a shower. She sat on the bed, wrapped in a towel, and forced herself to take a couple of deep breaths. Gran was okay, Simon was okay. It was going to be all right.

Kath had left T-shirts, sweatpants and a skirt with a drawstring at the top, which would pretty much fit any size, along with a pair of open sandals. There was also a cotton nightdress and a note, saying that she should call her and let her know if there was anything else she needed. Sara smiled. The resemblance in tone to Reece's, kind but brooking no argument, was striking.

She dressed in her own jeans and one of Kath's T-shirts, and padded barefoot along the hallway and into the open-plan living area. Reece's car was still parked out front, but the house was silent and there was no sign of him outside on the veranda either. She took a deep breath. She knew exactly where he was, and it was the last place that she wanted to have to go and find him.

The door was slightly ajar, and she tapped on it nervously. Not a sound. Frowning, Sara cautiously craned her neck around the door to see inside.

He was lying on the bed, fast asleep. His boots, jeans and heavy shirt had been slung in the corner in the approximate direction of the laundry basket. It was as if he'd stripped down to his boxer shorts and then lain down, thinking just to close his eyes for a few moments, until it was time to move again.

His skin was smooth, golden. One arm thrown out to the side and the other rested across his chest. Sara caught her breath and for the first time allowed herself to stare at Reece. He looked so peaceful. The temptation to join him there on the bed, feel the steady, reassuring swell of his chest against her cheek, was almost irresistible.

Stop this! Peaceful he might be, but that wasn't what was freezing her to the spot. He was so beautiful. The snapshots that she'd already dared to glimpse—his chin, his brow—were nothing in comparison to being able to look for as long as she liked at the whole thing.

Just a moment more. One minute, to fantasise that she wasn't who she was, and he didn't live ten thousand miles away from where she had to be in another couple of weeks. It didn't work, and a minute wasn't enough. Sara drew back, and headed for the kitchen.

She'd made coffee for herself and sat in one of the wicker chairs on the patio with a book from the stack on the breakfast bar. She'd reckoned that she ought to wake him, and then chickened out and read another couple of chapters. Finally she decided that food would probably do the trick.

The amount of chopping, clattering and general commotion that it took before she heard his footsteps in the hallway attested to how tired he'd been. As did the fact that he was still half-asleep and had clearly forgotten that having company generally meant you didn't walk around the house half-naked. Sara concentrated on not slicing her finger along with the vegetables on the chopping board. She'd already seen what Reece had to offer, and there was no point in staring at what she couldn't have.

'Ready for something to eat?' She flung the words over

her shoulder and then gave in to the inevitable and looked in his approximate direction.

'Uh? How long have I been asleep?' He ran his fingers backwards through his hair in a lame effort to tame it a little.

'It's two o'clock.'

'What?' He straightened, suddenly seeming to come to. 'We should be at the hospital by now. Sara, I'm sorry. Why didn't you wake me?'

'Because you were asleep. How do you like your steak?'

He stared at her as if she had just landed in his kitchen from outer space. 'What?'

'Kath left some steak in the fridge. I hope you weren't planning on saving it for anything else?'

'No...no, of course not. What about Simon?'

'I called him and told him we'd be with him later on this afternoon.'

He grinned. It was the kind of easy, open grin that melted your heart, set it sizzling like butter in a pan. 'How is he?'

'He says he's fine. I'd like to see for myself, though.'

'Yes, we'll go as soon as we've eaten.' He tried to see what she had on the cooker. 'What's that you've got there? Smells great.'

Sara stepped in front of it. 'Wait and see. Are you hungry?' She was getting a crick in her neck. Fixing her gaze on his face, not allowing it to wander down to his chest, to the tiny line of sun-bleached hairs that disappeared into the waistband of his shorts, was making her jaw throb.

He grinned. 'I could eat a horse.'

'Bad luck, then. That's not on the menu. You've got ten minutes to have a shower if you want to.' Sara hoped that was enough of a hint to get out of her hair and stop distracting her. Maybe put some clothes on.

'Oh. Yeah, thanks.' One hand wandered to his chest and stayed there, as if he had only just realised that he had no shirt on. He turned quickly, and Sara allowed herself just enough of a glance in his direction to confirm that the view from the back was as good as that from the front. 'Pink.'

'What?'

'The steak. Pink but not too bloody, thanks.' He threw the words over his shoulder and disappeared.

He was back in five minutes, thankfully wearing a clean pair of cargo pants and a shirt, his short hair already half-dry. Banished once more from his own kitchen, he busied himself with laying the table in a shaded part of the veranda.

Sara laid his plate down in front of him and he grinned appreciatively.

'Looks good! If I'd been awake, I would have thrown myself in between you and the cooker.'

'In case my cooking's like Simon's?'

'Yeah.' He waited for her to sit down, and cut into his steak. 'This is just perfect.'

Steak with a black pepper sauce, potato gratin and green beans. Nothing fancy, but all done from scratch. 'Good. Thanks.'

'I could get used to this.' He tried the potatoes and nodded with approval. 'Obviously Simon missed out on the family cooking lessons.'

'Yes. Missed out on a lot.' Sara stopped herself. She didn't want to say anything to Reece that Simon wouldn't want him to hear. 'How long have you known him?'

'Ten years. He was working on the architect's plans for an extension to the hospital where I was working. Kath was there to meet me, and he tried to chat her up in the canteen.' Reece was grinning.

'So you found my brother trying to hit on your sister…' Sara laughed. 'How did that go?'

'Oh, pretty much as expected. I thumped my chest and growled a bit, and Kath kicked me under the table. Simon had told her that he was only just off the plane, and before I knew what had hit me, she'd roped us both in for a trip up to Sydney with her friends.'

'And did Simon and Kath ever…?' Sara waved her hand to indicate whatever it was that might have happened between the two of them.

'Nah. Kath's interest was purely humanitarian. We've both been in that situation enough times—new place, no friends—and she was just trying to make him feel at home.' He grinned. 'Kath does that.'

Reece did too. He'd taken her in without a second thought. 'Thank you. For looking after him.'

Reece gave her the smallest of nods in acknowledgement. 'So what about you?'

'Me?'

'Who looks after you?'

The question floored her for a moment and she stared at Reece, not sure quite how to answer. 'No one.'

'Surely there must be someone.' Reece was gazing at her intently and Sara felt her cheeks flush. 'Or haven't you told Simon about him yet?'

Suddenly, and quite unaccountably, she felt the need to defend herself. As if being single made it okay for her to have looked at Reece and wanted him, even if it was impossible, and she'd rather be dangled over a tank of hungry sharks than admit it.

'There's nothing to tell.' There was no time for a man in her life. When she wasn't working, Gran took up all of her spare time. A man couldn't be expected to stay with a woman who could only give him about five minutes of her undivided attention per day. 'There's been no one since before my mother died. And Simon's my only close family.'

Apart from Gran. Simon seldom asked about her, probably assuming that she still lived independently, and Sara didn't dare tell him any different until she could be more sure of his reaction. She could just about understand him staying away when their mother had been ill, but if he acted the same way with Gran, Sara would never be able to forgive him. And if Simon wasn't to know just yet, then telling Reece would be foolish.

They ate in silence for a while. 'Simon talked a lot about going home when your mother was ill.' Reece had clearly been giving some consideration to which bombshell to drop next.

'Did he?' Sara couldn't conceal her surprise. Simon had pretty much covered everything he'd had to say to her in one line of an email. He wasn't coming back. It would be hypocrisy to do so when his mother hadn't spoken to him for more than ten years.

'Perhaps he's been saving it. Until he sees you.'

'Maybe.' Maybe not. The last two years had been tough. First her mother had been diagnosed with cancer, and then her grandmother had fallen and broken her leg. Sara had given up her job, her home and, one by one, most of her friends in order to move back to her mother's house to take care of them both. She had never quite understood why Simon had stayed away.

'Give it time.'

'I thought I'd done that already.'

'Then give it some more.' He was holding her in his gaze. It felt almost as if he was cradling her, keeping her from any harm.

'Yeah, I suppose so.' She may as well say it. He'd obviously heard most of it from Simon already. 'I don't want you to think that it was all Simon's fault. Mum wasn't the easiest of people to live with. We each dealt with it differently. I gave in to her on the things that didn't matter and held out for the things that did. But Simon couldn't do that. They used to have the most awful rows.'

Reece nodded her on. He seemed to understand that she both wanted and needed to say this to someone. And he was all she had right now.

'It all came to a head when Simon said that he wanted to travel for a year after he'd done his degree in architecture. Mum had been pushing him away for years and then when he did leave she was so angry with him that she never mentioned his name again, even when she was dying.'

'Simon told me that your father leaving had a pretty big impact on her.'

'I don't remember that. I was just a baby.' Gran had told her about it, though. 'I'm told she just shut herself off from everyone, became totally focussed on showing that she was better off without him. She threw herself into work and built up a successful company from nothing. She used to say all the time that my father was unreliable and weak…' Too much information, perhaps.

'And that's what she said about Simon too?'

'Yes.' It felt good to be able to say it, even if it was hard. Sara swallowed down the lump in her throat. 'It's not true, though, is it?'

'No. That's not the friend I know.' The look in his eyes was almost unbearable. Liquid blue, as if she could somehow plunge into his world. Luxuriate in the safety of those cool, soothing waters. 'And you and Simon kept in touch. That has to say something, doesn't it?'

'Yeah. Not sure what…but, yes, it says something.'

He seemed to realise that she'd had enough, and that she couldn't talk about this any more. He nodded towards her plate. 'Eat. It's been a long day already, and it's not over yet. And this is too good to waste.'

'Thanks. There are some more potatoes in the kitchen if you want them. I always make too much.' She reached for his plate, but he was already on his feet.

'I'll go. You want some?'

'No, I'm fine with this, thanks.' Sara went back to her food, smiling as she heard the sound of a pan being scraped from the kitchen. She loved cooking, and having someone with appetite enough to scrape the pan was a welcome novelty.

'Do you like Australia?' When he returned to the table, he seemed as intent as Sara was on lightening the mood.

'I love what I've seen so far.' She shrugged. 'Simon and I have been keeping ourselves to ourselves since I arrived. You and Kath are the first real Australians that I've met.'

'Well, I hope we've not let the team down.' He grinned at her then looked at his watch. 'We'll get going as soon as we've finished lunch. Simon will be wanting to see you.'

CHAPTER FOUR

AS FAR as appearances went, they'd fallen effortlessly into an easy routine. Up early so that Reece could do the forty-kilometre round trip to drop Sara at the nearest station before he went to work. Catching the train into Melbourne to spend time with Simon, then shopping and a tram ride back to Flinders Street Station, and home to cook for Reece.

The truth was a little different. Waking early and wondering if Reece was awake yet. Imagining the lazy flutter of his eyelids followed by the first sight of those clear, almost iridescent pools of blue. Three early nights in a row to escape the magnetic pull, which seemed to grow stronger as the sun fell in the sky and the moon rose.

The smile she liked best, held tight in her imagination during the day, was the one he gave her when he arrived home each evening. Today it was broader, more expectant, as if Reece had a surprise for her. 'We're going for a day trip tomorrow.'

'Really? Aren't you working?'

'No. It's Saturday tomorrow, in case that had escaped your notice. I've swapped shifts with one of the other doctors in the practice, and I have three days off.'

Something about the tone of his voice told Sara that he'd done that for her and she flushed with pleasure. 'That's great. So where are we going?' The distance to the local shops and the station was almost enough to be called a day trip at home.

'We're going to Simon's place.'

'The authorities have issued the all-clear?' She always waited until Reece got home so that she could check the news reports with him, telling herself that he could explain the things she didn't understand. But in truth she'd been living in a bubble, cushioned in his world, and now reality was calling. Earth to Sara. Time to wake up now, and get to grips with life.

'Yes. There are no more fires in that area now, and it's safe to return.'

'And the house? Do you know what's happened to the house, Reece?'

He shook his head. 'The fire went through that area, but I haven't been able to find out what happened to Simon's house.' His look of frustration told her that he'd tried. 'The house is surrounded by grassland, and there aren't too many trees on the property. The worst fires didn't get that far so there's a good chance that it's not badly damaged.'

He was giving her as much encouragement as he could, but he couldn't tell her what she wanted to hear. But at least she wouldn't have to wait too long to find out. 'Thank you. That sounds promising.'

'I found out where Simon's car is as well. We can pick it up on the way, it'll give you some mobility.'

Slowly the bonds that tied her here were unravelling. A car. And if everything went well, a house to live in too. For one brief moment Sara wished that Simon's house was somehow uninhabitable, and then cursed herself for her petty selfishness. 'So Trader and I might be out of your hair, then.'

'No. I said a day trip. You can't go back there.'

'Why not? If the fire's already been through, then there's

no more danger, is there?' The thought of a lonely house, in a blackened landscape, frightened her. Served her right. How could she have even thought about the possibility of a problem at Simon's house, however small and easy to fix, just so she could stay on here?

'That's not the point. We'll go back to the house, find out what's happened and salvage what we can. Then we come back here.'

He was giving her orders. She'd had enough of those from her own family, and Reece wasn't going to start that with her. He was about to turn away when she reached forward, catching the sleeve of his shirt. 'I'm grateful for everything you've done, but I can make my own decisions.'

'Not with this, Sara.'

'I'm not afraid.' Okay, so she was afraid. But she wasn't about to give Reece any more reasons to keep her here. 'If the house is okay, I'll stay there.'

'Right. So you know where to go to get petrol for the car, do you? Or where to get food if the local store is closed? The power's almost certainly off, so you'll have no running water, and you can't rely on the phone working either. What happens if you have an accident when you're on your own up there?' The tension lines had reappeared around his jaw, and his eyes flashed warning signals.

Trader slunk past them and out onto the veranda. He at least knew when to fold with Reece, but Sara wasn't ready to throw in her hand yet.

'Stop trying to frighten me, Reece. Lots of people will be going back to their homes. Why can't I be one of them?'

'Because you're alone. And you're not used to the terrain here, or the dangers. The emergency services have enough to do at this time of the year, without having to keep tabs on you.'

'So I'm a liability?' His words had stung her. He made

her sound like the kind of person who just did as she pleased and let other people pick up the pieces.

'You will be if you go back to the house. Simon would be the first to agree with me.'

'I imagine he would. Simon isn't my keeper, you know.' Sara felt herself flush. She was being unfair and Reece probably knew it just as well as she did.

Her outburst shocked them both to silence for a moment. When he spoke, Reece's voice was suddenly calm. 'You've been under a lot of stress, Sara.'

If he only knew. 'Don't patronise me.'

'I'm not patronising you. I'm asking you to stay here.'

There was an urgency in his tone that told her this was more than just a decision based on common sense. More than just a friend of the family, who was looking out for her safety. She should put a stop to that one right now. 'What for?'

Before she could take another breath, he had looped his arms around her waist, pulling her hard against his body. Before she could get used to the jelly-legged, head-swimming sensation that having him close to her produced, he was kissing her.

Reece knew he shouldn't be doing this. She was his friend's little sister. She was a guest in his house. She was also irresistible, and she'd pushed him too far.

She tasted sweet, with a tang of the chilli tomatoes that were simmering on the cooker. Yielding and yet fiery all at the same time, and he wanted to explore both of those options. Her body pressed against his, her fingers leaving trails of pure, excruciating pleasure. He took his mouth from hers, just for one moment, to allow himself to catch his breath, and a little sigh escaped her lips. He caught it in another kiss.

He backed her against the refrigerator door and she shivered slightly as her bare shoulders touched the cool surface, grinning upwards and reaching for him again. Pulling his head down towards hers, for one more kiss, this time her eyes open and staring into his. Dark and full of things that he wasn't sure he wanted to know about but simply couldn't resist.

There were about a million reasons why he shouldn't be doing this, but right now he couldn't think of any of them, because Sara was unbuttoning his shirt. Her fingertips found his skin and he gasped. She raked one nail gently across his chest and he felt his whole body shake.

A fridge magnet clattered to the floor and his itinerary for next week fluttered after it. No problem there. The foreseeable future had just changed.

'Kiss me again, Reece.'

He obeyed willingly, and she rewarded him by sliding her hands upwards, across his shoulders. A little sigh, and a shudder of pleasure that reverberated against his own aching body.

The phone rang.

No way! The sky could be falling in around their ears as far as he was concerned. He was busy.

The answering-machine kicked in. *'Reece. Pick up. It's an emergency.'*

They both froze. 'Go and get the phone.' She pushed him away from her, and Reece turned and snatched the handset from its cradle.

'This had better be good…'

It was good, all right. Or bad, whichever way you wanted to look at it. By the time he'd finished taking the message from his surgery, Sara had turned and was busying herself at the cooker.

'You have to go?' She'd clearly been listening to his side of the conversation, even though her back was to him.

'Yeah. I'm sorry, Sara.'

'What for?' She turned her eyes on him, dark and suddenly thoughtful. The moment had been well and truly shattered.

'For starting something I can't finish.' Reece wasn't sure whether the apology was for the starting part or the not finishing, but he could keep that open for the time being. 'One of my patients needs a home visit.'

'Would you like me to come along? Perhaps I can help.' She had already clapped the lid onto the saucepan and taken it off the heat, and was untying the strings of the butcher's apron that she wore. A trace of regret tingled through Reece's already inflamed nerve endings. He'd been looking forward to getting her out of that apron himself.

He forced his attention back to her question. Doubting her judgement had already gone down badly once tonight, and anyway he wanted her with him. 'Yes. That would be great. Thanks.'

They drove in awkward silence. Reece was used to being flung together with people and then letting go. The feeling that Sara might be ready to stand on her own two feet now, and that it was him who wasn't ready to let go, was unfamiliar and vaguely unsettling. When she finally did speak, her tone was measured.

'So what's the matter with the patient you're going to see?'

'Two-year-old child. Feverish, vomiting, listless.'

'Probably just a stomach bug, then.'

'Probably. Just as well to make sure, though.'

'Yeah. Absolutely.' She seemed to relax back into her seat slightly. 'Do you do this kind of thing a lot?'

He smiled at her. 'What, visit patients? All the time.'

'No, I meant get called out in the evenings.'

'Sometimes. We're pretty busy at the moment. And I'm a doctor in a semi-rural practice. When you're part of a community like this, the lines between off duty and on call tend to get a little blurred.'

'I imagine it has its compensations.'

It did. Knowing all his patients by their first names. Not being the 'new guy' who was just about to leave anyway. But it made him feel uncomfortable as well. He functioned better when he wasn't tied to one place.

'I said that I imagine it has its compensations.' Her voice cut through his reverie.

'Yeah, I suppose…' The possibility of staying put for long enough to find out was the one thing that Reece never talked about. The one part of his life that wasn't up for grabs. 'Yes, it does.'

The atmosphere in the car had turned from awkward to impossible, and Sara was glad when Reece turned into a driveway and drew up outside a large, sprawling house. As soon as he had grabbed his bag and got out of the car Reece was looking forward, though, on to the next thing. He was about as capable of hanging onto the past, even the very recent, mind-blowing past, as she was of growing wings and flying.

The front door opened before they got to it, and a young woman about Sara's age was standing at the threshold. Reece motioned Sara inside, introducing her briefly, and she followed him through to a child's bedroom.

'What's the matter, Ava?' He knelt down next to the child, who was whimpering fretfully.

'He's been sick. And he's feverish.'

'Any bites?'

'I don't think so.'

'Okay, let's take a look at him.' Reece turned to open

his bag, drawing out a pair of surgical gloves, and Sara kept her eyes on the child. She'd heard those high, keening cries before, but it could well be nothing. Leaning forward, she brushed one finger against his hand. Cold, even though the boy's flushed cheeks attested to him having a high temperature. Then she saw it.

'Reece. He has neck retractions.' She'd seen that rictus arching before too. She just hoped that Reece would react a little better to the suggestion than the doctor back in London had a few months ago. That time, a child had almost died before the doctors had accepted that Sara was right.

His gaze met hers and he nodded slightly. He'd got the message. 'Has he been arching his back, Ava? Throwing his head backwards?'

'Yes, a little. He's been wriggling around, he's not very comfortable at all.' Ava was looking back and forth between Sara and Reece, questions in her eyes.

'Okay, Ava. Come over here and let Reece take a look at him.' He had heard what she had to say and there was no more that she could do. A paramedic deferred to a doctor, that was the way things worked. Sara guided Ava over to a chair in the corner of the room and knelt down on the floor next to her.

The boy whimpered as Reece examined him. 'He's been like this all evening,' Ava confided to Sara. 'What's the matter with him?' Ava's instinct was telling her that something was badly wrong with her son, and that was just as telling as the indications that Sara had seen for herself.

'We don't know yet. But Reece will find out.' She wanted to tell Ava that her son was okay, but she knew better than to lie in this situation. She also knew better than to say the word 'meningitis' until there was a fuller diagnosis. Instead, she took Ava's hand, waiting while Reece worked.

'I think you're right, Sara. Call an ambulance—the

phone's in the hall.' He had made a careful examination
of the boy and now he threw the instruction at her over
one shoulder.

'What's the number?'

'Three zeros. We're at 211 Flowers Road.' Reece turned
to Ava, who was now shaking visibly. 'You were right to
call me, Ava. Now I'm going to tell you exactly what's happening and I want you to listen to me carefully.'

Sara hurried into the hallway and stabbed at the numbers. Quickly she reeled off the information that was asked
of her, giving Reece's name as the doctor in attendance.

'They said twenty minutes.' Sara had no idea about
whether that was a good response time or not. Out here
the distances were so much greater and while there was
not so much traffic for an ambulance to negotiate, everything was so much further apart.

'Good.' Reece looked at his watch. 'They'll be making
good time if they get over here so soon. I'll write a letter
for you to take with you, Ava. Where's Dan?'

'Over at his folks' place, helping with the vines.' Ava
shrugged miserably. 'They're pretty busy right now.'

'All right, I'll give them a call and get them to find him.
Don't worry, Ava, he'll be here.' He laid his hand on Ava's
arm and she looked up at him gratefully.

'Thanks, Reece. If he's not back…'

'If he's not back by the time the ambulance gets here,
we'll wait and send him on after you. Don't worry.'

By the time the ambulance arrived, Reece had written
detailed notes and Sara had been sent to pack a few things
for Ava so she could stay the night at the hospital. Ava sat
with her son, never taking her eyes off him, as if by sheer
force of will she might make him better. Maybe she could.
Sara had seen stranger things.

Ava's husband arrived just as the ambulance crew were

settling their patient into the back of the vehicle. As Dan got out of his van, Reece caught his arm, saying something to him, his insistent stance demanding that the man listen before going to his wife and son. Then he let him go, and the family was swiftly installed in the back of the ambulance, ready to leave.

Reece stood, his hands in his pockets, watching the ambulance disappear. It was almost as if it carried his own family.

'He'll be okay.' Sara wanted to touch him, but didn't dare. After what they'd done this evening, no touch from her could be construed as pure consolation. And what they'd both wanted to do was hovering between them now, like a wayward genie that had popped out of a bottle and refused to be crammed back into confinement again.

'Yeah. I hope so. That was a good spot there, Sara.' He said the words awkwardly, as if even that might be construed as being inappropriate.

'Thanks. For listening to what I said.'

'Why shouldn't I?'

She shrugged. 'Oh, you know. Doctors don't always listen to paramedics.'

'A good doctor listens to everyone.'

'Yeah. Good doctors do that.'

He grinned, dipping his head slightly in a gesture of acknowledgement. In the last two hours they'd gone from housemates to almost-lovers and now they were colleagues. And colleagues seemed to be the only one of the three where they both knew what to do and how to act. Maybe, from here, they could work their way through to being friends, so that when the time came for them to part, they could both do it well.

It sounded like a plan, anyway. It was the only one that Sara had, so it had better work.

CHAPTER FIVE

REECE was gratified to find that when Sara climbed into his SUV the following morning she pointedly did so without her large leather handbag slung across her shoulder. The few clothes that she had were still back in his guest room, and when he offered her his set of keys to Simon's house, she had waved them away. He was slightly ashamed at the swell of pleasure that it gave him to pocket them.

There was another battle to face, though, and that was the one that had been raging within himself. They'd been studiedly polite with each other throughout their meal last night, as if that was going to somehow erase the softness of her lips, make him forget how good she smelled and tasted and felt. And after she'd conjured up an urgent excuse for an early night out of nowhere, he'd found his own bed a little too large and much too lonely.

Fair enough. If that was what she wanted, then he would do nothing to make her feel uncomfortable. Restraint was the watchword for today.

Trader was about as jittery as he was, seeming to understand that they were on their way home, his tail thumping rhythmically against the back seat of the SUV as they drove.

'It looks...okay. Does it look okay?' Sara was peering out of the window intently.

'It looks fine. The fire didn't even get this far.' They still had over an hour's drive in front of them and she was nervous already. She'd start to see the devastation soon enough, and Reece knew she would deal with the reality much better than she would her own fears and imagination.

'No.' She seemed to settle a little. 'I'm glad it didn't reach that house over there, it looks like a nice place. The owners must be relieved.'

He grinned. Sara's glass always seemed to be half-full, even if it was with someone else's good fortune. 'Do you like it here?' He'd intended to change the subject, ease both their nerves, but as soon as the question had been asked, Reece realised that it mattered to him. It mattered a great deal.

'I love it. It's so…' She seemed lost for words for a moment. 'I feel free here. As if I can see a long way into the distance.'

'Yeah? Not so much in the way, I guess.' His fingertips were tingling.

'It's not that. It's the light. So clear, I feel as if I could almost touch it.' She was smiling now and it was hard to keep his eye on the road.

'Not as exciting as London, though.' He shouldn't press the point. He shouldn't be wondering what she might say if he asked her to stay on for a little while.

She shrugged. 'London's different. It's got a lot going for it, and so has this place.' She seemed to be thinking about something. Maybe weighing up the pros and cons. Reece almost held his breath. 'You must have seen pretty much all of Australia.'

'Not all of it. Quite a lot, though.'

'But you're home now?'

The question took him by surprise. Reece tried to decide where exactly might be classified as home, and came up blank. 'Not really. I came here to be with Kath. She had postnatal depression after she had her second child and she and Joe needed some support.'

'She's better now?' She swung round to look at him.

'Yeah. Took a while, but she's fine.'

'Does that mean you'll be moving on, then?'

Reece reckoned up the time in his head. 'I've lived in the same place for two years and three months now. That's pretty much a record for me.'

She laughed, shaking her head. 'All right, then, what's your favourite part of Australia?'

'Can't say, really. Everywhere has something to recommend it.'

'Hmm. Yes, you're right. There are so many wonderful things in the world.'

She had a knack of making things wonderful. After her first day in Melbourne she'd described her tram ride to Reece with such infectious enthusiasm that he'd thought that the next time he took that familiar route it would seem new and exciting. 'You must have travelled a bit. Europe's right on your doorstep.'

'Oh, nowhere, really. Italy…France.' She sounded almost wistful. As if somehow they were places that were out of her reach, although there was nothing stopping her now from going wherever she wanted. 'What about you?'

'New Zealand, of course. India, Indonesia, Japan…' He reeled off the list of countries and she laughed delightedly. 'I've not got as far as Europe yet, but I'll make it there one day.'

'You should.' That hint of sadness again, which was shaken off almost straight away. 'Simon said that you and Kath travelled a lot when you were young.'

'Yeah. My father was an entertainer, so we were on the move most of the time.'

'Really?' That touch of wonder again. 'What did he do?'

'He was a magician. He even had his own TV show.'

'What? So you know how to do magic tricks?'

Reece laughed. 'A few.'

'Show me!'

Suddenly a few simple conjuring tricks became a precious legacy from a childhood that had forced Reece to leave almost everything he'd cared about behind. 'I can't while I'm driving.' Reece wondered whether she was going to make him stop the car and produce a coin from her ear right this minute.

'Well, you can show me as soon as we get back to your place this evening.'

He grinned. His place this evening sounded like a promise with possibilities. 'You're on.'

The terrain was beginning to change. Yellow and green gave way to patches of burned-out land, and Sara stared out of the car window, trying to comprehend the vastness of it all. Great swathes of charred, black ground, the odd patch of untouched earth, which made the destruction wrought by the oncoming flames seem random and all the more chilling.

The smell of smoke still hung in the air, and she could glimpse the roof of Simon's house as Reece sped towards it. At least the place still had a roof. That seemed like a good sign, and she held onto it, not daring to ask Reece. He wouldn't lie, and for the next few moments, at least, hope was better than the uncertain truth.

The wooden outhouse, only fifty feet from the house, was an unruly pile of cinders with just a few charred structural beams still upright. The fire had taken the grassland around the property, but the house was untouched.

'Reece...' Sara couldn't help but reach across to him, and she felt his hand grab hers, holding it tight while he steered the SUV up the bumpy track towards the house with the other hand. 'Look, it's okay.'

'Yeah.' He sounded as relieved as she was, and Sara realised that he had shared her fears. 'Looks as if the fire was losing some impetus by the time it got here. The fire-break around the house was enough.'

'If you hadn't come for me...' Tears pricked at the sides of her eyes. Even though the house was untouched, Sara could only imagine the terror of being stranded there alone as the fire surrounded her.

'Don't think about that.' The car came to a halt outside the house and he turned, taking both her hands in his. 'It might be a bit of a mess inside, but don't worry about that. We can fix it.'

'Yes...yes, we can make it just the way it was before.'

He nodded. 'That's the spirit. Stay here for a moment with Trader while I go and check the place out.'

'I'll come with you...if that's all right.' Even though it went against all of her instincts, if Reece insisted she stayed here, she'd do it.

'Sure.' He reached into one of the compartments in the car door and drew out two pairs of heavy workmen's gloves, grinning as he handed her one. 'Whatever made me think you'd stay put?'

Trader, on the other hand, was told to stay and grudgingly lay down on the back seat of the car, his tail thumping out a message of rebellion. Reece caught Sara's gloved hand in his, whether as comfort or as a way of keeping her from straying she didn't know. She didn't much care. It was a world away from the way that their fingers had frantically twined together last night, and a welcome reassurance that today Reece could somehow make everything right.

Reece tested his weight on the boards of the veranda

before he let her follow him. Everything that he kicked or thumped with the heel of his hand was firm and solid.

'Looks as if Simon did a pretty good job when he designed this house. These fireproof boards have held up pretty well.' He gave the veranda one more kick to illustrate his point.

'I'm glad I wasn't here.' Sara looked at the blackened landscape and tried to imagine it burning. She couldn't. Some things were just beyond imagining.

His eyes were following the progress of a small flock of birds, dipping and wheeling in the distance over what was probably a source of either food or water. 'You did all the right things, Sara. Pulled the shutters down in case you had to stay. Packed up Simon's things in case you got the chance to go.'

'I don't know about that. I was pretty scared.' Perhaps she should have just left it. But she couldn't help wanting more from him.

'Anyone with an ounce of sense would have been. You handled yourself well.'

'Apart from locking us out of the house, that is.' Sara shrugged and turned away from him.

She heard his chuckle behind her. 'I'd have forgiven you anything at that point. You looked so cute in your jeans and your nightie. A bit like a wayward fairy who had lost her way in the bush.'

Sara heard the sound of the shutters as he pulled them up over the front door, and she turned, watching him. Waiting to see what he would do next, almost afraid of going into the house.

'It's a little stale in there.' He pushed the door open and the smell from the house hit her. A little stale didn't cover it. The place stank.

For a moment her courage failed her and Sara hesitated.

He seemed to understand, pulling off his glove and reaching for her, his fingers brushing the soft skin on the inside of her wrist. Sara thought she saw an echo in his eyes of the thrill that the contact gave her.

'Leave the door open. It'll air out.' He made no comment when Sara decided to follow him around the perimeter of the house, watching while he pulled the rest of the shutters up.

When he got to the back door, he unlocked it and propped it open to get a little more air into the house. By the time they had worked their way back to the front, the smell of smoke and decay from inside seemed to have lessened a little.

Everything inside looked tired and worn, from the onslaught of the smoke. Reece made for the kitchen, with Sara hard on his heels. She didn't need to follow him around any more, but somehow his bulk and the certainty of his movements were reassuring.

The fruit in the bowl was rotten and stinking. Sara left his side and inspected the food in the fridge, which was beginning to smell, a dried watermark on the floor from where it had defrosted.

'I'll go and get my tools from the car and see what I can do about fixing the front door.' He hesitated, silent questions in his eyes.

Sara nodded. He'd taken her the first few baby steps and she was ready to do this alone now. 'Thanks. I'll see what I can do about cleaning this mess up.'

He'd brought everything she needed. Waste sacks, cleaning sprays and even two large canisters of water, which he heaved from the car and rolled into the kitchen, telling Sara to go easy with it as it was all they had, apart from the drinking water they'd brought. She set about emptying the fridge and cleaning away the black dust that covered every exposed surface, while Reece clattered around at the front door.

When she wandered through to find him, not entirely satisfied that the kitchen was clean but confident that she'd got the worst of it, he'd almost finished with the door.

'What do you think? Once it's filled, sanded and painted, it'll hardly show.' He ran his hand across the wood he'd pieced into the doorframe where the lock was smashed, testing the alignment with his fingers.

'It looks great. It won't show at all.' She grinned at him and he nodded, seemingly now satisfied with his work.

'How are you doing?'

'I've pretty much finished in the kitchen. Have you got Simon's list?'

Reece pulled the list out of his pocket. 'There's the computer he uses for work and his back-up drives…I'll get those and see if I can clean up a bit in his office. Some bits and pieces from his wardrobe…' He twisted his wrist, flipping the sheet of paper towards her. 'Bring as much as you can fit into the car. We can wash clothes and bedding when we get them back home.'

Sara took the list without touching his fingers. 'Sure.' She'd given in to the need to touch him too much today already. Now that she was feeling stronger, her head was throbbing from trying not to think about how a comforting touch could so easily turn into a caress.

As soon as she had taken refuge in Simon's bedroom, Sara began to think more clearly. She simply couldn't give in to temptation where Reece was concerned. Ten thousand miles was nothing in comparison to the distance between their lifestyles. He was a free spirit, and she had made the choice to stay put and look after Gran.

She didn't regret it for a moment, but experience had taught her that it was better not to think about relationships.

If Tim, her last boyfriend, who had never gone anywhere unless absolutely necessary, reckoned that caring for her mother and grandmother had made her boring, then Reece wouldn't last ten minutes.

She sighed. Tim hadn't been that much of a loss anyway, she'd hardly missed him when he'd left. Reece would be, though. And what you didn't have, you couldn't miss.

She sank onto the bed, shrugging to herself. *So don't do it. Just don't. That's the easy way out of this.* Kissing goodbye to the thought of his caress might be the most obvious course of action, but it wasn't as easy as it sounded.

'Forget about that, there's work to do.' She muttered the words through gritted teeth and her body automatically obeyed. Sara opened the wardrobe and sorted clothes into neat piles on the bed. She went to the bathroom for Simon's shaving kit. Rummaging through the heavy workboots to find the soft-soled sneakers he'd asked for, Sara jagged her fingers on a sharp edge, right at the back of the wardrobe.

Investigating more closely, she drew out a large, metal banker's box, sliding it onto the carpet. It was heavy. Papers perhaps. If so, they should take these too. There was a lock on the box but it hung open, with two keys taped to the side, so whatever it was couldn't be private.

She opened the lid and found neat piles of papers and photographs. Her own face smiled out at her from a trip to France three years ago. Gingerly Sara picked up the stack of photographs, flipping through them. They were all of her, photos that she'd sent over the years. Postcards from when she'd been on holiday. Every single thing that she'd ever sent Simon.

Their mother was there too. Press cuttings from English papers that Simon must have had subscribed to. Articles about the company, even advertisements from the recruitment section. A page spread of their mother, accepting the

Public Relations Manager of the Year Award, carefully folded so that the creases in the paper didn't run across any of the photographs.

She jumped guiltily as Reece appeared in the doorway. 'Have you got any bags of clothes that I can pack around the computer to steady it in the car...?' He broke off as Sara looked up at him. Her bewilderment must have been written all over her face. 'What's the matter?'

'Nothing. Nothing. I...' She had no idea how she should react to this. She wanted to cry, but a lump of concrete in her chest seemed to be stopping her. 'Have you seen this box before?'

'No. Why?' He watched as she closed the lid of the box. She should leave it.

'Nothing. It doesn't matter.' She got to her feet and started to slide the piles of clothes into plastic sacks. Subject closed. It made no difference, anyway.

'Since it's nothing...' he walked into the room and sat down on the bed, watching her for a moment '...you won't mind if I look inside the box, then.'

CHAPTER SIX

THE unfamiliar, awkward sensation of not knowing what to do next had turned Reece's hands into heavy, clumsy things that he didn't recognise. He'd been trying his best to give Sara the support she needed, balancing that with the space she wanted. But his instincts had been warring with his conscious mind for so long now that he couldn't be absolutely sure about his motives for anything any more.

She was obviously upset. She had that strange air of being just about to burst into tears, without actually doing so. And tears or not, he wanted to comfort her but he couldn't do that unless he knew what the matter was. An abrupt gesture of her hand indicated that he could do whatever the hell he liked, and Sara turned away from him.

'Did you know he had all this?' Finally she spoke.

'No. I didn't.' Reece could have guessed, though. He didn't have a box like this in the bottom of his own wardrobe but everything, every scrap of paper, every last memory of his own brother, still followed him wherever he went, stored in a large manila envelope.

'Why did he do it?' She was pacing now, and it was difficult to tell exactly who she was angry with. Perhaps she didn't even know. 'Why couldn't he have come back? Mum would have seen him at the end. I know she would, whatever she said.'

'I don't know. We all deal with things differently, Sara.'

'How hard would it have been just to make some sort of effort to see us, instead of locking us away in a metal box?' Swiping her hand across her face, she threw herself back down onto the bed next to him. 'I guess I didn't mean that.'

'I guess that you did, and I don't blame you.' She still wouldn't look at him, but her body seemed less taut now. 'Have you and Simon talked about your mother yet? Why he didn't come home?'

'No. I've been meaning to mention it, but...' She shrugged. 'I don't know if that's ever going to happen.'

Reece took a deep breath. He'd been keeping out of this, reckoning it was best to let Simon and Sara work things out between themselves, but now might be the time to re-visit that assessment. 'You're more like him than I thought.'

It was deliberate provocation, and it worked. Better than he'd anticipated.

'What do you mean by that?' Her face flushed with anger.

'Simon walks away. It's what he does. If something's emotionally difficult then he'll let it slide. But you...' Reece decided to go for it. If Sara was half the woman he thought she was, she'd rise to the challenge. 'I had you down as being stronger than that.'

She stared at him, clearly not sure whether to take what he'd said as an insult or a compliment. 'I'm not...I'm not strong...'

'I think you're one of the strongest people I've ever met.' Her doubts about herself would have been almost laughable if they hadn't tugged so fiercely at his heart.

'So it's me that has to do all the running, is that what you're saying? Why can't Simon do something?'

'It's not fair, but that's how it is.' His words had a whiff of hypocrisy. 'Can I tell you something?'

She sensed his reticence, and it seemed to calm her. 'Yes, of course.'

Carefully, tentatively, he reached back into his past. 'It wasn't just Kath and I when we were kids. We had a brother.'

'Oh?'

'My mother died just after Kath was born. Dad remarried and my stepmother had a son, about my age. We grew up together and we were like brothers. I guess that travelling so much threw us together. It was me, Kath and Stuart, and we didn't need anyone else.'

She nodded for him to go on, resting her hand lightly on his.

'When I was fourteen, my dad and stepmum divorced.' He shrugged. 'She found him with one of the dancers from the show and walked out. I was confused and angry and I wouldn't speak to Stuart when he wanted to say goodbye. I didn't see him again.' He laid her hand back in her lap. It was okay. Really, it was.

'What I'm trying to say to you, Sara, is that families get split up for all sorts of reasons. People act badly. They make mistakes. I haven't seen Stuart for twenty years and I often wonder what became of him.'

She swallowed. 'Reece, I'm sorry...'

'It doesn't matter. I'm telling you this because you have a chance to mend things between you and Simon. If I had that chance with Stuart, I wouldn't waste it.'

She looked at him, wide-eyed and knowing. As if her gaze could pierce him, right to the heart. 'Have you ever tried to find him?'

'Yeah, I've tried. Sometimes I think that I'll go to a new town, pop into the local chemist and bump into him.' He shrugged. 'Not particularly likely, though.' Reece hadn't realised how much it would cost him to say that. How bad it felt to finally admit that he would probably never find his brother. He could feel himself beginning to shake and he got to his feet and walked over to the window, staring out at nothing in particular.

He felt her arm brush his. Whatever he was looking at out there, it seemed to have captured her attention too. 'I hope that someone's looking after Stuart. Being a friend to him, the way that you and Kath have been to Simon all this time.'

'Thanks. I hope so too.' He felt suddenly lighter. As if in trying to convince her that she was not alone, he'd finally convinced himself of that fact.

He had to make some space between them. If he didn't, he was going to do something stupid. Start believing that kissing her last night had been the sanest thing he'd ever done, and that he should repeat it. Up here, it would be nothing short of a miracle if the phone interrupted them.

'What do you think of this?' He turned quickly, and in the absence of anything else to busy himself with began to stack the piles of Simon's clothes into the case that lay open on the bed. 'We'll close the box up, lock it and take it back to my place for safekeeping. If the time comes when you and Simon want to look through it together, then it'll be there for you both.'

'Yes. Thanks, I'd like that.' She was wiping at the grime on her face with her fingers, producing a streaky effect. Not many women could have carried that off well, but somehow she looked just fine. Impish. Reece tried not to think about the mischief she could get up to, but it was too late. Desire had already ignited, deep in his gut.

'Okay, then. We'll pack the car, and then we can clean up before we get back on the road.'

'Wash?' Her face brightened. 'I thought the water pump wasn't working?'

'It isn't. But I've got some more water in the car.' He grinned at her obvious pleasure. 'One basinful each.'

'One basin is plenty.' She tugged at her T-shirt, now caked with soot. 'I'm glad now I took your advice and brought a change of clothes. This stuff gets everywhere.'

'And since we'll be more or less presentable, there are some nice wineries on the way back. Perhaps we can stop and I'll buy you a late lunch.' He might not be about to give in to his other fantasies, but they had to eat.

'No.'

Reece felt a trickle of cold sweat down his back. Perhaps he'd gone too far after all.

She laughed. The sound of her laugh was like the gentle patter of rain on leaves, breaking a long, hard drought. 'It's my shout. You've been so good to me, Reece, the least I can do is buy lunch.'

'Right. Fair enough.' He could handle that. 'Never turn a lady down when she's paying.'

Reece had driven past three wineries, which for some reason weren't good enough, and settled on a fourth, turning into a wide driveway and parking the car in a space surrounded by vines. They walked together through the light, airy restaurant space and out onto a wide, shaded veranda at the back.

'Is this okay?' He scanned the space, still apparently making up his mind about whether his choice was the right one.

'It'll do.' Sara sat down at the nearest table before he got the chance to spend another ten minutes deciding which had the best view. Reece hadn't initially struck her as the kind of person that it was all that easy to tease, but he was looking distinctly uncomfortable at the moment. 'It's lovely. Sit down before you take root there.'

Once she'd looked at the menu and pronounced it varied enough for her taste, declared the view across the vineyard delightful and confirmed herself to be not too hot or too cold, he loosened up a little. Sara stretched her legs out in front of her, slipping her feet out of her sandals and relishing the feel of the sun on her toes.

'So are you going to show me some of those magic tricks? Or do you need special equipment?'

'They're called props. And, no, you don't need any, because it's really and truly magic.' A grin hovered on his lips.

'Go on, then.'

He produced a coin from his pocket, holding it up for her to examine and then closing his fingers around it. 'I expect you've seen this one before. Keep your eyes on my hand.'

'I'm watching you carefully.' Sara fixed her eyes on the hand he held the coin in.

He chuckled, blew on his hand and then opened it, splaying his fingers wide to show her that the coin was now gone. Then he reached forward, a slight tremor in his fingers as they brushed her ear, making her flush red.

The coin clattered to the floor. His gaze was all for her now, and hers for him.

'Astonishing.'

He smiled, leaning across the table towards her. 'You missed the bit at the beginning. When I told you to watch carefully, I'd already switched the coin to my other hand.'

'I'll look a bit closer next time. Aren't you supposed to give the coin to me so I can check it's the same one?'

'Yep.' He didn't move. The magic going on here was the real kind, no smoke or mirrors. One touch of his gaze, a slight movement of his hand towards hers, and she could feel that slightly giddy sensation of being lighter than air.

A waitress broke the spell, unloading two glasses of

wine and a platter of food from her tray. 'Hey.' She bent down and picked up the coin. 'Is this yours?'

Reece grinned up at her. 'Thanks. Belongs to the lady.'

'Ah, right.' She laid the coin on the table in front of Sara. 'Enjoy your food.'

'Thank you.' Sara surveyed the seafood platter. 'This all looks wonderful.'

The waitress grinned and nodded when she heard Sara's accent. 'There's a guestbook on the bar where you can write what you think of our wine.'

'Thanks, we will.' Suddenly it was *we* and not *I*. As if they really had somehow melded together for a moment, and it wasn't just an illusion brought about by the seductive heat in his eyes.

He seemed to feel it too. Spearing some of the best bits from the platter and reaching over to drop them on her plate. His fingers brushing against hers as they both reached for the bread at the same time. The sun, the breeze and Reece's easy, open smile were working on her heart. If she could talk to Simon, what other impossibilities might she accomplish? Today she could do anything. Just for today.

That evening, Reece sat in the visitors' lounge at the hospital, the newspaper folded in front of him, ignoring the partially completed crossword. He didn't have the heart for it at the moment. Sara had already been with Simon for an hour and a half and the debate over whether he had pushed her into this too soon or just encouraged her to do what she already knew was right wasn't going well.

He had positioned himself carefully so that he could see along the corridor that led to Simon's room. When he saw her, walking slowly, her face creased in that worried look that seemed almost a matter of habit when she thought no one was looking, it was all he could do not to jump to his feet and hurry to meet her.

'How did it go?' He tried not to make the question sound too insistent.

'Good. I said what I had to say, and Simon responded to it.' Suddenly she smiled, and Reece breathed again. It was like the sun rising over the hills, with its bright promise of a new day.

'That's great.' He wondered whether he should ask where things stood now and decided not to. It was enough that she was smiling. 'Would you like me to get you a drink, or do you want to go now?'

'Let's go.'

Reece stood and made to follow her towards the exit door, but she stopped suddenly, catching his arm. 'We're okay with things. I mean, more okay than we were. It wasn't easy, and Simon said a lot of things that I didn't particularly want to hear. They needed saying, though.'

'I'm glad. Things like this, you can't mend them in one go. All you can do is make a start.'

'And we made a good one. Thanks, Reece. For your advice.'

Her words stung. He'd advised her to talk honestly with Simon, but he hadn't been entirely honest with her. The things he'd done today, getting close to her, trying to lift her spirits, hadn't been entirely selfless. They were the things he'd been longing to do. His motives had seemed solid enough at the time, but in retrospect they didn't stand up to very much scrutiny.

'Any time.' He ignored the hypocrisy of that statement too. This urge to be with her, all day and all night, wasn't appropriate either. She was a guest in his house, dependent on him, and she had a lot to cope with right now. She needed support, not someone else to mess with her head.

'Let's go home.' She stretched her arms out, working loose the tension in her shoulders.

'Yeah, it's been a long day. I'll pick up a take-out and a DVD rental on the way and we can just relax in front of the TV.'

She brightened immediately. 'Mmm. A shower and then food on the sofa with a film. Heaven.'

CHAPTER SEVEN

A BRIGHT, clear dawn did little for Reece's sense of disappointment in himself. Sara had fallen asleep halfway through the film, and two hours later, when she hadn't stirred, he'd carried her through to her room. He'd resisted the temptation to change her into her nightdress, deciding that she'd be comfortable enough in her sweatpants and T-shirt, but he'd not been able to find a good reason not to take her socks off. And after the swell of longing that brushing her ankle with his fingers had engendered, even that had seemed like an unpardonable intrusion.

The morning found him staring uncertainly at the contents of the refrigerator. Since she'd been here, the plastic food containers that usually lay undisturbed at the back of the cupboard had migrated to the fridge. All of them contained something, and he had little idea what.

'What are you looking for?' Reece jumped guiltily as he heard her voice behind him.

'Not sure yet. I'll know when I see it.'

She laughed and Reece turned in surprise. As laughs went she had a great one, but it was always cut short, as if she'd remembered that there really wasn't much to laugh about. This one seemed to run its course.

'There's bread in the cupboard and some fruit sliced in the second container on the left. Juice in the door, and...'

She slid past him and flipped open a cupboard, reaching for a packet from the top shelf. 'Look what I got.'

'Ah! Coffee beans. I thought we'd be back to instant when the ground coffee Kath brought over ran out.' He saw that there was another, similar packet stowed away behind the first. 'And you stocked up.'

She grinned at him. 'From the state of your coffee grinder, it looked as if you hadn't used it for a while.'

'That bad, eh?'

'Nothing a hammer and chisel couldn't fix.' She was playful this morning, and it warmed Reece's heart to see her like this. It started him thinking about what she could so easily be if that nebulous, unknown burden that she seemed to carry around with her was lifted. 'Sit down. I'll make breakfast.'

'You don't need to do that...' She'd been cooking for him ever since she'd arrived here and Reece was painfully aware of the fact that he'd eaten better in the last week than he didn't know when.

'Sit.' She was irrepressible and quite irresistible. 'I don't want you messing up your own kitchen. You can do that when I'm safely out of the country.'

She made breakfast and Reece came back for seconds in what was becoming almost a private joke between them. 'I could get used to this, you know.' He leaned back in his chair, full and ready for the day. Usually he left the house hungry and stopped off at the coffee shop on his way in to work.

'Maybe you should.' Her dark eyes found his gaze, and for a moment the world seemed to open up, full of possibilities. 'It's just a matter of organisation. Keeping a shopping list.'

'Yeah. Guess so.' Reece had never made a shopping list in his life. Neither of his stepmothers or his father's live-in girlfriends had ever made shopping lists either, let alone keep stocks of food in the cupboards. It was one of the byproducts of living in a different place every couple of months. Learning the lesson about not getting too attached to anything or anyone. 'I never really thought...'

He'd never really thought about a lot of things. About the single flower, taken from the garden and put into a vase between them on the table. About the smell of home-cooked food and how that curled around his senses, welcoming him home in the evenings. How two chairs, tilted towards each other on the patio, were so much more sociable than straightening them neatly.

The phone shrilled from inside the house and Reece rose, hoping that it wasn't a call from the surgery. He had other plans for today.

It was Simon, and he sounded as cheerful as his sister did. 'Some of the guys from work are coming in this afternoon. We were thinking of watching the game together and I reckoned that Sara deserved a break.'

Simon was playing right into his hands. 'I can take her out somewhere.' He found himself lowering his voice conspiratorially.

'That would be great. Would you mind?'

'Of course not.' He ignored the chorus of voices at the back of his head. He was doing a favour for a friend. Where was it written that had to be an irksome duty?

'Yeah. There were loads of places I was hoping to take her, and she hasn't got to see any of them yet.'

'Okay.' There was one person who still needed to be convinced. He could drop Trader off at a neighbour's and have Sara all to himself for the day. 'Well, I'll leave it to you to persuade Sara that it's okay for her to take some time off today.'

* * *

The rest of the day was hers. And what a day it was. Sara supposed that Reece pretty much took these bright, clear days for granted, and that he took the feeling of freedom that they seemed to engender for granted too. She didn't. She was enjoying every moment of them.

'Where are we going again?'

'You'll see.' Reece seemed to be taking pleasure in the fact that she'd lost her bearings completely. 'Again.'

'Can't you show me on the map?'

'What for? I know the way.'

'I'm a tourist. I need a map.' She shot him a pleading look. 'Suppose…'

'Suppose what?'

He had a point. 'I don't know. Suppose anything. Suppose you got electrocuted in a freak lightning storm and lost your memory.'

'I'd look in my wallet for my address. Suppose you take the day off. Let someone else cover all the eventualities for a few hours.'

That generally wasn't an option, but since it was now, there was no real reason why she shouldn't take it. Sara settled back into her seat. 'Okay.' At first she'd hated being so dependent on Reece, having to trust him for practically everything. Some time over the last week, though, it had become suspiciously easy.

'Really?' As he raised one eyebrow, the car kicked down a gear, attacking the steep incline of the road as if it too didn't quite believe her but was pressing on regardless.

The road wound, climbing all the time through dense woodland. Sara caught glimpses of rolling hills, which Reece drove past without slowing, and Sara twisted in her seat, trying to get a better look. Finally he did slow, pulling into an off-road car park.

'Are we here, then?' Sara got out of the car before Reece had a chance to start the engine again.

'We're here. Would you like to go for a walk?'

'Thought you'd never ask.' The forest around them was spectacular. Massive trees, giant ferns. 'I've never seen anything like this before.'

He seemed pleased at the way she was looking around, drinking it all in. 'Put your boots on and we can explore a bit. How are you with heights?'

'Fine. As long as my feet are firmly on the ground.' Sara covered her discomfiture by opening the back door of the car and pretending to look for her walking boots.

Reece watched while she laced them up and caught up the daysack he'd brought along. 'Let's go this way, then.' He turned resolutely and started to make his way towards the far end of the car park, twisting round when he realised that Sara wasn't with him.

'What about this way?' She jerked her thumb towards the signpost that pointed towards the trail that wound upwards and disappeared amongst the trees.

He hesitated, and Sara leant back against the car, folding her arms. So what if she didn't like heights very much? She wouldn't be coming back here any time soon and she was determined to see everything while she had the opportunity.

'You might find it a bit…challenging.' He still seemed unsure.

'Good. I'm in a mood for a challenge.' She was used to planning the easiest possible way to do anything with Gran, and this felt like an opportunity to stretch her limbs.

He grinned broadly, striding back over to where she stood. 'Okay, then. A challenge it is.'

Reece took her hand, leading her along the trail. On one side of them the ground suddenly fell away, only a sturdy handrail and a couple of feet of ground between them and a dizzying drop. 'Okay?'

She gripped his hand tightly. 'I'm okay.' She took hold of the handrail, testing it, and when it didn't give she took a step forward. Not too bad. With Reece on one side of her and the railings on the other, she felt almost safe. Sara took another step and then let him guide her forward.

Awe took over from fear. On one side of them was the canopy of the forest. Below them was dense vegetation, with the tops of the trees and the sky above them. It was breathtaking.

Reece was at her side, keeping up a steady stream of information. He pointed out the tall mountain ash and the myrtle beech trees, the giant ferns and various mosses. Every part of this ancient, gigantic forest seemed to fascinate him as much as it did her. She let go of the handrail and fished in her bag for her camera.

'Stop a moment. I want to take a photo.' Before she had even thought what she was doing, she motioned him forward. 'Go and stand over there. I need something to show how big the trees are.'

'You go, then.' He took the camera from her. 'Or do you just want to stay here and I'll take one?'

'No, no, I want that big one over there.' Sara walked ahead of him to stand in front of the tree she wanted. Reece backed up to get as much as he could into the frame, and Sara smiled for the camera.

A few exchanged words with a middle-aged couple who were passing and he handed the camera over and came to join her, standing next to the balustrade. Sara inched closer and he put his arm around her.

'Beaut!' the woman exclaimed delightedly, and clicked the shutter. Sara grinned and heard the camera click again. 'Here you are, doll.' The woman came forwards and handed her the camera, smiling at them both. 'You make a lovely couple.'

Reece watched, amused, as Sara thanked the woman awkwardly and then reviewed the photos with shaking fingers. 'Don't we just.' She jumped as his lips brushed her ear, and then he drew back, letting her put the camera back into her bag.

They had explored the trail together, and then a longer trail, which wound through the forest floor. Sara held her breath as Reece pointed out a lyrebird, which took fright almost as soon as she caught sight of it and made for the safety of the undergrowth. They paused to stand beneath gigantic ferns that looked like something out of a set for a prehistoric movie.

Reece drove to the summit so she could get the best view of the densely wooded hills that surrounded them, and then came the long drive back down again, marvelling at the dark shapes of the trees against the sun, now falling towards the horizon.

'Did you like it?' They'd been almost silent in the car as Sara had determinedly tried to drink in every sight and sound of the day.

'Out of this world.' She laughed. 'Almost literally.'

He smiled. 'It's something else, isn't it? Makes you feel very small when you think that some of these trees have been growing for nearly four hundred years.'

'Do you think they'll be there in another four hundred?'

'Who knows? With a little luck, some good management and the will to do it. I hope so.'

'It matters, doesn't it?'

'Yeah. It matters.' He slowed the car, giving a cyclist who was freewheeling down the steep gradient a wide berth. Another car shot past them, and Sara stretched automatically to look in the rear-view mirror.

'Stop the car!'

He didn't ask why, just jammed his foot on the brake. As soon as the car skidded to a halt, Sara jumped out, running back up the road for all she was worth. She could hear Reece behind her, and by the time she got to the spot where she had last seen the cyclist, he was at her side.

'Over there. That car that overtook us must have just clipped him and sent him off the road.' He pointed to where the thin trails, left by the bicycle wheels in the wet grass, disappeared over the edge of the steep incline, beyond the swathe of vegetation next to the road. 'Stay here.'

Reece jogged over to the edge of the incline and Sara followed him, dropping to her knees and crawling to the edge. For a moment vertigo almost threw her forward and then she caught sight of the cyclist, focussing on him, and the world began to steady again.

'There he is.' She craned over as far as she dared to get a good look. 'He's not moving.' The cyclist was lying on a broad shelf about thirty feet down, seemingly unconscious. Edging another few inches forward, she saw blood in the area of his shoulder.

Reece's hand was on her shoulder, pulling her back. 'Take my phone and call the emergency services. I'll go and get the car.'

By the time Sara had made the call, and received a promise of a rescue team as soon as possible, Reece had backed the SUV as close to the edge of the incline as he could and had jumped out. He was rummaging in the back for something.

'Have you got anything to help us get down there?' Reece had cleared out the boot of his car yesterday, in order to fit in as many of Simon's possessions as possible, but it appeared that most of the things that had been removed had managed to migrate their way back again.

'Ah!' Reece had obviously found what he was looking for, and reached in, dragging a coil of rope from the boot. 'I thought I put this back in here again.' He coiled the rope carefully, checking it as he went, and looped one end of it around the towbar on the back of the car.

'I'll go.'

He froze. 'You will not.'

'This is my job.'

'Not in this country it's not. You're staying here.'

'No, Reece.' She pulled at his shoulder, turning him round to face her. 'Look at it rationally. If you go down there, I don't have the strength to pull you back up again. The safest thing for both of us is for you stay at the top and lower me down.'

He broke away from her roughly, striding over to the edge of the incline and looking down at the man below them. 'You're no good with heights, Sara.'

'That's when I'm on holiday. At work I've been on roofs, ledges, you name it. People don't just get injured on the ground, you know.' Sara knew that Reece would understand that. It was one thing not to choose to stare down a thirty-foot drop. It was quite another when there was a job to do.

He turned and walked back to the car. He was more pig-headed than she'd given him credit for. Then she heard him curse under his breath.

'All right, then.' He had pulled a climbing harness out of the car boot and he began to wrap it around her body and legs, pulling the straps tight. 'Do anything stupid and you won't need to worry about falling. I'll throw you over the edge myself.'

'Fair dues. Just concentrate on not dropping me.' The grim humour calmed her nerves.

He clipped the rope to her harness and checked every-thing thoroughly. In almost any other situation his hands on her body like this, treating it as if it were his and there was nowhere he couldn't touch, would have taken her breath away. Now it was just reassuring that he was being so thorough.

'Right. I'll have to lower you down the first ten feet, but then it's not so steep. See if you can get a handhold, and guide yourself down. When you get down there, don't take the harness off and keep your helmet on, whatever happens. You stay attached to the rope at all times, right?'

'Right.'

He rolled his eyes. 'I must be mad, letting you do this…' He got hold of the ropes that he had fixed firmly to the back of the car. 'Okay, off you go.'

CHAPTER EIGHT

HE LOWERED her down, slow and steady, until Sara could get a handhold on the muddy incline, which was tangled with tree roots and branches. She scrambled down, and Reece played the rope out, ready to take the strain if she slipped.

'Okay. I'm down on flat ground now. Give me a few feet to work with and tie the rope off.' Reece's assent floated down and he disappeared for a moment.

'How is he?' His head and shoulders appeared again, straining to see.

'He's breathing.' Even though the light was fading quickly, Sara had already performed her initial checks. 'Seems to be coming round.' She bent over her patient. 'I'm a paramedic and I'm here to help you. Can you lie still for me?'

The man's eyelids fluttered in a gesture of assent, and Sara called up to Reece. 'I need a torch.' She could feel something sticky under her hands in the region of his shoulder.

'Coming down to you now.' She looked up and saw a large bag, suspended on a rope, being lowered towards her.

'Good. Got it.' She reached the bag and pulled the zipper. It was Reece's medical kit from the car, along with an assortment of other items. Reece couldn't be accused of having the tidiest car boot in the world, but he did have a lot of useful things in there. She grabbed the lantern torch and switched it on, setting it down next to the man.

'He's bleeding from a wound on his shoulder. I'm taking his jacket off for a better look.' Sara cut the Lycra cycling jacket and blood plumed out over her hands. 'I need something to pad the wound.'

She hoped that Reece would read the situation from that. Sara didn't want to shout that she had a bleeder on her hands while the man was conscious and might panic. The last thing she needed was for him to start thrashing around and tipping them both over the edge.

'Look in the bag.' He'd got the message. 'In a blue plastic wrapper.'

She snatched the packet out of the bag, tearing off the wrapper and packing the wadding against the wound. 'Okay, mate, this will hurt a bit, but try and stay still.' She applied pressure, and the bleeding began to slow.

With one hand she felt in the bag, searching for the things she needed, while she still kept up pressure on the wound. Reece was above her, and she could feel his gaze. Watching over her, and her patient, keeping them both safe.

He sent a blanket down and Sara wrapped it around the man. She kept him talking, telling him her name and finding out that he was a student, studying chemistry at Monash University. Together they crouched on the exposed ledge, as the minutes ticked by.

'I can see headlights.' Reece's voice again, floating down on the breeze. 'The rescue services will be here soon.'

'Hey, Patrick. Hear that? Looks like you and me are about to go up in the world.'

Patrick tried for a smile and failed, his eyelids fluttering down. 'Is it me, or is it freezing up here?'

It was cooler now that the sun had gone down, but Patrick had also lost a lot of blood and he was weak and in shock. Sara crouched over him, trying to shield him from the breeze with her own body. 'Is that better?'

'Yeah.' He managed the smile this time. 'Either I'm on death's doorstep or it's my lucky day.'

'It's your lucky day. Most of my patients get told to lie still and stop complaining, but I've taken a liking to you.'

'Right. So I'm not about to die or anything.' Patrick's ashen lips moved in a whisper.

'Nope. You've got a wound on your shoulder, but I've stopped the bleeding now and you're going to be fine.'

'Thanks. Don't suppose you can see my bike anywhere?' Now that Patrick's fears about his own mortality had been quelled, his thoughts were on his expensive racing bike.

'That's not in such good condition.' Sara could see the back wheel hanging from a tree root, and the rest of it must have gone over the side. 'Not quite as resilient as you are.'

'It's…insured…' Patrick's eyelids drooped downwards, and Sara looked desperately upwards, towards Reece.

'Not long now.' As he called down to her, his body was suddenly silhouetted against the glare of headlights. 'Just hang on there for another few minutes.'

She could hear Reece's voice and the sound of activity on the road above her. Sara crouched over Patrick, holding him tight.

Lights, the sound of motors and shouted instructions, and a carry cot came bumping down, followed by two men. They worked quickly, almost without a word, putting Patrick into the cot and winching him upwards to the waiting medics. Then, after what seemed like an interminable delay while activity at the roadside centred around Patrick, it was Sara's turn, and she half climbed, half let herself be pulled up to the top of the incline.

Reece was there. Steadying her when she stumbled to

her feet and guiding her away from the edge. Unclipping the rope, unbuckling her helmet and taking it off.

'Where is he?' Sara looked around wildly.

'Already gone. The ambulance guys wanted to get him to hospital as soon as they could.'

'Did they say…?' In the failing light, Sara had not been able to see Patrick's condition properly towards the end.

'He's in good hands. We can call the hospital to see how he's doing, but I checked him over quickly when he got to the top, and you stopped the bleeding in time. He'll be fine…'

Reece broke off, turning as someone called his name. 'Back in a minute.' His half-smile made the prospect seem delicious. Sara watched as he strode over to the mountain rescue team, who had finished loading their vehicle. A few exchanged words and he let them go.

'They've got another call. Gotta rush.' They were plunged into semi-darkness as the headlights of the rescue vehicle arced round, finding the road and tracing a path away from them.

'Bye, guys.' Sara intoned the words softly, giving a little wave at the receding headlights, and then turned to face him. Almost bumped into him, he was so close.

'Sara.'

'Yes?'

'Tell me you're not going to do this to me again.' He started to unbuckle the straps of her harness. This time there was nothing to divert her attention from the feeling of his hands against her body. Or maybe it was just that Reece seemed to be lingering over the task this time.

'Do what?'

He sighed. 'I've known you less than a week, and in that time I've had to collect you from the path of a bush fire and dangle you over the side of a mountain…'

'It was only thirty feet.'

'This is a mountain. It says so on the map.' He snapped open the buckle at her waist, letting the harness fall at their feet, and tucked one finger into the front of her jeans, pulling her towards him.

'Thought you didn't need a map.'

'Don't change the subject.' He curled his arms around her shoulders in a slow action that was nothing short of pure male possessiveness. Nothing could hurt her here, except perhaps the man who seemed to want so badly to protect her.

'I won't do it again. Unless…'

'Unless nothing. Or I'll take you home and lock you in your room.' His eyes were glistening in the half-light.

'Oh, yeah?'

'Think I wouldn't?'

'You might try.' He might be heavier than her and a great deal stronger, but there was no question who had the upper hand here. One move from her, one word, and he'd back off.

She reached towards him, her fingers brushing the front of his shirt, and the light in his eyes turned from humour to dead seriousness. 'I've already crossed this line once, Sara, and I've been thinking about it ever since.'

'Me too.' If he didn't kiss her now, she was going to have to kiss him. And she wanted more than anything for him to make the first move.

His lips touched hers, brushing them lightly. He tasted and then he took, and then came back for a second helping.

'I want more than this.' The finger that traced the line of her jaw told her exactly what he wanted. It was almost painful, that slow arc of desire, which burned through her with nowhere to go. Nothing to slake the heat that it produced.

'I…I want…' She wanted what she couldn't have. Long nights alone with Reece. Time to work through the attraction that flared between them, explore it, let it lead them wherever it was going to. Instead, she had less than two weeks, and that wasn't even close to being enough.

She could have listened to the voice of reason, but right now reason didn't seem to have much of a point to make. Reece was hers for the taking. All she had to do… She knew exactly what she had to do.

'No promises, Reece. I can't make any promises, you know that.'

'I know. Neither can I.' He chuckled quietly. 'Maybe just one.'

'Which one would that be?'

'Don't you know?' He backed her against the car, lifting her off her feet, his hands splayed around the seat of her jeans, supporting her weight. Tonight he was all hers, and he wouldn't disappoint her.

'I know. Kiss me again.'

'Thought you'd never ask.'

He kissed her as if all the hunger that had been building between them, all the uncertainties of the last few days could be set to rest by just this one kiss.

They couldn't, though, and she wanted more. Here by the roadside, on the damp grass, on the back seat of the car, she didn't care. She just wanted Reece. 'I don't suppose you have a condom in your car.' It seemed a reasonable enough request—he seemed to be able to produce almost everything else from the glove compartment, or under the seats, or from the capacious boot.

'Nope.' He didn't even pause for thought, and Sara suspected that even if he did, he wasn't about to use it here. 'Going to have to wait.' He kissed her again and all rational thought melted in the heat of his desire.

'Don't know if I can.'

'You can.' His hand found her breast, brushing it lightly

through her clothes. Closing around it, his mouth forming words of approval against hers as he explored its shape and feel. 'A short drive between the starter and the main course only makes you hungrier.'

It was *not* a short drive home, even though Reece was a lot heavier on the accelerator than normal. But driving with him in the darkness, the companionable silence hanging between them softened her hunger for him, turning it from a 'take me now or else' thing into something that suffused her mind as well as her body. Something that took its time, waiting, trembling at the thought of what might happen next, at the same time as revelling in it.

Reece skidded into the driveway and came to a halt. No time to park the SUV neatly alongside the house. No time for second thoughts but, then, Sara had none.

Reece hustled her into the house and switched on the hall light. He'd already pulled his shirt over his head, and his mud-caked boots had been left behind on the porch, next to Sara's. 'Let me see you, beautiful.'

'Hmm. You may have to catch me first.' She broke free of him, dancing backwards along the hallway, peeling off her sweater as she went and dropping it onto the floor.

'So it's like that, is it?'

'Yep…' Sara turned and darted away from him as he made a lunge in her direction. She sped into the kitchen and then doubled back when he blocked the entrance, ducking under the breakfast bar. By the time she had made the lounge and done a couple of turns around the sofa, they were both laughing. 'Slow, Reece. You're too slow.'

He vaulted over the sofa and grabbed her, in a cross between an embrace and a rugby tackle. 'Now who's slow? Ouch… No, honey, not the face.' Sara's arms were flailing, reaching for some kind of hold, and she had caught him square on the jaw with her elbow.

Before she could breathe, he had her on her down on the sofa, spread out beneath him, her arms pinned above her head. A grin curled his lips as slowly he started to unbutton her blouse with his free hand. She wriggled in his grasp, squealing with laughter, and he quieted her with kisses.

'You too.' She wanted him out of his clothes.

'Yeah?' He released her hands, pulling her blouse off. 'You've got a bit of catching up to do first.' One hand reached behind her back and before she knew it he'd got the catch on her bra undone.

'Hmm. Very impressive. Where did you learn to do that?' She slipped out of it, and his gasp of pleasure made her shiver.

'Sleight of hand. I can do magic, remember?' He was trailing his fingertips across the soft skin of her stomach.

'So you can.' Sara gave herself over to his caress. He wanted to see and touch and kiss then touch again. Gently he pulled off her muddy jeans and then gathered her up in his arms, to carry her through to the bathroom. He turned on the shower.

'Reece. Reece, wait.'

She pulled at the button of his jeans, snapping it open, and he grinned. Tugged the zipper and slid the fabric down over his hips, and he groaned at the touch of her fingers. Tonight that golden body was all hers.

He kept her under the shower just long enough to wash off the mud and sweat from the evening. Reece wanted to be clean for her, to do this properly, but he knew that they had to do it now. Even a moment lost was a moment that they'd never have again. He lifted her up, carrying her through to the bedroom, and she laughed with delight, wrapping her legs around his waist and kissing him so hard that he lost his balance and they crashed down onto the bed together, his arms only just breaking his fall in time so he didn't crush her.

'Now. Now.' Her body was urgent beneath his. Soft and giving, but insistent beyond all thought of resisting her. Trembling, he moved one hand down, between their bodies, to find out whether she really meant it and found that she did.

'Wait.' He would show her who was the stronger. He kissed her, nuzzling at her neck and breasts, and she cried out with frustration. Arched beneath him, her body was begging for his.

He'd reckoned on having the willpower to take it slowly, but he'd reckoned wrongly. When she cried out for him, he couldn't wait any longer. There was one short moment of stillness when he knew that this was the only place in the world that he was supposed to be, and then she choked out his name and pulled him with her into a place where thought and will had no say in the matter.

Reece tried to gather his thoughts, tried to give a name to what had just happened between them. It was no good. He kissed her flushed cheek and she nuzzled against him. The smell of her sweat was intoxicating. The feel of her skin. There was no name for this feeling. His body knew, but his mind had temporarily given up on him.

He folded her in his arms, feeling her heart beat against his chest. 'Sara...I'm sorry.'

'What?' She pulled back from him suddenly, and he thought he saw her eyes glisten with sudden tears. 'What for?'

'I meant to...' Dammit there was no way of putting this tactfully. No way that he could think of, anyway. 'I meant to go a little slower.'

'Oh. I thought you meant...' She dismissed whatever

she had thought as if it didn't matter, and grinned at him. 'Any slower and you would have killed me.' She wrapped her arms around his neck, kissing him. Her kiss told him everything, more than her words, and the warmth of sudden and complete happiness tore a chuckle from his throat.

'Maybe next time.'

'Next time?' Her fingers trailed across his skin, wandering playfully. 'There's going to be a next time, is there?'

'Sooner than you think if you keep doing that.'

CHAPTER NINE

REECE had opened the sliding doors that led onto the veranda, and the warm night breeze had played over their bodies as they'd made love, slept and then made love again. As dawn broke, he lifted her onto his lap, face to face, supporting her back with one arm.

'Do you think we made that?' Light was slanting across the bed, turning his skin from russet to gold.

'The sunrise?' He thought for a moment. 'Why, do you think it'll stop if we do?'

'Maybe. Do you want to risk it?'

He shook his head, laughing. 'Don't think we should.' His fingers found the nape of her neck, caressing its curve. 'Did I mention that you have excellent postural alignment?' He nuzzled her neck, kissing it, while his fingers trailed down her spine. 'Very sexy.'

'No. Think you left that out.'

'Hmm. Remiss of me.' His hand swept the length of her back, cupping her head, and Sara shivered at the sensation. 'Little bit of tension. Just here.' He kissed her shoulder.

'Really?' Sara reckoned that every single muscle in her body had quivered with tension and then relaxed under his caress at some point during the night. If he'd missed one, it certainly hadn't been for want of trying.

'Yeah. Here, let me…' His fingers found the knots in her shoulders and started to work at them. 'How's that?'

'Little bit more. I don't think you've quite reduced me to jelly yet.'

He grinned. 'Give me a chance.' He dug his thumbs in, and Sara shuddered.

'Yeah. That's good.' She wrapped her arms around his neck. 'You have very talented hands.'

'My hands thank you. If there's anything they can do for you, they'd like you to feel free to ask.' He curled his arms around her, the warmth of his body making her shiver.

'Just that. I like that.' Kissing him was almost automatic. Her lips seemed to form in the shape of a kiss of their own accord, against whatever part of his skin was closest. 'What do you like?'

'Didn't I tell you?'

'Tell me again.'

He chuckled, lazily. 'I love to feel you come. It's like…' He nuzzled close, whispering in her ear.

Sara giggled. 'It is not.'

'It is. Can't think of another way to describe it. What, you don't like the idea of warm honey…?'

'Bit messy.'

'Uhuh. So beautiful and yet so practical.' His teeth nipped her ear wickedly. 'You want to let me feel that again?'

'There's no honey in the cupboard. I didn't know you liked it.'

'Ah. Literal as well. You're sweet enough…'

Words gave way to thought, and thought to action. Sara had not thought that she had any more to give, but somehow, from somewhere, it seemed that she did. His slow hands, those soft lips found a wellspring of feeling locked deep inside, and coaxed it gently to the surface.

He took his time. Advancing slowly and then retreating. Surrounding her with warmth and cutting off every retreat until there was nothing in her world but him. When he finally coaxed her body into surrendering to him, it was more complete than she could ever have imagined. Devastating in its intensity, demolishing everything and filling her up again with the sweetest sensations.

She turned her face from him. He mustn't see.

'Hey. Hey, what's this?' With astonishing alacrity, he seemed to snap out of the post-coital blur that had gripped him.

'Nothing. Nothing.'

'It's okay. Whatever it is…'

It wasn't okay at all. In Sara's experience the one thing most likely to make a man feel awkward was a woman's tears. And crying after sex definitely wasn't a good look. She rolled away from him, onto her side, screwing her eyes shut in an effort to stem the tears.

She felt him kiss her cheek. 'You could share it with me, you know.'

'Share what?' She twined her fingers with his, pulling them to her lips and kissing them in a desperate attempt to convince him that everything was all right.

'That I'm so damn good in bed that it brings tears to your eyes.'

She couldn't help laughing. It seemed that all her emotions had suddenly escaped from lockdown and were bubbling in her chest, ready to break free at the slightest thing. 'Perhaps that's it.'

'Ah. Knew it.' He pulled her close, and she turned towards him, snuggling into his chest. 'I'm not afraid of your tears, you know. You've been strong for so long now, you should give yourself a break and just let go for once.'

There actually wasn't much choice about it. Her chest

was heaving now, trying to gasp out the sobs, but they wouldn't come. Then the dam broke, and she cried. It seemed like the first time in years that she'd actually sobbed her heart out, and it probably was.

Whether by accident or design, he'd unerringly found the source of that throbbing ache, which seemed to follow her around wherever she went. 'I don't want to be strong, Reece. Just for one day, I want to be…' She couldn't say it. Just for one day, she wanted to be the one who was nurtured and cared for.

'Make it today.'

'I can't…' Gran still needed her. She couldn't just fall apart and forget that.

'Why not? You've got to put it down some time. Last night, I thought you were a strong, beautiful woman…'

'Guess I've disabused you of that notion, then.' She quirked her lips downwards. Red eyed and sobbing wasn't her best look.

'Yes, you have. You're a strong, beautiful woman, who has joy and passion and who wants to break free.'

She'd done that last night when she'd fallen apart in his arms. Sara wondered whether he knew it or not. 'Last night was… I loved it, Reece. Every minute of it.'

'Yeah. Me too. And I love it that you couldn't hide your tears from me.' He grinned at her. 'And today is officially your day off. You get to sleep late, and I'll make breakfast.'

He would take no arguments. And when he wrapped her in his arms, drawing the sheet over her, she couldn't think of any place she'd rather be. Or when she'd felt so relaxed. Serene almost. Like the calm after the storm. She began to float, and then drifted into a deep, dreamless sleep.

When she woke again it was almost lunchtime. The smell of fresh coffee and bacon drifted in from the kitchen, along with the sound of Reece whistling tunelessly.

She lay on her back, smiling. The sweet scent of their lovemaking was still on her body, and when she reached out she could still feel the warmth under her fingertips where he had lain beside her.

'What are you doing?' she shouted through to the kitchen. Sara didn't want to move just yet.

'None of your business.' His head popped around the doorway.

'Oh. Okay.' She shrugged lazily.

'That's the spirit. Just keep that up, and let me take care of you today.'

Warmth enveloped her, and she stretched languorously. 'So you're in charge, are you?'

'Yep. And don't forget it.' He ducked as Sara threw a pillow at him, and she heard his chuckle fading along the hall.

She'd demolished breakfast, and Reece had run her a bath. Sara added something from one of the bottles of toiletries that Kath had left and then slipped into the scented water. Twenty minutes later, after he had showered, dressed and washed up the breakfast things, she was still there, and he figured that must be a good sign. Up till now the only time she'd stayed still and relaxed for as much as twenty minutes had been when she'd been asleep.

'I called Simon.'

'Yeah?' She stretched lazily. 'Suppose we'd better get going.'

'No need. He's got some other people visiting this afternoon, and he suggested that you come in tomorrow.'

She pointed her finger at him, narrowing her eyes. 'No, he didn't.'

Reece shrugged. She was too quick for him, and he supposed he'd better just accept it. 'No. Actually, he didn't.

But he does have some other people going to see him this afternoon...'

'After you called them, no doubt.'

'After I called them, if you're going to split hairs, and Simon says that you're to take a break.'

'You told him I needed a break, did you?'

'No, I told him that you'd kept me up all night, leading me astray.'

'I led *you* astray!' She was laughing now, her grey eyes bright and full of zest for life. 'You were the one doing the leading, I'll have you know.'

He loved it that she seemed so free, so happy. And Reece allowed himself the delicious thought that it was, partly at least, his doing. 'Since you're so good at tagging along, how about getting out of that bath and coming to the beach with me?'

She was on her feet in a second, the water slopping over the rim of the bath and onto his shoes. 'The beach! I haven't been to the beach yet, and I've been wanting to go.'

'The beach it is, then.'

True to form, Reece didn't take her to just any old beach. He'd picked the exact one he wanted and drove for miles, past a selection of other beaches, before he reached a wide swathe of sand, turquoise ocean crashing onto the shore. They walked a little way, clambering over the rocks, until they reached a sheltered cove, where they could swim and soak up the sun.

They found a place to eat later then drove home. As the sun fell in the sky, he made love to her again, tenderly marking the end of this perfect day. One moment. One day that she could catch and keep, through all the others that lay ahead.

CHAPTER TEN

'So what's on the itincrary tonight, then, sis?' Simon grinned at Sara.

'Tonight I'm staying in Melbourne and we're going for a meal.' Maybe she and Reece would stop off at the beach on the way home, as they'd done last night. Lie flat on their backs, hand in hand, watching the stars. She couldn't get enough of the stars here, so bright in the night sky.

'I guess I'll be breaking the party up when I get out of here in a couple of days, then.' Simon's steady eyes left Sara in no doubt that he was only half joking.

'What party?' Did that sound like a suitable response? Something that someone who had definitely not been partying every night for the last four days might say?

'You tell me.'

It was uncomfortable sometimes, having an older brother. Sara had forgotten all about that, but she was fast becoming reacquainted with the feeling. 'If you mean Reece and me...'

'I doubt that Trader's found himself a lady friend.'

The old anger tasted bitter. Sara tried the breathing thing, taught to her by one of her girlfriends, who had learned it from her relationship counsellor, and yet again it failed to work. 'Reece was a friend when I needed one.'

'Ouch.'

'I don't mean it like that, Simon.' Sara forgot the breathing and decided that honesty was the best policy. 'Just because you're my brother, you don't get to tell me what to do. Or vet my friends, for that matter.' She grinned at him. 'What you do get to do is to be there for me. Be happy for me when things work out, and pick up the pieces when it all goes south.'

'Pretty raw deal, if you ask me.' The brother that Sara remembered was still there. The one who knew her, and understood that she needed to draw the line somewhere.

'Yeah. Want the job?'

'I'll think about it.'

They were getting there. The realisation that they'd come a long way but still had a way to go felt much more healthy than glossing over things. 'Nothing's perfect, you know.'

Simon laughed. 'I thought you were, sis.'

'I might be the exception to that rule.'

'You just might.' Simon paused, running his finger idly up the side of the walking frame that stood next to his chair. Sara knew that motion.

'What? Spit it out.'

'I thought I didn't get to say…'

'You get to say. I just don't have to listen if I don't want to.'

'Right.' Simon rolled his eyes. 'You know Mum was difficult to live with at best.'

'I know.'

'And we both dealt with it differently.'

'Yeah. We did.'

'Then let me be the eldest for a minute here.' Simon's face—so like her own, according to all the nurses—became earnest. 'If a girl…woman…like you happened to get involved with a guy like Reece, you know what I'd say to him?'

'Hypothetically speaking?'

'Naturally. If this hypothetical couple happened to become hypothetically involved, then I'd tell him to watch out...'

Sara's eyebrows shot up. 'Him? Thanks for that thought.'

'Because my sister's a fabulous, intelligent, beautiful woman, but she draws lines around herself. She's done it ever since she was a kid. Mum never got to you the way she did to me because you had your own internal world where you kept yourself safe from her.'

'Have you been reading that stack of women's magazines in the patients' lounge again?' Okay, so she'd wanted honesty. Just not this kind.

'I'm serious, Sara.' There was a hurt look in his eyes.

'I know. I'm sorry. Mum didn't take you seriously, did she?'

'No, not particularly. But that's for another day. Today...' He shrugged. 'I'm taking Reece up on his offer to stay at his place for a while, just until I'm on my feet and I can drive again. I know I can't manage on my own at home at the moment.'

'And you just wanted to say?' Sara tipped her head towards his, in a remembrance of the way that he'd comforted her when she'd been little.

'I just wanted to say that Reece is a nice guy. If you like him, this is not the time to be falling for Mum's propaganda.'

If only it was that easy. The cold, hard truth suddenly reared up, slapping Sara in the face. She'd been forgetting about all of the tomorrows and just concentrating on her todays with Reece, but that couldn't last for ever. 'It's not that easy.'

'No?' Simon seemed disappointed. 'I thought you might say that. Any particular way that you can think of to make it easier?'

'Don't think so.'

'Right.' Simon seemed lost in thought. Maybe this was the time to tell him about Gran. Maybe not. She'd decided not to tell him just yet, and she shouldn't just blurt it out on the spur of the moment. She should think about it.

'Hey.' She leaned forward, taking Simon's hand. 'Thanks for looking out for me, big brother.'

She could see how much it meant to him. He'd not been her big brother for a long time now. 'Well, don't leave it all to me. Try looking out for yourself for once.'

In another life, maybe. Another time. 'I always do.'

Simon looked at her, narrowing his eyes. 'Sure you do. Whatever made me think otherwise?'

The search for some kind of suitable reply was abruptly halted as Reece appeared in the doorway. 'Not interrupting anything, am I?' He must have seen the look on Simon's face.

'No,' Sara got in before Simon could open his mouth. 'Where have you been?'

Out of the frying pan and into the fire. Sara didn't want either Simon or Reece to know that she'd noticed that Reece was late and that she'd been mentally counting the minutes for the last half an hour. Reece didn't seem to mind, and she kept her eyes on him, away from the *I told you so* look that Simon might be giving her.

'Just helping out with the preparations for the open day tomorrow at the surgery. Mary has a virus and I've managed to convince her that she's not well enough to be serving tea tomorrow, so we're trying to find someone else.'

'Sara can do it.' Simon had clearly not yet quite got the hang of when a brother ought to keep quiet.

'You'll be here, though, won't you?' At least Reece appeared to be offering her a choice in the matter.

'Not necessarily,' Simon cut in again. 'Maggie was going to come in over the weekend. I'll give her a call and tell her tomorrow afternoon would be good.'

'Maggie? I thought...' Reece tailed off abruptly. Obviously wondering whether Simon's on-off girlfriend had featured in Sara's conversations with her brother yet.

'You said that it was all over between you and Maggie.' Sara turned on her brother.

'Yeah, that's what I thought too. Apparently not.' Simon made a lunge for the table beside his hospital bed, wincing as he did so, and his phone clattered to the floor.

Sara picked it up and handed it to him. 'You could have just asked for it.'

'Spoils all the fun. Anyway, the physio said that I needed to establish my limits in the short term.'

'Yeah, that means doing what you can do, not what you want to do. There's a difference.' Reece glared at Simon.

'She said I should sit up for a few hours each day. And she works me pretty hard when she comes to see me...'

'That's because it's her job and she knows what she's doing.' Reece's eyes softened. 'Your job is to do as you're told.'

In the limited time that she'd seen the two of them together, Sara had already noticed an element of the big brother in Reece's relationship with Simon. To an outsider, Simon seemed the more settled of the two, with a house and a thriving architectural practice. But it was Reece who stepped in and called the shots when the going got tough.

Simon capitulated with a shrug and a grin. Maybe, one day, she'd have that kind of relationship with her brother. Until then they'd just fight things out between them, each trying to go their own way.

Simon was dialling, a smile on his face, and Reece rolled his eyes. 'I can't keep up with those two.' The words, sotto voce, were almost whispered in her ear, while Simon talked animatedly on the phone.

'Is she…?' She hated having to ask, and suddenly resented Reece for knowing Maggie when she didn't.

'Maggie's great. You'd like her. I'll get her to come over as soon as Simon gets home, and we can all have a meal together.'

'Thanks. I'd like that.'

Reece nodded and caught Simon's attention. 'Give Maggie my love. Tell her that she's to come over next week, before Sara goes back home.'

'Sure.' Simon spoke into the phone. 'You heard that?' He nodded, listening to the voice on the other end of the line. 'She says what about Tuesday?'

'That's good for me. I'm away on Monday night, with the travelling clinic, but I'll be back by Tuesday afternoon.' Reece looked at Sara and she nodded. He'd seen the problem and fixed it straight away. No messing around or arguments, and everyone seemed to be happy.

'Right.' Simon said goodbye, promising to call later, and laid the phone on his lap. 'So Maggie's coming over tomorrow afternoon, and Reece has his tea lady.' He gave Sara a wink.

'Hardly.' Reece shook his head. 'If you want to come along tomorrow, I could do with a bit of help with my first-aid demos. We can get someone else to make the tea.'

'Are you sure? I don't mind making tea.' From what Reece had said, the day was designed to combine some basic health education with family activities, and it sounded as if it was going to be fun. Sara had been thinking about popping in before going to see Simon in the afternoon.

'Someone will step up for that. I can use your qualifications elsewhere.' He winked at her.

'That's settled, then.' Now that Simon had got an outcome that he was happy with, he seemed to be tiring. 'So where are you going to eat, then? Sara's all dressed up for somewhere nice, so I hope you're not going to take her for a burger, mate.' Simon ignored the look that Sara flashed at him.

'Chinatown to eat, and then I thought we could go for a walk.' Reece grinned. 'Show Sara some more of the city by night.'

'Sounds great.' Simon picked up the nurse's call button pointedly. 'Think I'll get back to bed and watch a bit of TV. I'll call someone to help me.'

'You do that.' Reece made for the door, shaking his head.

By the time Sara arrived at the surgery, the open day was in full swing. Reece had got up so early that she'd hardly registered his going, and she'd busied herself around the house for a while, before taking Trader for a long jog. After hesitating over what to wear, she had settled for a pair of loose linen trousers and a pretty white top, which looked vaguely professional without being out of place on a casual fun day.

There was plenty of room for a marquee, which had been erected beside the main building, and several other smaller canopies, which shaded the refreshments table staffed by a horde of very capable-looking women and the children's face painting stand. The sun was out, and it seemed that half the population of the surrounding area had turned up, attracted by the prospect of supervised games for the children and a sociable afternoon for adults.

Sara made for the marquee and slipped inside. Working her way past the clusters of people, responding awkwardly as total strangers smiled and said hello, she caught sight of Reece.

He had obviously not worried too much about looking professional. Even in the unlikely get-up of a top hat and a bright waistcoat, he looked deliciously handsome, like a travelling showman who had just happened on the gathering and decided to join in. He was working the crowd like a professional, and Sara saw him bend and produce what looked like a chocolate coin from the ear of a solemn youngster.

'Hey!' He'd caught sight of her, and was trying to extricate himself from the group of children that had formed around him, but they wouldn't let him go.

'Reece.' Sara made her way towards him. 'What are you doing?'

It was pretty obvious what he was doing. None of the children gathered around him were likely to be afraid of going to the doctor any time soon.

'Mr Marvo, if you don't mind.' His eyes were shining and he was grinning broadly.

'I thought you were meant to be doing first-aid demonstrations.' Sara smiled back at him across the heads of the children.

'That's later. I get to transform magically into Dr Fletcher at about three o'clock. In the meantime...' He reached into a cardboard box behind him, which had been painted black and covered in silver stars, and pulled out a brightly coloured scarf, which he draped around her shoulders, and a flat black disc. With a quick flick of his wrist, it became a second top hat, which he offered theatrically to Sara. 'Would you do me the honour of being my assistant?'

The children chorused a 'Yes!' and Sara gave in.

'Just as long as you're not going to saw me in half.'

Reece chuckled. 'Nah. Although it's a thought. I could

stitch you back together later on as part of my first-aid demo.' He put the hat on her head, adjusting it slightly to what felt like a jaunty angle.

'Is she Mrs Marvo?' the solemn child piped up.

Reece hesitated for a moment, and then his mouth curved in a smile that wasn't all for the children. 'Yep. Now, let's see if we can find a magic wand, shall we?'

CHAPTER ELEVEN

HE'D sprinkled stars, produced a whole truckload of chocolate coins, which had been eaten just as quickly as they had appeared, and made sure that he'd greeted and talked to every family who arrived in the tent. His hat now resided on the head of a three-year-old boy, who had fallen over and then forgotten his tears as Reece had picked him up and produced yet another coin from nowhere.

'What do you think?' For a moment he was free of the demands of the children and he gave that moment to Sara.

'It's great. Everyone seems to be having a good time.' They were strolling together around the open space behind the marquee, which had been set aside for organised games for the children, in the hope that they would let off a little steam before the first-aid demonstrations.

He nodded. 'Yeah. The practice manager organises this every year. We're a part of a community here, and those ties are very important to the practice.'

'Not to you, though?' Reece had already talked about his plans for the future, and even though they seemed to change on an almost daily basis, the one consistent thread was that he would be moving on some time soon.

'Yeah, they're important to me.' He shrugged. 'Everywhere has its communities.'

She shouldn't care about this. She would be leaving

soon. She was the one who was moving on, not him. Somehow it would have made it easier to leave and wish him well if she had somewhere she could visualise him when she got back home.

'Don't you ever feel that you want to settle down, though? Be with people you've known all your life?'

'I haven't known anyone my whole life. Apart from Kath.' He jogged a couple of steps to retrieve a ball that had whizzed in their direction and lobbed it back towards the boy who was chasing it.

He made friends easily, fitted in so seamlessly everywhere, that it seemed as if he'd been there for ever. But Reece's real loyalty was reserved for a very select few. Kath. The brother he'd lost. Maybe Simon and a few others. Sara didn't want to think about which category she fitted into. It didn't matter, anyway.

'Your father—where is he?'

'Doing the rounds in Western Australia. Got married again last year.' Reece shrugged. 'His fourth wife.'

Sara didn't quite know how to react to that. Her mother had scarcely even allowed a man into the house after her father had left, let alone approved of one, so she'd never had the opportunity to find out how she would feel about having a stepfather. 'Did you go to the wedding?'

He grinned. 'Of course. Kath and I flew up there for the week. It was a good time.' He gave her a quizzical look. 'My dad's a law unto himself. He's a nice guy and he was a great dad when he was around, but he's never going to be the one who's there for either Kath or me. We've both learned to accept that.'

Perhaps that's what she should do with Simon. 'Do you think…Simon…?'

'No.' He rounded on her with an intensity that almost made her jump. 'Simon's not like that at all. You and he have been through a difficult time, and he's not always been able to be there for you, but in his heart that's what he wants.'

'You know that?'

'I know it. Don't ever doubt it, Sara. You both just need a bit of time to learn to trust each other again.'

He seemed so sure. Almost committed to it, as if it was a cause that he needed to fight for, right there along with her. She trusted Reece's judgement and he was no liar.

'Hmm. I guess I wouldn't be here if I didn't believe you.'

'Guess you wouldn't.' He leaned over, his lips close to her ear. 'I'm glad you are, though. As assistants go, you're by far the most beautiful I've ever seen.'

Sara dug her finger surreptitiously into his ribs. 'Watch it, Marvo. I've heard all about you magicians. All that sleight of hand doesn't fool me.'

'Not what you said last night.' He was so close. She could smell his scent, almost feel his hands on her body. Suddenly she was engulfed in the pure, sweet sensation of just wanting him. 'You know that top hat really suits you. I could…' He left the thought unspoken, trailing his finger down her spine.

'Don't.' Her knees were beginning to wobble, and she didn't want to have to cling to him for support, not in front of all these people. Maybe Simon was right. Maybe she did put people in boxes. If that was so, then Reece was in a dark, velvet-lined box, which emitted sunshine every time she opened it. 'Not until later, anyway.'

He grinned. 'Is that a promise?'

She could make that promise. For tonight, at least. 'Yes. It's a promise.'

She was still trembling when Reece seated her beside him and started the first-aid demonstration. Thankfully, he was the one who knew most about suncreams, sunburn and sunstroke, and the first ten minutes required no input from her. By the time he'd moved from bites and stings to cuts, she was feeling a little more in control of herself, and she demonstrated the pressure required to stem bleeding, almost indifferent to his touch.

Their audience watched politely, but question time revealed that there was an appetite for something more dramatic. Broken bones, choking, heart attacks and drug overdoses, and then the fifty-thousand-dollar question.

'What if someone's not breathing?'

Reece called a halt. 'Okay, all of these things are serious medical conditions, and the first thing you need to do is to call for help. Calling the emergency services is the most important thing you can do and the best way to help anyone who's in any of those situations.'

'But isn't there something that you can do in the meantime?' A woman with a young child on her lap spoke up.

'Yes, there is. And a first-aid course with a registered provider will teach you exactly what you should do.' He picked up a clipboard from the table next to him. 'You can sign up for a course here. If everyone in this community attends a course then it's not a matter of *if* someone saves a life, it's *when.*'

A buzz ran around the audience, and Reece took the opportunity of passing the clipboard and a pen to someone in the front row. It began to circulate, gathering names as it went.

'What do these courses cover?' A question from the back.

Reece held up a pile of leaflets. 'It's all on here. Some guidance on simple first aid and details of what the course will teach you.' A grin spread across his face. 'And since we have a paramedic here, I guess that she can show you some of the basic steps better than I can.'

A couple of children in the front row began to clap, and Sara shot Reece a withering look, which he ignored. 'For the purposes of this demonstration, I'm going to be the victim...' he paused theatrically to make the most of the laughter '...I mean, the patient.' Before Sara could protest he was on the floor at her feet.

She glared down at him, folding her arms, and Reece propped himself up on one elbow, addressing the audience. 'Now, the first thing to do is to get help. Call for an ambulance, and when medical personnel arrive, you should let them take over.'

The temptation to let him just lie there and see how long he could hold his breath was almost overwhelming. On the other hand, 30 people were waiting to see what she was going to do next. 'Right, well, obviously, if the patient's talking then he's probably breathing.' She got on her knees, and pushed him back down onto the floor.

A shimmer of laughter ran around the audience. That was okay. If they laughed about it, they'd remember it. If they remembered it, someone might be in the position to save a life one day. 'Follow the instructions on the leaflet.' Sara went through each of the numbered points in turn, rolling Reece into the recovery position and pretending to clear his mouth.

'Now, if the patient still isn't breathing you can try this simple technique. Lace your fingers together like this...' Sara held her hands up for everyone to see '...and apply pressure here.' She laid her hands on Reece's chest.

'Not too high, or you'll crush the windpipe. Right on the...' Reece fell silent, gasping as Sara pushed hard, expelling all the air from his lungs.

'You see what that does?'

'Think I'll try that on my husband.' A voice came from the back of the group and everyone laughed.

'Yeah, it's useful for that too.' Sara grinned. 'Now, let's go through the checklist again…'

Reece woke the next morning, completely satisfied. The open day had gone well, Sara had obviously enjoyed herself and she was in his arms, still fast asleep. Last night he'd learned that sleeping with a woman wasn't just a euphemism for making love. Sleeping with someone had a whole wealth of meaning all on its own.

They'd got home late, both exhausted from clearing up after the surgery had finally closed its doors to visitors for the day. They'd stripped off their clothes and fallen into bed. He'd curled his body around hers, pulling her close, no hesitation in touching, even if it wasn't for sex. And they'd stayed close all night, as if that was the way that they were meant to be, and everything was all right with the world.

'Hey, you.'

'Hmm?' She shifted slightly in his arms, still half-asleep.

'Are you awake?'

'No.' She pulled his arm around her, cradling his hand in hers against her belly. 'Still dreaming.'

Longing gripped him, squeezing so hard that he almost cried out. He wanted in on those dreams of hers. Wanted to be a part of her, waking and sleeping. His fingers slid downwards, his whole body tense now, gauging her reaction. One sign from her and he'd stop.

She sighed and he felt her body relax against his. Almost melting into him, as if it were possible for the liquid sunlight spilling into the room to somehow fuse them together in its touch.

His other hand cupped her breast and she stretched in his arms, like a cat luxuriating in the heat of the sun. 'That's nice.'

Her speech was still slurred from sleep and she seemed

to be making no effort to come to. The realisation hit Reece
that she didn't want to wake up just yet. Did she really trust
him that much?

'Shh, sweetheart.' He dropped a kiss on her neck. 'You
don't need to do anything. Just let me touch you.'

Her soft, sleepy laugh seemed to be laced with the music
of bells. 'Hmm. Don't stop, then.'

Reece felt something prick at the side of his eyes. Not
tears. Surely not. He dismissed the thought and concentrated on the matter in hand. He knew the caresses that
would send pleasure rolling through her, the ones that
would make her sigh, and those that would make her
scream. She'd already given herself to him, trusting him
to do this right, and all he wanted to do was to show her
that she hadn't been mistaken.

Slowly, gently, he made his move. Waited until each
breath was a sigh and then took the pace up a notch. She
squeezed her eyes shut, fingers reaching for something
to grip tight and latching onto the sheet that still covered
them.

It was all for her. Her submission had turned him into
her slave and everything he did was for her pleasure.
Watching for each twitch of the muscle at the side of her
face. Listening for each sigh, gauging whether it was deeper
than the last.

Rolling her over onto her back, he pulled the sheet away
from her. Tasted her sweat. Felt her shiver as his breath
cooled and then reheated her skin. Found that the scent of
her arousal seemed to change, grow sweeter, the further
he pushed her.

'Reece.' Her hands were fluttering across his back now.
'Reece, please.'

'Do you trust me?' He wanted to hear her say it, more
than anything in the world, apart from one thing. They'd

promised not to talk about love, and he wouldn't break that vow now.

'I trust you.' Her words sent him spinning, light-headed, into a new world of desire.

'Then let me make love to you.'

'Please...yes...'

Reece had always reckoned himself a considerate lover, but this was something different. This complete detachment from his own pleasure, his only thought being for hers. 'I can't breathe without you, Sara.'

'You don't have to.' She seemed to know that she had broken his will completely. 'Make love to me and I'll breathe for both of us.'

He had a true heart, and a free and giving spirit. Sara didn't just trust him, she loved him as well. But that wasn't any part of the bargain. Love meant promises and there was only one promise that she could make to Reece. When the time came she would let him go. Not try to drag him into her life, her responsibilities.

They lay on their backs, watching the line of sunlight move across the ceiling.

'Probably about time for breakfast.' Sara had discovered that this was the perfect way to start any day. Waking up with Reece. Feeling him touch her. Showering together and then making breakfast.

'Yeah.' He rolled over, propping himself on his elbows. 'I love sex in the morning.'

She dug her fingers into his ribs. 'I noticed.'

He seemed to be weighing something up. 'And in the evening.'

'Noticed that too. How are you with lunchtime?'

'Lunchtime? Haven't tried that yet.'

Sara grinned. She'd bet that he had, but it was nice to

think that he was suspending judgement until they'd done that together. 'Only about four hours to go.'

He grinned. 'Yeah. I could take you down to the beach, swim a little, and we could give it a go.'

'Oh, and we can find a deserted beach on a Sunday in the middle of summer?'

'Good point. I'll take you up into the mountains, then. Or out into the desert and build a shelter for you. Wait until the sun hits the top of the sky and then drag you into my lair.'

'And you'll do all this by noon, will you?'

He laughed. 'Another day, maybe.'

There weren't many more days left. Simon was going to be out of hospital tomorrow. And she was going home next weekend. Somehow when Sara had been able to tell herself that there was more than a week to go, it had seemed like for ever. This time next week she'd be on a plane, on her way home.

There were days, though. Today and then five whole days. 'Okay. What do you say we go to the beach anyway? Can we find one where we're allowed to let Trader off the lead?'

'Yeah, sure. Let's do that.'

Reece had been wondering about the best time to ask. About how to ask. Whether to mention it casually over a meal some time, as if the idea had just occurred to him and he hadn't been obsessing over it for days now, or whether to get her somewhere quiet, where they could discuss things properly.

The morning's lovemaking had been more than special, it had been somehow transforming. And if he still couldn't bring himself to contemplate the idea of knowing exactly where he'd be in a year's time, he couldn't contemplate knowing for sure that he and Sara would be apart either.

It was going to have to be the beach. They'd walked for miles and he'd chosen a secluded spot, where Trader could run free. Reece had spent half an hour spinning a ball as far as he could throw it, and then Trader had decided that was enough and had lain down at Sara's feet.

'There's something I wanted to ask you.'

'Yeah? Ask away.' She was watching the ocean, following each wave as it crashed against the shore then ran up the sand towards her.

'Would you...?' He chickened out. 'Do you like it here?'

'You know I do.' She turned to him, her short hair blowing in the breeze, her face tanned now from the sun. 'What's all this about?'

He had her attention now, and there was no going back. 'I thought that if you wanted to stay a little longer...until Simon's better maybe...then you could both stay on at my place, there's plenty of room.'

The light suddenly went out of her eyes. He'd messed this up. He should have told her straight away that *he* wanted her to stay. In Reece's experience, if you asked the wrong question then you seldom got the answer you wanted.

'I can't, Reece. I have to go home.' Her gaze fell from his face, dropping to her feet, where Trader lay, and he looked up at her, sensing that maybe he was the subject of the conversation.

Reece took a deep breath to steady his nerves. 'Sara, I want you to stay. I think...' This wasn't working either. 'You're the best thing that's happened to me in a long time, and I know that you feel it too. I want us both to have the chance to find out where that might lead.'

When she looked at him again, her eyes were full of tears. Reece hated seeing her cry, but maybe this time... Maybe this time it meant yes.

'We said no promises.'

'Right. And I'm not asking you to make any promises now. Just to maybe stay around a little longer. Take one day at a time.' One day at a time was the sum total of everything he knew how to give. And he'd give it willingly to her.

'I can't. I would if I could, but...' She trailed off, staring at the ocean.

Maybe he should have done this somewhere else. Somewhere where Trader and the broad horizon didn't have such a call on her attention. Reece caught her by the shoulders, twisting her around to make her face him. 'Sara...'

She faced him, her lips trembling. 'No. I can't. You don't understand.'

She was right about that, at least. The urge to promise her everything just to make her stay battled with the sure knowledge that he couldn't keep such a promise. 'Explain it to me, then.' If she told him that she didn't care for him then he'd know she was lying.

She looked at him, lips pressed together, eyes blazing behind the tears. If he turned away now and left it at that, Reece was under no illusions that she would never mention it again. He didn't give up so easily.

'Look, it's okay to say no, but at least give me a reason. I'll tell you now that I'm not going to stop asking, not until you do.'

She scrambled to her feet, calling Trader to heel, and starting to walk back along the track to the car. Reece wondered whether he should just let her go, give them both a chance to cool off a bit, and then got to his feet. Cooling off wasn't going to help. Nothing was going to make any difference, not until he got an answer.

Sara had known this was coming ever since this morning. How could he not have asked? And how could she have denied that being with him was the thing that she most wanted in the world?

'You could at least tell me what I've done wrong.' His voice hissed in her ear.

Typical! 'Stop it, Reece. Why does it have to be about you all the time? Can't you see any further than that?' Sara froze, stopping so suddenly that he almost bumped into her. Her mother's words had flown from her mouth before she'd had a chance to bite them back.

'I'm trying to. You're not giving me much help, though.'

'No... No, I'm sorry.' She made to start walking again but he caught her arm.

'So tell me. Is it that you don't care for me?' The look on her face told her that he didn't think that for a second, he was just goading her until she gave him an answer. He held her in his gaze for long moments while Trader circled patiently, waiting for them to finish and start moving again.

'Say it, Sara. All you have to do is say it, and I'll forget about this right now.'

She couldn't. Wouldn't.

'Say it.' His voice was gentler now. He knew. There was no point in saying it now, he'd never believe her.

'No. You can't make me say that.' Sara grabbed at the last remaining straw she had. 'No promises, Reece.'

'I made no promises to care for you, or to want you to stay. I didn't make any promises not to either. That's what it's like when you begin a relationship.'

'That's not what I meant.'

'I see that now. You'd already made a promise to leave.'

'Yes.'

'Who to?'

They'd been here before. Come round full circle and ended up with the same question. The one that Reece was always going to return to if she didn't tell him.

'I don't want you to tell Simon.'

A shadow fell over his face. 'I won't.'

He didn't need to promise. In any case, that word had already been used and misused enough between them, and Sara didn't want to mention it again.

'My gran. She's booked into a nursing home while I'm over here. The only way that she's getting out of there and back home is if I go back to London.'

'You look after your grandmother?' His face was grave. Concerned. It was okay, he didn't need to be. Sara didn't want his concern.

'Yes, she has a flat on the ground floor of my mother's house. She doesn't get about much these days. She's ninety.'

'And Simon doesn't know?'

He was just asking. Sara wondered why this felt like an interrogation and put it down to her own guilt. 'He never asked and I never said anything. He's had enough on his plate recently.'

'And you were afraid of what his reaction might be.'

Reece was good. Took the facts, wove motive around them and generally came up with the right answer. Sara wondered if he'd ever considered a career in intelligence. 'Yes, if you must know.' She started to walk. Somehow it was easier to do this when she wasn't rooted to the spot, staring up at his face. 'I made a decision that I'd stick with Gran and look after her, and I'm happy with that. I can't stay here.'

She didn't have Reece's gift for saying just exactly what she meant, but the message seemed to get through. He was walking beside her, thinking hard. Suddenly he seemed to come to a decision. 'I can't go with you, Sara. Not like that.'

'I know. I'd never ask you to.'

'Does this mean that we're done here?'

'Yeah. I guess it does.'

The walk back to the car was a blessing in disguise. Reece spun pretty much anything he could find along the way high into the air, keeping both Trader and himself busy and on the run. Sara took the time to compose herself, try to forget that she'd just refused what seemed like the offer of a lifetime.

It couldn't work. Tim had broken his promises to her and walked away unscathed, but that had been different. If Reece did that, it would destroy his integrity, and she couldn't take that away from him. She loved him too much to change him.

'Reece.' He'd managed to avoid any eye contact with her on the long walk back to the car, but it was best to deal with this now. Get it over with. 'I was thinking that I might spend some time back at Simon's place. Just a few days, to sort things out there for him.'

'I'd prefer it if you didn't.' He still couldn't quite meet her gaze. 'You know I have to go upcountry this week for a few days. I may need to extend the trip a little and Simon shouldn't be left alone at my place. Kath's back from holiday tomorrow and if there's anything you need...'

'There's nothing I need.' He was doing the decent thing. Or running away. Sara couldn't quite picture Reece running away from anything, but maybe she was deluding herself. Maybe her mother had been right about some things.

He opened the passenger door of the car for her, and she saw a flicker at the side of his face. Tension. Loss, maybe. A small curve of regret on his lips. Her mother had never met Reece, so how could she ever be right about him?

'It's the best thing all round. I'll leave this afternoon.'

'This afternoon? I thought you were going in the morning.' He'd said he would leave on Monday morning and be back on Tuesday evening, when he'd told her about the clinic that the doctors in the area staffed on a rotation basis.

'I have to start early. It would be a lot easier to drive up there this afternoon.'

He was leaving her. Sara wanted to cling to him, beg him to stay, but she didn't have a leg to stand on. How could she ask him to stay when she was going to be leaving for good next week, and she had just told him that this would be the end of things for them? 'Okay. Yeah, sounds sensible.'

'You'll be all right to pick up Simon tomorrow?'

'Of course. I said so.' She had to get into the car now, before she broke down. Before she promised him anything, in return for another few days, and then broke that promise and left anyway. 'It's okay, Reece.'

He closed the passenger door behind her then let Trader into the back of the car. Swung into the driver's seat, with that easy, restless grace of his. So free. It would be more than a crime to try and change Reece. He was fine just as he was. If she couldn't have him, that was her problem.

'It's not okay.' He paused before putting the key into the ignition, eyes far away, somewhere on the horizon. 'But it's the only thing to do.' His face showed one momentary flash of bitter regret and then he started the engine.

CHAPTER TWELVE

He'd been gone for three days. Sara had picked Simon up from the hospital and brought him back to Reece's house, letting him take the spare room while she slept on the sofa. Kath had called in, back from her week away. Maggie had come to dinner and Sara had cooked. It was all done in a kind of daze, as if she were living in a bag of cotton wool, able only to hear the voices around her as muffled, far-away sounds.

Then Reece called. Sara picked up her phone from Kath's kitchen counter, excusing herself with a smile, and slipping out into the darkness of the garden. 'Hello.'

'Hey. Where are you?'

'Simon and I are over at Kath's. Did you try the house?' Small talk. Anything, while she steadied herself in the wake of the giddy sensation of having everything suddenly snap into sharp focus.

'Yeah. I reckoned if you weren't there you'd be with Kath. Are you on your own?'

'Yes.' Sara sat down on the steps that led from the veranda to the garden, the darkness of the evening folding her into its warmth. Alone with Reece. Only this time he was just a far-away voice. She pressed the phone to her ear, straining to hear every word, every intonation. Each unspoken thing.

'How are you? Is there anything you need?'

'Fine. There's nothing I need.' If she closed her eyes and concentrated, that might almost be true. He could almost be here, sitting next to her.

'And Simon?'

'He's good too. Trying to do too much, of course, but he's mending well. Maggie came over last night.'

'Yeah?' Sara could hear the smile in his voice. 'Do you like her?'

'Yes, very much. Simon's planning to come to London for a visit later in the year, and she might come with him.'

'That's great.' The question hung in the air between them. 'So you…?'

'Yes. I told him about Gran. I reckoned in the end that he had a right to know, she's his grandmother too. It went better than I thought it would.'

'I imagine it did. So he's offered to help you?'

Sara smiled into the darkness. She'd missed talking things through with Reece. The way he seemed to know what was bugging her before she'd even said it. 'Yes. I turned down financial help, and said yes to the video conferencing. Gran's going to love being able to see and talk to him regularly.'

Reece's chuckle sounded down the phone. 'Sounds like a plan. I'm glad it's worked out so well.'

She had Reece to thank for that. He'd pushed her into getting things out into the open with Simon, and he'd been right to do so. It had been Reece's trust that had helped her to mend her broken family when her own had not been enough.

She could almost feel him breathing. Long moments of silence, like the ones when they held each other, but this time, instead of feeling that they could last for ever, they slid through her fingers like quicksilver.

'You're not coming back, are you?' She knew now what he had called her for. If he was coming back in the morning, he could have waited to hear all this, face to face.

'No. There are some things that need to be done here. Now is as good a time as any to do them.' At least he didn't make excuses and pretend that staying away was anything other than his decision.

'You should stay, then.' She'd already given him everything she could, a lot more than it was safe to risk, and there was nothing more left to be done.

'Yeah. I'll call Kath and Simon in the morning and let them know. Kath will keep an eye on Simon until I get back.'

'Thanks.' At least she didn't have to face Kath or Simon's questions about why Reece was staying away. He was trying to make this easy, but not even Reece could accomplish that. Some things were just the way they were and couldn't be changed.

'Sara, I—'

'Don't say it, Reece.' Whatever it was, she didn't want to know. 'We did what we did. Let's just let that speak for us.'

He heaved a sigh, but it was impossible to tell whether it was one of relief or regret. Probably a little of both, if her own feelings were anything to go by. Relief that he wasn't going to make this harder than it was. Regret that it had to be done in the first place. 'It speaks for me, Sara. Better than words ever could.'

Maybe he was going to make this more difficult than it needed to be after all. If he had begged, then she could have resisted him, but this silence, with the memories of his face torturing her, was worse than anything. 'Me too.'

'I'm going to hang up now.' His voice again on the phone. He seemed to know that she couldn't.

'Yes. Thank you.'

There was a short, cracked laugh on the other end of the line, which gave the lie to the joke. 'Anything for a lady.'

There was an abrupt click and the phone went dead. Sara strained to hear beyond the silence, and there was nothing. He really had hung up. She thumbed the button to cut the call from her end, and laid her mobile down on the decking beside her. Voices and laughter sounded behind her, in the house, and suddenly she was plunged into deeper darkness as someone switched the light off in kitchen.

Shadows pressed in around her, imprisoning her, like the sliding walls of the haunted house in the old horror film that she and Reece had watched together. This time there was nobody to hold her tight, though. No handsome adventurer to gather her up in his arms and save the day. She felt her back bend as the suffocating weight that she had almost grown used to not having to carry any more settled back onto her shoulders.

Reece craned over the glass-and-steel balcony at Tullamarine Airport. He could see Kath's head below him, bobbing amongst the crowd, alongside Sara's. He fixed his eyes on her dark hair, almost wishing that she would look up. Just so he could see her face, one more time.

There was no point in him being here. She couldn't stay, and he couldn't see himself learning how to put down the kind of roots that would allow him to go with her. All the same, he'd driven a long way to get here, and had raced through the airport, desperately searching for the boarding gate for the eleven o'clock flight to London. Then he'd frozen. There was only one thing left to say and that was goodbye. He couldn't bring himself to do that either.

The women hugged, and Kath started to speak. He knew what she was saying, it was what Kath always said when they parted.

'We'll say goodbye and we won't look back.' Kath's hand went to her chest. *'I'll hold you in my heart until I see you again.'*

Sara nodded and said something. Her own hand went to her heart, and Reece found himself mouthing the words. *'I'll hold you in my heart.'* He wouldn't see her again but he could deliver on the first part of the promise.

The women hugged again and, too quickly, Sara turned away. The downward slope of the wide walkway gradually swallowed her up, first her feet, then her body and finally that dark mop of hair. He kept his eyes fixed on the spot where she'd disappeared from view. Maybe she would sense his presence, turn and walk back again.

'What the bloody hell do you think you're doing, Reece?' He'd stared at the walkway for so long now that it seemed to have burnt its way into his retinas, and Kath's voice shattered his concentration.

'Hey. Looks as if I've just missed you.' It wasn't a matter of wondering whether he looked guilty or not, more like how guilty he looked. From the look on Kath's face, it was guilty as hell.

'Pull the other one. Have you driven down this morning?' Reece nodded and Kath frowned at him. 'So you drove all that way just to hide around a corner and not say goodbye. What's going on?'

Kath had a right to ask. She'd filled in for him, looking after Simon and Sara while he was away. The trouble was, Reece didn't have an answer. He wanted a few moments more to stare at the spot where he'd last seen Sara, fix it in his mind, but he knew he had to go now. He couldn't stand guard on this place all night, and Sara wasn't coming back. He turned and met Kath's questioning eyes.

'Was she all right? This morning?'

'She was fine. A bit teary at having to leave Simon, but

that was…' Kath broke off as light dawned. 'Reece. What did you do?'

Reece forced a smile. 'You want a blow-by-blow account?'

Light dawned on Kath's face. 'No. Too much detail.' Her gaze dropped to his hand, where he held his phone, his keys and the small, blue box. 'What's that?'

It didn't matter now. 'Here, take a look.' He handed her the box and Kath opened it.

'Reece! That's beautiful!' Kath looked around wildly and then started to tug at his arm. 'Go and give it to her. Quickly, the flight's not leaving for another half an hour. You could flash your doctor's badge and say there's a medical emergency and that she's forgotten her pills or something.'

The thought that Sara would be here, within reach, for thirty minutes more was almost too much for him to bear. 'No.' He laid his hand on her shoulder. 'No, Kath. It's too late, and it won't change anything. She has reasons for going, and they're good ones. I won't make things any more difficult for her.'

'But this is so pretty.' Kath took the gold chain out of the box, holding it up so the heart threaded on it dangled, sparkling in the overhead lights. 'Surely you want to give it to her?'

Not any more. He'd thought it was a good idea, a sign that he cared and that all the things he'd said to her hadn't been just hollow words, but as soon as he'd seen Sara here, he'd known that he had to let her go. He'd always travelled light, and he had to give her a chance to do the same. He shook his head, unable to find the words that made any sense of it. 'We said goodbye already.'

Kath's hand flew to her mouth. 'That night, at our house, when she took the phone outside…'

'Yeah.'

'She seemed…'

'How did she seem?' He was still hungry for every last little piece of information about Sara.

Kath shrugged. 'She was sitting outside on her own for almost an hour. In the end Simon went and brought her in. She was very quiet, I thought she was tired.' She grimaced, tipping the chain back into the box and closing it.

'Why don't you take that?'

'What?' Kath pushed the box back into his hand. 'Not on your life, Reece. It's not meant for me.'

'It's pretty. Shame for it to go to waste.'

She huffed at him. 'It went to waste when you decided to stand here watching Sara go instead of coming downstairs and giving it to her. If you don't want it then you can throw it in the Yarra.'

Maybe he would. Sara was gone now, and he couldn't imagine having any other use for the pretty, heart-shaped pendant. If Kath wouldn't take it off his hands then it would be better if it was never worn by anyone.

'Where's Simon? Do you have to get back for him?'

'No, he's at my place with Joe and the kids so there's no need to rush back.' Kath linked his arm with hers. 'Coffee. I'm buying.'

'Sounds ominous.'

'Don't worry, I'm not going to give you the third degree.' His sister laughed. 'Not unless you want me to.'

'There's nothing to say. Sara and I were together and now we're not.' It was much, much more than just that. But however hard Reece had thought about it, however many options he had gone through in his head, he'd still come back to the same conclusion. He couldn't follow her, knowing that she was tied to one place. He'd never been able to resist the lure of the open road before, so how could now be any different?

'And who decided that?'

'It was mutual.' Now that Reece thought about it, he wasn't sure who had decided. It had been an instinctive reaction on both their parts, something that neither he nor Sara could change. 'Thought you weren't going to give me the third degree?'

'It was a rhetorical question. I don't expect an answer.' Kath fished in her pocket and drew out a ten-dollar bill, holding it up in front of him. 'From the look on your face right now, I've got ten that says it's not as over as you think it is.'

'Put your money away. You'll lose.'

'Well, I'm not afraid to try... Hey!' Kath protested as he whipped the note out of her hand.

'Then don't be a sore loser. Sara and I are done. We won't be bumping into each other in the street and deciding to give things another try any time soon. It's over.' Reece said the words with as much finality as he could muster, and turned, scanning myriad airport signs to find one that pointed to a coffee shop. 'Suppose I get to buy now.'

'You suppose right. And I want a sandwich, I'm starving.' Kath was obviously bent on not leaving Reece any change from his win. If you could call it a win.

'Sure. Is this an end to it?'

'You've made up your mind?' Kath knew him well enough to know that if he had decided on something, he wouldn't go back on it.

'Yeah.'

She shrugged, twisting her mouth in an expression of regret. 'It's an end to it, then.'

CHAPTER THIRTEEN

'HEY, Gran, it's only me!' Sara shouted at the top of her voice, so that her grandmother would hear her.

'Obviously. Who else makes all that noise?' Her grandmother's clear blue eyes regarded her from the chair by the window.

'Well, I wouldn't have to if you'd wear your hearing aids.' She unwound her scarf from her neck and took off her gloves. 'How was your day?'

'About twelve.'

Sara laughed. 'That many?'

'Sally loves her murder mysteries.'

'Oh, and you don't, of course.' Gran loved a good murder, particularly if it was solved by a woman over sixty. 'So the body count's twelve. Everyone brought to justice all right?'

'Of course. They always are. I wanted the one with the blue eyes to get away with it.'

Blue eyes. Reece. Sara swallowed down the now familiar feeling of loss and sat down, pulling her boots off. It had been a month now since she'd looked into those eyes. When was she going to pull herself together and find something else to daydream about?

'What about yours?'

'My day? Zero body count. That makes it a good day, Gran, in my line of work.'

Her grandmother nodded sagely. Small, white-haired and dressed neatly in a matching blue cardigan and skirt, with a bold printed blouse and a pretty necklace. Gran still liked to look nice. 'Well done, dear.'

Gran made it sound as if she had personally wrested everyone she'd been called to see from the jaws of death. Sara decided not to tell her that her last call had been to someone with a minor ear infection. 'So, have you eaten yet?'

Gran looked at her watch. 'Yes, I expect so. Sally left something for you in the fridge.'

'Oh, she's a star. I'll just go and see what I've got.'

Sara padded through to the kitchen and pulled the film from the dish that Sally had left. The woman was worth her weight in gold. Caring, sensible and a fan of murder mysteries. It cost almost as much as Sara earned in three shifts a week to have her look after Gran, but that wasn't the point. It gave Gran a change of scene and someone else to talk to, and Sara got to keep the job that she loved.

She put the dish of lasagne into the microwave, and popped her head around the door of the sitting room. 'Would you like a cup of tea?'

'No, I've been drinking tea all day.' Gran beckoned to her. 'Someone phoned.'

'Yeah? They didn't try and sell you anything, did they?'

'No. It was a man. He wanted to speak to you.'

'Did he? Who was it?' Sara wasn't holding out much hope of finding out. If Gran hadn't happened to be wearing her hearing aids, she wouldn't have been able to hear properly, and writing a message down wasn't so easy with arthritic hands. Whoever it had been would probably call back.

'He left a message.' Gran produced a piece of paper

from the table beside her and focussed on it. 'He wants to speak to you and he'll call back.'

'Oh, that's okay, then…' The microwave pinged and Sara turned.

'Simon's friend, from Australia.'

She spun round so quickly that she almost fell over. 'Who?'

'He's a doctor, you know. We had a very nice chat.'

'Yes, I know.' Reece had called her. It must be six in the morning in Australia. The flood of pure, perfidious joy that shot through her body, suddenly putting something to eat and a sit down right at the bottom of her list of priorities, turned to fear. She'd agreed with Reece that they'd make an end to it. No contact. He wouldn't have gone back on that unless it was something important.

'Did he say what it was about, Gran?'

'He wants to talk to you. I told him you'd be home at seven and he could pop round if he wanted.'

Right. Reece obviously wasn't going to be popping round, but perhaps he'd call back. 'Did he say anything about Simon?' The only reason that she could think of that Reece would be calling would be if something had happened to Simon.

'He said that Simon is fine. He made me write that down.' Gran handed the paper to Sara.

Dr Reece Fletcher. Simon is fine. Popping round after seven.

All written painstakingly in Gran's tiny writing. It must have taken for ever to shout the message down the phone to Gran and wait while she found some paper and wrote it down, and Sara wondered how much the call had cost him.

'Okay. Thanks, Gran. I guess I'll hear from him, then.'

'Is everything all right?'

'Yes, of course.' Sara managed a smile, and grabbed the phone from its cradle. 'I'll just go and get my supper. Did you want a cup of tea?'

'Yes, I think I would. Thank you, dear.'

'Right. I'll be back in a minute.'

Sara hit the kitchen, pacing. What did Reece want? Maybe she should call back. She shook her head. He'd said he'd call back and hopefully he'd make it soon. She wanted to hear his voice. She just wanted to hear his voice.

It was probably nothing. Sara flipped the kettle on, and put a teabag into Gran's china cup, spilling the hot water into the saucer as she poured it. The phone rang and she grabbed it.

She took a deep breath, trying to sound composed. 'Hello.'

This is an important message about personal injury compensation. If you have been...'

There was no point in shouting at the voice on the end of the line, it was a recorded message. Sara cursed it under her breath, jabbing at the button to end the call.

Her heart was beating so fast that Sara wondered whether she might be about to faint. Planting her elbows on the worktop, she put her head in her hands. Deep breaths. That was better. Her hands were shaking as she tipped the hot water from the saucer and finished making the tea, but she was under control. Just about.

The doorbell rang. 'What now?' Sara muttered under her breath, deciding to let whoever it was wait. She had more important things on her mind. Tucking the phone into the pocket of her cardigan, she took the tea through to the lounge.

'Who's that at the door?'

'No idea. Probably someone selling something that we

don't want.' Sara supposed she'd better answer it. 'Back in a minute.'

She flipped the porch light on and put the chain on the door, opening it a few inches. The dark shadow that had been hovering halfway down the front path, obviously unsure of whether anyone was in or not, advanced into the pool of light and Sara jumped back, slamming the door closed.

'Sara?'

It was Reece's voice. That made sense, as it was him standing on the doorstep. 'Reece?'

'Yes. Are you all right?'

'Yes…of course… Just let me take the chain off the door.' Good. At least her wits hadn't completely deserted her and she had managed to come up with an excuse for shutting the door in his face. Other than the obvious. Disbelief and joy fought with panic and lost hands down.

Her trembling fingers fumbled over the chain and Sara took a deep breath. 'Seems to be stuck. Sorry, won't be a moment.' Another deep breath.

'That's okay. Take your time.' His voice was gentle. Like warm syrup, flowing over her nerve endings.

'Right. Got it.' She slid the door chain free, took another breath and opened the door.

'I'm sorry if I startled you. I spoke to your grandmother on the phone earlier and she said—'

'Yes. I know. I thought that she'd got it wrong and that you were going to call back.' Sara pushed the phone handset deeper into her pocket, until such time as she could unobtrusively get rid of it. Reece didn't need to know that she'd been carrying it around with her in case she missed his call.

'Is this a bad time?' He didn't move.

'No.' She swung the door wide, stepping back. 'Come in.' *What on earth are you doing here?* would have been a bit more to the point, but they could get to that one in a minute. Sara closed the door behind him. 'So…you're here.'

'Yes. I'm here.'

CHAPTER FOURTEEN

SARA had clearly opted for observation, prior to diagnosis and action. She stood in the hallway, looking more beautiful than Reece remembered, pulling her thick, knitted jacket around her as if it was a shield. He had thought that seeing her again might bring him to his senses and make him realise that not even Sara could live up to the picture of her that he had been holding so tenderly in his imagination for the last month. That was obviously not going to work.

So much for Plan A. That was okay, he had a back-up. He also had a number of carefully thought-out opening lines at his disposal, but none of them seemed adequate for the moment. Maybe it was the sudden change in temperature from the doorstep to the hallway that was making his head swim.

'I'm here to see you, Sara. I'd like to talk to you.' It was neither witty nor heartwarming, and didn't bear the faintest resemblance to anything that he'd anticipated saying, but at least it was honest.

'It's a long way to come.'

She seemed just as much at a loss as he was and Reece reminded himself that she'd had no time to prepare for this. If the truth be told, neither had he. He simply hadn't anticipated that seeing her again would make him feel this way.

'That's how much I want to talk to you.' Damn. That

sounded like emotional blackmail. 'I was here anyway, and...'

She sensed the lie immediately. 'Yeah, yeah. And you just decided to drop by.'

'I should have phoned first.'

'You did.' She smiled and suddenly the sun came out. It had been four days since he'd seen the sun and he was already missing it. 'I just didn't get the message.'

He only had to reach out. The city that had greeted him had been cold, grey and claustrophobic and, despite his habitual optimism about new places, so far nothing had changed that initial reaction. And here, after a long, cheerless ride on the Underground, he'd found everything that he needed.

'It's good to see you, Sara. But I really just stopped by to let you know I was here. Maybe I can give you a call in the next couple of days.'

'No.' She caught his hand, and the heat of her fingers was almost painful after the freezing temperature outside. 'Stay for a while.'

'Thanks. I'd like that.'

He couldn't tell who reached for whom first. All Reece knew or cared about was that Sara was in his arms, and he could suddenly breathe again. This was the complete opposite of what he'd come here for but, then, staying away from her hadn't gone as planned either. Nothing had worked to slake the longing that had burned in his chest for what now seemed to have been the whole of his life.

It was more of a hug than an embrace, thick layers of clothing insulating them from each other. Just like friends who hadn't seen each other in a while. Somehow that was worse. The closer he was to her, the more he realised just exactly what he'd lost.

'Hey. It's okay.' He stroked her hair, making sure not

to let his finger stray to her cheek. It wasn't okay, but that was what he was here for. Somehow he had to find a way to lay the ghosts that swirled between them and give them both a chance to get on with their lives.

'If you can stay a while, we can talk after Gran goes to bed.'

'I've nothing else planned.' This was the plan now.

'Sara?' A thin, clear voice floated out into the hallway and she moved in his arms, twisting her head around.

'Just coming, Gran. I've got someone for you to meet,' Sara shouted back at the top of her voice, and warmth flooded through Reece. He would have waited outside until she was ready to talk to him, she hadn't needed to invite him in.

'Do what? If it's that doctor again, tell him to go away.'

She rolled her eyes, grinning up at him. 'It's okay, she doesn't mean you.' Reece let her go, and she hurried to the open doorway. 'It's not *your* doctor, it's a friend of Simon's that I met in Australia. The one who phoned, earlier.'

'Well, ask him in, then. What are you doing with him out there in the hall?'

'He's just taking his coat off.' She disappeared into the room, her voice softly conspiratorial now. 'Put your hearing aids in, Gran.'

Reece took his coat off quickly, hanging it on the post of the dark stairway, and she was back again, beckoning to him. 'Come in. Reece, this is my grandmother, Lily.'

Lily was dressed neatly, her silver hair carefully combed and styled. Reece knew how much work it took to achieve that, and he knew how much love it took to achieve the bright smile that she gave him when he was introduced. He'd seen it often enough in the women who gave him tea and reeled off a list of medications by heart when he visited his elderly patients.

He could see the fatigue that slowed Sara's movements from time to time as well. The way she leaned back in her easy chair, her gaze never leaving him, while he answered Lily's questions about Australia and his life there.

'You've come at a very good time.' Lily gave him an approving nod. 'I'm off on a little journey myself tomorrow, so Sara will have some time to show you around.'

Reece tried not to look at Sara and failed. She had reddened slightly, but she said nothing. The least contentious way forward seemed to be to concentrate on Lily's journey rather than Sara's free time. 'Where are you going?'

'I've decided to go back to the care home I stayed at when Sara was in Australia. It's a nice place and I'm well looked after there. And Sara will have some more time to herself during the week.' Lily's tone brooked no argument.

'This is still your home, Gran.' From the look on Sara's face Reece could see that she was not as comfortable with the idea as her grandmother was.

'Yes, and I'll be coming back every weekend.' Lily and Sara were obviously going over old ground here. Revisiting it again and again until they were both comfortable that the other was happy with it.

'Sounds like the best of both worlds.' Reece knew he shouldn't really be venturing an opinion on this, but he wondered whether Sara had spoken to anyone else about her obvious reservations.

'I hope so.' Her grey eyes were thoughtful, but she seemed pleased with his comment. As if she cared about his opinion. Suddenly it was important to him that she did care.

She seemed to relapse into her own thoughts, while Reece talked to Lily, only breaking in when it was obvious that her grandmother was beginning to tire. Lily bade him goodnight, and the two of them left Reece in the small sitting room.

'Right.' Sara breezed back in on a tide of warmth and energy, light years away from the slow, measured pace that she lived at when Lily was awake. 'Gran went out like a light when I put her to bed, so we can go upstairs.'

'If you want to stay down here, just to make sure she's settled...'

'No.' Sara grinned at him. 'I have technology for that.'

She led him into the hallway, catching up his coat and running up the stairs. The door at the top of the stairs opened into another world. A confection of architectural features that Simon would have been proud of, and which Sara didn't give a second look as she showed him into a large kitchen.

'Wow! This is...' He had imagined Sara in a range of different environments, but this hadn't been one of them. Downstairs, her grandmother's living quarters were a little old-fashioned but cosy and welcoming. This was sleek, beautifully designed and about as homely as a high-class office building.

'Yeah, I know. Not really me, is it?' She produced a pink gizmo of some kind from the kitchen drawer and flipped a switch on the bottom of it, holding it to her ear before she planted it in the middle of the shiny centre island.

'Baby alarm?'

She nodded. 'Gran's got a call button, but she doesn't always press it when she gets up in the night. This is my back-up surveillance system. Are you hungry?'

'I've eaten. Don't let me stop you, though.' He'd seen a plate of food in the kitchen downstairs, but she'd tipped it into the bin before he'd been able to enquire whether it was her dinner.

'I'm fine. I'll make coffee.'

She busied herself with an industrial-looking coffee-maker, and opened the freezer, pulling out part-cooked French bread and putting it into the oven. Suddenly the shiny, sterile kitchen started to look, and smell, like home.

'So.' She plumped herself down on one of the bar stools, next door but one to where he was sitting. 'What brings you here, Reece?'

She'd brought him. 'We didn't get to say goodbye.'

She nodded, suddenly solemn. 'No, we didn't. That doesn't mean we didn't both agree on the best course of action. I haven't changed my mind about that and I'm guessing that you haven't either.'

'That's not my point. We knew we had to finish it, but neither of us could bring ourselves to do it properly.' Whatever properly was. At the moment all that Reece knew was that they hadn't achieved it yet.

She shook her head in a sudden display of impatience. 'So you've flown ten thousand miles just to say goodbye to me, have you? Couldn't you have phoned?'

'No.' He laid his palms on the cool marble counter top in front of him. 'Can you honestly tell me that a phone call was enough the last time?' It hadn't been enough for him. It had left him a prisoner in his own home, bound to a house that he didn't even care about, just because she'd been there. The world had shrivelled around him, and there had been only one place to go if he wanted to find his freedom again.

She pressed her lips together tightly, jumping to her feet and marching across to tend to the coffee. Frothing the milk and banging the jug rather too hard on the counter top, so that she spilled some of it.

'Can you?' He was more sure of his ground now. He knew Sara. If she'd been that certain that parting was the best thing to do, she would have been kinder. If she screamed at him and threw things, he knew he was in with a chance.

'What? What do you want me to say, Reece?'

'Just give me an answer. Do you feel as if we really said goodbye?'

Sara wanted to shake him. Hard, until it knocked some sense into that thick head of his. She'd kept the emotion of seeing him again pretty much under control while she'd had Gran to concentrate on, but suddenly it reared up, smacking her in the face. 'We didn't need to... Oh!' Her gesture of frustration, anger, she didn't know what, had flipped the jug over and there was milk everywhere.

'No?' He jumped as she slammed the metal jug into the sink. 'Are you sure about that?'

Of course she wasn't. Sara grabbed a tea towel and dabbed ineffectually at her cardigan, then gave up and turned her attention to mopping up the spilt milk. She could almost feel his gaze on her back.

'I really don't know why you came here, Reece. There's nothing more to say.'

'Can you face me and tell me that?' His voice was closer now, right over her left shoulder, and Sara jumped. 'If you can face me and tell me that there's no unfinished business left between us, I'll go.'

She couldn't do that. Wouldn't do it. And he obviously wasn't listening to her silent agonised pleas for him to back off. He reached around her, and took the dishcloth from her hand, throwing it into the sink.

'Look, Reece, this isn't the time. I've got a lot on my plate right now...' She puffed out a breath and turned to face him. Tried not to look into his eyes. 'Tomorrow's going to be a busy day, and I'm truly not sure how I'm going to do everything that needs doing.'

Some of her anguish must have showed on her face because he stepped back. 'Is there anything I can help you with?'

'No. I can manage.'

'I don't doubt it. That doesn't mean that you're not allowed to accept some help.'

'It doesn't mean that I have to either.' Tears began to prick in her eyes. She didn't have to cry either. Whatever he did, and whatever he said, there was no rule written down anywhere that said she had to cry.

'And you're feeling guilty?'

Of course she was feeling guilty. Guilt went with the territory. 'It's the best thing for Gran. It's what she wants.' Sara took in a gulp of air. She knew exactly how this must look to Reece. She'd left him, telling him that she had no choice, and now he'd turned up to find that Gran was on her way to a care home. 'Things haven't changed, Reece. She still needs me.'

'I know that.'

'She's made me her legal guardian, and I need to be here to see to things for her. Make decisions for her if ever she can't make them herself. And there are the day-to-day things. Shopping, visiting…' Sara broke off. She was protesting too much and this was beginning to sound like an excuse.

'Hospital appointments, taking her out to see her friends. Giving her the reassurance of being there so that she knows she has choices.' He grinned. 'I know, Sara. I've never had to care for someone like this, but I know what it entails.'

'I just don't want you to think…' She didn't want Reece to think that she had lied to him. That it had been easy for her to walk away from him. 'I know how this looks.'

'It looks as if you let your gran do things in her own time. You helped her stay in her own home for as long as she wanted to, and now she's ready to go somewhere new.'

His eyes were darker that she remembered. Maybe a trick of the light. A deep, swirling blue that seemed to penetrate right into her thoughts, sifting through the hopes and fears that she kept so tightly under wraps. 'Thanks. For understanding.'

Reece turned away from her, one hand sweeping through his hair. That familiar tousled look that set the memories of sunlit mornings playing again in her head and almost made her choke with grief.

'I just wish I understood how to respond...' He sounded almost angry. Uncertainty wasn't Reece's style, and the emotion was obviously exasperating him.

She had no answers for him right now, and Sara knew that was dangerous ground. She needed a few minutes on her own, away from that magnetic pull of his that turned her thoughts upside down. A clatter sounded from the baby alarm and Sara silently thanked Gran for her good timing. 'Wait a minute. I'll be back.'

She spent a little more time downstairs than she strictly needed to, sitting by Gran's bed until she was asleep again. Tomorrow was going to be a tough day, both physically and mentally, and she would have given anything to have Reece with her. But it wasn't fair on either of them.

'We have to manage without him, eh, Gran? However hard it is.' She whispered the words so as not to wake her grandmother, tears rolling down her cheeks as she did so. This was no good. She had to go upstairs and face Reece, tell him the lie that she hadn't been able to tell him earlier. She crept silently into Gran's small kitchenette and splashed cold water onto her face, drying it carefully with a piece of kitchen towel.

She hadn't heard his footsteps on the stairs but the front door, clicking shut, made her jump. Sara's first instinct was to go after him, until she realised that Reece had done just exactly what she'd wanted him to do. He'd gone.

Upstairs, the kitchen was empty. The newly heated bread had been taken out of the oven and lay cooling on the hob. The baby alarm was in a slightly different place from usual. Sara picked it up and reddened when she found that it was still on. She could have sworn she'd switched it off before going downstairs.

There was one cup of coffee, by the bar stool where she'd sat, made just the way she liked it. A note, folded over in the saucer.

He'd written just two words, in the centre of the page. 'Until tomorrow.'

CHAPTER FIFTEEN

SARA was a sitting duck, and she knew it. She couldn't rush Gran out of bed, or get her washed and dressed any faster, and once that was done, she needed to finish packing up the things that her grandmother wanted to take with her. All she had left to do now, though, was to load up the car, give Gran a cup of tea and then they could go.

She'd allowed herself to hope a little too soon. Just as she'd finished stacking everything in the hall, Gran picked up her extending grabber, catching the net curtain deftly between the pincers and pulling it to one side.

'Go and let Reece in, dear. He looks absolutely frozen out there.'

'Right. I dare say he's just popped in for a cup of tea.' Like hell he had. He looked cheerful and ready for action, and the mortifying thing about it was that, despite all her resolve of the previous night, Sara was actually glad to see him.

At least he had the grace to look a little sheepish when she opened the door. Didn't even attempt to come inside, even though she stood back from the door in an indication that he should.

'Can I move those for you?' He indicated the boxes and cases in the hall.

He was here, ready to work, to give her the support she

needed. She should just accept it. There was nobody she wanted more right now, and anyway she could no more turn him away than tap him with a wand and make him disappear.

'Thanks.' The one word constituted an agreement between them, and he nodded slowly. 'I'll bring my car around to the front door.' Sara picked up her car keys from the hall table.

'That's okay, I can do it…if you'd like me to.' He was carefully drawing the lines between them. Making the boundaries clear. Reece, the man whose second nature was to act rather than to ask, was deferring to her.

'That would be great. I was just about to make some tea for Gran.' She pointed across the street. 'That's mine, the red one.'

'Stick shift?' He grinned slowly.

'Yeah. Think you can manage it?'

'I'll do my best.' He took the keys, without even brushing her palm with his fingers, and another line was drawn. Jokes were okay. Even an exchanged smile. No contact, though.

The truce held. Gran left her home on his arm, guided safely to the car, while Sara followed behind at a discreet distance. Gran might be over ninety, but she still preferred a young man's arm to her ugly, grey walking frame.

'It looks like a nice place, Lily.' Reece walked Gran to the front door and left her with the job of pressing the bell. 'You'll have to show me around.'

'If you like.' Gran batted away the carer who came to greet her and started to make for the dining room, Reece supporting her all the way. 'Come and see in here, I think you'll find the view interesting.'

Being relegated to second fiddle, left to park the car

and get Gran's suitcases out, was nothing short of a delight. Reece was professing interest and approval for everything Gran showed him, and if he didn't notice the second glances that he got from women of all ages, Gran certainly did. For the moment she was the belle of this particular ball, and when you were ninety, you didn't let chances like that slip away easily.

'I'll call someone and get a cup of tea.' Reece and Gran had finally made it to Gran's room, where Sara was hanging her clothes in the wardrobe. 'Or would you prefer coffee, Reece?'

'Coffee would be great, if it's not too much trouble. Shall I call someone?'

'No, that's all right. I'll do it.' Gran was installed into her chair and was fiddling with the call button when a carer popped her head around the door, smiling.

'Everything all right?' The question was aimed at Gran, and Sara kept her mouth firmly shut. When she looked at Reece, he was doing the same.

'Yes, thank you. Only we'd like some tea, please. And a cup of coffee for Reece.'

'Sure.' The carer winked conspiratorially in Gran's direction. 'Make sure the workers have a break, eh, Lily? Get more out of them that way.'

'Quite.' Gran beamed back and Sara felt the muscles across her shoulders relax by one more notch. Every small kindness was like a balm spread over her fears for Gran.

'Right.' Reece picked up Sara's car keys from the bed, seemingly confident that she wouldn't object. 'I'll go and fetch the rest of the things from the car.'

He'd given Gran the instructions for the flat-pack chest of drawers and had spread the various bolts and screws out on the table next to her, so she could sort them into piles. Once that had been assembled, he'd taken the new TV out of its box, plugged it in and tuned it, while Sara had sat with Gran, drinking tea and admiring the clarity of the picture.

Then it was time to go. Sara knew that Gran would be fine. She knew this was the best thing for her. That didn't matter, it was still tough to leave her. Reece kissed Gran on the cheek and said goodbye, leaving Sara alone with her.

'It's time for you to go. I'll be all right here.' Gran stroked her cheek.

'I know. If I thought for one minute that you wouldn't then you'd be coming straight back home with me.' Sara didn't want to let go of Gran's hand. 'There's some flower arranging in the activities room this afternoon, if you fancy it.'

'I've got flowers.' Gran indicated the bunch that Sara had put on the windowsill. 'There are plenty of people here, I won't be lonely. Don't you be either.'

'Me? I'll be fine. Anyway, I'll be seeing you tomorrow, and we'll have the weekend together next weekend…'

'And in the meantime, you go and have a good time with Reece. Now give me a kiss, darling, and off you go.'

'Do you think she'll be all right?' Sara had done three months of research before she'd allowed Gran to come here while she herself was in Australia. Talked to people, visited different care homes, read reports. Gran had liked it, and had wanted to come back. But suddenly Reece's opinion seemed more important than all that.

'I think it's a great place.' He was leaning against her car, waiting for her. 'This isn't an end for Lily, you know.'

'Have you been talking to the manager here? That's exactly what she says.' Sara could feel herself beginning to relax.

'I did meet her while I was downstairs.' He grinned. 'Nice lady. She was telling me how she's working on strengthening links with the community here. Bringing people in so that the residents can still engage with different kinds of people, follow their own interests.'

'Yes. You didn't tell her that you do magic tricks, did you?'

'No. Why?'

'You'll be roped in for an afternoon's entertainment if you do.'

He chuckled, his eyes dancing. Ever since he'd been here, he'd seemed so controlled, so tightly reined in. Suddenly here was a glimpse of the free spirit she loved so much. 'Maybe I'll volunteer, then.' He pursed his lips, seeming to come to a decision. 'I'd offer to take you for a late lunch, but I've got two problems.'

'Yeah? I might refuse. What's the other problem?'

'First, I've no idea where to find a decent eatery around here and, second, you'll have to do the taking, because you've got the car keys.' He knew that there wasn't much chance of her refusal.

She dangled the keys in front of him. 'Does that make things any easier?'

He grinned. 'Yeah. One down, one to go.'

The problem, it seemed, was not with Reece's driving but with Sara's directions. She had meant to guide him past the underground station and then on to the multi-storey car park, so that they could walk to the high street and make their choice of where to eat. Instead, she'd got them stuck in a long tailback of traffic.

'Is it usually this bad?' He seemed to be taking it in his stride, but Sara was getting agitated.

'No, not at this time of day. There must be something going on up ahead, this lot's not moving.'

'Can we go another way?' He indicated a side road.

'No. That's just leads you into a one-way system that comes out on the other side of where we want to go.' She craned her neck, trying to see what was going on up ahead. Maybe an accident. Maybe she should go and see.

Reece was obviously thinking the same. 'Slide over, I'll go and see what I can see.' He got out of the car and Sara climbed across into the driver's seat.

'Anything?'

'Nothing that I can see. This jam seems to go right up to the next corner.' He jumped back into the passenger seat of the car. 'I don't hear anything—' He broke off as the unmistakeable sound of an emergency siren came from behind them.

The car was nosing through the traffic, switching lanes, using every inch of space to get past the stationary cars. Sara swung the steering-wheel, ready to turn out of its path, and was blocked by another car, inching its way along the inside lane.

Reece wound down the car window and leaned out. 'Can you move? We need to get out of the way, mate.'

The driver of the other car ignored him, inching forward still, taking advantage of a few feet of empty space in front of him to get just that little bit closer to wherever it was he was going. Reece gave a huff of impatience and was about to get out of the car when Sara stopped him.

'Leave it.' She manoeuvred the car so that she was almost touching the one in the next lane. 'They can get through there.'

'Can they?' Reece twisted round to check the oncoming vehicle's path.

'Yeah. Piece of cake.'

She turned and seemed to recognise the occupants of the emergency vehicle, flashing her headlights as it nosed past. Reece recognised the signal. I'm here. Ready to help if you need it.

It looked as if they did need it. Sara's mobile rang and

she pulled it from her bag, sliding it into the hands-free clip on the dashboard. 'What's up?'

'There's been a fire. Just around the corner in the high street. We'll know more when we get there, but there may be multiple casualties.' A man's voice crackled down the line.

'Okay, I'll see you there. Save a few for me.'

'Right you are.'

She glanced across at him, and Reece nodded. No need for words, there was no way that either of them would be continuing their journey to take a leisurely lunch now.

The lights changed up ahead and she switched on her hazard lights, changing lanes and cutting through the traffic to turn left. The junction up ahead seemed to be semi-organised chaos, vehicles trying to turn and being diverted on ahead by a couple of policemen, and Sara stopped at the tape that was stretched across the road.

'Paramedic. Let me through.'

One of the policemen nodded and waved her through, and Sara accelerated along the few hundred yards of empty road that led to a large department store. Reece could see fire trucks and an ambulance, along with other emergency vehicles. Great gusts of black smoke were issuing from the open mouth of the store.

They were both out of the car as soon as she cut the engine, and Reece followed Sara over to where one of the paramedics from the car that had passed them was unloading the vehicle.

'Jack. What's the story?'

Jack shook his head. 'We're not sure yet. Some kind of electrical fire probably, the whole street's shorted out. Two already on their way to hospital and we've got some minor cuts and burns, shock and smoke inhalation. There are an unknown number of people in there still, trapped in a lift between the basement and ground floor. The fire crews are working to get them out.' He seemed to notice Reece for the first time. 'Who's this?'

'He's a doctor.' Sara's voice was firm.

'Done any emergency work?' Jack's gaze was laden with suspicion.

'I'm in general practice at the moment, but I was a flying doctor in Australia for three years. Before that I worked in the emergency room in several different hospitals.'

Jack nodded. 'Okay.' He reached into the back seat of the SUV. 'Here.' He handed Sara a bright yellow jerkin with the word 'Paramedic' across the back. ''Fraid we haven't got anything that says "Doctor". You're the only one we've got here.'

'That's okay. I'll manage. Where do you want me?' Reece knew where he needed to be. The situation up here was under control and there was no one seriously injured. The stranded lift was an unknown quantity. This was Jack's operation, though, and he had no wish to challenge his authority.

Jack nodded, and a hint of a smile crossed his face. 'Inside with Sara, in case there's anyone injured in that lift.'

'Right you are.' Reece took the heavy medical bag that Jack proffered and started towards the entrance to the shop. Behind him he could feel Sara's presence and hear Jack's shouted instructions for the firefighters to let them through.

'Sorry about that.' Sara caught him up and was half running to match his stride. 'He shouldn't have—'

'He should. Jack's trying to deploy everyone where they can do the most good. He needs to know who's got what experience, and he doesn't have time for social chit-chat.'

She grinned at him. 'Yeah. Only Jack doesn't have much time for social chit-chat at the best of times.' She offered him the jerkin. 'Do you want to be the one with the badge?'

Her pace didn't slacken and she hardly looked at him, but he could see the side of her mouth twist.

'Nope. You're the fully paid-up member of the NHS, not me. I'm just an innocent bystander.' He grinned at her. 'You get to be the official help.' Despite the seriousness of the situation, Reece wanted to smile. They were a team again. Two people, acting as one. He felt almost light-headed with excitement.

She nodded and pulled the jerkin on over her thick, padded jacket as they followed one of the firemen through the blackened doors of the store.

'We've opened the lift doors at ground-floor level and the lift's stuck lower down.' Their guide briefed them as they walked. 'The emergency engineer got here in record time after we called, they're based just around the corner. He's checked out the shaft and the cables and there's a team downstairs now, working on the doors in the basement. Hopefully the lift car is far enough down that we can get whoever's in there out that way.'

Their feet clanged on the metal treads of the stationary escalator as they hurried down. 'The fire didn't reach the lift shaft, though?' Reece didn't want to think about what they might find in the lift car if it had.

'No. There'll be some smoke down there but hopefully not too much.'

The basement was in complete darkness, so they only had the light from their torches to guide them. Smoke hung in the air, and Sara felt her eyes begin to sting as she followed Reece to where a group of firemen were working.

They were prising open the doors to the lift shaft. One last heave and they gave, opening into darkness. She heard Reece curse under his breath. The floor of the lift was barely eight inches from the top of the doors.

'All right. Looks as if we'll have to go in from the top.'

One of the firemen stood back, surveying the gap. 'No one's getting out through there.'

'If we can get the inner doors open, at least we can talk to the people inside. Maybe give them some help if they need it.' Reece spoke up and the fireman swung round. 'We're medics.'

The fireman nodded, and Reece helped him to sweep the display from a raised dais and drag the dais over to the mouth of the lift. 'Okay. The engineer says that the lift's not going anywhere, so it's safe to reach through if you can get your arm in there.' Together, they prised the inner doors open.

Voices came from inside the lift and, almost in slow motion, a woman's hand reached out, as if somehow she could grasp the freedom of the open space outside.

'Okay. It's okay.' Reece took the woman's hand, in his, guiding it back inside the lift. 'There's been a fire but it's out now, and there's nothing more to worry about. The fire service is working to get you out. I'm a doctor. Is anyone hurt in there?'

'Yes. There's a man who fell when the lift stopped, he says he thinks he's sprained his wrist.'

'No one else?' Reece was craning to see inside the lift, and Sara handed him a torch.

'No, I don't think so. It's dark in here.'

'Here.' He handed his torch through to the woman inside the lift, and Sara passed him another. He turned to her.

'I can't get my arm through. Can you try?'

Sara stripped off the bulky jerkin and her coat, throwing them onto the floor. 'Give me a leg up.'

He bent down, half lifting her up onto the dais. Sara reached into the lift, finding that she could easily slip her shoulder inside.

'Good work.' Reece grinned at her. 'I'll pass anything

you need up to you, and if you can do your best to see inside…' He jumped down from their perch and opened the bag of medical supplies, checking to see what was there.

Sara stretched her neck to get some kind of view. Feet, and then a woman's face, her cheek pressed to the floor of the lift.

'Hey, there.' Sara grinned at her. 'My name's Sara, I'm a paramedic. How many are you?'

'Five. Two men, three women. I'm Claire.' The woman had obviously emerged as the leader of the small group, and she was doing her best to look after the others, even though she was plainly frightened.

'You're doing great, Claire. I want everyone to sit down on the floor, please…' There was room enough in the large lift, and the air would be clearer lower down. 'Now, I need to see everyone.'

'Right. The torch beam jumped, seeking out its target. 'This is David, he's hurt his hand.'

From what Sara could see, David probably hadn't just sprained his wrist. He was sitting on the floor, cradling a swollen hand, his face drawn. He gave a tight grin and a nod. 'Okay, David, hold on there for just a minute and I'll get back to you. What about the others?' She needed to see everyone first to assess her priorities.

Claire shone the light at each of the others in turn. Hannah, a young woman who was unhurt but worried about her baby, whom she had left with her sister on the ground floor. A young girl, Becky, who was pale and quiet but otherwise seemed okay, and pronounced herself to be fine. Mike, who was dressed in the uniform of a store assistant. Then Claire herself, middle-aged and capable.

'That's good. The firefighters are working above us to get you out of here. As far as I know, everyone got out of the store, but we'll see what we can find out about Hannah's family.' Sara twisted round.

'I saw a woman with a baby outside. She had a green coat. Redhead.' Reece was standing right behind her. 'The baby was crying, that's why I noticed them.'

'Hannah? Does your sister have red hair and a green coat?' Hannah's face brightened and she nodded. 'Okay, we think she's outside and she's got your baby with her.' She could hear Reece behind her, talking to one of the firemen. 'We're going to radio through and check.'

Sara turned back towards Reece. 'There's a guy in here called Mike, who works for the store. The firefighters might be looking for him, if he was noted as missing when they did the employee roll call.'

'Okay, we're on it.' Reece signalled to the fireman standing next to him, who was listening intently to the chatter on his radio.

Sara gave a tentative breath of relief. No major casualties. Nobody seemed to be panicking. So far so good. She flipped the beam of her torch back to David. 'Right. Let's take a look at that hand of yours.'

Claire helped David to slide to the front of the lift, and he gingerly held his hand out for her to examine. 'Did you hit your head when you fell? Feel dizzy at all, or sick?'

'No, no and yes.' David coughed, wincing as he did so. 'It's just the smoke in here.'

'Yeah.' Sara could identify with that. The smoke was beginning to get to the back of her throat and her eyes were stinging, but fresh air was filtering into the lift and the fine mist inside was clearing. 'Well, I don't think that's just a sprain, you may have broken a couple of the small bones in your hand. I want you to try and keep it still and we'll sort out a sling for you to make it easier for you to climb. Don't try hanging on with that hand, get the firemen to help you.'

'Right. Thanks.' David grinned at her. 'Don't suppose…'
He broke off as a painful, laboured wheeze came from the
other side of the lift car.

CHAPTER SIXTEEN

SARA flipped the torch around in the direction of the sound, and its beam confirmed her fears. Becky was slumped forward, her head almost touching her knees, battling for air.

'We need to get out of here. Now!' Mike, the store assistant, chose this moment to try and assert himself, pushing past David and jamming his contorted face as close to Sara's as he could.

'Get back. I can't help her with you in the way.' Sara snapped out the order, hoping that the firmness of her tone would be enough to calm him. It was all she had. A girl could be dying just feet away and in front of her very eyes, and she could do nothing other than hope that the people who could reach her would stay calm and respond to her instructions.

Mike lunged back into the corner of the lift, his shoulders shaking with emotion, and Sara turned her attention back to Becky. 'Becky, do you have asthma? Nod if you can't speak.'

The teenager nodded, her chest heaving, and Claire scooted over to Sara. 'What do we do?'

'Support her in an upright sitting position. It's really important for you to be calm and reassure her. Get someone to look in her bag and you look in her pockets, you need to find her inhaler. Do it quickly.' Sara spoke quietly so that Becky wouldn't hear. She had no time to turn and ask for Reece's help, and he could do nothing more than she could. She could feel him there behind her, though, and that steadied her.

'Right.' Claire did as she was told, passing the teenager's handbag to Hannah, who started to fish around inside it.

'Quickly, Hannah.' She wasn't going to get anywhere with the large bag just dipping her hand in and feeling around. 'Empty it out…carefully…'

Hannah had tipped the bag upside down in a jerky movement and its contents went everywhere. The inhaler bounced and rolled across the floor and Sara made a grab for it, almost toppling off her perch as it spun towards her, out of the lift and downwards. Reece's hands on her waist stopped her from falling and she spun round to see where the inhaler had gone.

He was down in the lift pit in one beat of her heart. He found the inhaler amongst the debris at the bottom of the lift shaft and then Sara breathed again as he swung himself out from under the lift. 'I'm going upstairs. Perhaps I can get down there.' Before Sara could even nod, he was running towards the escalator.

Sara passed the inhaler back inside the lift and willing hands transferred it to Claire, who was sitting next to the Becky, supporting her. 'How do I use this?' She turned the inhaler over in her hand.

'Just give it to her. She knows how to use it, let her do it herself.' Sara nodded as the teenager took the inhaler and used it. Her breathing seemed to ease a little and Claire held her, comforting her. 'Good. That's good. Well done.'

It was medicine at arm's length. It was unbearably frustrating that she couldn't even touch her patient, but it seemed to be working. She flipped her eyes across to where Mike was sitting in the corner, and saw that David was talking quietly to him, his uninjured hand laid on his shoulder in a loose gesture of camaraderie. She grinned at David, and he winked back at her.

They weren't out of the woods yet, though. The sooner Reece could get to Becky and find a way of getting her out of the smoky atmosphere the better.

A couple of thuds, which seemed to come from the ceiling of the lift car, and everyone looked up expectantly. Everyone apart from Sara, who was still staring at Becky, trying to assess the rapid rise and fall of her chest and willing her to breathe. A small, hopeful murmur of excitement ran around the car as the ceiling hatch opened and a pair of legs appeared.

'It's okay, sweetheart. You're going to be fine, the doctor's with you now,' Sara called to Becky, and thought she saw some reaction.

Reece lowered himself into the lift, grinning, and Sara left her post. Now that he was there, he would do what was necessary, and there were things in the medical bag that he could use.

'Oxygen?' When she climbed back up to the opening, he was sitting next to the teenager, supporting her. He didn't look in her direction and Sara wondered whether the same radar that had told her that he had her back was operating for him.

'Here.' She slid the portable oxygen kit over to him and he reached for it.

A brief grin. Just enough to let her know that she was showing up bright and clear on his radar. 'Thanks.'

He unrolled the kit with one hand, giving the mask to the teenager to hold, while Claire shone the torch so he could see. 'Okay, sweetheart.' He guided the mask to the Becky's face. 'This will help you. You know what to do.'

His gaze met Sara's for a moment. The teenager was

responding, but not as much as either of them was happy with. Wordlessly, Sara slid the epi-pen and the intubation kit towards him, and he nodded. Just in case. There was no need to frighten their patient any further by voicing the need for them, but if it got to those last resorts, Reece might need them quickly.

'Well done, Becky. You're doing well.' He was holding her tenderly, reassuring her every step of the way. Almost coaxing the breaths from her, willing the blocked airway to clear, so that life-giving oxygen could reach her lungs. Sara tore her gaze away from them. This was no time to be thinking about Reece, or how she wanted some of that tenderness. Some of that reassurance that everything was going to be okay.

Turning to David, she smiled at him. 'How are you doing?'

'We're okay here.' His eyes slid to one side, towards Mike, who was sitting quietly now. 'See to the girl.'

'The doctor's got that under control. How's the hand now?'

'I've got a spare one, I can climb out if I need to.' Along with the others in the lift car, David had clearly divined what the next step was going to be.

'Sure you can. How's the pain?' It was a delicate balance. Sara would have had no hesitation in administering pain relief straight away in normal circumstances, but David still needed to focus. Too much pain would rob him of that focus, but so would too many drugs.

'It hurts.'

'I can give you pain relief, but you need to keep your wits about you.'

David grinned at her. 'I'll keep my wits for the moment. When I get out of here, you can give me as many drugs as you like.'

'Me too,' Mike piped up, and then quietened down again when Sara ignored him.

'David, I'm going to pass you through a sling and the doctor will put it on for you. It'll make it easier when they come to getting you out.' It was obvious from the sounds of activity going on above them that the fire crew was working on creating a safe passage upwards and out of the lift.

'Don't bother him. I can manage.'

'I'll help you.' Hannah slid over towards Sara, taking the sling when she passed it through, and gently slipping it over David's head, fixing it as Sara told her to. He winced with pain and then relaxed.

'Is that better?'

'Much. Thanks.' His head snapped round as the sound of wheezing came from the other side of the lift car. Reece was reaching for the teenager's inhaler again.

'Hannah, get that piece of paper, will you?' Sara indicated a scrap of paper in the pile from the teenager's handbag. 'Roll it up...a bit tighter than that... Yes, that's right.'

'Thanks.' Reece took the rolled-up paper, using it as a makeshift spacer between the inhaler and the teenager's mouth. It would keep the medicine in place between breaths, and what Becky needed right now, more than anything else, was her medication. 'Breathe now, sweetheart.'

Becky's hand found Reece's arm, tightening around it. She was hanging on, as if the mere fact of holding onto him would help her to breathe. 'That's right. Squeeze my arm when you're ready to take another breath.'

The tips of her fingers whitened as she squeezed hard, and Reece worked the inhaler again. 'That's right. You're doing beautifully. Two more puffs.'

The wheezing had stopped again and Reece was gently replacing the oxygen mask. 'Better now?' Becky nodded, and something that looked like a smile ghosted across her lips.

A ladder dropped down through the hatch in the ceiling, and a fireman climbed down, bringing with him the harness that would be needed to get Becky out. Another fireman appeared and started to marshal the other occupants of the lift up the ladder, one by one, while Reece helped to strap the teenager into the harness.

'We're on our way up.' He gripped Becky's hand, in a signal that she wasn't going anywhere without him, and she managed a grin. 'That's the ticket.' He smiled back, and the fireman connected the harness to a cable, ready to winch their patient upwards.

'Sara...' The one word betrayed him. He may have been working without even looking her way most of the time, but it didn't mean that he hadn't known that she'd been there. At times like these, ignoring someone, letting them get on with their job, was the deepest form of trust.

'I'll meet you upstairs.' Sara scrambled down from her perch, shouldering the straps of the heavy kitbag, and made for the escalator as quickly as the darkness and the weight of the bag would allow.

The muscles in her legs were screaming for mercy by the time she got to the top, but she didn't stop. The smoke in the basement and in the lift shaft had been clearing as it had drifted upwards, but here it was still heavy in the air. Reece had already freed Becky from the harness and hoisted her up in his arms, hurrying towards the exit.

Dropping the bag, Sara ran ahead of him towards the open shop doors. 'Coming through,' she yelled at the group of people between them and the waiting ambulance. There was no less urgency now, in the cold air, than there had been in the smoky atmosphere. Reece made the back of the ambulance, and waiting hands guided them both inside.

The doors closed in her face and Sara stared at them. She should go back, collect the bag and check on how the others were doing, but something stopped her. She needed to see Reece. Just for one moment.

The doors opened again and he stepped down from the ambulance. The smile on his face told her all she needed to know. 'She's okay?'

He nodded. 'Now that she's out of there, she's breathing a lot more easily. I told her I'd go with her to the hospital. Will you see if you can find my jacket? It's by the lift opening on the ground floor.'

'Of course. There's some more for me to do here, but I'll meet you there.'

He nodded, his blue eyes flashing with something that looked like relief. If there had been no unfinished business between them before, now there was plenty. Being parted from him now, after they'd done so much together today, was like having one of her arms wrenched off.

'Thanks. Only I don't know where we're going.'

'I do. Wait in the coffee bar on the east wing for me.'

'Sure. See you later.' He climbed back into the ambulance, closing the doors, and she lost sight of him.

She found Reece where she'd told him to wait, sitting in the cafeteria, half a cup of coffee in front of him.

'Hey, there. How are you doing?'

'Fine. How's Becky?'

Reece grinned. 'They're keeping her in overnight, but she's okay. I saw David come into A and E too. Four broken bones in his hand. They're splinting it and sending him home.'

'That's good. I checked everyone else over and they're fine.' Sara grinned. 'Hannah's little boy is a real sweetheart.'

His gaze caught hers and they locked. Held. The way they had back at his house in Australia. The way she had relived in her dreams ever since, and had tried so hard to avoid in the last twenty-four hours.

'Are you going to finish your coffee?'

He shook his head. 'No. I do have to pay for it, though. When I got here I realised I'd left my wallet in my jacket, and I had to beg for credit. One pound twenty. I had a bun as well.'

Sara got her purse out, leaning towards him. 'So how did you get Irene to give you credit?' The lady who ran the Friends' Coffee Bar was a treasure. A very stern treasure who made it an unbreakable rule never, ever to give credit.

'She was very nice about it. I explained what had happened and said that you'd be along to rescue me any time now, and she gave me one free cup of coffee and then came over and took an IOU from me for a second cup and a bun.' He was smiling now. His shock of blond hair and mischievous eyes told Sara exactly how he'd managed to get Irene to break her unbreakable rule. He'd just charmed her into it.

'You got a free cup of coffee?' Sara whispered the words at him in case anyone overheard and started a rumour.

'I'm not supposed to tell anyone.' He looked over his shoulder furtively. 'Perhaps you should give me the money and wait for me outside while I go and pay.'

'Okay.' Sara pressed a coin into his hand and he squinted at it. 'There's two pounds. Meet me outside and we'll go back to my place and I'll make you a decent cup of coffee.'

'I'll just get my jacket from your car and then I've got to get going.' The refusal of her invitation felt like a slap in the face and Sara reminded herself that just last night it had been her telling Reece to go. 'But I was wondering if you were free tomorrow.'

'Yes…' She'd answered before she had bothered to think. 'Why?'

'Thought you might like to do something. I've got a tourist guide and an Oyster card.' He made it all sound so innocent.

She should say no. On the other hand, he hadn't abandoned her when she'd been alone in Australia. And they did need to talk. Perhaps he was right, and it would be better to do that after a night's sleep. 'Okay. Where do you want to go?'

'I don't know yet. Any ideas?'

Sara thought for a moment. 'I'll meet you at Green Park Station. Come up onto street level and I'll meet you by the exit on the same side of the road as the park. Can you get there all right?'

He nodded. 'I'll find it. What time?'

'One o'clock. I'll go and see Gran in the morning and I'll take you to lunch.'

'No.'

'No?' The ends of her fingertips began to tingle. They'd had this conversation before, hadn't they?

'My shout.' He grinned, getting up and making for the serving hatch to pay Irene before she had a chance to argue.

CHAPTER SEVENTEEN

'So, what do you think? Do you like it here?'

That was his line surely. Then Reece remembered where he was and realised that he was the tourist, not Sara. You'd never have known it from the way she'd been acting but, then, Reece had learned something today. Back in Australia, he'd thought that her keen interest in everything around her had been because her surroundings had been new to her, but he'd been wrong. She was like that all the time.

'Yeah.' He weighed up the pros and cons, finding it impossible to compare this with his homeland. 'Yes, it's... different.'

She laughed. 'Cold?'

'Yes, cold. I assume you do get a summer?'

'Course we do.' They'd stopped walking, and the stiff breeze from the river was making her cheeks flush pink. 'Most years.'

He laughed. Free and clear, allowing his chest to expand and take in air. It seemed so much easier to do that when Sara was around. 'It's amazing.' The London Eye towered to one side of them, turning so slowly that it was impossible to track. All the same, it turned, and in the space of half an hour passengers got a full three-hundred-and-sixty-degree view. 'Such a lot to see.'

'That's why I made you walk. It's much better than just going from place to place on the Tube.'

She'd made him walk all right. And after the exertions of yesterday and a broken night's sleep, he was beginning to ache. But it had been worth it, and Reece had felt he'd seen the best of the city, glittering proudly under a cold, clear sky. Or maybe it just seemed that way because Sara was there.

A thought struck him, and suddenly he couldn't get it out of his head. As they'd walked across Westminster Bridge together, she'd told him about how gold rings and coins, centuries old, were washed up on the shores of the river. 'Will you stay there for a moment? I just want to go back onto the bridge to get a photograph of the river.'

'Hmm? Yes, of course.' Her attention had been diverted by a pavement artist, who was putting the finishing touches to a chalked image. 'I'm just going to go and see what this guy's doing.'

Reece strode back onto the bridge, walking almost to the centre of it. This was the place. Turning, he saw Sara raise her head and wave, as if she knew that he was looking at her. He waved back and he thought he saw her smile.

Training his camera lens up the river, he took a couple of shots, managing to get one of the Houses of Parliament with a red bus going past. Then, reaching into his pocket almost furtively, his fingers found the gold chain with the small heart threaded onto it that had travelled with him ever since he had failed to give it to Sara.

It was time to let go of this. He'd brought it with him, thinking that a goodbye was the only thing that they had left to do. Maybe that was true and maybe it wasn't. He could no longer hold himself to it, though. His relationship with Sara was too multi-textured, too full of possibilities to bind himself to just one outcome. He had to let go.

Leaning on the wide parapet, looking out over the water, he let the bauble drop and it spun downwards, glittering in the low sun. He thought he saw it hang in the water for a moment before it sank, but perhaps that was just his imagination. Reece turned and walked back towards the bank, without looking back. One day the shifting waters would probably throw it back up onto the river shore again, but he would never know about it.

When he rejoined her, she was still studying the chalked image on the pavement. 'I guess it'll be getting dark soon.'

She looked at her watch. 'Yes.' She seemed to be turning something over in her mind. Probably the same thing he was. They could only pretend for so long that there was nothing more that needed to be said. 'We should talk, Reece.'

'Yes. We should.'

'My place?' The two words seemed like water to a dying man. He'd come here to find some way of breaking free, and yet the only time he felt free was when he was with Sara.

There really wasn't a choice in the matter. 'Yes. Your place.

The house was dark and quiet. Last night it had seemed unbearable, walking up the front path, with no glow from Gran's window to welcome her home. Sara had no plan. No idea what she was going to do next, whether she was going to let him stay the night in the spare room or call him a taxi after they'd eaten. She'd work that one out when she came to it.

Dropping her keys on the kitchen counter top, she made for the coffee-machine. 'Fancy a decent cup of coffee?'

'Love one.' He grinned. 'That's quite a magnificent beast you have there.'

'This?' She indicated her espresso machine. She'd never quite got the hang of which lever to pull when. 'My mother had this installed for when she entertained. She never used it, just got the catering staff to do the honours.'

'Did she entertain a lot?'

'A fair bit. Only ever for business. She reckoned it was easier to talk people into things over a meal, a decent vintage and properly brewed espresso.' Sara watched as coffee dripped into the cups.

'Probably right. Only if you brew your espresso for that long, it'll be bitter.'

Sara kept her back turned to him, so he couldn't see her grin. 'Oh, and so you're an expert, are you? The man with no coffee beans in his cupboard and a grinder that needed to be excavated before it would work.'

'Just because I don't drink decent coffee, it doesn't mean to say I don't know how to make it.' His voice was closer now, and a bead of cool sweat ran down her spine. 'I had a part-time job as a barista when I was at uni. Little place in Melbourne where they used to do speciality coffees.'

'So you can probably show me where I'm going wrong, then.' She kept her eyes doggedly on the machine.

'Yeah. We'll have to start again, though, right from the beginning.' He fetched the milk from the refrigerator while Sara knocked the grounds from the filters into the bin.

His arms reached around her, picking up the tin of coffee beans that she'd taken out of the cupboard. All she had to do was to lean back a little and she'd be touching him. It would be the sweetest, most delicious thing that she could imagine.

He kept her in front of him, inside the circle of his arms, while he ground the coffee and filled the filters, tamping them down just so hard and no more. 'Your espresso needs to be filtered for less than a minute, any longer and it gets bitter. So start with the milk.' He moved away from her for a moment to froth the milk, signalling to her when the time was right to press the brew button. Then he whipped the cups out from under the filters and put the milk jug in front of her.

'Now I have to hit it, yes?' She could feel him again. His body against hers, his fingertips resting on the counter top on either side of her.

'No, you tap firmly. Don't bash the jug down as if you're trying to beat it to death.' Sara tapped the jug on the counter top to settle the milk and he laughed softly. 'Bit harder than that. Three times.'

'Three?'

'Yeah. I always do it three times.'

Somehow he made that sound like a proposition. Sara swallowed hard, and tapped. 'Very good. Now tip the cup to coat the inside with coffee.' He reached for one of the cups, showing her what he meant, and Sara did the same with the other. 'And tip the milk in slowly. That's right.' He waited for her to tip the milk into both cups. 'All you need now is chocolate sprinkles.'

'Hmm. Think I'm out of sprinkles.' She summoned up the courage to turn and face him. It was just as she'd thought. His eyes, dark and delicious. His body taut. And that smile was just downright dangerous.

He shook his head. 'What about amaretti biscuits? Something sweet to go with the coffee.'

'Sorry. None of those either.'

'Too bad.' He was so very close. 'Guess I'll just have to go to the source.'

He kissed her. Lightly on the lips. Warm. She could feel his warmth, tingling through her body. They'd gone too far already, but all Sara could think was that it wasn't far enough.

'Hmm. Perfect.' He kissed her again, and this time she felt his hands, laid lightly on her hips. It was too late to do anything now other than just enjoy this moment. And the next.

'It's chilly in here…' Sara hadn't changed the thermostats on the radiators yet, and Gran's flat was probably as warm as toast, while up here the heating was turned down low.

'Yeah. And I don't know about you but I'm starting to ache like hell.'

There were two ways of taking that. Probably both pretty accurate right now. Sara's legs ached from the stairs yesterday and the long walk today, and the rest of her… The rest of her just ached for him. 'I've got the very thing for that. Bring your coffee.'

She took him upstairs to the big master bathroom. She normally used the en suite shower in her bedroom, reckoning that the big spa tub was no good for just one person, but now it was just perfect.

'Not quite sure how this works.' She fiddled with the levers. 'I've never used it before.'

'Let me.' He set the temperature and twisted one of the taps, setting hot water gushing into the tub. 'Now, anything else I can help you with?'

They floated together in the warm bubbles, his arms wrapped around her shoulders. Slowly they were pushing the boundaries, taking one at a time. At first they'd just looked and not touched. Now they were touching, without caressing.

'Are you sure that you live here?' Reece was staring ruminatively at the ceiling.

'Yeah. Course I do.'

'It's just that you don't seem to know how anything works in this house.' He stroked the side of her face with his finger. 'I was just wondering whether the real owners were going to come home any minute and ask what we're doing here.'

Underneath the lightness of his tone was a serious point. One that Sara had wrestled with for a while now. 'It's never really been my home. Bit too much like a show home for my taste.'

'Hmm. It's not the kind of place I'd imagine you living.'

'No. I don't imagine me living here either. But for the foreseeable future…'

'You'll stay here because your gran's flat is here. And if you sell this place, you won't be able to bring her home.'

He understood that, at least. 'Yes. It's not the home that I chose, but it's where I've ended up.'

'Where would you rather be?' He said it as if there was a choice.

'I've got a cottage of my own. Not as posh as this, all the furniture's secondhand and it's small and some way out of London, but it was mine.'

'Not any more?'

'I'm going to sell it. It's stupid to keep two places on, and I was going to send the money to Simon. My mother left everything to me, but I don't want it. He should have something.' She'd hung onto her own place way too long now in the hope that somehow she would be able to return. It just wasn't practical, though. It was too small to give Gran a decent-sized bedroom and sitting room on the ground floor, and the money would come in handy for Simon.

'You could make this place yours.' He seemed to be considering something. 'You made my place into a home and you were only there for two weeks.'

Did he really think that? When she'd left Reece's house, it had felt like leaving her own home, but she hadn't re-alised that he'd felt it too. As if somehow what they'd shared there had seeped into the bricks and mortar of the place, making it special.

She didn't really want to think too much about that. 'Yeah. You'll be moving on soon, though.'

'I have already.'

'Moving on for good, I mean. You're like one of those fish that suffocates if they stop swimming.'

'I think you mean a shark.' He splashed some water in her direction.

'Or a tuna. You could be a tuna if you preferred.'

He snorted, obviously unimpressed with the choice. 'I'll let you know.' He pulled her into his arms, and the water rocked in the tub. It seemed that the ban on caressing was now over. 'In the meantime, what about those aches and pains?'

'Still a little achy.'

'Hmm. Want me to rub them better?'

Reece had hardly noticed the decor when he had carried her into her bedroom, making a wrong turn out of the bathroom and having to get her to point the way. He hadn't noticed anything much, other than the deep hunger that penetrated his bones and left him unable to do anything other than just what he was doing now. Making love to her. Holding her in his arms while they merged into what seemed like one being. Moving as one. Feeling as one.

When he woke up, though, some time in the middle of the night, light streaming through the open door from the hallway, he did notice. The walls were painted a shade of rich caramel instead of the bright white of the rest of the house. Wooden furniture and soft earth shades on the curtains and bedspread. Sara's unique way of blending colour and texture, the way she'd arranged the iridescent, polished agates on her dresser, which made the room soft and welcoming. The rest of the house was about as welcoming as an ice hotel.

She appeared, holding a glass of water. Still naked, even though she was shivering slightly from the cold air outside the room.

'Come back to bed.' The words felt possessive. Greedy for the endless possibilities that they held. Reece had wondered whether his memory had been taunting him by enhancing the delights of making love with Sara. It hadn't. If anything, it had left a few things out.

'Sorry. Did I wake you?' She scooted across the room and dumped the water on the bedside table, before sliding in beside him.

'No. Ow—your hands are cold! And your feet. What on earth have you been doing?'

'I went downstairs to get some water and put your clothes in the washing machine. They were in a soggy pile on the bathroom floor.'

'So I can't leave, then?'

'They'll be dry by the morning. It's a washer-drier, runs on an automatic cycle.'

Clean, dry clothes, so he could leave in the morning. There were times when her practicality was downright distressing. 'Okay. Guess that means that I'll have to make the best of my time, then.' There wasn't really a great deal of choice in the matter. Her hands were sliding up his thighs, deliciously cold, leaving trails of pure desire in their wake.

'You like that?'

'Love it. That's one thing this climate has in its favour.' The cosy warmth of her bed. The tantalising coldness of her fingers against his skin, tracing their way lightly towards his groin. 'No...wait, Sara...'

She didn't listen to him, and sudden pleasure gripped him, pulling tight on his senses. 'No?' She was teasing him now, and pure delight shot through his body, turning his blood to fire and making his eyes snap upwards in their sockets

A low growl escaped his throat, and he tipped her over onto her back, covering her with his bulk. The primitive male in him surfaced, revelling in her softness, the slim lines of her frame, clamouring to take her for his own. 'Come here…'

She giggled, letting out a squeal as he pulled her legs around his waist, goading him further by planting her cold feet right in the small of his back. 'No, you come here…'

Sara woke to find herself locked tight in his arms, his body curved around hers. That was fine. Right now, the last thing she wanted to do was move.

When he woke up, he made coffee for them both, and they lay together, talking. She planned out his stay in London, suggesting things to see, places that he could go that were off the usual tourist circuit. He redesigned her house, suggesting she throw out the white leather sofas in the lounge and replace them with the warm, earth tones that she loved.

'I can't. They're designer sofas, my mother paid a fortune for them.'

'Do you ever sit on them?'

'No. If I want to sit down, I either sit with Gran or I come up here.' She indicated the easy chair in the corner of the room, next to her books.

'So they've already gone to waste.' He shrugged. 'I imagine you could sell them then someone else will appreciate and use them.'

He had a point. If she sold them, she'd probably be able to redecorate the whole room with the proceeds. But something in the back of her mind wanted to revolt against that logic, turn it on its head. Why make this place look like a home, when really it wasn't? She'd never wanted to come back here, and now that Gran was gone, the only thing that made it feel like home was Reece. And he would be gone soon, and whatever colour the walls were, or however many soft furnishings she changed, the place would still be sterile and unwelcoming.

'I guess.' It was time to get out of bed now. Time to face the things that she'd been so unwilling to face last night. 'Your clothes will be dry now, and I really should move if I'm going to see Gran this afternoon.' She looked at the clock. It *was* already this afternoon. 'Would you like me to print out some information from the Internet for you? About the places I told you…?'

She couldn't go on. It hurt too much. The look of reproach in his eyes seared through her like a red-hot knife.

'So you're not going to do any more sightseeing with me, then?'

Sara reached for her thick dressing gown and pulled it on then perched herself on the edge of the linen chest at the foot of the bed. 'No. I don't think I am.'

He nodded slowly. 'Is there anything I can do to change your mind?'

Everything he did changed her mind, that was the problem. 'I think we've just proved that being friends doesn't really work with us. We just end up…' She couldn't say it.

'We end up here. Is that so terrible?'

She couldn't look him in the eye. Whatever she found there, it would be enough to stop her from doing this. 'We've done everything that we can do, Reece. There's no future in this, and I want to say goodbye now, before things start to go bad between us.'

'And that's what you really want?' If he felt anything, he was giving none of it away. His face was like a mask, suddenly devoid of emotion. None of the disbelief and exasperation that he'd shown when he'd asked her to stay in Australia and she'd said she couldn't. None of the sheer, bloody-minded determination to sweep all her objections aside when he'd arrived the night before last.

'You and I are different creatures, Reece. We live differently, and neither of us can change who we are.' She was going to cry in a minute. She had to get out of here before she fell into his arms, sobbing and pleading for one more day. Another night. One more moment, even.

He didn't move. Didn't even try to argue with her. Sara stood up, feeling the muscles in her legs pull as she did so.

'I'll always care for you, Sara.' She had almost reached the door before he spoke.

'Thank you.' She didn't turn and face him, afraid of what she might reveal. Afraid of what he might see in her eyes. 'I know.'

It was like a landslide. It had started so suddenly, and now that it had gathered momentum it was unstoppable. Merciless in its swift path, flattening everything as it went. He showered and dressed in less than ten minutes, and two minutes later he'd put his jacket on, picking his wallet up from the kitchen counter where he'd left it last night. Checking his pockets to make sure he'd left nothing behind, so he wouldn't have to come back.

'I'll hold you in my heart, Sara.'

It was what Kath had said at the airport, but he'd left a bit out. *Until I see you again.* Sara bit her lip. Sensible. That wasn't going to happen. She put her hand over her heart, the way she'd done with Kath. 'I'll hold you in my heart too, Reece.' Maybe one day she'd see him again. In about a thousand years' time, when there was no question of her wanting him any more.

He kissed her on the cheek, turning quickly. Maybe he

didn't want to see her tears any more than she wanted to show them to him. Sara squeezed her eyes shut, wrapping her arms tightly around herself, until she heard the front door close.

'No.' Suddenly she couldn't believe what she'd done. Running to the door, she pulled it open, only just remembering to grab her keys. Barefoot and still clad only in her dressing gown, she ran up the front path, her feet stinging from the frost on the pavers.

She caught sight of him, striding away. As he turned the corner she thought he would look back, but he didn't. It was only then that she realised that she didn't know the name of the hotel he was staying at and for one giddy moment she knew that if she ran after him, he wouldn't ignore her and just keep walking.

It wasn't the freezing weather or her bare feet that deterred her. It was the ice around her heart. If she stopped him now, she would just face this moment again and again, until finally the pain of parting obliterated everything else. Sara turned and walked back into the house, closing the door behind her. She was ready to cry now. At least she could do that.

CHAPTER EIGHTEEN

IT HAD been a tough week. For the first few days Sara had slept in the tiny spare room in Gran's apartment, along with Gran's collection of porcelain dogs and a stack of boxes of things that were no longer used but couldn't possibly be thrown away. She'd ventured up to her own room for long enough to strip the bed and open the windows to the freezing air, in the hope that this might erase the memories that Reece had made. It was no use. However hard she tried not to think about him, he was still there, in the very air that she breathed.

Three days' work had at least diverted her attention slightly, although the evenings were still as empty and sorrowful. And a thick fall of snow on Friday had occupied her in clearing the sloping drive that led to the house, so that she could get her car up to the front door when she bought Gran home on Saturday morning.

'Who built the snowman?' Sara put on a smile for the carer who answered the door and gestured towards the large snowman built outside the window so the residents could see it when they passed on the way to the dining room.

'Oh, one of the relatives. The gardener helped as well, I think.'

'It's nice.' One of the things that Sara liked about this

place was that practically anything was cause for celebration. A birthday, a public holiday, a fall of snow. Everything was marked by as much joy as the care staff could manage to inject into it. 'Is Gran in her room?'

'No, she's in the small sitting room, playing bridge.'

'At eleven o'clock in the morning?' A thought struck Sara. 'She hasn't been up all night playing, has she?' Gran had a habit of sleeping during the day and then sitting up till late at night.

'We had to make her go to bed. And the card sharps got together again this morning for a last game.'

'Right. Thanks.' Sara supposed that she would have to wait, at least until this rubber was finished. That was okay, she had nothing else to do.

She called in on Gran, and then went upstairs to her room to pack her things for the weekend. Opening the door, she thought she caught a hint of Reece's scent. Her senses had been playing those cruel tricks on her all week.

'Hey, Sara.'

She dropped her car keys, and they jangled onto the carpet. Tried to gulp in a breath of air, and failed. 'What are you doing here, Reece?'

'Lily said I could wait here for you.'

In some ways, it was a worse intrusion than if he'd shinned up the drainpipe, climbed in through the window and settled himself down in Gran's easy chair. 'What, so you took advantage of a ninety-year-old woman to...?' To see her. He could only have done it to see her. Sara tried to not to think about it. She didn't need to feel that kind of joy, not right now.

'No.' He stood up. Stiff, uncertain. Formal somehow. 'I told Lily that I wanted to see you.'

'What did you have to go upsetting Gran for?' The blood

had started to pump around her body again now, and Sara felt her cheeks flush. Maybe it was just the heat in here.

'It wasn't like that, Sara. I dropped in during the week with the photos of Simon that I promised her the other day.'

Sara bit her lip. He had promised the photos, and she knew how much Gran wanted them. All the same, he shouldn't have told Gran about their personal business. 'And, what, you just happened to convince her that this was a good idea?'

'She asked me if she would see me at the weekend and I said no. This was her idea.'

It just got worse and worse. Her own grandmother was conspiring with her ex-lover. 'Right. Well, you've seen me. You and Gran have both got what you wanted, so you can go now.'

'There's something I want to tell you. I can tell you now, or I can meet you later and tell you. Any time and any place you like.' It sounded like someone arranging to meet for coffee, but this was unmistakeably an ultimatum. The tension in Reece's tone, the tightness in his face left Sara in no doubt that he would catch up with her sooner or later.

She sighed. This was turning into a nightmare of goodbyes. The first had been bad enough and the second had almost torn her apart. She doubted that this one would be any better. 'Look, we can't talk here.' She couldn't take Gran home when she was in this state either. She'd better get it over and done with. 'We'll take a walk. Outside in the garden.' Maybe the cold would encourage him to keep this short.

'Okay.' He caught his jacket up from the back of the chair and put it on. Wound a thick scarf around his neck and put on a pair of gloves. He'd learned one thing, at least, during the course of the week.

The cold outside hit her full in the face, and she snuggled

into her warm, padded coat. The thought struck her that she'd worn this coat not just because of its warmth but because it was red. Something to make her look a little more cheery for when she saw Gran.

'Do you like the snowman?'

'Yes, it's great, isn't it?' Sara answered before the significance of the question struck her. 'Is this your handiwork?'

He grinned suddenly. Just for a moment before that tense, solemn look returned to his face. 'I'm a tourist. Can't resist a little snow.' He trudged along the path that led around the building, taking care to walk where other people had already left their footsteps. Like a child who didn't want to spoil the pristine white of the undisturbed snow.

Sara waited. He'd wanted this, not her. She wasn't going to ask what it was all about, that would sound as if she wanted to know.

'I want to buy your cottage.'

'You can't.' If that was all it was, the answer was simple. 'I've already got an offer on it. Came in last week. Full asking price.'

'And you've accepted the offer?'

'Yes, I have.'

'Good.' He was kicking at the snow with the toe of his boot, not looking at her.

'Is that all?'

'You're going to throw in the carpets and curtains as well?' He looked up at her suddenly, and the full force of his blue eyes hit her. Like an iceberg, smashing against her, dragging her under.

'You… Reece, you didn't.'

'I'm afraid I did.' He wasn't afraid at all. He'd decided to do it and had just gone ahead and done it. She knew him well enough to know that.

'So you've been poking around in my cottage, have

you?' Suddenly the thought of him there was more than she could bear.

'The estate agent phoned and asked you first.'

'Yes, but she didn't say that it was you who wanted to look around.'

He nodded, turning the edges of his mouth downwards. 'No, she didn't. I told her that I didn't want her to give anyone my name until I was ready to make an offer on a property.'

'Right. So you trick your way into my house, and then make a cash offer. I suppose that's as bogus as you are.'

'Just because I don't own property, it doesn't mean to say I don't have savings.' He couldn't keep up the hurt look that he flashed her for very long and a grin started to spread over his face. 'In fact, it looks as if the two are mutually exclusive—even small cottages don't come cheap.'

'I know how much my cottage costs. What are you planning on doing with it?' It was a theoretical question. She wasn't going to sell to Reece and that was that. Asking price or not.

'I'll need somewhere to live. I need a work permit and a job as well. I've got those in hand too.'

This was ridiculous. Some kind of mad gesture that was all going to come to grief in the end. 'No, you don't need a work permit because I'm not going to sell you my house and you're not getting a job. It'll just make everything much more complicated when you move on.'

'It will, won't it?' His forehead was creased with stress. She knew that look, and there was something he wasn't saying. 'Sara, you said that I'd suffocate if I stopped moving.'

'Yes. You would.' It was the truth, and he needed to see that before he made a mistake that would not just break her heart but break both their souls.

'Have you ever been to Mexico?'

'No.' She stamped her foot in frustration.

'I want to show you the Caves of the Sleeping Sharks in Isla Mujeres. The water there is so rich in oxygen that reef sharks rest motionless at the bottom of the caves. They don't need to stay swimming in order to breathe.'

She could feel her tears. Sara wondered whether they might freeze and stick to her face. 'That's just a story, Reece. It doesn't mean to say—'

'It does.' He turned on her with such certainty that she almost backed away from him. 'When you left Australia, I was just about to leave Victoria. I couldn't. I couldn't leave the house where you'd been, or the places we'd seen together. I was trapped, like a man in an underwater pocket of air, trying not to breathe too much. The only place I could come, the only place where I could breathe again, was here, with you.'

She stared at him. He really was serious about this.

'The only way that I can think of to show you that I'm serious about this is to just do it. I know you don't believe me now, but let me show you.'

'What, by nailing your feet to the floor, Reece? That's what buying property does. It's a commitment.'

His shoulders seemed to relax a little. 'Exactly. That's exactly what I'm doing, because I don't need to be anywhere else. You are all I want and everything that I need. If I have to nail my feet to the floor to show you that, then...' He grinned. 'Pass the hammer.'

'You don't know what you're doing, Reece. There's Gran to think about. I don't have time...' She trailed off. 'It's not fair to ask you to stay when I don't have the energy or the time to devote to a relationship. I tried that balancing act a long time ago, and I failed.'

He stopped short, looking at her with reproach in his eyes. Maybe she shouldn't have brought up the thing with

Tim. It wasn't the same at all. Reece wasn't the kind of guy who would sit on the sidelines, let her do all the work and then complain that she was never around.

'He was a fool, then. He didn't love you enough.' He threw the words at her, disgust in his voice.

'No…I suppose he didn't.' Some of Reece's no-holds-barred straightforwardness seemed to have rubbed off on her. 'And to tell you the truth, I probably didn't love him enough either. I love you, though, and that's why I'm not going to let you stay.'

'We'll look after Lily together.' He shrugged. 'If she'll have me.'

'Oh, she'll have you all right.' It was all or nothing now. She had to call his bluff. Sara didn't want to even think about his answer, but she had to know. 'Marry me, then.' She threw the challenge down, and it lay freezing at their feet.

She couldn't bear the shock in his eyes. 'Sara, I'm not ready…'

He'd done just what she'd thought he would, and yet had hoped against impossible hope that he wouldn't. Baulked at the last fence. There was nothing more to say. If this was what it took to make him realise that staying was just a crazy plan that he'd never be able to stick to then so be it. Sara turned and walked away from him.

'Wait.' He caught her arm and she pulled it away. There really was nothing left to say. 'Wait!' His tone was almost harsh, and his hand closed around her arm again, this time unyielding.

'Let me go.'

'Never.' He pulled her back towards him, banding his arms around her body, and she struggled vainly to get free. 'I'm not ready to ask you properly. I don't have a ring and I haven't wined and dined you yet in the best restaurant in town. I left all that until later, because I reckoned it might take me a while to prove myself to you.'

'You don't need to prove yourself. All I need is your word.'

'Then you have it.' He pulled her close and she felt his body relax along with her own. 'We'll get married by special licence.' He paused. 'Can you do that here?'

'We will not. I want a proper wedding, with Simon and Gran there. Do you think that we could get Kath and Joe to come over?'

He let out a short, barking laugh of disbelief. 'Try keeping her away. In fact, it'll be interesting to see how long she manages to hold out before she starts sending you cake ideas.'

'Sounds good. Be nice to have something a bit different. I want a beautiful dress and a cake…' She tipped her head upwards and kissed him. 'I want you.'

'You've got it. All of it, I promise.' He bent closer, his lips grazing her ear. 'I think we've got an audience.'

'Gran?' Sara didn't even look. Gran was safe and sound inside and this moment was hers.

'Yeah. Along with a growing crowd.' He chuckled. 'I may not have a ring but I've got witnesses.'

'Reece, what are you doing? Get up.' He'd fallen to his knees in the snow. 'You'll get wet and then you'll freeze to death.'

'Better answer me quickly, then.' He resisted all her attempts to pull him to his feet, and closed his hands around hers. 'I want to make a home with you, Sara. I want to fill it with all the love I can give you, and share that with Lily. I want to make babies, and have our children grow up knowing that there's a wonderful world out there but that there's a place where they can always come and find us…'

He stopped, searching her face. This was Reece all over.

When he made a promise he made it comprehensively, missing out nothing.

'Sounds wonderful.' Sara smiled at him, willing him on.

He nodded. 'I want to love you and make you happy. Will you marry me, Sara?'

He'd missed nothing out. 'Yes, Reece. I'll marry you.' She pulled him up, out of the freezing snow and this time he made no effort to resist her, holding her tight against his chest and kissing her, to the faint, muffled sound of applause from the sitting-room window.

There was one thing she wanted, but Sara knew she couldn't have that. 'I want this to last for ever.'

'It will. It'll be in my heart, whenever you want it.'

He'd done the impossible. She could move now, instead of standing here shivering in the magic of the moment. She could walk away from it, knowing that Reece would be with her.

The sound of a sharp rapping on the window caught her attention. The senior carer was beckoning them. 'Ah. It's nearly time for morning coffee, and that looks like an invitation we can't refuse.'

He chuckled. 'Sounds like a plan. I'm losing the feeling in my fingers.'

She stripped off his glove, tucking his hand inside her coat. 'Better?'

'Much.' They started to walk together around the building, back to the main entrance.

'I guess this means the sale on my cottage just fell through.' She grinned up at him.

'Not necessarily. If you want to live there and Lily's happy with it, there's plenty of room at the back. We could build an extension for her, have it designed especially for her needs.'

She shrugged. 'It doesn't matter any more. We can clear the house out, make it ours. Plenty of space for visitors.'

He chuckled. 'I've a feeling we'll need it.' He turned to her, pulling her against the side wall of the building, out of sight of watchful eyes. 'Now, before we go and share, I want one more kiss.'

* * * * *

A sneaky peek at next month...

Medical Romance™

CAPTIVATING MEDICAL DRAMA—WITH HEART

My wish list for next month's titles...

In stores from 1st March 2013:

☐ NYC Angels: Redeeming The Playboy – Carol Marinelli

& NYC Angels: Heiress's Baby Scandal – Janice Lynn

☐ St Piran's: The Wedding! – Alison Roberts

& Sydney Harbour Hospital: Evie's Bombshell
   – Amy Andrews

☐ The Prince Who Charmed Her – Fiona McArthur

& His Hidden American Beauty – Connie Cox

Available at WHSmith, Tesco, Asda, Eason, Amazon and Apple

Just can't wait?

Visit us Online

You can buy our books online a month before
they hit the shops! **www.millsandboon.co.uk**

0213/03

MILLS & BOON® Book Club

2 Free Books!

Get your free books now at
www.millsandboon.co.uk/freebookoffer

Or fill in the form below and post it back to us